Praise for Morag Joss's Spellbinding Mysteries

FRUITFUL BODIES

"The most persuasive chronicler of the city perhaps best known to some as Jane Austen's stamping ground."
—*London Times*

"Joss has a remarkable talent—reminiscent of early P. D. James—and a gift for creating wonderful characters and relationships."—*Yorkshire Post*

"Morag Joss writes with razor-sharp, wry observation."
—*Bath Chronicle*

FUNERAL MUSIC

"An exquisite crime novel.... If rich, gorgeous Sara sometimes seems too perfect to be true, the book's supporting cast is nicely fleshed out with human idiosyncrasies and tangled cross-purposes. Even better are Joss's lyrical evocations of Bath, which becomes the book's most compelling character."—*Publishers Weekly,* starred review

"*Funeral Music* earns the favorable Ruth Rendell/P. D. James comparisons Joss has received. . . . Not many mysteries about professional musicians show how their combination of detail and passion make them ideal detectives, but Joss knows just which strings to pull."—*Chicago Tribune*

"A very dark and disturbing mystery. . . . Joss has created an excellent ensemble of characters. . . . *Funeral Music*'s well-plotted story compares to those by Patricia Cornwell, James Patterson and Phillip Margolin. . . . Each turn of the page skillfully peels away another layer."—*Fresh Fiction*

"It is always a pleasure to welcome a new and exciting talent to British crime writing, and Morag Joss's distinguished debut demonstrates an interesting setting, characters, both sympathetic and villainous, who are drawn with wit and perception, good writing and a plot which combines tension with credibility."—P. D. James

"As well plotted as Ruth Rendell and with all the psychological complexity you find in the great P. D. James, *Funeral Music* is an exceptionally accomplished first novel. Beautifully written, it manages to be witty and touching at the same time. . . . Music lovers will admire Morag Joss's expertise and anybody who loves Bath itself has to buy this novel for the setting alone."—Bel Mooney, *Bath Chronicle*

"Both literate and sardonic, filled with persuasive characters."—*Sunday London Times*

"The skilful plotting, strong sense of place and colourful but credible characters would alone mark this book out. What makes it not only convincing crime writing but also a fine novel is its lively sense of social comedy and sharp wit."—*Good Book Guide*

"Well written and well plotted, with a good Bath background."—*Evening Standard*

"A promising first novel. The author writes well and has a keen sense of place. Her evocation of Bath is very convincing."—John Boyles, *Tangled Web*

FEARFUL SYMMETRY

"*Fearful Symmetry* makes the elegant city of Bath a venue for fear and suspicion. A mesmerising psychological thriller."—*London Times*

"The characters are presented in sharp detail, while their various relationships offer a complex set of variations on the theme of love, all adding a rich substrata to the skilful unravelling of the intricate plot in this accomplished and satisfying novel."—*Good Book Guide*

"*Fearful Symmetry* is in the finest tradition of British whodunits—constructed with page-turning skill, witty and touching in equal measure, and displaying the crucial awareness that corruption looks innocent and lives next door."
—Bel Mooney

"A welcome addition to the crime writing genre, there are enough twists and turns to keep you guessing throughout."—*U Magazine*

"Larger-than-life characters inhabit this absorbing mystery. . . . The plot twists and turns to an unforeseen conclusion."—*Family Circle*

HALF BROKEN THINGS

Winner of the prestigious Crime Writers' Association Silver Dagger Award

"Sad, funny, original and wise."—*Literary Review*

"A work of fiction that sets its author on the path to greatness."—*London Times*

"It is a fantastic moral exercise as well as a gripping novel." —*Scotland on Sunday*

"This is a top-notch example of British psychological thriller writing."—*Manchester Evening News*

Also by Morag Joss

FUNERAL MUSIC

FEARFUL SYMMETRY

And coming soon in
hardcover from Delacorte:

HALF BROKEN THINGS

FRUITFUL BODIES

Morag Joss

A DELL BOOK

FRUITFUL BODIES

Hodder and Stoughton UK edition published 2001

Dell mass market / August 2005

Published by Bantam Dell
A division of Random House, Inc.
New York, New York

Dell is a registered trademark of Random House, Inc., and the colophon
is a trademark of Random House, Inc.

ISBN 0-440-24243-6

Printed in the United States of America
Published simultaneously in Canada

www.bantamdell.com

OPM   10 9 8 7 6 5 4 3 2 1

FOR

FIONA, GAVIN AND NEIL

ACKNOWLEDGEMENTS

Lots of people helped. John and Yvonne Cullum very kindly allowed me to turn their beautiful house into a clinic for the purposes of this story. Hamish Denny hunted out huge amounts of arcane information crucial to the plot, despite being busy either sculpting or operating on animals. Fiona Scott-Lockyer found time to show me round the Royal Albert Hall when she had the builders in. The Soil Association was very helpful, as was Howard Morrish of Dove Farm Foods.

The late and much missed Alex Kelly was the source of the (true) story on which Chapter 10 is based. Iain Burnside helped with the Rachmaninov as well as with James, and his emails also meant that most days I began work laughing. I must thank also Olive and Bob Heffill, for sharing their knowledge of Japan and the Japanese, and Keith Shearn, former Superintendent of Bath Police, who with his wife Lyn now runs an excellent B&B on which the one in this book is *not* modelled.

I am immensely grateful as ever for the support, advice and patience of Judith Murray at Greene & Heaton and Kate Lyall Grant at Hodder. And Tim and Hannah were, it should go without saying, their saintly, selfless and long-suffering selves throughout the year of writing, for which I do, truly, thank them most of all.

A LIST OF MUSIC PLAYED IN THIS NOVEL

Brahms	Variations on a Theme by J Haydn—The St Anthony Variations
Dvořák	Cello Concerto in B minor Op. 104
Rachmaninov	Preludes Op. 23: No. 4 in D
J S Bach	Adagio from the Toccata, Adagio and Fugue in C, BWV 564
J S Bach	Suites for Violoncello: No. 1 in G major, BWV 1007
Beethoven	Seven Variations in E flat major on *Bei Männern, welche Liebe fühlen* from Mozart's *Die Zauberflöte*
	Twelve Variations in F on *Ein Mädchen oder Weibchen* from Mozart's *Die Zauberflöte*
Saint-Saëns	From Carnival of the animals: The Swan
Fauré	Élégie in C minor Op. 24

BATH
CITY CENTRE

Royal Crescent

Lansdown Road

Camden Crescent

To St Catherine's Valley

To Limpley Stoke
via
Bathampton

River Avon

The Paragon

Walcot St

Russel St

Bennett St

Brock St

The
Circus

Gay St

George St

Milsom St

Queen
Square

Royal Photo Soc.

Broad St

Green St

New Bond St

Pulteney Bridge

To Bathwick
and the
Sulis Clinic

The
Abbey

Roman Baths

Manvers St

To the Station

PART 1

CHAPTER 1

SOMETHING WRONG WITH the lipstick. Joyce's fingers, which were feeling twice their normal size, swivelled the base again and the thumb of puce lard twirled down out of sight and then welled back up out of the tube at her. She stared as it shimmered and wavered, eluding focus. Sniffing, as if this could somehow improve her eyesight, she gave it a push with one finger and inspected the smudge on her fingernail. That looked solid enough, so maybe it was only her lips that were wobbling. She wiped the finger down the front of her jacket and with another sniff looked firmly into the mirror that was held by a piece of wire to the handle of the cupboard above the Baby Belling. She sucked in a deep breath and tried to maintain a steady pout. But her reflection was telling her that the problem was not just getting her lips to hold still long enough to put the stuff on, it was the question of finding them first. They were developing a tendency to slip into her mouth and stay there, stuck to her dry teeth.

They had never been that great anyway. The gene pool of Monifieth in 1927 had not been overstocked with luscious Aphrodite mouths in the first place, and seventy-odd years of Scottish consonants, east winds and chewing politely had not fleshed Joyce's out any. Across the crumpled page of her face her lips looked like two horizontal curly brackets of the sort that Joyce as a little girl had practised whole jottersful of at Monifieth Elementary School, along with sevens with wavy tops and treble clefs. Joyce allowed herself a moment's recollection of the perfection of her treble clefs with an involuntary satisfied purse of her lips, before giving herself a shake. It was another tendency she recognised; if she grew for a moment inattentive, her mind would pull her back to a past so distant that even Joyce herself viewed it with scepticism. For how could they have been real, those treble clefs? She must concentrate on the here and now. She leaned in towards the mirror again, took another deep breath and stretched out her lips to receive a straighter gash of *Bengal Blush*.

Worse. Her mouth now looked like a newly stitched scar and time was getting on. She would have to allow extra for the underground walk, changing from the Northern to the Piccadilly Line at King's Cross, especially in her best kitten-heeled shoes which had been a good fit for the first eleven years but now slowed her down because she tended to walk out of the backs of them. That was the trouble with having Scottish feet, which were longer and narrower than Englishwomen's, she had read somewhere. It sounded finer somehow, longer, narrower feet; yet another little superiority in which one could have taken a pride if more people had known about it, although it did make for a wee problem going any distance in the kitten-heeled shoes.

She considered wiping all the lipstick off but *Bengal Blush* was the finishing touch, being the exact shade of her suit, the Pringle two-piece that she'd had for, well, did it matter how long, it was a classic. A classic re-interpreted for the modern woman, she remembered being told when she bought it in Jenners on Princes Street in Edinburgh, where it was called not a suit but a costume. Ladies' Costumes, Second Floor. And the jaunty little poodle brooch for the lapel, she'd bought that in Hosiery & Accessories on the way out, unable to resist the picture she made of a professional woman with the style and means to travel from Glasgow to Edinburgh to buy her clothes, no Sauchiehall Street for her. And from Jenners! New stockings too, six pairs on a whim although by this time she was mainly showing off to the salesgirl and the girl had known it, the tone of her 'certainly madams' carrying by then the merest acidity, the wee baggage. But she was getting off the point again. Concentrate on the here and now.

Joyce began to busy herself around the bedsit, collecting purse and keys and, from a suitcase under the bed, her good handbag and chiffon scarf. Only when she had gathered everything up in her arms did a sound from behind the one armchair, followed by the rattle of Pretzel's claws on the linoleum under the sink, remind her that she had not left him any food and he had trodden in his water bowl again.

'Och, Pretzel, was that Mummy going away and not leaving you your tea?' she said.

She dumped her amassed accessories on the floor, mainly into the pool of spilled water, and opened a new tin of dog food while Pretzel's rattling on the floor grew animated and the entire brown tube of dachshund torso wriggled in anticipation. The warm, already half-eaten smell that arose from the tin reminded Joyce's innards that she was in need of sustenance too. As she stooped to put down Pretzel's tea on the floor under the sink, where the smells of drain and warm dog were waiting to mingle with the scent of braised horse and gelatine from the bowl, her stomach, signalling its emptiness, pushed out a little shudder which puffed up through her guts and out of her mouth in a quiet, inflammable belch of vodka vapour. Sour saliva flooded the inside of her cheeks. Her throat puckered and she swallowed a mouthful of neat bile. No, not food. Something else. But there was only the remaining vodka in the bottle in her bag and she was supposed to be keeping that for when she felt the need, or for later on (whichever came sooner, if there was a difference) but what the hell, what was wrong with now? Here and now. She didn't need to get there till the second half, anyway.

Some time later she closed the door and concentrated hard on the here and now of getting the key, which seemed to be trembling, into the keyhole, which wouldn't keep still. From inside the room she could make out the burble of the television which she had switched on so that Pretzel would be less lonely, and thought she could hear Carol Smillie. Pretzel liked Carol Smillie. Joyce sighed with satisfaction as the key finally turned, and set off carefully down the stairs, her good handbag over her arm. Her slept-on, unbrushed hair, her bare, varicosed legs and the rickety *Bengal Blush*, all things which she had consigned to the there and then, concerned her not at all.

CHAPTER 2

SARA WAS FEELING sick in the usual way, that was to say, not quite unpleasantly so, and it was such a familiar feeling that it would have unsettled her to be without it. She had done her warm-up, showered, changed into the dark brown silk dress and fixed her face and hair, also in the usual way, which meant about an hour before she really had to. So she had walked about the dressing room, switched the radio on, cracked her knuckles, practised deep breathing, switched the radio off, made some faces in the mirror and asked herself why she did this for a living.

Outside, she could hear the hum of people who had leaked out of the Prommers Bar and were lining the stuffy corridor around her dressing room door. They would be leaning on the walls fanning themselves with programmes, knocking back warm drinks and waiting for the second half, in complete if not comfortable relaxation. She would give anything, *anything* to be one of them, to be in a summer top and sandals at a concert, sipping heartburn-inducing house wine in the interval, the biggest challenge of the evening being the momentous decision on the way home between Chinese or Indian.

Feeling sorry for herself, she clipped on her diamanté

earrings, the only jewellery she would wear with this slinky, chocolate satin dress, and turned her head to watch them catch the light of the dozen or so bulbs round the dressing room mirror. The earrings were too large for real life, and too showy even for some musicians she could think of, the professional mice who would consider the playing of the Dvořák Cello Concerto at the Proms as a grave undertaking whose solemnity was not to be compromised by any flippancy in what they might call 'the earring department'. Sara smiled to herself in the mirror. All the more reason to wear them, then. She liked the frivolous note they struck, and the question they raised—brassy or classy?—which led to the next question—who cares?—as long as the Prommers enjoyed the bit of sparkle. What they made of her playing was up to them, once she had given them her best. The one-minute bell sounded and the hum in the corridor began to subside.

Now her shoes were on and she had, out of a mixture of superstition and supreme practicality, worked out the exact spot (a little above her knee) on the front of the dress where she needed to pick up the fold in her right hand and raise it before she took the first steps out on to the stage, if she were to avoid standing on her hem, ripping the dress, falling on hundreds of thousands of pounds' worth of Peresson cello and impaling herself on her bow. The audience would love that.

The sick feeling was still there. She swigged some water from the glass on the dressing table, made her way over to the green velvet sofa and perching on the arm (she did not want to walk on stage with even one satin crease across her stomach), she rang Andrew on her mobile.

'Hello. It's me.'

'Oh. Hello.' Silence.

'Look, I'm sorry.' Sara sighed, less with regret than with the effort of apologising when she did not feel she had been at fault.

''S all right,' Andrew replied, unenthusiastically. After another silence he added, 'Me too. I'm sorry. But I have to put the kids first, don't you see?'

Sara did, but she also saw that Valerie, Andrew's ex-wife, should not have insisted that he look after them tonight at two hours' notice. And she also saw that the result, her own barging angrily out of the house to drive up to London alone, was utterly understandable.

'Andrew, I do wish you were here.'

'Look—well, never mind. So, are you ready? Are you all right? I've got the radio on. First half was good. I do like those St Anthony Variations. But everybody's waiting for you. How're you feeling?'

'Sick. Doing my deep breathing.' She found herself smiling, as if he had just walked into the room. 'It's lovely to hear your voice,' she added.

'Oh darling, it's lovely hearing you. I'm just so sorry I'm not there with you.'

'Well, I suppose I'd have booted you out by now anyway, if you had been here. I need the time by myself, just before.'

'Time to feel sick in, you poor beast. Look, you'll knock 'em dead. Live from the Albert Hall. Enjoy it.'

Sara smiled at the unnecessary reassurance. 'Oh I will, I will. I'm ready. I'm always like this before I go on.'

'And look, drive back safely, won't you? I'll be here.

The M4 should be fairly empty this late, but don't do anything silly. I'll see you later. Break a leg. I love you.'

'I will. Love you too. Got to go. 'Bye.'

There was a knock on the door. 'Three minutes, Miss Selkirk.'

'Thanks,' she called back. And she was grateful, not just for the call but because, as it always did, in that instant her sick feeling vanished. She stood up, stretched her arms up over her head, took two deep breaths and realised she was still smiling. Now the odd jumble of furniture, the pipes running under the ceiling and the fuggy warmth in the dressing room, that made her think she was in the bowels of a very old cross-Channel ferry, ceased to command any of her attention. With her cello in her left hand she crossed the now empty circular corridor that ran right round the building, and joined the leader and conductor in the passageway that led up and on to the stage. They exchanged kind nods and good wishes. The cue that told them that the orchestra had finished tuning came, and the leader made off up the ramp. Two stewards held open the double doors and nodded him through. The applause drifted back to Sara. Simon was looking at the ground. With a raising of the eyebrows and a gesture of the hand, he invited Sara to precede him. Now. She beamed at him and they exchanged a wink. Breathing deeply to control her excitement, she picked up the fold of her dress and stepped forward into the dark tunnel.

Her arrival on the stage brought applause and whistles. Smiling broadly, she wove her way through the orchestra, followed by Sir Simon Rattle, and bowed to the audience, taking in the vast arena, the promenaders' floor with the fountain in the centre, the rows of stalls, behind them three crimson-curtained tiers of boxes, and higher, staggeringly high now, the circle and the colonnaded gallery. Then she turned to the orchestra and inclined her head towards them before taking her seat, thinking that really, she was quite stupendously, outrageously lucky, the luckiest person by far out of all the hundreds in this vast auditorium. To walk out of the darkness into this beautiful bright light, about to play the Dvořák Cello Concerto with this wonderful orchestra, to know with certainty that this thing that she was being allowed to do was what she was *for*, made her feel excruciatingly privileged. What *was* all that nonsense she had been thinking ten minutes ago?

She tuned quietly to the orchestra and nodded to Simon on the rostrum. And now she was to be allowed a few minutes listening to the opening Allegro before her first entry. Another thing she liked about the Proms, she thought, tingling with pleasure, was that you see the audience properly. The arena lights were kept on throughout and were placed so high in the roof that from where she was sitting she could see everything, instead of being half-blinded by stage lights beaming on to her from a darkened auditorium. She looked round again, enjoying the pace of the Allegro, her left hand rehearsing her first fingering. She felt momentarily, madly, gratefully in love with *everyone*, Simon naturally, but everyone else too, from the most pedestrian rank and file players, including the reptilian brass section, the worried-looking BBC crew, the stage technicians, the stewards, the corporate toffs in the boxes, down to every last one of the Prommers: the daffy girls, the skinny blokes, the earnest music teachers in sandals and bifocals, the students, the tourists, the oddballs, even that crazy one in the awful pink suit. She glanced up at

Simon and they exchanged a look, a mixture of *yes I'm ready, isn't this wonderful*, with perhaps a fleeting hint of *what are you doing later* which they both knew was the occasion, rather than themselves talking. He really is sexy, she considered, smiling, at least with a baton in his hand. God, save me from conductors. Concentrate. Concentrate, it's me in eight bars. Her eyes darted back to the pink suit.

The pink suit. That suit. Pink suit, pink suit, oh God it couldn't be. It couldn't. Watch, only six bars and I'm in. My God, it is. That pink suit. Two bars. Damn, I haven't missed it, have I? It is her. Have I? She's covering her eyes. Oh God, now, *now* . . . I'll be late . . .

*   *   *

NOT UNTIL the Finale did Sara dare to look again. Steeling herself for the sight, she saw that she had been correct. The emaciated creature in the pink suit was Professor Cruikshank, Sara's cello teacher from the time she had arrived at the Royal Scottish Academy of Music as a student in 1978 until she graduated, with most of the prizes, in 1981. Somehow, in the intervening years, the imperious, gifted and universally respected professor had become a bag lady.

Even in the minutes since Sara had first spotted her and nearly fluffed her entry, Joyce seemed to have liquefied a little. She was standing in the midst of a knot of people near the front, and was now bending unnaturally forward from the waist, like a melting snowman. She seemed to be holding her head up towards the stage at a difficult angle and the mouth was working gently. The large black handbag, surely very heavy, seemed to be pulling her arm almost to the ground. As Sara watched, Joyce dropped out of the audience altogether, sinking softly and noiselessly out of sight, her small body apparently too weak to withstand gravity any longer. Sara stared in disbelief as the Prommers, instead of going to her aid, created a circle around her and ignored her. Were they just going to leave her on the floor? Surely nobody, least of all the chummy Prommers, would ignore an old lady who had fainted? Sara was on the point of jumping to her feet and stopping the orchestra when the young man who had been standing nearest Joyce turned to his friend, raised one hand curved as if cupped round a glass, and made a swigging gesture. The friend raised his eyes.

So that was it. At the 1999 Henry Wood Promenade Concert given by the City of Birmingham Symphony Orchestra conducted by Sir Simon Rattle with cellist Sara Selkirk, Professor Joyce Cruikshank was lying unobtrusively pissed on the floor of the Royal Albert Hall. Sara turned her attention back to the music. No point in taking it personally and she had a concerto to finish.

CHAPTER 3

ALEX COOPER WAS washing her pants to Dvořák on the radio, sloshing water on the floor, rubbing, wringing and stacking up the multicoloured little twists of cotton around the taps. Nice colours, she decided, more intense when they're wet and seen against the bright white of the basin. They had lost the dusty look they had sitting on her dry haunches, next to her unloved, waxy skin. Practically the only coloured clothes she had now, they were, and terribly tatty, defeated-looking. Still, what did it matter, she thought forlornly, rubbing a smear of hand soap on an apple green gusset. There was nobody to see her knackered knickers, either on her or anywhere else. And even if (big if) *he* did, he would probably just let his gaze settle on them for the few seconds it took to decide to turn her down, the way he had that time when she had stood at his door wearing the long T-shirt, Calvin Klein's Obsession and little else. Alex let the water out of the basin and waited for the little coda of misery which always followed thoughts of him to pass.

At least Dvořák seemed to know all about it, she thought. Good cellist playing it. Lived near Bath, Alex knew that. She had passed her in the street once, last winter. If it hadn't been her it was someone very like her, slim and strong-looking, with long dark hair and big eyes that seemed to be looking miles beyond you, the sort of person who looks so successful as well as nice that you could just kill them. Alex knew that all she needed was a bit of success with something: work, or a man, *something*, and she could be like that too. Life was unfair.

Alex picked up the radio and wandered out of the bathroom to escape the atmosphere of misery she had filled it with, annoyed with herself for allowing even a knicker-washing session to have led to thoughts of Stephen Golightly and the Sulis Clinic. Again, she told herself that she had her own life to lead. It was a pity that her room confronted her with just how poorly she was leading it.

Not that it was a bad room, but it was small and not really hers. Her own African batik hanging on the wall and funny cactus lamp did not detract sufficiently from the truth that she lived in somebody else's house, surrounded by somebody else's misplaced confidence with colour, in this case peach and cobalt blue. At twenty-three Alex felt she deserved to be more than a lodger, living by her landlady's rules about noise, hot water and the electric fire. She turned up the radio and wondered what Sara Selkirk got paid just for sitting there playing the cello.

Back on the subject of what Alex deserved, she deserved *one*, a decent place to live; *two*, a proper job, and she certainly had *not* deserved what Stephen Golightly had done to her. Or not done. Alex knew—she could *tell*—that he had liked it when she had taken a bit of initiative and shown up in the T-shirt and had liked, too, watching her humiliation as he had feigned flattered surprise and refused to take her up on it. And she definitely had not misread things the way he later claimed in his patronising, fatherly way. So it was his fault, not hers, that she no longer had items *one* or *two*, because she couldn't have stayed at the clinic after that, even though the job had been just what she wanted, not with him living right next to her and practically laughing at her with those blue eyes. But nor could she, obviously, let anyone know the real reason for her leaving so suddenly. It was so humiliating. Even now, the huge, massive lie she had told to explain her departure seemed smaller than her own embarrassment at the truth. Alex ran over again in her mind her sudden and emotional exit from the Sulis Clinic and confirmed to herself that she had done what any normal person would have done. You had to survive in this world. They were the weirdos, not her.

But somehow in the muddle of quitting her job and moving out she had still held in her mind, for some point in the future, a picture of Dr Golightly coming to see her and saying something, saying that he had been wrong, he understood and please would she go back, *something*. She had not quite grasped at the time that she would not see him again, ever. Three months later, the bleakness of the idea could make her cry though it was not that, it was the Dvořák, only the Dvořák that was doing it now.

It sometimes comforted Alex to think of herself as offended rather than humiliated, so she now asked herself rhetorically what the hell he thought he had been playing at. And while maybe she shouldn't have told that lie and said what she said to Ivan on the day she left, it *was* Dr Golightly who was sending out the signals and *she* was the one who had had to give up her job and the little apartment. Her indignation grew as she banged about making toast in the corner of her room and opening a jar of some snotty stuff to spread on it, so that she was already quite angry when her landlady thumped on her door and told her to turn down the radio and that personal items were not to be left in the bathroom.

CHAPTER 4

I T WAS SO awfully hot in there, dear,' Joyce was saying from the sofa. 'So silly to faint like that. So sorry. I've never cared for the heat.'

Sara raised her eyebrows. Joyce had been flat out and snoring on the green velvet sofa since Sara had had her carted in and put there at the end of the concert. She had done three calls, showered, changed into jeans and a shirt, said her thank-yous and goodbyes to Simon, joined some of the orchestra for a drink and a sandwich in the Artists' Bar, returned to the dressing room and shaken Joyce awake.

'You're not suffering from the heat. You're drunk,' Sara said. She pointed to the dressing table where the empty vodka bottle stood. 'That was in your bag. What's been happening to you?'

Joyce eased herself into a sitting position. 'Happened? I just fainted with the heat, dear. You know.' She turned yellow, watery eyes on Sara. 'Nothing to do with you, dear. So sorry. I'll get out of your way now.' She rose and swayed like someone trying to stand on ice-skates for the first time, and peered at the bottle, no doubt, Sara thought, to check that it really was empty. Then, with a wan little wave of both hands which seemed to mean that she was finding the presence of the vodka bottle just too mystifying to think about any longer, she declared, 'Right then, I'll away home now.'

'Wait, wait. Where do you live? How are you getting home? You're probably too late for the tube, you know.'

They looked blankly at each other. Joyce's mind did not work fast enough to lie about being able to take a taxi, nor could Sara humiliate Professor Cruikshank by giving her the fare.

'Wait. I've got my car. I'll take you. You can direct me, I guess, can't you?'

In the car it became clear that she couldn't. Joyce travelled by tube and had no above-ground homing instincts at all, nor could she focus properly on street names.

'If you could just get me to the Angel, dear? Northern Line. I'm in Colebrooke Row, just behind.'

'The Angel, Islington?' Sara said, trying not to sound weak with dismay. 'The Angel. Right.'

As they drove, Joyce tried to reassert some professorial authority.

'A very fair attempt, dear, really quite good in places. But your legato was always a wee chink in your armour, I remember, always a chink. Need to work on upper arm strength and flexibility. So necessary for Dvořák, I remember using those very words to you. Did I not? And was I not right, too?'

In the dark, Sara smiled, glad that at least on some level the intolerable old bitch had not softened. It had been appalling to see and hear Professor Cruikshank so abject. Now, the lips writhing with self-certainty and the old hands gripping the top of the large handbag on her lap had restored the queenly demeanour Sara remembered. Had Joyce at that moment lifted one languid hand and circled her wrist in her cuff towards the cheering populace it would have seemed natural; certainly her indifference to the extent of the favour Sara was doing her in making at least an hour's detour from her route to the M4 was regal enough.

Joyce sank down further in her seat and fell asleep, her hands loosening their hold on the handbag. As Sara drove on she began to think that Joyce's circumstances (starting with the address in Islington) could not really be so very bad. There would be some sensible explanation for the vodka business. And for the pink suit. In fact, she now recalled hearing, a few years after she herself had left, that Joyce had retired a year or two early which surely meant that she had arranged matters comfortably for herself. She would have had a good pension after a lifetime at the Academy. Then there was the grand flat in the red sandstone terrace in Kelvinside, with Art Nouveau glass in its bay windows, brass door plates and skirting boards a foot high. Sara breathed in and suddenly smelled again the mixture of biscuits and beeswax that pervaded the place and saw again the high drawing room where she, marooned on a chair on the Turkish rug in the middle, had had her technique and musicianship subjected to three years of Joyce's excoriating tutelage.

Nearly twenty years later she could feel almost the same fear creeping into her that had sometimes overwhelmed her then. She had been nervous, conscious of the honour which, she had been given to understand (Professor Cruikshank left one in no doubt), had been accorded only to a few star students over the years. And although it did not feel quite like simple generosity, by summoning Sara to the flat for her lessons in the evening instead of teaching her during the day, Professor Cruikshank was in effect giving her unlimited time. Instead of the Academy's timetabled one-hour session, the evening lessons were never less than two and frequently more, and were followed always by Professor Cruikshank's tea ceremony, its intended message of reward for hard work overshadowed by the gaucherie of its delivery by someone who was not a natural hostess.

While Sara put away her cello Professor Cruikshank would leave the room and return wheeling a trolley covered with a clean and ironed tea towel. Underneath would be the teapot, cups and saucers, plates, milk, a basin of sugar cubes with sugar tongs and a plate of at least two kinds of home-made cake or biscuit, all on a perfect tray cloth. Only her thin smile would betray the pride she took in her baking, for Professor Cruikshank would, with a wriggle of the lips and an inclination of the head towards the trolley, say only 'almond shortbread' or 'Viennese fancies' or 'macaroons'. The manner amounted almost to a formal introduction, to which Sara felt the proper response would be to nod to the short-bread and reply 'Sara Selkirk, how do you do'. But she learned that a long *oh*, carrying an inane degree of surprise, was all that seemed required. Once early on and after a par-ticularly long and fractious session, Sara had tried to duck out of the tea, but Joyce's 'You'll just take a wee cup,' had been not an offer but a command. So tea was ritually enjoyed, Sara sensing that quiet compliments about the shortbread or the cake were appropriate even though the professor would of-ten dismiss them in a way that also dismissed Sara as a com-petent judge—'No, it's heavy', or 'No, needs a drop more almond essence'. Then Sara would set off with her cello strapped on her back, invariably in the dark and most often in the rain, to catch two unreliable buses and an underground back to her own dreadful flat on the other side of the city, a journey about which Joyce knew and cared nothing.

It had never occurred to her at the time but Sara knew now that the arrangement must have been, if not quite a breach of rules, then at least not strictly official. There were rumours in college of the cruel routine kind about Joyce's sexuality, just the kind of rumours that would circulate among the heartless parochial young of Glasgow about a single, middle-aged, unattractive and aloof woman. Of the substance of these rumours Sara neither experienced nor witnessed the slightest evidence. The discomforts of the lessons at the flat were rather those of finding her efforts perpetually inadequate to Joyce's demands and the feeling, which in three years never quite left her, of slight embarrassment that she was there at all. Because her teacher's manner towards her invited no deeper warmth, indeed Joyce seemed quite uninterested in her as a person and never volunteered anything about herself beyond the provenance of some of her recipes ('Mother's shortbread called for rice flour'), Sara felt always that in coming to the flat she was straying on to ground where she had no business to be. It was like eating a poke of chips off a high altar.

Skipping over the question of why she should have, Sara calculated that after selling the Kelvinside flat, Joyce must have bought a smaller but probably delightful place in London. Colebrooke Row, N1 seemed to prove her right, its mainly Georgian houses and long strip of communal garden down the centre looking even more prosperous in the generous glow of private outside lighting. They had just turned into it off the main road and Sara was noticing one of the nice things about London, the leaving of a busy road for a street filled with houses that is filled also with a beautiful hush. Little or no traffic disturbs the birds in the daytime and at night, you suddenly hear the sound of your wheels on dry leaves. She slowed the car to a crawl and woke Joyce.

'Joyce, we're here. What number?'

'Augh . . . gh,' Joyce gurgled, her mouth slapping sleepily over her teeth. 'Anywhere's fine, just here. Here'll do,' she said, thickly. But it was late, the street was long, Joyce was tired and Sara was kind.

'The number, what number?' she insisted.

'Eighty-one. Down the end.'

It was actually beyond the end. The road, lined with stuccoed, burglar-alarmed houses with original fanlights, grilles behind the barred windows and expensive plant tubs chained to their steps, came to an apparent end with St Peter's Street cutting across it. But beyond it, Colebrooke Row continued with another short terrace of houses which had escaped the gentrification of the rest of the street. Most of them were of unadorned brick and dark with dirt. The plant tubs were plastic, the phoney Georgian doors were off-the-peg from Doors 'R' Us or some such place, and the metropolitan, crime-phobic manner of doing up houses to resemble extremely pretty prisons had not been necessary or possible here. As Sara pulled over to park, her dismay at realising that Joyce lived somewhere in this lot was interrupted by a wail of anguish.

'Oh! Oh no! Pretzel! My wee Pretzel!' Joyce was pointing with a shaky hand at a dark mound on the pavement near the railings. It looked like a heap of discarded boxes. She was out of the passenger door before the car had quite stopped. At the sound of her voice something moved from the heap, got up and started barking.

The dog was tied to the railings outside number 81 by a rope attached to its collar. What seemed to Sara odd, but

which Joyce appeared not to have noticed, was that surrounding the dog were two suitcases, several full bin liners
tied with string, three boxes of books, a table lamp, a
dozen or so Tesco bags, a box of crockery and, propped
against the railings, an upright cello case with an envelope
addressed to Joyce sellotaped to it. Sara ripped it off and
pulled Joyce to her feet, pushing the excited dog away
with her foot as forcefully as she could without quite kicking it. She regretted it at once, sensing saliva on her shoe.

'Open it,' she said, although what had happened did not
really require explanation.

As she read, Joyce moaned. She handed the single sheet
of paper to Sara with a guilty glance and crouched down
once more to Pretzel.

TO WHOME IT MAY CONCERN

Owing to Non paying of Rent you owe Us and Other
matters since before Easter and even before
we are giving you notice to get out as of
immediatly We have been patiant for months now
its beyond a joke You were Warned about the Dog
several times by myself when I called for Rent
also my wife mentiond other important Matters re
Cleaning ect and also my son NB. That time you
threatend us with the Dog he warnd you he would be
changing the locks well now he has

You were warnd you brought this on your self you
only should of paide Rent on time and got rid
of Dog. P.S. we are keping Rug and T.V. in line
of Rent still owing our selvs.

Sara looked again at the jumble by the railings, then at her watch. Nearly one o'clock. She opened her mouth to speak and, looking down, took in Joyce's thin back in the light of the yellow street lamp, the hair like a wispy old dishcloth dripping over her collar and the snuffling noise that might have been coming from her or the dog. She closed her mouth again. It was a stupid question. Of course Joyce didn't have any friends she could go to.

'Don't worry,' Sara said instead. 'We'll get most of it in, give or take a Tesco bag.' Joyce straightened up and dared to look hopeful. 'You can stay with me. For a few days, anyway, until you're sorted out. You'll have to come back to Bath with me.'

Joyce turned tremulous eyes to Sara. 'Thank you,' she said, her lips finding the words difficult to say, perhaps through unfamiliarity. She was shaking now. The chill of the street and the night were stealing into her body and even the bedsit's electric fire that smelled of burning dust would have been welcome. She overlooked for the moment that she had no money for the meter in any case, but to break down now because she was out on her ear and debarred even from that much comfort would have been self-pitying, a characteristic that Joyce Cruikshank had never tolerated in others and was not now going to permit in herself.

'I think I'll just sit tight in here while you load up,' she said. She toddled round to the passenger door and opened it. Before she got in she called across the roof of the car, 'Oh, and you'd be wise to walk Pretzel up to the garden for a number two, dear. We don't want him doing it in the car, do we?'

Indeed we don't. But Sara still found it difficult to

explain to Andrew on her mobile exactly why, after finishing the performance of the Dvořák Concerto at a quarter to ten, she was still, at ten past one in the morning, three hours from home and in North London, waiting on the end of a rope for a dachshund to shit in the bushes.

CHAPTER 5

HILARY GOLIGHTLY FELT that she knew herself in mind, body and spirit, after more than a couple of decades thinking about it. She did things thoroughly on the whole, being a constructive sort of person, and her interest in what she called personal growth had moved on since she had begun to talk in such terms mainly to annoy her dad, who had been impatient with concepts such as karmic energy and psychic wellbeing after a lifetime in chiropody in the Harrogate area. Hilary was well up on her body rhythms, attuned both to her own and, after ten years of marriage, also to Ivan's, but while he continued to sleep like a boy (a very indulged one) and wake up loose-limbed with a mind emptied, usually with pharmaceutical help, of ordinary care, she was waking earlier and earlier. She knew she had undergone some change. So of late she had taken to lying until morning came, listening to the incessant summer rain and praying, although she was too practical to address any particular deity, that the change she felt in herself was the one she craved and for which she had risked so much.

What had not changed, unless to increase, was her sense of being responsible for Ivan, of being the stronger one, as well as older by eight years. She was still ever watchful for the signs that might warn of another of his episodes. She needed these hours spent beside him, but alone. Silently, in the dark before the day came, she was collecting her faculties in preparation for the next big thing, gathering enough strength for both of them. It was a habit formed early in their relationship, during his first episode, but there was something else now that was making her protective, cautious of mind and more careful in her movements.

The last Friday in July was wet and cold and Hilary rose silently, exchanged her nightie for an indigo sack dress and went downstairs, there being no reason now, except the fear that she might be mistaken, to delay. Gazing across the kitchen sink to the grass and the vibrant parsley patch, she pondered. She felt responsible in a way that was as yet untouched by anxiety, stronger in some way and paradoxically more vulnerable. Oh yes, and as sick as a dog. She turned on the cold tap and held her wrists under the water, a natural, healthful remedy for nausea she had read about and which today, as on the preceding six days, did not work. She turned from the sink and lit a cigarette, which did. As she stood puffing, letting blue threads of smoke weave into the dry clump of hair that fell over her face like a trailing plant with a bushy habit, she thought again about her parents.

The smoking, too, had started in defiance of Dad. Its unoriginality as a gesture now depressed her as much as it had enraged him. Hilary had been fifteen. Mum's personality had long been submerged in deference to both of theirs; she had shrunk into the role of ineffectual referee, fretting between them and clucking that their problem was that they were too alike. Hilary and Dad had been too busy hammering it out over boys, O levels and her hippy nonsense, refining their acknowledged, mutual stubbornness through several purifying stages of animosity, to notice Mum much at all. By the time Hilary lit up her first No. 6 in front of him they had achieved such a fragile, invisible perfection of hatred that they both took trouble to preserve it.

The fags had been stupid, Hilary saw that now. And Dad might even have been softened by grandchildren, but he was dead, and Hilary braced herself sensibly with the thought that it was impractical to mope over impossibilities. She thought of Stephen, Ivan's father, so different in every way, and imagined his joy. She must choose just the right moment to tell him herself. If. She sank into a chair at the kitchen table, stubbed out her cigarette, opened the box and pulled out its contents and the instructions. There was a lot to read. Ivan would not stir for a while yet.

Checking that the sleeping silence she had left behind in their bedroom was still undisturbed and that the dining room was empty, Hilary quietly closed both doors to the kitchen, lifted her dress, squatted on the floor and squirted the 'few drops of early morning urine' demanded by the leaflet into the tiny plastic container, designed by a man. She accomplished it with more ease than she expected and was silently congratulating herself when, rather too late, she realised that the leaflet had said nothing about where she was supposed to put the rest of it. The leaflet designer obviously assumed (naively, Hilary thought, for how often is a pregnancy test uncomplicated by who is or is not meant to know, and so *not* done on the quiet) that a person would be in the loo. But she hadn't

been able to use their bathroom because Ivan might have
staggered in for his early morning pee, and if she had pre-
empted that by locking the door she would have made him
suspicious. Cursing quietly, still doubled over and with her
pelvic floor held as tight as a fist, Hilary gathered her dress
up in a wad in front of her, waddled on splayed feet to the
back door, stretched up and unlocked it (a feat in itself),
made it outside and finished her pee in the herb garden,
sprinkling the chives. She stretched up to her full height
with a sigh of relief and surveyed the morning with defiant
dignity. Although she had no belief in an afterlife beyond a
faintly Buddhist question mark in her mind about continu-
ity, she looked up at the sky and hoped that her father had
not been watching. Now that he was dead she had, in an
effort to think kindly of him, grown fond of picturing him
looking down on her from a peculiarly Yorkshire Heaven, a
sunny place a bit like Castle Howard on a nice afternoon
with fresh tea and proper cakes and spotless toilets.

   Hilary returned to the kitchen in time to hear the
sound of the door into the dining room being opened and
closed. So she'd got the main part of the business done just
in time, although Mrs Takahashi would hardly be likely to
wander into the kitchen. She would be tidying her boring
little tourist's uniform of polo shirt and little denim skirt.
Next she would be taking up her position at the small table
overlooking the bird bath where no birds ever came, staring at the stainless steel cruet and the artificial primulas in
the cut-glass vase, waiting for the breakfast that she would
not eat. The woman was getting on Hilary's nerves.
Hastily, she carried out the rest of the instructions involving the dropper and the test tube, and placed the test tube
in its little stand on the high shelf with the jamjars and

Tupperware. Then she wiped her hands, filled and switched on the kettle, lit the gas and reached for the frying pan.

A quarter of an hour later she sank back into her chair at the kitchen table, grateful that she'd made it to the dining room and back without throwing up, and irritated beyond endurance at having to make the effort again. For the fifth morning in a row she had swallowed hard before cooking and serving Mrs Takahashi her bacon, sausage, tomato and egg, and unless today was going to be different most of it would come back on the plate, just pushed around a bit. Hilary had wondered momentarily whether to ask, on the second day, if there were some other thing that Mrs Takahashi would prefer for breakfast, but she had managed to stop herself. It was not, as she justified first to herself and later to Ivan, as if she was running the Ritz. Besides, the B&B was only a sideline. She and Ivan had their own proper jobs at Ivan's father's clinic, the Sulis, and it was only right that they put that first. They owed it to Stephen and he relied on them.

But the justification for Hilary's breakfasts, once rehearsed and ready, had not been called for. Mrs Takahashi had not complained and it was not because she could not speak English. She could when she wanted to. It was rather that she seemed, most of the time, not to want to. Where breakfast was concerned she certainly was not, scrawny little thing, driven by anything so basic as appetite. With mounting annoyance Hilary had continued to dish up the breakfast that she might have saved herself the cost of buying and continued to do without the lie-in she also could have done with. It had not occurred to her to ask Ivan for help with either.

On Tuesday, when the Traditional Bath Breakfast Platter had again come back rearranged but uneaten, Hilary had washed the egg yolk off the sausage and saved it, warming it up on the Wednesday, when it had come back still untasted but cut in two. The tomato was on its third day now. Hilary lit another cigarette with the satisfied thought that what Mrs Takahashi didn't know was that the parsley sprig on her plate this morning had also garnished Tuesday's, Wednesday's and Thursday's. It was a nice touch, parsley on a breakfast plate, and it never lasted less than a week if it was rinsed off after each trip to the dining room and kept in the fridge. She swallowed, flicked her ash into the puddle of lard in the still-warm frying pan on the table and looked at her watch.

Only another fifteen minutes and she would know. On no account must Ivan's hopes be raised until she was sure, because if she turned out to be wrong it could set off another episode. She fingered one nipple under her dress to check that it was still as abnormally hard and tender as it had been for a week now. The sensation brought a delicious recollection of all those frantic and frequent attempts at conception, mixed with the fear that all that side of the business might now be over. But there was no reason why it had to stop now, just because its purpose had been achieved. She would give up the ciggies the moment it was confirmed, but it would be hard to give up the sex. And anyway, suppose she wasn't. In fact, she often felt something like this just before her period, which had been late before, and she had only felt sick, not actually thrown up. It could even be the start of the menopause.

A slight cough from the dining room signalled that Mrs Takahashi had finished. Hilary balanced her cigarette on the side of the table and went through, waving her arms to disperse the smoke that followed her. Mrs Takahashi looked up meekly and offered the smiling and bowing that courtesy demanded and which by now Hilary could hardly be bothered to return. The dining room was freezing and Mrs Takahashi, even with her cardigan slung around her shoulders, seemed to have grown even smaller with the cold. But it was midsummer, the end of July, and you didn't go round switching on fires in July, not even this cold and wet one. The trouble was this room got no sun, but July was July. In Harrogate, where July often felt like November, you put another layer on. You didn't wear it round your shoulders.

'Any plans for today? Will you be wanting a lift down into town again?' Hilary's questioning bore the roughness of interrogation rather than polite enquiry.

Mrs Takahashi half shook her head in a gesture of non-committal. Very odd woman. 'Today I am tired. Today I shall stay here and perhaps walk in this area.'

Hilary nodded. 'There's the towpath along the canal, that's a nice walk. Don't go all the way round by the road, you can get to it through our land. Just go up through the vegetables, there's a way through. The vegetables are nice at this time of year. If you like vegetables. You're welcome to wander.'

Hilary returned to the kitchen with the plate and took in a rack of cold toast. People did go on holiday alone, so perhaps it had not been all that odd when Mrs Takahashi had turned up without a reservation last Sunday and booked a room for the week. They were seldom full, being too far out for couples 'doing' Bath and too small for families wanting countryside diversions. Their situation wasn't all that countrified anyway, being close to the railway and the canal. Most people stayed only one night, including a proportion of those who booked two and cancelled the second after experiencing the first, a statistic that Hilary did not bother herself about. She was an artist first, and her work at the Sulis was the next important thing, after supporting Ivan with the smallholding. With a self-justifying sniff Hilary deposited the toast on Mrs Takahashi's table and exited.

Nevertheless it was slightly strange that Mrs Takahashi, apparently such an organised little woman, would just wash up on the edge of Limpley Stoke with a huge suitcase and no plans. And it had seemed odd that she had then spent half the time in her room, the smaller one which, like the dining room, got no sun. On the first day Hilary had given Mrs Takahashi a lift down into Bath straight after breakfast, dropping her at the abbey before going on to work at the clinic. Mrs Takahashi had done the usual tourist things, that evening showing them the leaflets of the places she had seen, with a display of nodding and polite English. On the Tuesday she had gone out again after her non-breakfast, leaving her room exquisitely tidy, and returned in the early evening a little dejected. With rather forced nods and smiles she had said she had simply been walking. On the third day she had stayed in her room.

On the fourth, yesterday, coming back from work at six o'clock, Hilary had heard the sound of weeping from behind her door. She would have left her to get on with it, but she might get a late arrival wanting the other room and what sort of advertisement for her establishment was that, the sound of sobbing from next door? Summoning the charm which was going to have to substitute for compassion, she had knocked quietly on the door and asked her if anything was the matter. Mrs Takahashi had apologised and bowed several times. Then a frown had crumpled her small face and she had struggled not to cry again. Hilary had hesitated. She would not venture any enquiry about the absent husband. She did not want to be told about the absent husband, to be thought of as a person who knew about breakups or breakdowns, as if it were written all over her face that she was some kind of expert. Ivan was fine now, that was what mattered, so she had simply said, 'Good. Well. We'll see you in the morning then. Eight o'clock for breakfast? Fine.'

'Very private people, the Japanese,' Ivan had said nonchalantly, when she had told him about it later at supper. 'Saw her round the garden today, trying to chat to Leech. Obviously at a loose end.'

'Can't think what she made of Leech. Still, I feel sorry for her,' Hilary had lied, as she rose to clear their plates. Really, she couldn't wait for Sunday when Mrs Takahashi's stay would be over. She had already decided that should she ask to stay longer she would say the room was already booked. But Ivan expected her to be caring about strangers in a baseless, general way and knowing this, she found that she could often sound as if she were. 'Poor little thing,' she had added, ruffling Ivan's hair on her way to the sink.

Ivan would be down in a minute. Hilary looked at her watch, sucked on the last half-inch of her cigarette and stubbed it out in the scooped-out tomato half on Mrs Takahashi's plate. It was time. She opened the cupboard and rose up on tiptoe to check the test tube for its little blue ring. Which wasn't there. It wasn't there. *It wasn't there*. A whole thirty minutes had gone by and the blue ring definitely wasn't there. Hilary turned from the cupboard and found that in the few seconds during which her back had been turned, somebody had changed the set. The world had been transformed into a warm, generous place, full of people dear to her. Suddenly she knew herself to be warm and generous too, a woman so heaped with blessings that she could not begin to count them all: she was an artist whose fingers were aching to sculpt, the happy wife of darling, damaged Ivan who was going to be so happy now. And Stephen would be so happy too, the most wonderful, generous father-in-law in the world, a brilliant doctor and so much more, a true healer. She scraped the tomato ashtray into the bin along with the rest of the debris on the plate and chucked her cigarette packet in on top. She would give this place a really good going-over. She would redecorate in the autumn. Leech would have to go, of course, which in many ways would be a relief. Perhaps Mrs Takahashi would like an orange for breakfast, or she could try her on grapefruit, or melon, perhaps strawberries, even Ivan's macrobiotic muesli. She must get the poor little woman to eat. She should perhaps switch to fruit herself, to prepare her body. Ivan would know what to do. She returned to the dining room.

'More tea or toast?' she offered. Just as she was about to make her offer of fruit tomorrow, she heard Ivan come into the kitchen. With a smile she cleared the last of the breakfast things away and returned. Ivan was getting himself a spoon, looking that sulky, little boy way he did in the mornings, an effect heightened by the checked blue shirt. Hilary dumped Mrs Takahashi's dishes on the table and sat down out of his way and watched as he mixed flakes, grain and dried fruit from five plastic containers in a bowl, added live yogurt from the fridge and a sprinkling of wheatgerm. She had grown used to his tranquillized lack of excitement over things and she had almost stopped noticing how she mimicked his mood with a detached flatness of her own. Despite her elation she said, in a sleepy voice that seemed to her quite natural for the circumstances, 'Pass us a banana, pet,' and pushed her bacon-scented hair off her face. If she announced it calmly, it would simply add to his joy.

Ivan was leaning against the sink eating his cereal, his long torso slightly, boyishly concave. He pushed himself on to his feet, took a banana from the bowl and tossed it to her.

'Ivan?'

He was in a good mood. In a bad one he might have ignored her altogether or just handed her the bunch. Encouraged, Hilary rose, crossed the room, took the cereal bowl and spoon out of his hands and put her arms round him. She whispered in his ear, 'Ivan? I'm pregnant. We're going to have a baby at last.'

Ivan said nothing at first, but by the slight tightening of his hands on her shoulders, and his muffled gulping as he cried into her hair, she knew that he had heard. And was overwhelmed with delight.

CHAPTER 6

ANDREW STOPPED ON the pavement at the corner of Green Street and said, 'I'm not sulking,' in a voice that made it clear he was.

Sara appeared not to hear. His eyes left her face and followed the direction in which she was looking. They both watched in silence as Joyce and Pretzel wandered ahead into the crowd in the sunshine. Both sides of Green Street in Bath were lined with trestle tables and awnings; plastic tables, chairs and umbrellas were arranged on the road down the middle and everywhere there were people, inordinate numbers of them in aprons selling and serving food and drink, and many more buying from the stalls, laughing in groups, sitting or standing with plates, glasses and carrier bags. Mingled with the scents of fresh fruits, wood smoke, garlic and grilling meat was an almost tangible layer of amused incredulity that this combination of sunshine, food and people was happening in England, and that was what gave the game away. In France, Italy or Spain it would happen every week and be called the market; in Bath it happened once a year on the last Saturday in July and was called the Bath International Taste Extravaganza, the BITE Festival.

'Good. Glad to hear it,' Sara murmured. It was a technique that worked with very small children, she believed, simply to swamp petulance with unironic good nature. It appalled her, if she thought about it, that she was using it on Andrew, so she refused to think about it.

Amid the crowd Joyce remained distinctive, her pink suit and chiffon scarf standing out against the vest tops and shorts of other people. A child, stooping to pat Pretzel, was gently pulled away by its mother. As she ambled slowly from stall to stall down the street, her passage eased by the undeclared *cordon sanitaire* that surrounded her, Joyce remained separate and alone, although the shy smile and wave which she was now turning to send Sara and Andrew's way suggested that she was not aware of this.

'Wave. Wave back,' Sara commanded. 'Smile.' Andrew obeyed, then turned to Sara. The smile died on his face as he saw that tears were running down her cheeks.

'Darling,' he began, taking her hand. 'Darling, I'm sorry.'

'It's all right,' Sara said. 'I'm fine. It's just so awful, seeing her like this. If you'd known how she used to be. We've got to do something.'

Andrew sighed. 'I know, but what?' His years as a police officer had shown him more than he had cared to see about chronic alcoholics and he would have described his pessimism over Joyce's chances of recovery as realistic. He also knew, after three years of loving the passionate, compassionate and downright bloody unreasonable optimism of Sara's view of people, that she would consider his view offensively cynical. He sighed again.

Sara was saying earnestly, 'Look, I know she's in a bad way, I know other people have probably tried. But don't you see? She hasn't sold her cello. She's sold everything else, bit by bit, but not that. There must be something in that.'

Andrew nodded. 'I know, I know.'

They had, since Thursday morning, been taking care of the now sober, wobbly, but far from contrite Joyce, and had pieced together her unedifying story. It followed the usual pattern: shortly after she had retired, and Joyce did not offer any reason why, the booze had begun to take over, bringing about the first of many losses, the respect of acquaintances and friends ('Just because I took a wee hoot mid-morning, dear. Some folk are awful narrow-minded.'). Next to go was any interest in anything except the next drink and the gradual selling off of just about everything she owned. Joyce had pointed out that three bottles of vodka a day for ten days out of every month soon mounted up, and had gone on to blame the Chancellor of the Exchequer for scandalous excise duty. Then had come the day she first collapsed drunk in public, which she described with vague arm waving and a short discourse on deplorably uneven pavements, marking the loss of her shame at what she had become. When they had reached the end of her sparsely detailed story Sara and Andrew had been surprised by the amount of energy that Joyce held in reserve for her firm denial that she was afflicted by anything more than 'a wee weakness'. Her friends had been faithless. She did not need to be saddled with owning a flat or furniture so why hang on to them. She tended to faint in the heat. A wee weakness, that was all.

Sara would have backed off at that point. Andrew had not.

'You call it what you like, and I'll call it a serious drink problem. And I want to make something clear. While you are a guest in Sara's house, you do not drink a drop, here or anywhere outside. Understood?'

Joyce had merely given him a huffy scowl. 'Who's he again, dear?' she had demanded, turning to Sara.

'Because if you do,' Andrew continued, 'I am going to make it my business to throw you out. I will not have Sara's kindness abused. Is that clear?'

Joyce had changed tack and assumed a ruffled, regal grace. 'I hope I know *my* manners,' she said. 'I would never let it be said that I outstayed *my* welcome.'

That seemed to amount to an uneasy agreement to Andrew's terms. Sara had looked pleased, as if a problem had been solved. Andrew had kept to himself the knowledge that it was a painless promise for Joyce to make at the end of a binge when her body would need time to recover before it could tolerate another drink. Before it would crave another.

He squeezed Sara's hand. 'No, she hasn't sold her cello,' he conceded, silently adding 'yet'. 'Of course we'll help her. I'm sorry. I'm just disappointed. We were going to have the day together on our own, that's all, and instead we've been clothes shopping for'—he substituted *a fucking hopeless, drunk down-and-out* for—'a long-lost cello teacher who's down on her luck. But it's fine,' he added hastily. 'She's not just your problem, don't forget.'

But it was Sara's house where Joyce was now staying, not *theirs*. He tried to think this without bitterness, but the fact that they still lived much of the time in separate houses reared up in his mind daily as an obstacle to complete happiness with Sara. He had bought a crummy little flat after his divorce from Valerie, which he was meant to be doing up (he had not lifted a paintbrush) while Sara still had Medlar Cottage, which was easily big enough for them both, as she pointed out, and utterly beautiful, which she didn't have to. But he had found he could not quite move in. Sara had bought the place with Matteo, and although he had died before he had spent any amount of time in it, it felt like someone else's territory.

'I know, but we could tackle the problem better if you moved in properly. Sell the flat,' Sara said.

They had had this conversation many times. Andrew paused, trying to find a variation in the script.

'Darling, I don't think Medlar Cottage would be right. Matteo—'

'Why do you have to be such a tomcat about it? Matteo didn't *spray* the place, you know.'

'It's not just that. I think I'd feel—well, swamped. After all it's not my house, it's *yours*. I can't explain it very well—'

'Oh? Swamped? By me, I suppose? Well, thank you. I'm not a black widow, you know. Do you have to be such a gorilla about territory? I don't see—'

'Darling—' Andrew cupped his hands round Sara's face and kissed her to shut her up. 'Cut the zoology. It isn't helping.'

They walked on, knowing they would return to the subject. They caught up with Joyce at the Fish Market stall. A family of Japanese was crowding round, amused by the sight of sushi in an English food market.

'Awful lot of tourists, aren't there?' Joyce said loudly, exempting herself from the category. 'They're everywhere.' As Sara and Andrew exchanged a look of longsuffering over her head, the family moved on.

'See that? What a price for kippers!' she cried, embarrassing Andrew into buying some. 'A kipper gives me awful heartburn,' Joyce confided in her loud voice as Andrew took his change, 'but the dog likes a head. Don't you, Pretzel?'

Sara smiled appeasingly at the stallholder and led Joyce gently by the elbow towards a table in front of the pub across the street, a suspiciously refurbished place now called the Snake and Ladder.

'Now—lunch. Are you hungry, Joyce?' Andrew asked, without a trace in his voice of anything other than generous good humour. He helped her into her chair and sat next to her. Sara, having wound Pretzel's lead round the table leg and encouraged him to lie in the shade underneath, took the other seat, kissing Andrew lightly on the head as she sat down, not just for his kindness but for concealing the effort of it. She took up the menu, whimsically decorated with snakes and ladders.

'There's grilled tuna or curried prawns on ciabatta, or gazpacho,' she told them, translating the witless themed offerings of python steaks, hot little vipers, and chilled snake soup. 'Or lasagne and chips.' Joyce's lips had almost disappeared in a grimace of uncertainty.

'I expect they could do something plainer for you,' Andrew ventured. 'An omelette, maybe, or soup?'

'To tell you the truth, I'm not a big eater.' Joyce managed a brave smile of apology, as if her wrecked stomach lining, still stinging after the ten-day vodka binge, were a mark of gentility. She leaned closer. 'But I've a sweet tooth. Would they have ice cream? Pretzel likes a wafer.'

'I'm sure they will,' Andrew said, beckoning the waitress. 'And what to drink? Mineral water, in this weather, yes?' Everyone seemed to understand that it was a rhetorical question.

After they had ordered, an atmosphere of waiting for

something settled a little sadly over them. Joyce peered round as if in search of something to talk about and took in the covered alley that ran down one side of the pub and connected Green Street and New Bond Street. Halfway down the alley was a side entrance to the pub, with a sign reading Lounge & Toilets. She rose from her seat, whispering to Sara, 'Just away to spend a penny, dear,' and had disappeared before Sara could reply.

Andrew and Sara sat on in silence for a few moments. 'Well, she did at least go to where the loos are. Not straight through the front entrance to the bar. Should I go after her?' Sara asked eventually.

'And do what? Stand over her while she pees to make sure she doesn't slip off to buy a drink? And suppose you stop her this time?'

'She does *want* to stop, though. She's as good as said so.'

'Ah yes, so she has. After she's swallowed so much booze she doesn't know what to do first—throw up or pass out.'

Sara gave an exasperated sigh. 'She needs help. And she didn't sell her cello.'

Andrew took her hand. 'We'll try to help. But don't be surprised if it doesn't work.'

'All right. But she still hasn't really explained why. I mean, if we knew *why*. Why would she suddenly start—'

She was interrupted by sudden high-pitched screaming from inside the pub. All movement in the street, except for heads turning in the direction of the noise, ceased for a moment. Andrew had already jumped up and was making straight for the side entrance. As she followed him Sara was aware of others behind her, also running.

The darkness in the narrow alley after the bright sunshine stopped her dead. Just inside the entrance of the pub Andrew turned to face her, blocking her way, talking over her head and demanding that the alley be cleared. Already people were backing up behind Sara; she could feel their breath, sweat and warmth as she was jostled forward. Beyond Andrew, Sara could see a young waitress, standing distraught but holding on, absurdly, to a tall glass of ice cream in one hand and a bowl of chips in the other, her deafening screams reverberating off the walls of the small space. Andrew turned back and stepped forward towards the girl. Sara followed. Deftly he relieved her of the ice cream and chips, turned back and handed them to Sara. One look from his eyes prevented her from demanding what the hell she was supposed to do with them. Andrew now had the girl by the wrists and he pulled her gently towards the entrance, turning once more to insist that the way be cleared. Her screams subsided as Andrew's voice, steady and gentle, told her she was coming outside and that everything would be fine in a minute. As they edged past, Sara stood transfixed, staring from them to the chips and to the ice cream in her hands, while the knot of people crowding the passage behind her melted out back in to the alley. Andrew turned to her and demanded, over his shoulder, 'Get her out. She's down there at the end.'

Sara made her way down the corridor. A door on the right led to the bar and lounge. An arrow on the wall above the word TOILETS directed her further down. At the end of the corridor was a door, facing back down to the entrance and marked PRIVATE. It was open, and a group of apron-clad young men stood some distance back in the kitchen, looking too stunned to venture into the doorway. Along with the smell of frying wafting from the kitchen came the thump of an inane and very loud radio.

'Christ! Turn that *off*, please!' Sara hissed.

A youth in the doorway straightened. 'Wha', the radio? Aw right. Don't notice it, 's always on.' He disappeared and the noise stopped.

In the blessed silence Sara looked further. On either side of the kitchen door another corridor, at right angles to the one Sara had just walked down and lined with tall cupboard doors, led off, left and right, to Ladies and Gents. Turning left, Sara came upon Joyce standing in front of the door marked Ladies. She had the knuckles of both hands in her mouth. She peered at Sara out of the gloom.

'Joyce?'

'I . . . I . . . was just . . . you know . . . kind of thing . . .' Her voice tailed away. The double doors of one of the built-in cupboards lining the passage were open. 'Just got lost. A . . . a . . . tourist. I suppose.'

Sara looked down. Lying half in and half out of the cupboard, with her face on the carpet right at Joyce's feet, was a small, dark-haired woman dressed in a denim skirt and polo shirt, with a cardigan round her shoulders.

Sara was still holding the bloody ice cream and chips. Resisting the urge to fling them as far up the passage as she could, she deposited them on the carpet behind her, trying to recall what to do when someone fainted. She crouched down to turn the woman over and undo a neck button. But on closer inspection, even in the gloom of the passage, Sara was at once struck by two things: the woman was dead, and she had been strangled with her camera strap.

Behind her, Joyce whimpered, 'Dear me, yes. An awful lot of tourists. They're everywhere, aren't they?'

CHAPTER 7

LEECH'S STOMACH WAS sending him the usual message about its being about time to stop for a bite to eat, but what was not usual was that Ivan had left him some lunch today. Ivan and Hilary didn't give him food regularly, he didn't think. Hilary called up the garden sometimes to say there was hot water if he wanted a bath, and sometimes there was something to eat on the kitchen table afterwards, sometimes not. Sometimes she washed clothes for him. It wasn't regular, or perhaps he was just bad at remembering. But it seemed that sometimes Ivan was chatty and worked with him in the garden, other times he was silent, at others just not there. What he was pretty clear about was that he, Leech, slept in the shed on the allotment, a big place full of seeds and plants and tools that he had found one day (when, no idea) on a day, anyway, on which he had wandered a long way along the canal path out of the town. They had put a folding bed in there after a while so that meant, he supposed, that they didn't mind. So, as far as his life had any pattern or content that Leech could point to and say yes, that is my life, he knew that he owned a sleeping bag and some clothes, he slept in the shed and worked in the garden, went with Ivan in the van sometimes, got his money from the post office. The shed had acquired a kettle and a mug and plates and he bought tea and UHT milk. He walked to Limpley Stoke in one direction and Bath in the other, along the towpath, when he needed bits and pieces, tobacco or food, a bottle of Coke. Not that he reflected on any of this, but he thought that Ivan did not usually leave him lunch.

Today, when Ivan had brought the food down for him, he had told him to work on the beans and lettuces until he got back. Stay here and do the beans and lettuces till I get back, all right? I'll be cutting the rye later today. Don't you touch it, I don't want you using the scythe. I'll do it later when the sun's been on it all day. Wear this, he had said, smiling and holding out the shirt, it's a nice shirt for you. And don't forget your hat. There were two white cotton hats on a nail on the back of the shed door and they each wore one on sunny days. Give me that T-shirt, it needs a wash.

It was so long since Leech had reflected on anyone's reasons for things that it did not occur to him now to wonder why Ivan had placed the plastic-wrapped sandwich, banana and bottle of Coke at the end of the patch where he was to work that day and told him it was his lunch. It had felt good to be given a gardening shirt to wear, though as far as he could remember (not far, he knew that much) Ivan had not done that before, either. As Leech weeded and hoed, he managed to sustain a mood of self-scrutiny long enough to realise that in his mind 'before' was, like all concepts relating to time, vague and amorphic, a word he had not realised he knew. 'Before' demanded the 'what' or it made no sense. Before what? 'Before' required a firm grasp of some notion of time previous and a recognisable period since, a then and a now between events, a space of time segregating all the sometimeses—the sometimes this, the sometimes something else—into recognisable memories that would sit obediently in their places in Leech's past and present, allowing themselves to be joined up into a continuum that would be his life so far. And Leech did not have any such firm grasp. On a good day he knew this, on better days he forgot he knew, as he forgot words such as amorphic. So those things that Ivan had not done 'before' might have been not done before yesterday, last week, last year or, for all Leech knew, the dawn of time. Meanwhile, his stomach was still telling him it was time to eat.

Settling himself on the ground at the end of the bean rows Leech pursued his mental exercise as he bit into the sandwich. He found to his pleasure that he had what felt like a clear recall of the morning. He had got up in a way that was familiar (encouraging him in the belief that he had done it that way many, many times now) and gone to watch the train. The train came every day, early, and he had got up and watched it pass—this, too, he felt with certainty, was something he often did. Then he thought he had walked down to wait behind the hedge at the house until Ivan came out. Today it had been different, because it was Hilary who had come out. She had come out to piss in the garden, which he did not think she had done before. No, that was wrong. That was yesterday. Or possibly not. Another day, anyway, if not today.

The sandwich, at least the wholemeal bread it was made with, was not good. Leech pulled out the white cheese and ate that, buried the remaining bread in the soil beside him, and ate the banana. He stood up to drink the Coke and walked along with it into the shed, wondering about the rest of the morning. He was wearing the blue shirt and white hat so yes, it must have been today when Ivan had told him to wear them, but that now seemed a long time ago. And he remembered, or his stomach did, that he had been hoeing a bean row when lunchtime came. Memory of anything between those two points had already slipped away like the dreams he sometimes woke up knowing he had been having, knowing too that they were already gone even as his brain clutched for recollection.

In a bundle of clothing at the foot of his bed he found his stuff and rolled a cigarette, sitting in the doorway. A lazy, afternoony warmth clung to the shed; it twisted the smells of never-quite-dry concrete and creosoted wood and burning match, rolling tobacco and banana skin into the air, and in the fly-buzzing, soft leaf-lifting, almost breeze-less calm Leech wondered if he might go and sleep for a while. Ivan's voice telling him to work until his return was receding into the already vanished morning. He sat in the doorway and looked out, swigging at the flat, warm Coke at the bottom of the bottle, sucking on his cigarette, while the scents of earth and cheese on his hands mingled with the smoke. Then, more as a pulse which moved the air than as a sound, he began to sense the whispering, metallic whipping of a distant train. He dropped the bottle and cigarette, hurried down the allotment to the far end, scrambled up the bank and through the hedge, across the brambly stretch of waste ground and up the steep slope of the embankment opposite. The steel noise was now beating from the rails in a quickening, hardening rattle. Leech scrambled upright and stood swaying, his eyes squeezed tight, as the diesel-hot wind lashed across his face, sucking him in, pushing him back, flapping the blue shirt against his chest, and behind his closed eyes he felt the lurching, dark train blot out the daylight as it rocked and whacked along the rails two yards from his feet.

CHAPTER 8

SARA TOOK STOCK. She was sitting on a bar stool opposite her chronically alcoholic house guest plus revolting dog, in love with a divorced, suddenly absent detective, and jealous of a corpse.

Andrew had leapt, with altogether too much zeal, Sara considered, into Detective Chief Inspector mode. Once he had delivered the screaming waitress into fresh air and the care of the pub landlady he had run back in, ordered Sara and Joyce away from the scene and shooed everybody out of the kitchen and into the lounge. There they had been instructed to wait. The sale of any more alcohol had been forbidden, and the bar staff were sullenly serving brackish pub orange juice that tasted of marmalade, and fizzy apple juice, gassy, sugary and innocent of apples. Sara sighed. Andrew obviously expected that they would be stuck here for ages and did not want any sozzled witness statements. Then he had disappeared, telling Sara that he would have to guard the scene until the investigating officers and forensic team arrived. A few minutes later they had turned up with the usual theatrical lights and sirens. At the sound someone had opened the pub's double doors and Sara had seen through the rectangle of brash white light that outside the sun shone as brightly as before but that the tables and chairs were being carted away so that police vehicles could park outside. The party was over.

Andrew did not reappear. Sara cast a look towards Joyce, who was rocking gently to and fro, crooning at Pretzel while with both hands she kneaded his ears over and over. Pretzel gazed back at her through wet eyes, the look on his face conveying perhaps deep sympathy, perhaps deep hunger, or perhaps the fervent wish that she would leave his ears alone. It was not clear who was trying to comfort whom, nor how successfully.

The pub furniture was depressingly dark and covered in fake Jacobean tapestry, the ashtrays were bright plastic and the beermats curling. Polystyrene models of ladders and snakes were stuck unconvincingly over the dark wallpaper. The lounge doors had been closed again and now no natural light reached them. The place should have smelled of warm, hoppy beer and plummy spirits, of red wine, wood smoke and roasting meat; instead it almost stung Sara's nose with the usual mixture of bar disinfectant, frying and fag ash.

At Joyce's side Sara seethed more with jealousy than anger. It had come at her once again and without warning, that dimension in Andrew's life that took precedence over anything to do with her. Another stupid corpse had jostled its way to the front and seized all his attention and until the stupid person who killed the stupid corpse was found, she knew she could expect little of his energy or imagination to be directed towards her or her needs. She felt sullenly that she was being elbowed out of her own relationship, and by a dead tourist.

She peered further into the gloom of the lounge, determined not to care who else was here or what they might think at being detained at the scene of the crime. The mainly young people, mostly men, looked completely, utterly ordinary: ordinary clothes, haircuts, accents and, presumably, drinking habits. They probably also had utterly ordinary tastes, opinions, jobs, homes, and she did not care how lazy it was of her to think so. She yawned. Yet someone, perhaps one of them, or one of the pensioner couples or quartets, or one of the pairs of young girls dressed for sexual combat, might be responsible for strangling the woman in the corridor. But Sara, yawning again, thought not. Most murders were domestic affairs. And unsatisfactorily married people go on holiday too, possibly more often than happy ones. She yawned again, tipped a practically empty bag of peanuts into her mouth and was rewarded with a throatful of gritty salt.

But it did seem now as if something was happening. Three uniformed police officers, accompanied by another man whom Sara recognised, recoiling, as Detective Sergeant Bridger, had entered the room. Two of them set themselves up at the bar with notebooks, and one by one the pub customers were called up and questioned. Nobody was kept for more than a couple of minutes, so Sara guessed that they were being asked only for their names and addresses, possibly also when they had arrived at the pub or visited the loo. One or two of the young men seemed to find the proceedings funny or embarrassing, turning to their friends, grinning or making faces, but most seemed to take their cue from the police officers who went about their job with undertakerly seriousness. Gradually the numbers in the place dwindled.

While this was going on Bridger and a female police

officer had installed themselves at an empty table. Sara watched as the landlord and landlady, with much head-shaking, were questioned in turn. The screaming waitress now seemed calmer but no more forthcoming, judging by the fifteen minutes it took Bridger to be appraised of all she knew. The WPO was now approaching their table.

Joyce glanced up from Pretzel's ears, looking old and frightened.

'I'm going to stay with my friend while you speak to her,' Sara blurted. 'That's all right, isn't it?' The WPO glanced back at DS Bridger. 'Should be,' she said. As an afterthought she added softly, 'Just insist, if you have to.'

But she didn't. Bridger gave Sara a cold but respectful smile which told her that while she was no more popular with him than she had ever been, he now knew her to be his boss's—what? This little problem was one that she sometimes scratched at. Girlfriend? She was a woman of thirty-nine. Lover? Such a private thing should not be pa-raded by a public label. Partner? She wasn't, not properly, nor did she like the business implication. Companion? The pensioners' choice, suggesting days out to factory shops and evenings in.

'Miss Selkirk is a close personal friend of DCI Poole,' Bridger informed the WPO. Friend, pronounced 'furr-end' to convey extra friendliness. As if it mattered now. Sara thought of Andrew and his desertion with a sudden wave of irritation.

'Now, Miss Cruikshank, I understand that after order-ing lunch'—Bridger was checking some notes, presum-ably information from Andrew—'you left your seat outside at approximately a quarter past one in order to go to the toilet. Would you please tell me exactly what you did when you got there?'

Joyce blinked a few times and her lips wriggled like two worms trying to free themselves of each other. 'I didn't go to the toilet. I went to the lavatory. And it's none of your business what a lady does in the lavatory,' she said. Sara drew in her bottom lip and looked at her hands. She had better not laugh, but God bless Joyce and Kelvinside.

'I mean, of course,' Bridger said wearily, 'after you'd used the toilet. Assuming you went straight to the ladies and er . . . used the facilities. What happened then?'

'I washed my hands, of course,' Joyce said primly. 'And then I tidied my hair and left the *lavatory*.' She patted her head in emphasis and Sara looked at her, knowing this to be a lie. The hair had obviously not been touched that day and looked more as if it had been ploughed than tidied.

'And then?'

'Those doors—there were doors in the corridor, going down the wall. She fell straight out, she fell *right out on top of me*.' Joyce looked round the table with indignant eyes, trying to enlist sympathy. 'The door must have been left open. Half open, anyway.' She seemed on the brink of complaining to the management.

'Did you see anyone else, either in the ladies' toilet or in the corridor outside?'

'No. Just me.'

'Really? Nobody at all? It's a busy day for the pub, after all. And there were a lot of people outside on the street who could have been using the toilets.'

'There wasn't anybody else. I was minding my own business. I don't go round looking at people in the lavatory, I'd like you to know.'

'And you say you think the cupboard door may have been open. What do you mean by that? Try to remember—when you came out and saw the doors, were they open or closed?'

'Did you not hear me? She fell straight out on top of me. So they must have been open. Or maybe half open. I think they may have been open, I'm not sure.'

'Were the doors open or closed when you went past them on the way in?'

'They were closed.'

'You're sure of that? They were definitely closed?'

'Yes, definitely,' Joyce said. 'They . . . well . . .' She had sensed a trap, too late.

'You see, if you're quite sure they were closed on the way in—obviously you could see them clearly—how is it you're not sure if they were closed on your way out?'

Joyce shrugged. 'It's no business of mine, what the doors were doing is nothing to me. I just . . .'

'If the lady fell out on top of you, you're saying, I think, that she must have been propped upright in the cupboard with her weight against the inside of the door? Which must have been closed, mustn't it, otherwise our lady wouldn't have been inside the cupboard at all, she'd have been on the floor in the corridor, wouldn't she?'

Joyce said nothing.

'Which suggests to me, Miss Cruikshank, that you must have opened the cupboard yourself. Is that what happened?'

Joyce was shaking her head vehemently. 'No, I didn't open any cupboard. I don't think I did . . . it's not what I . . .' She turned to Sara. 'Can we go home now, dear? Pretzel wants to go home.'

'Look, she's had a bad shock,' Sara said. 'You can't go on with this.'

'What would I be opening a cupboard for? It's not my cupboard.'

'Will you please tell me why you opened the cupboard, Miss Cruikshank?'

'I . . . I wasn't just . . . I don't do that kind of thing . . . I wouldn't . . .'

'Look, what's the point of this?' Sara demanded. 'How dare you put her through this? Can't you understand what it must be like to have a corpse fall on top of you out of a cupboard?'

Joyce had covered her face with her hands. She gave a quiet wail, which Pretzel answered with a protective bark. He scrambled to his feet and took up a wriggling guard in front of her knees, dancing up and down on his splayed front feet and growling softly. Bridger sighed. This would have to be followed up later at the station, with any luck when Poole's 'close personal friend', aka his bit of fanny, and the fucking dog weren't around.

'Yes, thank you, Miss Selkirk, I think I can,' he said. 'If Miss Cruikshank doesn't wish to continue, we can speak to her another time. But we shall need to interview her again.' He had deliberately omitted to say, 'as a witness', but this seemed to satisfy Selkirk, who was leaning back with her arms folded. God, she was so bloody superior, all big eyes and no tits. 'And I understand that Miss Cruikshank is staying with you, isn't she? Well, we'll call and arrange for her to talk to someone at the station, assuming you have no objection. Now, if I may detain you for another few minutes, perhaps we can go on to what you saw when you came down the corridor. Assuming your dog doesn't mind?'

Pretzel slithered back down to the floor and rested his chin on Joyce's foot. Ten minutes later, Bridger dismissed Joyce and Sara generously, after hearing Sara's account of finding the dead woman and Joyce in the corridor. He even managed a smile as he watched them make their way, with the bandy-legged dog, back out into the sunshine. Selkirk wouldn't be looking so superior much longer. He would crack the old soak's pathetic story about the corpse falling on top of her out of the cupboard, because Bridger's instincts were telling him something quite different. Cruikshank was a down-and-out with a drink habit, and the Jean Brodie accent and the presence of Selkirk didn't alter that. She'd opened that door, all right. But she had been opening it to stuff the corpse in. Because, coming across an easy touch in the toilet, a Jap woman even smaller and weaker than she was, she'd gone after that expensive camera, maybe the wallet, too. That black stinking handbag was big enough to stash them. In all likelihood the Jap had left her stuff on the side of the basin when she was washing her hands or looking in the mirror, people never learned. Anyway, she had presumably seen Cruikshank trying to lift the stuff and put up a struggle, more of a struggle than Cruikshank had bargained for. Perhaps she hadn't meant to kill her, but after she had, she'd tried to hide her in the cupboard. If she'd managed it, the body wouldn't have been discovered for hours. It was risky, but less risky than leaving her in the toilet. They'd just ordered lunch, hadn't they, so she was going to be stuck there for a while and unless she hid it the body would be discovered within minutes, while she was still there. And she had already been in the toilet too long to rush out pretending she'd just found her dead. If she'd been lucky she could have got her into the cupboard in a few seconds, but then the waitress had appeared and spoiled that little plan.

Bridger beamed with such sudden amiability at WPC Frayling that she looked over her shoulder expecting to see someone else. She had never seen him so pleased.

'We'll have her charged within twenty-four hours,' he told her.

'You're very confident,' she said. 'Think you've got the evidence, then?'

Bridger performed a drum roll on the table with his fingers. 'Oh, we'll get the evidence. I know she's guilty. I'm a lateral thinker, and I'm talking with ten years' experience here. Experience and instinct.'

Yes, he had a good feeling about it all. He did not go on to explain to Frayling that although his instincts had let him down in the past, this was different. It was different because this time, and for the first time, Detective Chief Inspector Poole was in complete agreement with his version of the probable course of events.

CHAPTER 9

IVAN AND HILARY Golightly opened the front door together, looking slightly frightened in the yellow light of the hall. It was raining again, and Ivan stepped aside to usher Andrew in under the dark and dripping doorway. They walked ahead of him down the narrow hall.

Their sitting room had the beige, slept-in look of early Habitat and Andrew noticed as he sat down that there had been more recent and thoughtful ethnic additions to the tweedy three-piece suite: pink and green cotton throws concealing, Andrew was sure, the worst stains on the elderly armchairs. On the back wall was the ubiquitous pine storage system containing a collection of books, plants, tapes, mugs, plates, telephone, pens and other domestic paraphernalia which suggested that much of the couple's lives were lived in this room. There was original art on the white walls, mainly unframed, abstract oils of which one could imagine people saying that they 'had something' and leaving unanswered the question of what. Art postcards in clipframes filled the sides of the modern tiled fireplace. On the mantelpiece and window sill were several cranky attempts at figurative sculpture, some in wire and plaster, others in clay or papier mâché, which shared the single virtue of being small enough to escape serious notice.

Andrew turned to the couple sitting on the sofa, concluding from the faint pride in Hilary's eyes that she had been watching his visual scan of the pictures and sculptures, and that they were hers. Ivan and Hilary were holding hands. She looked a good few years older than her husband, in her mid-forties judging by the grey streaks in her long, frizzy dark hair, and much more solid. She had a wide, sensual mouth and very large breasts which Andrew felt sure she would refer to as her bosoms, happier with the notion of maternal safety than of pneumatic sexuality. She was of his mother's type, women for whom there exist two states of being: very, very busy or very, very tired. Such women look as if they work harder than their husbands, Andrew had noticed, especially if the husband is of Ivan Golightly's sort: fair, tall and thin, with impractical hands and large, intelligent, frail eyes. Andrew suddenly remembered, in the way that he quite often did when he really should be thinking of other things, a remark of Sara's. She had said (he suddenly also remembered that at the time she had been naked in bed and sipping a cup of tea, watching him dry himself after a shower) that his body looked as if it had been designed for two things: rugby and sex, and what a good thing he didn't bother with the rugby. Andrew felt that she might judge Ivan Golightly's body to be designed for chess and poetry. As if that were relevant. He coughed to signal the start of proceedings.

'Now, you reported Mrs Takahashi missing at nine-thirty this evening. What made you think she was missing at that time? It's not terribly late to be out, after all.'

'Well no, it's not,' Hilary said. The sense of solidity was

•

strengthened by a nasally sensible Yorkshire accent. She stretched forward on the sofa to make her point. 'It's just that she's been out all day, since before nine this morning. And she comes back before seven, usually. She's been sat in her room for the past few evenings. And well, she . . . she, look, I don't pry, but she . . .' She stole a look at Ivan. 'She was on her own, she didn't get up to much, what with the weather so changeable. So . . . so I rang the police station, just in case . . . you know, an accident, run over, what with the traffic driving on the other side . . . or worse. She had seemed a bit upset, you see.'

'Upset? In what way?'

'My wife is very sensitive to other people,' Ivan said, gazing at her with a look that made Bambi look like a Komodo dragon. He stroked her hand. 'She can sense things about people. She's very intuitive.'

Hilary seemed to know how silly this must sound. 'Well I don't know if it's that, or what. I heard Mrs Takahashi crying in her room, Thursday night it was. I asked if she was all right and she said yes. You can't pry, can you? But she wasn't happy. I do get feelings, vibes, sometimes,' she said, stoutly. 'And sometimes people try to do away with themselves, when they're upset, don't they?' She glanced at Ivan.

'Especially now,' Ivan said, fondly. 'Heightened intuition, it's well known.' He turned to Andrew with a look of sleepy pride. 'My wife is having a baby. We only found out yesterday. We've waited so long. We're so thrilled.' The interlocking fingers resting on the sofa squirmed and tightened.

'Oh, Ivan, don't. We should be thinking about Mrs Takahashi.'

'That's lovely news. Congratulations,' Andrew said, with a nod rather than a smile. 'Got three myself.' He was unwilling to pursue the matter of Hilary's intuition—which he did not believe in, hers or anybody's—and she had in any case given him several quite straightforward reasons to account for her uneasiness about Mrs Takahashi's safety.

'Now, I'm afraid,' he began. He took in their concerned, gentle faces and judged her certainly, him less so, to be a non-panicker, which would make the next bit easier. 'Now, I'm afraid we do have reason to suspect that Mrs Takahashi may, I stress *may*, have been involved in a serious incident which took place in Bath this morning. I would like, of course, to be able to eliminate the possibility if I can, and that means finding some identification for Mrs Takahashi.' He paused. 'A photograph, ideally. So I would like to have a look in her room, and if possible locate her passport.'

'Oh my God,' Hilary exclaimed, raising her hands to her face. 'You've got a body, haven't you? Oh my God.'

Ivan stood up. 'You're not to upset yourself. You stay here. I'll take the inspector along.'

The room was adequate and unpleasant, heavy with the scent of a syrupy room spray which mixed with, rather than disguised, the gingery, inflammable smells of nylon carpet and furniture glue. The Golightlys had fixed up the room for B&B guests on minimum outlay, with dismayingly twee bedroom furniture with plastic gilt handles. Under the ugly light of an overhead bulb in a white fringed shade the woman's unremarkable possessions were set out with precision on the dressing table, a reddish, synthetic veneer-eal surface one scratch away from raw chipboard. Andrew found the passport in the dressing table drawer

and flipped it open. The woman in the photograph, looking with a half-smile towards some focal point slightly to
one side, was about five years younger than the blue-faced
corpse in the mortuary, but it was the same face.

Hilary stood in the doorway. 'She's died, hasn't she?
You've got a body. You think Mrs Takahashi's dead. Don't
you?'

Andrew turned and nodded. 'It's possible, Mrs
Golightly. There was a fatal incident in Bath this morning,
and we'd like to rule out Mrs Takahashi if we can. We'd like
your assistance with identification, though of course her
next of kin—' Just then Ivan swayed on his feet and sat
down heavily on the bed, turning to his wife with a face
that was stunned and white.

'Oh, Hil, how can—I didn't think we'd have to do that
kind of—'

Hilary came forward protectively and placed her arm
across his shoulder. 'My husband isn't good at taking
shocks. He mustn't be given sudden shocks, he reacts
badly. Poppet, come back to the lounge with me and sit
down.'

'No, no, I'm fine. Fine now,' he said, standing up.
'Don't worry about me. You're the one who needs looking
after.' They exchanged another of their looks. All four
hands were now earnestly kneading one another.

Hilary looked at Andrew, who appeared to be waiting
for something. 'You don't mean right now? It's after
eleven. Do you really want my husband going off to iden-
tify a body at this time of night?' She looked up at her husband with concern.

Andrew pursed his lips, feeling almost nauseous. Perhaps it was jealousy. It was of course late, in other people's

terms. He tended to lose sight of that kind of thing, but if he were honest, the reason he was still calling on people at close to midnight had less to do with dedication to his job than with postponing the moment when he had to return to his depressing flat, because he had been assuming, with a combination of gloom and angry pride, that he would not go back to Medlar Cottage that night. He was still feeling piqued at how Sara that afternoon had in the space of a minute grown so remote, extinguishing any glimmer of sympathy or understanding for the position in which his job placed him. Suddenly all he wanted was to get back to her, the unreasonable, adorable, demanding bitch, and he still had to deal with Cathy and Heathcliff here.

'It is late, but if you're agreeable, sir, I'll take you over to the mortuary now. Best if we can get the ball rolling. We don't want any unnecessary delay in informing next of kin, and confirming the identification, as I'm sure you'll understand.'

It was horribly easy to say the right thing sometimes, Andrew reflected, as he drove down the hedge-lined lane that skirted the village of Limpley Stoke and turned the car on to the main road. Ivan sat beside him, calm. Andrew had come straight out with the right words, about next of kin and all that, when what he actually meant was let's get on with it so that I can get back to the person I love most in the world and who I have upset yet again and who I am terrified might suddenly have decided she doesn't want me. But the official, responsible thing came pinging out of his mouth, even out of his brain, more automatically (as well as more grammatically) than any expression of his personal wishes, and that was exactly what froze Sara into an unresponding block. Whether his job had begun to change him into a machine or a monster he was not sure, but his responses to things too often fell short of simple human ones. It was true that he did not wish any delay in identifying the body. But it was also true that he wanted Ivan Golightly's confirmation of Mrs Takahashi's identity within the next hour, so that he could be back with Sara to begin convincing her all over again how much he loved her.

CHAPTER 10

*

'YES, THAT'S NICE. Nice, lyrical opening phrasing you're giving us, yes, this lovely phrase—tyaa da daa tyaa da *dum*!—that's quite good . . .'

It wasn't, actually, it was barely kind of adequateish, but for the sake of everyone present—for the crowd of about a hundred (very respectable for a Sunday morning masterclass), for Tom who was in the back row openly reading the *Scotsman*, for the aspiring pianist herself and, Christ knew, for himself—James Ballantyne was trying to move the thing on, so that he could get off the stage as fast as possible. There were three others chosen from Scotland's music conservatoire—Caledonia's finest, Tom called them—waiting to have their well-rehearsed renditions of Rachmaninov taken apart and put back together in public, but after this one perhaps he could call a little unscheduled interval and see if ten minutes' lying down would ease the pain in his stomach. Actually, if it went on like this he was going to have to lie down, interval or not.

He sucked in a breath silently and mopped at his forehead, reminding himself that the young woman at the piano was not responsible for his pain, nor was it constructive to hate her quite so wholeheartedly because she couldn't play Rachmaninov.

'So in this one, the opus 23, No 4 in D, isn't it, when we come on to this new melody, Morag,' James avoided even thinking about Tom's face as he spoke her name. Backstage, just as James had been pretending he felt fine, Tom had looked up from the programme in horror. 'Your first one's actually a Morag. I didn't think people were really called that.'

Morag was pushing back her velvet hairband (James could find no words to express his view of velvet hairbands on women of twenty-two) and nodding. The light was glinting off the lenses of her glasses, making it impossible to see her eyes, but the anxious working of her long top teeth on her bottom lip told James she was concentrating.

'I think it may be calling for serenity, certainly, but perhaps also something more languorous . . . tyaa da dyaa?'

'Uh-huh. Languorous,' she echoed.

'First, I want you to try giving us more at the beginning. Pull it out even more, as you come to the end of the first melody, it is all but exhausted, yes, but you move on slowly, wait, caress the phrase, let it grow even bigger, there's going to be more . . . tyaa da da TYAAH . . . you see?' There was a short snorting sound from behind the *Scotsman* at the back of the hall. He would kill Tom later.

'Right, uh-huh . . . Emm . . .' Morag seemed reluctant to start playing. James sighed and as he did so a pain like teeth ripped at his insides with such savagery that his face crumpled.

'And *then* we come to this, nice and languorous. So try thinking . . . suppose you try to think'—he rose slowly to his feet, gently holding his side—'of the kind of languor Rachmaninov wants here. This is the opus 23 after all, still intensely passionate, still echoing the idiom of the second piano concerto. He wrote this, didn't he, in the summer of 1903. At the family's summer estate, at Ivanovka, I believe. Still a young man, wasn't he, and newly married. In love. *Langoroso*. How would you feel languorous? What would *you* do to feel languorous?'

Morag put her head on one side and pushed her glasses up on to the bridge of her nose. 'Well . . . em, maybe when you have a bath . . . really, really hot . . . with, em, Radox . . .' James closed his eyes. Morag tried harder. 'And . . . and then, em, you know, just relax . . .'

'Morag, try picturing Rachmaninov—young Sergei—and his new wife, Natalya. In the summertime, at Ivanovka. Go on, just for fun. Imagine—it's hot. The sun's beating down outside, it's afternoon, imagine you're Natalya . . .'

James's pain was sending him over the top now. Anything to get his mind off it, he didn't care what. One miserable piano student gets embarrassed, who cares? 'This piece is not for virgins. You're not a virgin, are you, Morag?' He looked hard at her, now pink and staring down at the keys, as the audience's giggles burbled round her. 'You're Natalya Rachmaninova, and Sergei, your new husband, he plays you like you're a piano. You've just spent four hours making love in the afternoon . . . the golden wheat is whispering on the steppe . . . there are ripe cherries in the orchard . . . can you imagine that?'

'I'm from Penicuik,' Morag whispered.

James ignored her. Pacing the platform now, and paddling the air with his arms he practically shouted, 'Try it again, Morag. Languorous, you see? Let's have some languor for grown-ups. Rachmaninov's not for virgins. Make it big, make it about *sex*, Morag. The languor in this piece is *post-coital*. Do you understand? Come on, Morag, make *love* to the piano.'

Morag was sweating visibly. She raised a timid hand, more to stop him than to ask her question. But James's sudden involuntary cry of pain and his heavy collapse on the stage all but drowned out her mystified, 'Em—with or without pedal?'

CHAPTER 11

THERE WAS SOMETHING teeth-grindingly irritating about students, Andrew thought. He had long since lost (he believed) any sense of inferiority at not having gone to university himself, but had not noticed that he had lapsed instead into a dull sense of superiority arising from an unexamined conviction that young people nowadays had things easier than he had. He was quite sure that he, when in his early twenties, would have been sufficiently awake if not sufficiently respectful of authority to give better directions than those he had taken from the tall girl carrying folders and a laptop, and which had now got him lost on the windswept brick and concrete campus of the University of the West of England. His annoyance hurried his pace past the flat glass walls on either side of the raised concourse and DS Bridger, who had driven all the way from Bath without daring to break DCI Poole's angry silence, had to take his hands out of his pockets in order to keep up.

The campus consisted of a half dozen or so visually unrelated buildings whose entrances had been concealed (surely deliberately) by their being placed either round the back, down the side, up or down flights of outside steps, or all four. Some were recognisable as entrances at all only by the delinquent huddles of wheelie bins outside. The buildings were connected by brick pathways, windy stairs and treacherous ramps arranged with Escher-like malice to necessitate the taking of long, pointless walks between destinations. Bright plastic-coated signs with arrows did not help much; no consensus had been reached about whether locations were to be identified by level (LOWER CONCOURSE 2 SPANISH AND LEVEL 3 >) or academic department (< PHARMACOLOGY LEVEL D SPANISH > LIFTS AND STAIRS) or function (LABORATORIES/DRAMA STUDIO > STRAIGHT ON LEVEL 1 < PHYSICS BUILDING) or by whimsical given names (BRUNEL GALLERY LEVEL A < > BECKFORD BUILDING/WILBERFORCE (STATISTICS) ANNEXE >).

'Sir, sir, this is us, isn't it?' Bridger walked over to peer at a single fluttering sheet of white paper stuck with masking tape to the outside of a window. Done in thick black marker pen, an arrow below the words 'UWE/BCTILHE Mycology Symposium' directed them inside. Growling gently, Andrew followed Bridger who, encouraged by his own initiative in picking up the trail, led the way, guided by a succession of handwritten notices which brought them up through several bleak stairwells, along corridors and past payphones, classrooms, coffee machines, pigeonholes, notice boards and administration desks to a pair of double doors marked BRITISH GAS (SOUTHERN) CONFERENCE SUITE on the top floor.

Just inside the doors, the smell of bacon hit Andrew like a wallop on the nose. From the corridor that stretched down past the empty reception desk came the clatter of cutlery mixed with the sound of piped music.

'Right. Safe to assume that's the conference dining room down there and the delegates are still having breakfast. Go on, Bridger, get in there and track down Mr Takahashi.'

Bridger reappeared a moment later, alone. 'Eh, sir, I've found him. He's still having his breakfast.' There was an exasperated silence as Andrew looked wanly past Bridger's ear.

'Just get him, Bridger.'

'Thing is, he still doesn't know, does he? That his wife's dead, I mean. Seems a shame, I mean, he's going to know soon enough, isn't he? Shouldn't we let him just finish his breakfast first?'

Bridger's newfound if clumsy compassion would have been, if Andrew had been curious, puzzling. 'Let's just get on with it, shall we?' he asked in tired irritation, leading the way.

The source of the bacon smell was more of a self-service cafeteria than a dining room. Of the twenty or so functional tables, each with four matching chairs, set out with only squeezing distance between, fewer than a third were occupied. Bridger nodded towards a dark-haired man hunched with concentration over his plate at an otherwise empty table. Mr Takahashi half rose for introductions and then bowed them into the seats opposite, smiling apologetically. His black hair was silvered; he looked at least twenty years older than the woman in the mortuary.

'Please, please.' He pointed downwards with his fork and beamed at his breakfast.

'Fond of our famous English breakfast, then, sir?'

Bridger said, with nervous joviality. Andrew scowled at him and cleared his throat.

'Ah, yes!' Mr Takahashi pointed downwards again. 'Very, very good, I am very fond of hash browns, also the bacon. Eggs—easy over, also. Sunny side up! Tomato, mushroom, all very good.' He began to eat with enthusiasm while still laughing at his fondness for the food, a disconcerting sight. He seemed quite lacking in curiosity as to why two police officers should have dropped in apparently to watch him. Andrew cleared his throat again.

'Mr Takahashi, we tracked you down by contacting your department at the University of Kobe in Japan. We understand from them that you and your wife came over here for a symposium.' Mr Takahashi was nodding happily as the next mouthful went in. 'Mr Takahashi, what do you know of your wife's whereabouts now?'

Mr Takahashi's chewing face began to frown. 'My wife accompany me. My wife is assistant to me in my work.'

'What work is that, exactly, Mr Takahashi?' Bridger asked, in a tone that Andrew thought inappropriately conversational as well as irrelevant.

Mr Takahashi speared three large mushrooms with his fork, folded a slab of fried egg over them and held the morsel up for their inspection. There was a glistening smear of fat on his chin and a gleam in his eyes. 'Ah. I am mycologist, mycology, very interesting subject. Also delicious!'

Just as the egg yolk on top was gathering momentum for its inevitable slide down the prongs and on to the handle, the forkful disappeared into Mr Takahashi's mouth with a clang and scrape on the teeth, and appreciative slurping noises. Andrew, revolted, thought that he re-

membered that in Japan it is polite to indicate enjoyment
of a meal. He closed his eyes briefly and opened them
again, trying to broaden his mind to accommodate the
spectacle before him. He even began to rehearse mentally
how he would amuse Sara this evening with an imperson-
ation of Mr Takahashi, hoping that by doing so he could
make it seem privately funny now, until the thought that
he would not be amusing Sara this evening at all because
she had all but thrown him out last night hit him so hard he
felt almost light-headed. After the business at the mortuary last night, when he had been trying to let himself quietly into Medlar Cottage at one o'clock, that fucking
dachshund (whose presence he had completely forgotten
about) had started up. So instead of tiptoeing upstairs and
explaining softly to his sleepy darling why he was so late,
he had been met by a barking animal, a dazed old lady and
a furious, exhausted Sara who had complained that she
hadn't expected him this late. He had gone back to the
flat. And instead of going straight round to talk to her this
morning and dealing with the only thing that really mattered to him, he had wasted hours trying to find this
bloody place and was now having to wait while the guy
finished his bloody breakfast. His pain hardened into rage
and he rubbed his eyes, resolving to speak to Sara the
minute he got back to Bath, just as soon as they'd booked
this grinning fool with the mushroom habit.

Mr Takahashi chewed open-mouthed as he prepared his
next forkful and continued, 'Mushrooms, very good for
breakfast. Also very good for studying, very interesting! I
am professor of mycology, representing Phytopathological
Society of Japan.' He swallowed his mouthful and the next
followed. 'All people here, we study for summer, all paid,

very international symposium, organised by British Council Trust for International Link in Higher Education.' He was delighted with himself for remembering the title of his host and benefactor.

Bridger at last seemed about to be getting to the point. 'Wouldn't have thought there would be that much to study. Is it your first visit to this country, Mr Takahashi? You see, I'm afraid we—'

'Ha, there you are not quite correct. Oh no, fungi is very, very big subject. All thallotypes, no chlorophyll, nuclear cells. Fruiting bodies, reproducing by spores. Fungal body is single-celled thallus or threadlike structure called hypha, hyphae together constitute mycelium—'

'When did you last see your wife, Professor Takahashi?' Andrew asked.

The professor's elation lessened. His chewing slowed to a cud-like rhythm as he considered how to reply. When at last his mouth was empty he said, 'I understand. She make complaint. She complain to English police?' A glance from Andrew stopped Bridger, whose mouth was already open, from speaking. They waited. Mr Takahashi put down his knife and fork.

'I apologise,' he said, bowing his head. 'I hope my wife will forgive my disgraceful behaviour. I was very wrong, I meant only to correct her attitude, but I apologise.'

'Please tell us what happened, Mr Takahashi.' Andrew reached across, took hold of Mr Takahashi's half-empty plate and slid it with its offensively congealing contents towards Bridger, who removed it to another table. Mr Takahashi's sorrowing eyes followed the plate and his look of contrition deepened. He sat up straighter and folded his hands in his lap. The cafeteria was almost empty now; the last stragglers, already in conversation, were leaving.

'I come with my wife to England, she assists me, she is photograph researcher for my work. But she is depressed. Perhaps she is not feeling well, homesick. Please understand that I am Japanese husband so it is my duty to stop this behaviour. She must have self-discipline to overcome her depression, I tell her this, she has no reason for unhappiness. So she must try to be happy. But my wife, she does not like this, so she go for a few days to Bath. She is very independent, like English, American wife, I say to her. We are very fond of English, American methods.'

'So what is this disgraceful behaviour that you hope your wife will forgive, exactly, Mr Takahashi?'

Bridger broke in. 'Excuse me, sir, Mr Takahashi, if you'll excuse us for a moment, I would just like a quick word with the Detective Chief Inspector. Won't be a moment. Sir?'

Andrew had no option but to leave the table and follow. Bridger halted a safe distance away. 'Sorry sir, but . . .'

'What the hell are you playing at, Bridger? Why are you giving him the chat like that? *"Is this your first visit to England?"* Good god, man, do you think you're working for the tourist board?'

'Sorry sir, but look, we've come to tell him his wife's dead, haven't we? We're supposed to be breaking the bad news and getting him to come and give a positive identification. I meant to say in the car, but shouldn't we have been in touch with the consulate? I mean, he speaks good English, but what if he didn't? We should have laid on an interpreter. He's in a foreign country, probably got no one here to turn to.'

'Bridger, haven't you heard a word he's told us? His English is perfectly okay. I haven't time to be fannying about with interpreters, I've got things to do back in Bath. He's admitted there was trouble between them. If he'd kept talking another minute he would have confessed he killed her, and you drag me away to talk about interpreters?'

'Sir? You really think he's a suspect, do you, sir? I mean, normally, of course, you'd expect a category C. I know you'd look first to see if it's a domestic, but this bloke's just an academic, a visitor. If you ask me we've got our killer, haven't we? That Cruikshank woman. You said so yourself. Sir.'

Andrew stared at him. 'That Cruikshank woman, Bridger, is, as I remember telling you, an unreliable and probably incurable alcoholic who quite possibly had a motive for killing Mrs Takahashi. Which doesn't mean she did. As for breaking the news, I'm not at all sure that we have to. I think he probably knows, for the obvious reason. Now, are you going to let me get on with this, or are you going to start recommending the Lake District?'

'Sir? But sir, if you think he is a suspect . . .' Andrew had already begun to walk away, but Bridger pulled at his arm. 'Sir—excuse me sir, look—if you're talking to him as a suspect, shouldn't you caution and arrest him? I mean strictly speaking, if he—'

'Let's just get on, Bridger.'

When they returned to the table, Mr Takahashi was still sitting upright but appallingly large tears had gathered in his eyes and were dripping on to his shirt. He looked up desperately.

'Sorry about that, Mr Takahashi. Now, I was asking you, I think, what there was that you needed forgiveness for?'

Mr Takahashi's lips tightened. 'I am trying to tell my wife she must cheer herself, be pleased. But she says she does not wish to spend her time with me in Bristol. I am older man than my wife. I am too impatient and . . . look, I am modern Japanese, I agree it is wrong to strike her, even one small slap.'

'How many times exactly did you strike your wife?'

'Oh, only one time, because she is behaving in stupid way, refusing to eat and crying! Only one! One slap across face, not so . . .' Mr Takahashi made his hand into a fist. 'Slap only. To calm her. But she—I have to, to stop her . . .' Andrew allowed him a silence, and after a long pause, got what he wanted. The man, inculcated in a culture in which confession, as the precursor of shame, carries the only hope of absolution, continued, 'She is very very angry, and she is small, so she take my hair, tight, and I take hers also and try to stop her. Not hard, just to stop her.'

'How did you stop her? You banged your wife's head against the wall to try to stop her leaving you? Your wife wanted to leave you and you tried to stop her, is that it? Is that what you're saying?'

'She is not leaving me. She is Japanese wife, I remind her. So she agrees she wants only to leave to have break, to have peaceful time alone. She is not disgraceful. This is what she says.'

Bridger's jaw was now slack with disappointment. He would have to brazen it out with Frayling. Perhaps he could dress up the idea of Cruikshank as prime suspect as Poole's idea, while he had been the one to put pressure on Takahashi.

Mr Takahashi was saying, 'This is all very unfortunate. And I feel truly sorry that my wife go to Bath. I cannot follow her, I am specialist in Ascomycetes, you see. I am giving paper on hymenium in *Tuber aestivum, Claviceps purpurea* and *Bulgaria inquinans*. I must go and prepare, I have to get my slides ready.'

'When did you last see your wife, Mr Takahashi?'

Mr Takahashi looked at his watch. 'Already it is nine fifty-two, I am speaking at ten o'clock. My wife, she is in Bath, as I say. She telephones on Friday and she say she want to see me. She will not come back to Bristol but instead I should go to Bath to talk to her on Saturday, yesterday. This is very unfortunate, very inconvenient for me because then I am going to miss important visit by symposium delegates to International Mycological Institute at Kew Gardens, I am not pleased to go to Bath instead.' His face had grown angry. 'My wife does not think of this, she does not care, she is lacking in respect. I go to Bath because I wish to apologise humbly, but she makes me more angry instead.'

'Tell me exactly what happened, if you would, when you arrived in Bath.'

'I get on train arriving in Bath. I am meeting my wife at 12.30 at the Royal Photographic Society. I tell her we will have lunch but she does not agree. She will not have lunch, perhaps only a beverage, but will meet me to tell me something important, this is what she says. So I say yes to meet her at the Royal Photographic Society.'

Andrew drew in a breath silently and waited for Mr Takahashi's confession that he had not been able to persuade his wife to come back to him, that when she had left to escape him he had followed her down the alleyway, lost his temper, grabbed her by the hair, dragged her through the side entrance and into the pub passageway where he banged her head into the wall, strangled her and stuffed her body into the cupboard. Nobody had disturbed him: there were no customers because the pub was not open and none of the kitchen staff would have heard a thing above the permanently blaring radio. Was it going to be this easy?

'But she is not there.'

'But you hit her. You said so. You met your wife and you hit her.'

'No. I unfortunately have difficulty in finding Royal Photographic Society and I am eight minutes late. I wait outside, but she did not come. I think she is very angry that I am late and she did not wait for me, even one minute. I wait until after one o'clock, but she did not come. So I came back to Bristol.' Mr Takahashi scraped back his chair and stood up. 'I am ready to be punished. My wife is right to complain that I strike her. It is most clear, she is angry that I am late, she think I do not care and do not keep appointment on Saturday so she has complained to the English police. But if she forgives me I too will forgive her for her behaviour to me. Please take me to my wife now, I wish to apologise to her and to forgive her.'

Andrew, knowing that he was a bastard to do it, also stood up. 'Bridger, inform Mr Takahashi about his wife, for the record. And then arrest him. I'll be outside.'

He turned, wove his way through the plastic-topped tables to the door and in the neutral air of the corridor outside Breakfast World, breathed in deeply. He had no stomach for the clapping-on of the handcuffs, metaphorically or actually, whereas Bridger clearly enjoyed his role as instrument of the law, which he did with all the magisterial pomposity that he could summon in his polyester-tied, five-foot-eight, ginger-topped frame. But already Andrew was despising himself for his squeamishness over what was, in the end, a procedural necessity, and was composing in his mind a slightly altered version of events to tell Sara in which he would figure just a little more heroically. He was, he realised, already preparing to bask in the light of vindication, hoping that she would be not only impressed by the early arrest but ready now to understand the point of his sudden and hurtful preoccupation with the case. And Andrew had no doubt that Takahashi had killed his wife, but nonetheless he was beginning to construct, also for Sara, a slightly defensive set of reasons for being so certain.

CHAPTER 12

JOYCE HAD INSTIGATED a daily routine for herself with more determination than was polite in a guest and had unpacked her bags and boxes a little too comprehensively for Sara's peace of mind. After her nasty shock in Green Street and possibly, Sara thought, in order to soak away in sleep a couple of hours each day and so shorten the time available in which to crave a drink, Joyce had also announced that she would take a little nap in the afternoons. When she informed Sara of this decision on the Sunday, she had added that she would be grateful if Sara would wake her at around four o'clock with a cup of tea.

Sara had been grateful. She had spent a miserable morning trying to be bright and normal, taking the car down to Bathampton and going for her usual run along the towpath, getting the papers and pottering enjoyably in a Sunday-ish way in an effort to show, ostensibly to Joyce, that Andrew's absence was a complete irrelevance. She was also showing Andrew, should he care to take an interest, that he was not the only one with people to look after. Joyce, declining the offer to be made comfortable and left with the papers, had for most of the morning followed her about, sitting or standing some distance off and watching

whatever she did with reproachful, judging eyes. Over
lunch, at which Joyce picked daintily, she had announced
her intention to lie down for forty winks. Sara was exhausted by the effort of cheerfulness and said something
insincere about managing without her.

On Monday Sara stood in the doorway of the spare bedroom with the tea, and the pile of new clothes bought on
Saturday which Joyce had until now declined even to try
on. 'Come on. They're not really jeans, they're black. And
the sweatshirt's a good colour for you,' she said, briskly.

Joyce, too sleep-befuddled to comment, unfolded herself from under the eiderdown fully dressed, and took
them obediently. Her lips taut with uncertainty, she began
unpinning herself from the pink suit. It was a long process
undoing the many safety pins which served in place of the
broken skirt zip but Sara waited, determined to get the
suit out of Joyce's clutches and burn it, whatever the jeans
and sweatshirt looked like. She had already taken away for
washing every other garment that Joyce owned and had
ended up binning most of them. When Joyce got down to
her underskirt and vest she turned away, offering a view
less of her buttocks than the place where her buttocks
should have been. She was so thin that the grey petticoat,
with a tattered hem of what once had been lace and was
now a nylon cobweb, fell from the back of her waist to her
scrawny knees like a flat dirty curtain. Sara, sensing
Joyce's embarrassment, looked conspicuously round the
room.

'I see you've unpacked, then,' she said. Joyce had replaced Sara's iron bedside lamps with her own, one with a
lampshade depicting a coaching scene and the other with a
peach nylon one that looked like a showercap recycled

from a pair of frilly trainer pants. She had displayed her
books—a few novels, dark-spined school prizes and texts
on music—in the small bookcase and stacked the overspill
along the skirting board. Several ornaments of the Delft
clog and brass dog variety covered the dressing table,
along with a beautiful rectangular box of dark wood, in-
laid with a Tree of Life design executed in soft pink
mother-of-pearl and silver. That and the cello propped
against the wall were the only items of beauty or value that
Joyce seemed not to have been parted from.

'I remember that box from your flat,' Sara said, wanting
to forget the dispiriting ugliness of everything else Joyce
owned.

Joyce's lips puckered up with satisfaction. She drew
herself upright in her wretched underclothes, walked over
to the box and lifted the lid. A strange, Eastern-sounding,
modal melody came twanking out of it. 'That's the
Egyptian national anthem,' she announced. 'And this box
was a gift to me from'—she looked regally at Sara—'the
Queen of Egypt herself.'

'Wow.' Sara now remembered being told something of
the sort years ago. She handed Joyce the green sweatshirt
and Joyce's head disappeared into it.

'The Queen presented me with it when I left,' she said
as she reappeared, blinking like an emerging pot-holer.

With deliberate nonchalance she went on, as Sara offered her the trousers, 'I was tutor to the Egyptian royal
family, you know. After the war. I was sent to Cairo. I
taught music to the princes and princesses for nearly two
years.' She was now holding the trousers the right way up
and persuading her right foot into the leg. The twanking
music box melody was starting over, slowing, each note

sounding with more *twwwww-* than *-aaank*, as the mechanism wound down.

'You'd find it easier sitting down,' Sara ventured, realising that Joyce was in danger of falling over. Suddenly it crossed her mind that Joyce had probably never worn trousers in her life, not so much as pyjama bottoms. She was a skirt and nightdress person, a lady, and had probably thought at one time, assuming she didn't now, that women in trousers proclaimed the coming of the Antichrist. But Joyce had them on now, and was busy tucking her petticoat into the waistband, which was loose enough to allow it.

'It's a beautiful box,' Sara said. 'What was the Queen like? Did she speak English?'

'The Queen? Oh, well.' Joyce was still tucking herself in. 'The Queen? Well, it was a while ago.' There was a pause during which Joyce opened her mouth and then folded her lips, and decided not to lie. 'Well now, I seem to remember now, yes, that's right. I got the box from a lady-in-waiting. The Queen couldn't be there herself. Affairs of state and so on, I suppose.' Her voice trailed off, the shining, imagined memory of the grateful queen entreating her to accept her gift growing dim in the dismal light of the fact that she had received the standard leaving present for minor servants via a secretary, and had only once in nearly two years met the Queen, in a room containing at least thirty others. It was not how she liked to look back on it and, for fifty years, had not.

'Well. But Cairo—that must have been fascinating. Here, don't forget your tea.'

Joyce sat down on the edge of the bed and took the cup as the melody stopped. 'Och well now, it was awfully dusty. I remember that, hot and dusty. Not a clean city at all. I never saw the slums, of course.' She blew delicately on her tea. 'Filthy. There was some sort of epidemic, when I was there, I remember that. People died. Mass hysteria. Though that was in the countryside, not the city, come to think of it. Anyway, all gone now,' Joyce said, with a dangerous wave of the free arm, stirring the silent air into which the last notes of the music box tune had lately vanished. 'All gone.' She sucked up some tea in her lips which, after sleep, were so loose they looked almost frilly. 'Tone deaf too, the wee tykes,' she added, after she had swallowed.

There was a silence save for Joyce's slurps. Sara sat down in the chair by the dressing table, feeling the full extent of her entrapment. Joyce would be up and about again in a few minutes, haunting every step she took. How long was she going to stay? And where would she go? Joyce obviously had some sort of income, although Sara had been so far too squeamish to get out of her exactly how much. She had said she had no relatives or friends, which Sara guessed meant none whom she had not, in the course of her descent, estranged beyond any possibility of reconciliation. Was Joyce quietly banking on not quite ever getting round to arranging things so that she could move out again? Sara knew that she could never, ever actually throw her out. She also knew that she could never, ever tolerate her as a permanent fixture.

And there was Andrew to consider, although when she did, Sara felt only a quiet panic that he did not want to live with her in Medlar Cottage, closely followed by dismay because she could, when she was being honest with herself, see his point about territory. Would Andrew even agree to come back as long as Joyce was here? And with Joyce as a sort of resident, half-malevolent, droopy-eyed house troll his reluctance was more than understandable; it was utterly reasonable.

'Joyce, what happened? What happened to you that made you give everything up? Why did you start drinking?'

Joyce looked at her accusingly, as if the questions were in the worst possible taste. She shook her head. 'Oh well. It was a while ago. Something upset me, that's all. A person. Here, and what about your er . . . I can't get his name. Where's he?'

'He's at work,' Sara explained patiently. 'What upset you? Who? Who upset you? What did they do to you?'

'Och, you know fine yourself how it is. You should know. Did you not have the same thing, with Matteo Becker? He died, didn't he? I saw it in the paper. Well, same thing. Someone died.' She swallowed some tea. 'Nobody you know.'

'I wish you would tell me. It might help.'

Joyce drank more tea as if Sara had not spoken. Sitting in the peaceful bedroom at that slightly head-swimming point in a summer afternoon when an old lady might decide that, as the day is all but gone, she will take the rest of it slowly, Sara realised that it would be cruel to displace the consoling effects of tea and warmth and quiet with unsettling conversations about the past and an insecure future. Joyce was so old, Sara noticed, that the drinking of her cup of tea was an activity which she carried out with care and concentration, without trying to do several other things at once. At what age, she wondered, does a cup of tea make us sit down? It was a trivial enough concession to age, Sara thought, watching Joyce, to claim a few minutes in which to sit and sip a cup of tea, and a modest enough hope that there might occasionally be someone else around to make it. Could she and Andrew find a way to keep her, for as long as it took? Was it callous to calculate that her malnourished, alcohol-abused and elderly body would not be around to inconvenience any of them for long?

'Now, dear,' Joyce said, sliding her empty cup cautiously back on to its saucer. 'Time you and I had a wee talk. You don't want an old woman in your house, I'm quite sure of that. And I need to find myself a wee place to stay. Although after what those terrible people did to me, robbing me of half my means, I'll need to content myself with maybe just a room. Then we'll be out of your way, Pretzel and me.'

Without a second's doubt Sara knew that Joyce was opening the way to getting herself clear of her in order to start drinking again. She also knew that she could let her, and that Andrew would probably say she should. The generous thoughts of Joyce enjoying her twilight years bathed in the golden light of her magnanimity, which only two minutes ago had been making her feel cornered yet rather good about herself, were now making her feel stupid.

'I'm not letting you go off to another crummy bedsit,' she announced, 'just so you can start drinking your way through the rent money again. I'm not letting you.'

Joyce managed to look both stunned and pompous. Sara bit her lip, because she was not at all sure exactly what she was going to let her do instead. What options were there? Whatever happened, if Joyce were to stay off the bottle, she would have to restore some pride in herself. Her little daily self-deceptions and habits of self-aggrandisement would not substitute for the self-belief and self-discipline she would need in order to live independently. 'You need to find something to do.'

'Do?'

'To keep yourself occupied, to have an interest.' Sara knew as she spoke how interfering she sounded and how futile her interference was, unless Joyce were to start doing something she really enjoyed. 'Your baking. Your wonderful baking? You enjoyed that, didn't you?'

'I don't bake now,' Joyce said, with finality. 'I am a musician, not a pastry cook.' She gazed past Sara as if she were invisible.

'Right. Well, suppose you start teaching again? Could you give lessons?'

'Teach?' Joyce's eyes travelled to the cello case against the wall. 'On that? Teach?'

'Go on, have a try,' Sara said. She rose, walked over to it and undid the clasps. 'When did you last play? Ages, I guess? Why not have a go now?'

Joyce was chewing her lips. 'Well, dear, I don't know . . .'

'Come on! Just a little try. You'll be rusty, of course, but a bit of practice'll sort that out. Haven't you missed it?'

The instrument was dreadfully out of tune. Sara pulled the dressing table chair to the middle of the room, sat down with the cello and after several minutes managed to get it in tune without breaking any strings. Gently she handed Joyce the bow, which she took from her as if the varnish were still wet. With a slight bouncing movement in her wrist she accustomed her arm once more to its weight and balance. Her fingers had found their correct places on it instantly. She looked at Sara with nervous hope and Sara smiled encouragement. 'I remember how you played,' she said. 'You were wonderful, technically brilliant. It's impossible to forget how, once you've played like that. It'll come back to you, I know it will. You remember the Bach Toccata, Adagio and Fugue in C? Suppose you try the Adagio. Go on.'

She helped Joyce into the seat, easing the cello towards her thin shoulder. Joyce set her lips in a brave line and adjusted her posture until she was sitting proudly straight. With her right hand she was gently stroking the honey-coloured wood of the instrument, reacquainting herself with its sleek hollows, her fingers remembering how beautiful it was. She tapped softly on the strings with her left hand and smiled at the sound, which seemed to invite her to play. She smiled hopefully up at Sara. Perhaps she was right. She could never forget how to play an instrument like this. The Adagio. Of course she remembered it, it was not even difficult. Joyce opened and closed her left hand several times, flexing her stiff fingers, tipped back her head, still smiling, and taking a breath as if she were going to sing, placed the bow tenderly on the string. With a last nervous, excited glance at Sara, she drew it across in the stately, sombre opening notes of the piece. Sara listened, unable to look at her. There was no mistaking it: the sound which was rising from the beautiful, long-neglected cello now in the arms of one of the country's most celebrated cello teachers was, truly and indisputably, absolutely bloody terrible.

The banging of the front door interrupted the noise and also allowed Sara, coward that she knew herself to be, to skip off with an apologetic smile without having to say anything. Andrew was in the kitchen, looking around crossly with his hands on his hips as if he were somehow angry with the room.

Sara raised her eyebrows and said, 'Trouble?' *Don't ask me how I am, will you?*

Andrew nodded, his face softening, acknowledging to her that none of it was Sara's fault. *Actually, it is. You make me so angry I can't think straight.*

'What? What's the matter?' Instead of hugging him, Sara stood with her arms folded. *Go on, hug me. Tell me I'm doing a great job looking after Joyce.*

'I've cocked up, that's what's the matter,' he said, rather aggressively. *Fat lot you care, you're so selfish.* 'We've got the bloke who did it and I cocked up the arrest. Possibly even the conviction.' He sank into a chair and turned away from her. Still she did not come and hug him. Perhaps she would if he held out his arms to her, but he thought on balance he would not and besides, she had already moved away and was topping up the teapot from the kettle.

'Tell me,' she said in a tired voice, reaching into a cupboard for a mug. *I've got problems too, you know.*

Andrew sighed and groaned. 'How long have I been doing this? After all these years, I can't believe that I got such a basic thing wrong. Maybe that's the point, it's Bridger's job, all that stuff, it's so long since I did it. I suppose you just get out of practice.' *Why aren't you sorry for me?*

'Why did you do it, then? Why didn't you leave it to Bridger?' *Why are you so stupid sometimes?*

Andrew did not reply, having no acceptable way of telling her that he had muscled in aggressively on Bridger's work rather than spend time dealing with his own problems.

'Have you found out who she is yet? Was, I mean?' *You're about to tell me anyway.*

'Oh, yes. Easy. Her B&B reported her missing. I went to take a look on Saturday night. That's why I was so late coming in, if you'd given me a chance to explain. I meant to call yesterday but all this came up. Look, Sara, about Saturday—' *It wasn't my fault.*

'Never mind about that. Go on. You went to her B&B?' *Yes, it was.*

'Tatty place just outside Limpley Stoke. Some kind of smallholding as well, they supply the Sulis Clinic and one or two other places. Ivan Golightly, he's the son of the bloke who runs the Sulis. Wife does the B&B, cheap and cheerless. The B&B, not the wife. Looks like Mrs Takahashi was trying to save money. She'd left her husband at a mycology symposium in Bristol.' *Okay*, don't *listen, then.*

'A what?' *I'm not.*

'Mycology symposium, some academic thing, that's not the point. He's a professor somewhere in Japan, Kobe. It's so straightforward, she was trying to leave him and he killed her.' *All right, fine by me.* His voice tailed off in weary gloom.

'*What* did you cock up? You still haven't told me.' *Fine by me, too.*

'Bridger and I went to see the husband yesterday. It's years since I did this basic stuff and I just forgot. I bloody forgot to caution him before he started talking about his wife. He as good as admitted he killed her, but that was *before*. And now he's got his lawyer and interpreter and all that and of course the lawyer's done the obvious thing and claimed that everything he said before he was cautioned is inadmissible. She's right. The bastard practically admitted it and now we can't use it. And I *know* the bastard's guilty.'

'How come you're so certain?'

'I told you, he was close to admitting it. He's a wife-beater. She'd left him. He admits he came to Bath that morning to see her, claims he didn't find her, but it's pretty clear he did, and he lost his temper and strangled her.'

'I always think of wife-beaters doing it behind closed doors. I can't see anyone strangling his own wife in a pub. In public.'

Andrew tried to hide his exasperation at Sara's now reflexive questioning of his judgment. While he admitted that it had been helpful before, it was not so now.

'They're visitors. They haven't really got a door to be behind, have they?' He sipped at the tea that she had now put in front of him, wishing that it were a glass of wine. As he swallowed, his insides griped with the thought that it quite easily could be, were it not for Sara's insistence on keeping Joyce here and declaring the house a dry zone so that there would be nothing lying around to tempt her.

'Anyway, look, I meant to come over yesterday after we'd got him in custody but of course as soon as we got back to Manvers Street the whole thing got complicated. The Japanese consulate and all that, interpreters. We had to get all that set up so his lawyer can't claim he doesn't understand what's going on. It took a while. And in the end I was so angry I thought it was better to keep out of your way. Angry with myself, I mean.' Well mainly, he thought, looking away, and meanwhile what was that bloody racket coming from upstairs?

'Oh, she's trying again! That's Joyce, she's practising,' Sara said, with too much enthusiasm. 'That's a good sign, isn't it? That she's trying, I mean. She's got a few years' neglect to make up for. Obviously.' It was so very obvious from the graceless sawing noises overhead that Andrew did not think he needed to reply, and he restrained himself also from saying anything peevish about what seemed to be Sara's waning interest in *his* playing. Instead, he drank some of his tea and waited to be asked if he would like to play something for her, because he did, very much, but even more than that, he wanted to be asked.

'So what happens next? Assuming you're right about him and he did do it.'

Andrew shook his head and sighed. 'He's on police bail pending further enquiries. We let him go back to Bristol to his damn conference. We've got his passport and he has to report to a police station every day. Meanwhile we're checking everything Mrs Takahashi did, everywhere she went, everyone she spoke to. And contacting her sister. There was a mobile in her room with the numbers she spoke to logged. Handy, that. She'd spoken to her sister in Japan three times since she came to England.'

'Anyone else?'

'Only her husband, on his mobile. They spoke on Friday around five o'clock, just as he says. He'd know we could check, so he hasn't tried to deny speaking to her or arranging to meet. He's just lying about when and where.'

'You sound very sure.'

'I spoke to the sister this morning. It sounded to me quite likely she didn't like her brother-in-law very much. She said Mitsuko—that's Mrs T—was upset about something. I couldn't grill her on the phone, mainly I was trying to explain to her why we can't release the body yet. She's coming over. I'll find out more when she arrives.'

'Don't the Golightlys know? Or anybody else she spoke to?'

Andrew shook his head. 'Bridger's been talking to them. He says they're pretty laid back, run their place very informally and they thought she was quiet but just let her get on with it. Hilary Golightly took her down into Bath in the morning a couple of times, including the Saturday. Ivan showed her round his vegetable garden on Friday, she didn't go far that day, went for a walk on the towpath and that was about it. The neighbour Mrs Heffer spoke to her too, on another couple of days, she can't remember which. They both liked cats. She's terribly upset. So are the Golightlys, they've cancelled all their B&B bookings.'

'And the PM?'

'Still waiting. How long *is* that going to go on for?' Andrew asked, casting his eyes towards the noise of Joyce's cello. Just then it stopped.

'And meanwhile your prime suspect's not admitting anything.'

Andrew grunted unhappily, finished his tea and asked for more in a manner that Sara thought a little too uxorious. She looked into his eyes in search of what she had ever seen in him. And if I don't find it within the next two minutes it's over, she told herself, feeling a mixture of desperate sadness and something like panic at being able even to consider the idea so coldly, almost as if she were not still in love with him (when she *was*). At that moment from above their heads came the deep, long-drawn-out, miserable belching sound of the cello's lowest open string. Andrew covered his ears. 'That'll be the *Queen Mary* leaving Southampton, then,' he said. As Sara burst out laughing he pulled her on to his lap and kissed her. Nothing husbandly about *that*, she thought, returning the kiss.

'I love you,' she said, eventually.

'That's good, because I love you too,' Andrew growled back in her ear, not a moment too soon. His hands were making their competent way into her clothes. 'How long have we got before she comes creeping in?'

Sara drew away and shook her head. Why could he not understand that having Joyce in the house was just the same as having his children around? It was out of the question, but she was saved from saying so by the sudden ringing of the telephone.

CHAPTER 13

'I AM NOT SLEEPING in a room with deadly nightshade dripping down the fucking walls.'

'It's not deadly nightshade, it's wisteria. And it's hand-printed. This wallpaper is hand-printed, it's very fine. Of its kind.'

Sara's eyes took in the painted branches of purple and green that hung down as if trapped but escaping from the join between the walls and ceiling. The room was huge, with vast windows on two sides, and was dominated by a canopied bed draped with swathes of matching green and lilac silk. The carpet was of the coolest pale green and the rest of the furniture, a dressing table, a sofa and two small chairs, was white.

'At least it doesn't look clinical.'

'It looks completely *private* clinical to me. It's like a country house hotel for rich hypochondriacs.'

'It's a naturopathy clinic, as you well know, and they consider the surroundings important. Beauty has a healing power, that's the theory. And it's run as a charity, some people don't pay anything, so they're not necessarily all rich,' Sara said, 'or hypochondriacs. That's what Tom says. And it's what I say, too.'

Between them, they had been selling James the idea of the Sulis Clinic solidly, ever since Tom had brought him back from Edinburgh late on Sunday and since his telephone call to Sara on Monday afternoon. He wanted James to try the Sulis because some years ago Tom's mother had spent a fortnight there and been cured, rather amazingly, of her diverticulitis. In a fortnight. Tom had seen it for himself. James had been unconvinced but also too ill and scared to object, and had agreed to the appointment with Dr Golightly in Bath on Monday morning.

'But look at these colours. I cannot sleep here.'

'Yes, you can. It's the best room in the whole clinic. The colours are very restful, if you give them a chance,' Sara said with determination. James was sitting glumly on the end of the lilac quilted bed. She joined him and put an arm round his shoulders. He sagged, his head dipped, he turned his face into Sara's chest and wept.

'I can't stay here. Don't make me.'

'You have to stay here,' Sara said gently, 'just for a while, a couple of weeks. While Tom's away on this case in Brussels. You know how reluctant he was to leave you and you promised him last night you'd give the Sulis a go. You know you're not well.'

'But I'd be all right at home. I'm feeling fine now.'

Sara eased herself away and, with her hands on James's defeated shoulders, looked him in the eye. 'You promised Tom. He wouldn't have gone otherwise. When the pain does come it's more than you can stand. You don't want a repeat of Edinburgh, do you? Do you really want another ambulance ride to A&E, just for the pain to disappear almost the minute you get there?'

The A&E doctor had sent him away with the

recommendation that James go to his own GP. Instead Tom had driven all night and marched James off to Dr Golightly's surgery for an appointment the following day because Dr Golightly, when he had been reminded that Tom was Lady Wallace's son, had found that he could 'fit him in' after he had seen his morning patients. Tom was still furious because James had kept from him the fact that he had been having the pains, on and off, for about two months. It was Tom who had explained to the doctor that James's own GP knew nothing of the problem because James (and this was said with a despairing look at the patient) had not consulted him about it. And they had both allowed themselves to be calmed by Dr Golightly's view, and by the way he expressed it, that James had an irritable bowel, illustrating the strange truth that even strong men in their forties would rather be told about a 'troublesome tummy' than intestinal inflammation, twisting, strangulation, blockage or obstruction. And to Tom's relief the doctor had gone on to suggest that the Sulis would indeed be an appropriate solution if James would consider going there.

'He'll go,' Tom had declared. Delicately, Dr Golightly had raised the squalid question of money.

'When patients come through my surgery door, of course, I'm just an ordinary part-time GP,' he explained, 'although when I treated Lady Wallace I was working very nearly full-time for the good old NHS. But I do also have the Sulis, though most of my NHS patients have never heard of it,' he had said. 'Run on naturopathy lines, a holistic approach. It's a special area of mine. Conditions such as IBS are often very responsive. But of course although it's not run for profit, it's private sector and fees do have to be charged. I take it that would be, er . . . no obstacle to, er . . . ?'

'None,' Tom had said.

And because he had to go to Brussels on Monday night he had rung Sara to ask her not so much to take James in to the Sulis as to make sure he went. And stayed. So now she was saying gently to James as they sat on the end of the bed in the Wisteria Suite, 'He doesn't want you on your own while he's away. We've got to get you better.' She gave James's shoulders a little shake. 'Haven't we?'

James looked back at her and for the first time did not try to hide the fear in his eyes. 'But what if something happens when he's not here? I mean . . . suppose it's not IBS? Suppose it's something like . . . something you don't get better from?'

Sara interrupted, reiterating old reassurances. 'There's no good reason to think it's anything other than an irritable bowel, Dr Golightly said so. You're very wound up, that's all, you know what the past six months have been like. It's stress-related IBS. So this is the best possible place you could be. It'll *make* you relax in a way you just wouldn't at home. Tom said Dr Golightly says you've got to change your pace, your diet, your outlook, and stop worrying. Then you'll be giving your body the right conditions to heal itself.' She did not add how utterly, desperately, she needed this to be true. 'Tom thinks Dr Golightly's a good egg. His mother's never looked back. And she's not easily fooled.'

'No, but she practically fell in love with him. Apparently everyone does. You wait till you've met him, you'll see why.'

'Don't change the subject.'

James nodded, conceding. 'All right, I know, I know. I'll stay. It's not your fault. I suppose I'll bloody stay.'

'And Tom will be in touch though they don't like you to have your mobile here. We just have to accept that he can't be here to look after you when you're ill. So you're going to stay here and be properly sorted out, once and for all. Lots of people come here and get better when nothing else has worked. Lots of them come regularly because they leave feeling so well. It's got a great reputation.'

'Not for its fucking wallpaper, it hasn't.'

'It's hand-printed.'

'It looks like deadly fucking nightshade. Or poison ivy.'

James was reverting, possibly even without noticing it, to the tense and aggressive posturing he adopted when he was hopelessly tired. Sara, now convinced that this was at least partly why he was ill, tried again. 'Tom says Dr Golightly set the place up for people just like you.'

'What, specially for people with IBS? Or suspected IBS, because nobody knows except Dr fucking brilliant Golightly?' It had swept over James again that Tom had walked out and left him here, and he had decided that he felt not grieved, but aggrieved by his abandonment.

'Oh, you've got IBS all right,' Sara said, rising and walking to the window. 'Irritable Bastard Syndrome. You're an awkward sod, you know that? Do you realise how hard you're making this for yourself?' Despairing, she looked out across to the city and the hills beyond, blind to the beauties of the view, framed as it was by the trickle of hand-printed wisteria down the sides of the window.

There was a knock at the door of the sort that is not asking if entry is permitted but giving a split second's no-tice that privacy is about to be violated. A white-uniformed nurse strode into the room, marched over to the other window and tugged at the sash cords.

'Afternoon! Oh, they do stick, these windows. I'll just—Ooof!' The window cracked open. ''Scuse me!' Sara stepped aside from her window and the nurse strode over and pulled this open, too, with much greater ease. 'That's better, need a bit of air in, don't we, Mr Ballantyne?' She turned with a matey smile to face James. She had the almost plumptious curves of a small fifty-year-old, with no-nonsense legs in white stockings and shoes, and black curled hair.

'Mr Ballantyne?'

James looked up meekly and met her gaze. Above the white of her uniform, her large brown eyes had a delicious lustre, like melted plain chocolate.

'Aw, sweetheart,' she said, tipping her head to one side and wrinkling her nose sympathetically. She walked over, crouched beside him and took his hands. 'You're not feeling too clever, are you? Never you mind, sweetheart, that's why you're here.' She patted his hands and stood up. With a nod and another nose wrinkle, a conspiratorial one, to Sara, she announced, 'I'm Sister Cartwright but everybody calls me Sister Yvonne, all right? And I'll call you James, that's if you don't like me calling you sweetheart, because I tell you now that's what I call everybody, all right?' To Sara's amazement, James was smiling up at her like a comforted child.

'And aren't you lucky getting the Wisteria Suite? Lovely, isn't it?' Her confident beam took in the whole room and its contents.

After a pause James said, 'Yes, it's lovely.'

'You are lucky Mrs Purdey was due to go this morning.

She was very happy here. She's gone off fit as a butcher's dog. Oh, except they're all vegetarian here, don't tell anyone I said that, will you?' In a stage whisper she confided, 'You do tend to get meat a bit on the brain here, though, if you're like me.'

James, a dedicated carnivore, giggled. Sister Yvonne checked the watch on her bosom. 'So, tell you what, sweetheart, we'll go down now and see Dr Golightly. He likes to see his new arrivals. I expect you'll be down for Scottish Douche and balneotherapy, for starters, but we'll see what the doc says. All right, chuck?'

James stood up and said, 'Yes, that would be lovely. Thank you.'

Sara followed them, open-mouthed.

As they made their way down the stairs Sister Yvonne pointed out various features with the proprietorial pride and closet ignorance of a National Trust volunteer. 'These are the main stairs, grand aren't they?' She waved an arm bountifully. 'There's a little staircase as well, for the staff, through a door down in the main hall. Built in 1828 originally, this house, by a chap called Henry Goodridge. Supposed to be Grecian influenced. But,' she lowered her voice, 'you tell me what's Greek about black wrought iron banisters and bright yellow walls. My Chris and me've been to Patsos *and* Athens and there's nothing like it there. English as roast beef and Yorkshire pud, I'd say—oh, there I go again! Meat on the brain. Dr Golightly's on the ground floor. Here we are.' She knocked at a door and turned to them. 'Got to wait,' she whispered. 'Dr G's rule. Might be with someone.'

But he was not, judging by the speed with which the door was opened. The welcoming bearded face looked so happy to see them that James feared Dr Golightly might burst into song. 'Here's Mr Ballantyne for you, Doctor,' Yvonne said, taking her leave. 'James, I should say. All right, James? I'll leave you with Doctor now but I'll be seeing you soon, no doubt.'

'Ah, no! Let's rather say here am I for James,' Dr Golightly laughed, ushering Sara and James in urgently, as if they were standing in the rain. 'Do come in and sit down. I'll just find your records.'

The room, although not nearly as large, had the same imposing high windows as James's room, here dressed by sweeping silk curtains in a restrained rust colour which exactly matched the carpet. It was arranged partly as an office, with a desk and tall filing cabinets, and partly as a consulting room. But evidently the consultations carried out here were only of the verbal sort conducted in the comfortable chairs where they were now being invited to sit. There was no high couch, not even a washhand basin with the soap, paper towels and ominously clean-looking implements that doctors need in order to do the kind of unspeakable things they routinely do to their embarrassed, half-dressed patients. Although grand the room exuded intimacy, even kindness. A clean and calming scent filled the air, its source, James assumed, being the small clay contraption on the table where a nightlight burned under a little pot. Aromatherapy, no doubt, a thing he had no time for, but the scent—lavender with something?—was wonderful.

Dr Golightly was turning to them from the filing cabinet behind his desk, holding a slim folder. Before he could speak, James announced, 'I should say at the outset, because yesterday I didn't get the chance, that I really don't see how you can claim that naturopathy is the answer to every medical problem under the sun.' He would not look at Sara.

Dr Golightly stopped, took off his metal-rimmed spectacles and looked at James indulgently. James stared back. Had he been feeling so bad yesterday that he had somehow managed not to notice what a perfect advertisement the doctor was for whatever quackery he was presumably about to flog him? Dr Golightly was both extremely tall and long-legged. He was straight and supple and moved with the grace of a young man, which James admitted to himself was impressive, guessing him to be in his late fifties. Probably just lucky genes, he tried to think, his good manners requiring some mental resistance to such a persuasively sexy body. But what was quite impossible to dismiss was a sense of wellbeing so powerful that Stephen Golightly seemed to embrace others with it, as if he were offering to share some quietly joyful aura of his own with other people. Never had James found a person's health so compellingly attractive. He felt himself almost blushing.

Stephen Golightly took a chair opposite and placed the folder on the low table between them. 'But of course it isn't. Whatever gave you the idea that it could be?'

James straightened up in his chair and looked embarrassed. He glanced over at Sara, who raised an eyebrow sternly at him. 'Well, this place,' he said uncertainly, 'the whole thing, it's . . . all very . . . big and . . .' He waved an arm hopelessly.

'If you mean it's all rather grand,' Dr Golightly said gently, 'I probably agree. But it's also a gracious building. Architecture matters, don't you feel that? I looked at several places, but I bought this one and set the clinic up here because it seemed to offer a haven—it's spacious, surrounded by trees, it's high, it overlooks the entire city. Didn't you feel that, up in the Wisteria Suite? I always hope that beauty helps people forget what's not really important and connect with what is. That's the true, the only purpose of beauty, to my mind.'

The intelligent eyes looked a little crestfallen and James, obedient to the same impulse not to disappoint that had prevented him being rude about the Wisteria Suite to Sister Yvonne said, 'Oh, of course, it is a wonderful house, yes. I just mean, naturopathy, I mean, if it's that great, why isn't everybody doing it?'

'But everybody shouldn't. There are many, many acute conditions for which conventional medicine is more appropriate, even essential.' He sighed. 'I'm not a zealot, believe me, either by inclination or experience. I lost my own wife eighteen years ago. She was forty-two and was so depressed she killed herself. Naturopathy couldn't help her, nothing could. I'm not offering cure-alls. And the approach we adopt here involves patients in their own treatment, so if you really feel—'

'Oh, look, I . . . I really am sorry . . . about your wife, I didn't mean—' And he was. Along with the sense that he had been brutal, he was taking in the news that Dr Golightly had been married. Not that his *not* being gay, no . . . no, certainly not, but . . . well, it did put a dispiritingly sterile slant on what could have been a rather diverting little crush on his doctor.

Dr Golightly raised a hand. 'No, please, I tell you that only to demonstrate that I am the last person to overlook serious symptoms, or to try to insist on a naturopathic regime for every condition. I am not offering miracles. I have a perfectly ordinary part-time NHS practice in town, as you know. But naturopathy is an extremely effective approach for conditions like yours, for patients who have the time and the means. That's an unfortunate fact of life, as far as I'm concerned. We're a charity, so when we can, we subsidise certain patients, but on the whole I can only suggest a stay at the Sulis to patients who can afford it. And even then I am very keen to see that they are not wasting their money. So I only admit patients who are well disposed to the idea behind it, of course, otherwise there's little point.'

There was a silence as Dr Golightly put his glasses back on and flicked casually through James's records.

'I am, really,' James squeaked. 'I mean, I will give it a go. It isn't unpleasant, is it? The treatment, I mean?'

Dr Golightly smiled, removing the top from his fountain pen. 'Heavens, no. Am I to take it then that you, James, are making a commitment to us? If so, we are ready and willing to make ours to you.'

'Yes he is,' Sara said. Her eyes told James to bloody well say so, too, which he did.

'Good,' Stephen Golightly said, looking up and holding James's gaze over the top of his glasses in a blue-eyed stare, 'then we'll start you on a Scottish Douche, twice daily. That's simply the application of hot and cold water up and down the spine, alternately, which tones up the spinal nerves and perks up circulation, followed by a salt rub.' James looked dolefully at Sara. 'And daily constitutional hydrotherapy.' In the stunned silence Dr Golightly explained kindly, 'That's body wrapping in cold, wet sheets, followed by hot packs on the neck, lower back and soles of the feet. To fight any incipient infection.'

James's stare at Sara grew reproachful. 'Is that all?' he asked.

'Oh no,' Dr Golightly said, ignoring the sarcasm. 'We have daily massages, yoga, therapeutic pool exercises, discussions on health and lifestyle, those are mainly with Sister Yvonne. Also daily art therapy run by a professional artist, who is my daughter-in-law, Hilary. We strive for a family atmosphere here, so you can appreciate it helps to actually have family involved. Although music therapy is sadly suspended temporarily, as we have a vacancy to fill there, but we'll be getting that going again as soon as we can.' He coughed a little apologetically. 'It can be a challenge, finding the right people. We had someone who left at Easter, before we could replace her. Now, what else do you need to know—ah yes, nutritional therapy. Almost the most important thing of all, particularly when the problem is a digestive one, like yours. We're vegetarian of course, and nearly a hundred per cent organic. My son Ivan manages our organic garden out near Limpley Stoke. We have three acres. All the main vegetables and fruit, herbs of course, and even a small cereal and seed crop, rye and sunflowers. We make all our own bread, wholemeal, mixed-grain and low-gluten, and our own pasta, too. No coffee is served. For you we'll go for the low salt, low fat, gluten-free and high fibre options and see how you do.' He bent his head and made some more notes, and looked up again. 'Do you have any questions?'

James had heard enough. He shook his head and rose, trying to look keen. Dr Golightly beamed his happy smile at him again and shook his and Sara's hands warmly. 'James, it's good to have you here, and I hope we'll soon have you restored in body and spirit. I'll let you go now. I expect you'll want to meet the other patients. Why not go along to the library? They'll be having tea.'

Visions of a pot of Assam, scones, jam and clotted cream swam giddily into James's mind, but Dr Golightly walked them to the door saying, 'Herbal, as you'd expect. Caffeine's a no-no, obviously. I suggest camomile or peppermint, with one of Ivan's celery and rye flatbreads,' and they swam right out again. 'Oh, and did I mention that we don't serve alcohol? Goes without saying, really,' he added, holding open the door and pointing further along. 'Library's that-a-way. Goodbye!'

That settles it, James thought, with a departing, stagey grin. Twenty-four hours, forty-eight maximum. Then he'd make Sara come back for him. She would take him home. Whatever Tom had made her promise, Sara was his best friend. She wouldn't let him stay here and suffer.

CHAPTER 14

IVAN PICKED THE blue shirt off the floor next to Leech's bed.

'What's this doing here?' he asked, pleasantly.

Leech, busy with a leather flail in the centre of the shed, looked up. He loved being spoken to by Ivan, even when he could not give an answer. He was smiling as he shook his head.

'What's this shirt doing here?'

Leech's head continued to shake as he mumbled through the scarf over his mouth, 'Don't know,' hopeful that he was about to be told. But Ivan only dusted the shirt off, folded it loosely and slung it over the handlebars of the bicycle which stood just inside the door.

'Haven't a clue, have you? Remind me to take it back to the house,' Ivan said, and Leech nodded his head happily. 'We've nearly finished,' he went on, dumping another load of cut rye on the floor, not realising that for Leech this was disappointing news.

Leech turned and bent back down to his work. Ivan had cut the rye crop late on Saturday, just before the rain, and armfuls of it were spread around them now on a huge canvas sheet that covered most of the floor. It had been outside drying for Leech was not sure how long, and to-day, with a thing that Ivan had told him was an old-fashioned flail, he was beating it until the chaff and grain separated. They had worked for a long time, for as soon as Leech had cleared the patch of floor in front of him Ivan would push along the next load. In between bringing in loads, Ivan would gather up the stuff that Leech had just done into wide shallow pans and cart it off outside. Then he would let the breeze carry away some of the chaff, and then he sieved and separated, working outdoors on a line of trestle tables that he had set up.

The air inside the shed prickled with floating, broken chaff that swirled up in the little cyclone made by Leech's circling arms; papery sharp, near-invisible needles danced up and cut into the inside of his nose. The back of his hand was streaked with smudges of mucus mixed with blood where he had scrubbed it against the itchy, stinging, broken membranes of his nostrils. His eyes were bloodshot and smarting. Ivan had told him to keep his mouth closed. Once when he forgot, he had sucked in a lungful of air that hit the back of his throat like a handful of thrown sand. Coughing, he had stumbled out of the shed and Ivan had given him Coke to drink and a scarf to cover his mouth. I told you to keep your mouth closed, can't you even remember that much, he had said, tying it at the back of his head for him.

It was hot work but he did not mind, for Ivan was here and was keeping him supplied with bottles of Coke and was even joining in the flailing occasionally, in between fetching and carrying loads and dishes of grain. And now they had nearly finished. Ivan had come back to the door-way of the shed and was motioning him to take the scarf off his face. Come on outside, Leech.

Leech's tobacco, papers and matches were waiting on
the ground outside the shed, next to a bottle of water and
a towel. Ivan waited until Leech had rolled a cigarette.
Here, he said, wetting a corner of the towel from the water bottle and holding it out. For your eyes. Press this
against your eyes. Leech solemnly bathed his stinging eyelids, laid the towel aside and lit his ciggie, blinking. Keep
your eyes closed for a bit longer, Ivan said, it'll help. You
can come down to the house for a bath, later. Go on, shut
them, relax. Leech lay his head against the wall of the shed
and smoked, watching red and yellow shooting stars exploding in the dark of his closed eyelids, as more tears
formed and rolled down his cheeks. He smiled in the silence, knowing that Ivan was near. Keep them shut, Ivan's
voice was saying, and hold out your hand. Leech, smiling
and obedient, did so, and a soft tickling sensation spread
over his palm. Speaking over the gentle rattling sound and
Leech's amused little sighs came Ivan's voice again. It's a
pure, organic, hand-produced crop, Leech. Leech tried to
look but was half-blinded by the sudden light and the tears
which again flooded his eyes. Don't open them, rest your
eyes. They'll be better soon. But you can feel it in your
hand, can't you? Not everyone could do what you've
done, stand for hours and hours threshing by hand, Leech,
you're a wonder. Ivan was saying that. Leech drew hard on
the cigarette, smiling again, as Ivan picked the grains out
of his hand and returned them to the bowl. Mustn't waste
any, there isn't a lot. A difficult year, what with the wet
spring and cold summer. But still, there's enough for—
oh, *ages*, Ivan was saying dreamily now. Ivan had a nice,
slow voice and Leech felt his sore eyelids grow heavier. He
sneezed and wiped his nose with the back of his hand. His

nose pricked as if he were sniffing pins, his eyes watered again and he drew hard again on his cigarette. Ivan was talking again. There's enough here to keep the clinic going for ages, he said. You've helped to grow and harvest this, Leech. That's your work and mine running through our hands. Leech removed the cig from his dry lips and struggled to say, for some of the paper had stuck, and Mother Nature's. It's Mother Nature's work, too. Ivan laughed then so that Leech laughed too, glad to have made a joke, for it seemed that was what he had done. You're quite right. Mother Nature's behind the whole thing, Leech. Indeed she is.

*   *   *

IT WAS hard not to be actually angry with the weather. Sara, leaning against the open door, looked out under the dripping eaves of the hut at the top of the garden and down through the white roses which climbed through the apple trees below, their waterlogged blooms hanging in the wet like used and scrunched-up Kleenex. Far away and above the treeline at the top of the valley, at seven o'clock on this August evening, the sky was thick and white. And out of its apparent solidity a steady cold rain was falling, greasing the paths that criss-crossed the garden and drenching again the six lime trees in the bloated meadow on the far side of the valley. Their water-laden leaves now gleamed indecently with the over-lusty, acrylic viridity of a fluorescent felt-tipped pen. It was only weather, but it had been fine all day until now, and it was impossible not to take it personally. Sara sighed loudly and turned back to Andrew who was sitting with his cello, his bow resting on his knee, staring at the music on the stand.

He looked up and said simply, 'I don't feel like playing. I only said I wanted to come up here so that I could be with you.' Sara smiled.

'You're not getting away with that. Come on, let's have a bit of your *Ein Mädchen oder Weibchen*.'

Andrew sighed and began the theme from the *Magic Flute* on which Beethoven had written twelve variations. Sara watched him as she listened, impressed equally by his playing and the sight of his long legs and his wonderful face when he was concentrating. There were, of course, little criticisms of his playing that she could think of but she had no intention of stopping him to make them, and so curtail her own pleasure. When he came to the end of the first variation she crossed to the music stand, closed the music and kissed him on the lips.

'Very good. You're very good, do you know that?'

'Yes. Actually you've no idea how good I can be.'

'Remind me.'

Andrew pulled away. 'If only. But you don't like to when Joyce is around, do you?'

Sara sighed, conceding. 'Seems as if she's been here for ever.'

'Well, you *did* take her on.'

'You should try to understand. It's no different from you and your children, really. Now we've both got people to look after.'

'It is, as a matter of fact, entirely different.' After a silence he went on, 'It's only a week, isn't it? Wednesday today. How much longer?'

'At least we're by ourselves for a while. Even with the rain it's nice to be up here by ourselves, isn't it?' She shivered. 'Isn't it?'

Andrew stood up and put his cello away as Sara moved the chair and music stand to the wall. Although it was not late she lit the two oil lanterns that hung from the roof and immediately their glow lent the hut the illusion of warmth. Andrew closed the half-glazed doors and pulled the tatty velvet chaise longue round so that they could lie wrapped together in the lantern light, watching the view of the soaked garden and valley through the streaks of rainwater hitting the glass. They lay in silence for some moments, relaxing in the gratifying absence of Joyce.

'She doesn't like being on her own for long,' Sara warned. 'It's as much as I can do to get away for an hour every day to run along the towpath. She'll come barging in soon.'

Andrew shifted under her and coughed. 'Damn,' he said, continuing to stroke her thigh.

'Tell me the latest about the case,' Sara said, after a minute. 'You know that's what's making you miserable. That, and this,' she added. She did not have to explain that *this* meant not the rain nor even the need to escape Joyce, but the growing mutual wish to make love right then and there, and the also unspoken risk that they were bound to be interrupted if they tried. The tension between desire and its constraint seemed to be twisting the very air they breathed. It would not be long, Sara thought, before they began to resent each other just for having the power to arouse each other so pointlessly. 'What's happening with the case?'

'It's police business. Confidential. I'm not meant to discuss it,' Andrew said rather officiously, wondering if perhaps they could, perhaps if they didn't take quite all their clothes off? Not ideal of course, but in the circumstances better than nothing. He shifted again and looked at his watch. They had only been up here ten minutes, after all.

'I know that. So?' So she wasn't even pretending to believe that that was his reason for not wanting to embark on conversation. She was waiting for his answer.

'We've had Mrs Takahashi's PM results,' he said in a tired voice, 'and it's exactly what I expected. Cause of death is asphyxiation. There's bruising to the upper arms and the skull injury that she sustained when he knocked her out cold against the wall or got her so punch-drunk she couldn't put up any real resistance when he strangled her. No fingernail evidence. We found a dent and a couple of her hairs stuck on the wall of the pub corridor, at just the right height. Oh, and she was pregnant. Just a few weeks. Sorry—you can't want to hear this.'

Sara had shuddered in his arms. For a reason she could not fathom, the fact of the poor woman's pregnancy suddenly brought her to life, so that the brutality of her killing felt like a new blow, becoming now also a new death. Not even the sight of the contorted blue face in the dim and grubby pub corridor had made her feel this. But now, the thought of a baby conceived never to be born, conceived to wither in its mother's belly, not knowing that it had existed but never quite lived, was unbearable. She was struck by the thought that Andrew had to face such appalling truths if not quite every day, then too often. As she watched the trails of rainwater sliding haphazardly down the window glass she wondered shamefully how she could have been so self-obsessed that she had refused even to try to understand this.

'What's next, then?'

Andrew considered in silence. Then he said, 'She was

killed no later than about ten o'clock that morning, according to the PM, probably earlier. Rigor was well established, and the stomach contents were hardly digested. Her last meal was fried egg and toast. Hilary Golightly confirmed the time she had breakfast, anyway.' Sara squirmed in his arms. 'Her husband claims he was meeting her at 12.30 at the RPS and got there slightly late, at 12.38. If we can find the evidence that he was in Bath earlier then that would be significant. Not conclusive, but significant, in the absence of anything better.'

'How are you going to get evidence like that, though? Bath's seething with people on Saturdays in the summer. Unless he spoke to somebody who remembers him? And wouldn't he take care not to do that, if he'd come to murder his wife?'

'Well, in the first place it's unlikely he intended to kill her. You wouldn't choose a passageway in a pub as the ideal murder location, would you? He probably lost his temper, though that said, it's an oddity that he went as far as he did with the strangulation. She'd have been unconscious long before she was dead and that's usually when an abusive husband stops. So he probably wouldn't have been trying to stay inconspicuous before he met her. There's security video footage from the town and the railway station to go through, and we're putting out appeals for information. People who were in the area from eight or nine o'clock onwards and may have seen him.'

'So—a swarthy photograph in the paper, then?'

'Oh no,' Andrew said, sounding almost shocked. 'That'd screw us up completely. We might want to do an ID parade, and that'd be out of the question if a photograph had been published earlier. You can see why.'

'I thought you told me identity parades were a nightmare?'

'They are, they are. And this one will be worse than most.'

'Because?'

'Because I'm bored stiff talking about it,' Andrew announced, rousing himself. 'And because it's a nightmare getting enough volunteers together, and then your suspect doesn't show up, any number of things go wrong, whatever. Anyway, it may not even happen. We need witnesses first, people who think they saw someone answering Takahashi's description at or near Green Street before ten o'clock that day. A long shot. Oh God, look,' he groaned, pointing outside.

An eager, wet face was peering in at them, bouncing up and down, its indecently pink tongue lolling. 'Just as well we kept our clothes on, then,' Sara said dolefully. 'We wouldn't want to embarrass Pretzel, would we?'

'I hate you,' Andrew said conversationally to the dog as he opened the door to let him in. 'I hate you because wherever you are, Joyce is never far behind. Ah, Joyce! There you are!' he called. 'Up here! We were just wondering where you were, weren't we, Sara?'

As they stood together watching Joyce struggle up the slippery path to the hut Sara whispered, 'Let's go to bed really early. At least she can't follow us *there*.'

Andrew squeezed her hand. He had been saving until the last possible moment the news that he was babysitting his children that night because Valerie, once again at deliberately short notice, had decided she needed an evening out.

CHAPTER 15

By THREE O'CLOCK on Thursday James, lying up at the top of the Sulis garden in the deep of the afternoon and surrounded by flowers and summer birdsong, felt he had read enough Coleridge to be able to appreciate that

> —far and near,
> *In wood and thicket, over the wide grove*
> *They answer and provoke each other's song,*
> *with skirmish and capricious passagings,*
> *And murmurs musical and swift jug jug jug*

but he didn't because in his exhausted stomach there was so much skirmish and capricious passaging that it felt as though someone with a pickaxe and a grudge was down there breaking boulders. After he had left his message on Sara's mobile he had tried to make himself relax by listening to the birdsong tinkling down from the high trees that bordered the clinic grounds, but had fallen instead into an agitated and distressing half-dream in which he was losing control of a masterclass made up of fledglings in velvet hairbands falling out of their nests. 'No! Come on! Give me swift jug jug jug, not *pring pring*! Get back in your nests! Sit up straight!' Shaking himself into wakefulness he tried to remember what he had been learning in the yoga class about relaxation and a sense of harmony with oneself and with the natural world. But all he could hear in the calling of the birds was a restless lament for how things ought to be but were not. Coleridge's *Poetical Works* lay open across his chest. The book on naturopathy lay on the ground beside him open at the page headed Health Is A Matter Of Nutrition.

It was a pity that Health seemed also to be a Matter Of Sharing A Dining Room With Intolerable People although, to be fair to them, James admitted to himself that had the food been more enjoyable and sustaining, the company of the others round the oval table at lunch would have been, too. The dining room itself was superb, another high-ceilinged room with full-length windows on two sides, carpeted in pale grey and with hand-painted murals depicting some kind of eighteenth century carnival with horse races. Parts of lunch had been good: the different kinds of lettuce, chervil, parsley and rocket had been wonderfully fresh, which was not to say they would not have been better with garlic mayonnaise. The carrot, courgette and tomato bake, with shredded raw cabbage, celery and cucumbers had also been very nice, though how much of such stuff could a person be expected to eat? The bread, a mixed grain slab with a crust like pebble dash, James had judged about as rewarding as eating eggboxes. And that, along with all the water he could drink, had been it. Where was his lump of Stilton? The smoked ham, the shavings of parmesan? The marinaded anchovies, the oil, the butter?

James had watched his four fellow patients approach their lunch with the solemnity of communicants.

'Isn't he a genius?' rasped the old woman sitting opposite. When no one had replied, she had turned to the man on her left, with the cravat tucked into the neck of his towelling robe, who had been staring at his plate. 'Warwick, don't you agree he's a genius? Ivan. He's a genius. With food.'

Warwick, still chewing, considered. 'Oh absolutely. Though truth to tell, Bunny, I don't go such a bundle on the raw stuff,' he said. 'And the bread's a bit heavy.' Sensing the old lady's dismay at the criticism he added, 'Oh, it's meant to be, one appreciates that. Full of cereals.' He picked up the untouched chunk of bread on his plate and weighed it in the palm of his hand. 'Rather filling, that's all. In fact, I think I'll keep mine for later. As is my wont.' Smiling with faint embarrassment, he wrapped the bread in his paper napkin and pocketed it.

The old lady nodded in the general direction of Warwick's dressing-gown pocket and said, 'I hope you're not skipping it. You must be sure you eat it. Everything's worked out for nutritional balance. It's a daily requirement.' Turning to James she said, 'Ivan and his father work it all out. Dr Golightly insists we eat well, whatever we're in for. Get the fuel right and the body will rejuvenate itself, you see. Better than a whole handful of antibiotics. I see you've eaten yours. Have you a troublesome gut?'

James was saved from having to reply by Warwick, who seemed anxious to convince that he was a true disciple. 'Oh, goodness me yes, Bunny's right. Solid goodness. Goes through the colon like a bottle-brush. I'll eat mine later, you see. I often get peckish around three o'clock.'

A little silence had then settled over the table, during which the old lady's jowls had fallen, rather miraculously, even further. As James looked at the other two patients who had so far said nothing, one of them, a big-boned, gentle-faced woman with hair the colour of parsnips, raised her eyes and met his look. She was chewing bravely, while tears gathered in her large green eyes.

'Oh Jane,' the old woman said. 'What's set you off this time? Not talking about food, surely?'

Jane shook her head and tears splashed on to her plate. 'Nothing. It's just—' The word 'just' had proved difficult to say with a mouthful of the challenging bread. She swallowed inelegantly and gave a little nod of apology to everyone. 'I was just thinking about my wedding. Today's our anniversary. I can't help it, it's my first as a . . . as a divorcée. It just reminded me. You see, it was three o'clock when we got married.' Confident of her charm, she trailed off into a pretty little sniff. Even her voice had been blonde, James thought as he remembered it, this seeming to him a charitable way to describe her tone of soft-brained inconsequentiality.

Nobody had known what to reply, perhaps because if something as innocuous as three o'bloody clock in the afternoon was too charged with painful meaning to be mentioned then it was surely dangerous to say anything else.

Warwick had resumed the earlier, less hazardous topic. 'Well, well. Nutrition's vital, of course. But you know me, Bunny. The creative therapy's the thing. Therapeutic self-expression—that's more me. That's my saviour, not the rabbit food.'

This remark stirred the other man, who had hairless pink hands and the face of a middle-aged cod, into speech.

'Oh yes. Thera-*peu*-tic's right. You're all right, you lot are, with Hilary,' he said, in a reverential Welsh accent. He turned to James. 'They're all right. Doing art. They get Hilary, the art therapist. Attractive woman. Only I can't really get on with the clay, not like these two. Dries my hands out, you see.'

James murmured with what he considered the minimum acceptable level of feigned interest, but the Welshman wet his lips and continued. 'Now the music therapy, I could have got on with that. Bit of a singer at one time, actually. I auditioned for the Swingle Singers once. I could have done with the music therapy, only there's none. She's left, the music therapist. Didn't tell me that when I booked, though.' He sat back and pursed his lips. 'I'm negotiating a refund,' he said importantly.

'There are plenty of other things you could do instead,' Bunny said, peering frostily along the table, 'only you don't. You could paint but you don't. You don't even swim. You just fall asleep by the pool in between massages. I think you're very unfair.' She glared at James as if to warn him that it would be intolerably bad form to side with the Welshman, who had now grown pink in the face.

'Rest is a fundamental need for my condition,' he pouted, and fell silent.

Warwick patted his sides. 'Results speak for themselves, don't they?' There was a murmur from the others. 'Anyway, it's the whole shebang, isn't it?' he went on, trying to draw them together. 'Diet, rest, self-expression. Physical and mental. The whole thing.'

The blonde woman, Jane, added, 'Yoga, hydrotherapy, massage, posture, breathing,' counting them off on lilac-painted talons. Her contribution over and clearly not expecting a reply, she had risen with a cool smile and swayed from the room as slinkily as her lumpy robe allowed. The Welshman's hungry eyes tracked her working buttocks until they disappeared behind the door and then he, presumably in obedience to some doomed libidinal impulse, had got up and followed.

'Ivan is a genius, anyway,' asserted the old woman, back on the subject with which she seemed to be successfully emptying the room. She pulled a reptilian hand from somewhere inside her towelling folds and held it out to James, displaying several rings as gnarled as her fingers.

'Mrs Bunny Fernandez,' she said. She leaned across the table and offered with the hand a close-up of her heavily made-up cheeks and a smiling top row of tea-coloured teeth. The black eyelashes flailing in the chalky face made James think of two spiders trapped in setting cement.

'James Ballantyne,' he said.

'Detoxification,' she replied.

Warwick leaned towards James. 'Bunny's a big fan,' he said. 'Comes every year. Three weeks of organic food, rest, art therapy, swears by it, don't you, Bunny?'

'Detoxification. Every August,' she assented graciously. James murmured with the impressed tone that was clearly expected. 'Essential,' she went on, 'for rejuvenation. I'm seventy-nine, you know.'

She certainly did not look that. James had put her closer to ninety.

'Warwick Jones,' the face above the cravat was saying. 'Practically indestructible, in need of pepping up.' He lowered his voice. 'Somewhat weakened constitution, you

see, once the Japs had finished with me.' He coughed to indicate that no answer was necessary.

'Warwick's liver is a battlefield,' Bunny said, importantly. 'He won't mind me saying. And you?'

James had been saved from having to return the confidence and mention his bowels by the sudden reminder
they had at that moment given him of their presence.
Whether it was the food or the conversation that had
caused them to reconsider their strategy of refusing to
budge for an average of four days at a time, however much
James besieged them with fig and senna extract, they had
clearly resolved after forty-eight hours at the Sulis to
abandon that tactic and go for complete evacuation. He
had left the dining room very quickly.

*   *   *

WITHOUT REALISING that he had been asleep, James now
awoke with a few seconds' disorientated puzzlement
about why there should be giant birds wearing glasses in
his bedroom. He was still under the gazebo at the top of
the garden. Stretching, he felt grateful for the sleep even
though it had brought unpleasantly vivid dreams. His
stomach still groaned painfully but he supposed, reviewing his mood and trying once more to ignore the birds,
which at least had returned to their normal size and were
back up in the trees, that he had felt worse before he came
here. Picking up the Coleridge again, he leafed through it.
How sweet, typical and nuts of Tom to stick this and other
volumes of poetry in his luggage. You're not to read fiction, he had said. You get too involved, you know you do. I
know you can't empty your mind, so at least fill it with
poetry. The book had fallen open at *Kubla Khan*, the only

Coleridge that James until that afternoon had ever read, apart from the *Ancient Mariner*.

> *In consequence of a slight indisposition an anodyne had been prescribed, from the effect of which the Author fell asleep in his chair at the moment he was reading. The Author continued for about three hours in a profound sleep, at least of the external senses, during which time he had the most vivid confidence that he could not have composed less than two to three hundred lines. Yet from the still surviving recollections in his mind, the Author has frequently purposed to finish for himself what had been originally, as it were, given to him.*

James smiled to himself as his eyes skated through the poem, trying to picture the gardens bright, the incense-bearing trees and sunny spots of greenery that had danced through Coleridge's brain during that prosaic-sounding afternoon nap. When Sara arrived he must ask if she could get hold of some *Anodyne* for him. He could do with a little milk of paradise, he reflected, as his stomach rumbled agreement.

CHAPTER 16

ANDREW DECIDED IN the end to submit with grace to the suggestion that he see Joyce back to Medlar Cottage, remembering Sara's own grace at being deserted for babysitting the night before. The three of them were standing in the entrance lobby of the police station. Sara was still holding her mobile phone. It was not usual, he had suggested mildly, for a chief inspector to drive witnesses around.

'Well no, but you *know* Joyce, don't you. She'd be happier. Sorry . . . only you see James has left this message. He's in the Sulis and he's practically demanding I go and see him. I've got to go, I really have. You will see Joyce home, won't you? Joyce, he'll get you back in time for your rest. Be nice to each other. I really must go.'

Distracted, she had gone, leaving Andrew looking at Joyce and wondering if he could find it in himself to think of her as some kind of irresponsible child or animal, something unlovable with hideous habits and redeeming qualities so deeply buried that one simply had to trust that they were there. Sara had brought her to Manvers Street Police Station to make her statement about the events in the Snake and Ladder on the previous Saturday. Joyce had repeated her story loftily although with perfect consistency to Bridger, altering nothing except perhaps the height of her contempt for the entire process. She continued to claim that the doors of the cupboard in the pub corridor had been closed. Somehow, on her way back from the lavatory the woman had just fallen out on top of her.

Eight days of daily baths, a good bed, Sara's careful cooking and no booze had restored in Joyce not just some physical condition but also a disproportionate *amour-propre*. It was extraordinary, Andrew had observed to himself, that such a scrag end of womanhood, barely five feet tall, could survey a roomful of police officers as if from a height. She managed to make you feel that she was inspecting you from a balcony.

But he would submit with grace. Grace in the immediate circumstances was appropriate, Andrew reminded himself as he smiled at Joyce, because later on he had every intention of getting Sara away from Medlar Cottage for a night. Ordinarily he might, despite the wary liking he had developed for James, have slightly resented Sara's rushing off so full of concern for somebody else, especially since this now meant breaking up his afternoon with a drive out to St Catherine's Valley to deposit Joyce. But he would submit with—had he thought grace? It was more like delirious joy, because he was already planning the evening.

'Right, then, your ladyship,' he said, determined not to be discouraged by Joyce's unsmiling eyes, 'your carriage awaits. Shall we?' He opened the heavy glass door of the police station with a facetious flourish, making a face to the desk sergeant behind the glass partition as Joyce scuttled under his raised arm into the sunshine outside.

They sat for a long time in a traffic queue in Walcot Street. Joyce and Andrew watched inexpressively without speaking as people went by, up and down the pavement next to the flea market, crossing the road in front of the stopped car with pedestrians' smiles, betraying their pleasure in having a practical advantage, as well as moral superiority, over mugs stuck in cars. Most were carrying, or displaying on stalls, the kinds of things that Walcot Street sold: pots, pictures and frames (sometimes together), bags and rolls of curtains and clothes, hangings, candlesticks, urns, fireplaces and objects that fell into no category except that of things to buy for a bit more than they were worth, put somewhere, look at for a bit and then go off. And it seemed that everything traded in Walcot Street, if not actually antique or second-hand, had been duffed up and rubbed down in order to look so. The people too, many of whom were young, had apparently been duffed up and rubbed down with the result that they also looked if not older then slightly thumbed. They were wearing clothes that were either so huge or so tiny that their bodies were swamped or barely covered. That, together with a soft look of benign puzzlement on their faces created the lovable impression that the dear things hadn't quite got the hang of finding the right sizes. Hair of varying styles and colours was on the whole odd or impractical, if not absent. Andrew smiled. Natalie would be among this lot in a few years' time. He made a mental note not to shout when she got her first navel piercing.

Joyce sniffed and rearranged her thin lips over her teeth, a signal that Andrew now recognised. She was going to speak. 'Well, it would appear that not quite *all* of your famous Georgian Bath is famous for its elegance,' she said, looking out. 'Just what are these people trying to achieve, going about like *that*?'

It was the kind of critical yet impersonal remark, delivered with that self-satisfied, superior, Scottish nasality that had in just over a week brought Andrew close to reviewing his position on handguns.

He sighed with open exasperation. 'I expect most of the people here are either students or traders. Perhaps they're achieving having a good time being themselves, being nice, ordinary people. I think you would find,' he said, trying not to hiss, 'that most of them manage to *achieve* keeping jobs and homes and relationships of their own.'

There was a crusty silence. Joyce said, 'You're not fond of me, are you? I can tell, you know.'

It was the most direct thing Andrew had heard her say, but he was not going to give her the satisfaction of a straight answer. The car ahead was moving now. As he put his car into gear and followed, Andrew said, 'Why do you drink?'

She did not reply, and began to rummage pointlessly in her handbag. As far as she was concerned nothing had been said.

'You opened that cupboard, didn't you? Not on the way *to* the Ladies', because you hadn't been in yet to check that there was nobody in there. On the way out. You checked the Ladies' was empty and then opened the cupboard because you thought there might be something to drink in there, didn't you?' Andrew's voice was quiet but not gentle. He edged the car forward.

'That's your theory.' Joyce sounded so offended that Andrew knew he was right and, perversely, knew also that because they both now realised it, there was nothing else to be said. Warning her off the booze again would be a waste of breath. The silence which followed became permanent, and by the time they had reached the cause of the hold-up, some nonsensical roadworks where a traffic island was being prettied up with fake cobbles, Andrew had lapsed back into his own thoughts. He didn't care where Joyce's mental travels had taken her to.

Because once he had got Sara out of the house this evening he was hoping that he might succeed in getting her to stay with him at the flat for a night. If Joyce was happy to rest alone at Medlar Cottage for an afternoon, couldn't she also be left to feed herself and put herself to bed? He was irritated not just by how little she ate of the food Sara prepared for her, but by her habit of repeating that she ate 'like a bird'. Sara had now forbidden him from mouthing *and drinks like a fish* over her head, but he now considered sourly that it would be an easy matter for one evening to leave a dropper of milk and a couple of worms for her in the fridge. He and Sara could buy some food and a bottle of wine and have the evening, a long, balmy one, to themselves. He would cook. The cooker in the flat worked, or parts of it did, albeit with an accompanying alarming smell (perhaps a salad would do, though). Really, the place wasn't that bad. All right, it was still an unloved, chilly box that he was supposed to be doing something about, but they could sit outside (ignoring the traffic noise) until late, and then he could make it better with candles. Yes, all right, he admitted it, the place was a dump next to Medlar Cottage, which he missed. Mostly he missed, since Joyce's arrival, not being able to make love in every room of the house. The absence of Joyce was the only thing his flat had going for it, at least until he got round to doing something about it (he would, he would) but he would make much to Sara of that undeniable attraction.

For Joyce had the knack of infiltrating an atmosphere so strongly with her own hangdog authority (she was even doing it now, in his car) that even empty rooms in Medlar Cottage seemed now not so much unoccupied by her as vacated only seconds before. And he was finding that she cramped his style not only as a lover but as a musician. How could he play the cello with her in the house, when he could imagine so easily what her tight-lipped, dismissive comments on his musical abilities would be? Thinking of it, he could practically hear the berating scratch of her consonants crackling in the air from room to room. And if he was being over-fanciful, which was what Sara said, then no flight of imagination was required to notice and silently object to Sara's confiscation of all alcohol in the house. He thought, with quiet savagery towards the silent Joyce beside him, of the empty wine rack and the empty shelf in the fridge to which he now mentally added other distasteful, daily reminders of her occupancy: the smell of Complan in the kitchen, pink, ragged lipstick prints on the edges of tea cups, used tissues down the sides of armchairs and that handbag, which stank of face powder, on the stairs. Not to mention the dog.

He coughed and tried unsuccessfully to pull his mind back round to work. Bridger had taken Joyce's statement with gloom, and though it pained Andrew to do so, he had sympathised with him. Had there been grounds to suspect her guilty of the murder, conviction would not have been difficult, for a drink-deprived alcoholic eventually grows confessional about most things. But the time of Mrs

Takahashi's death seemed to rule Joyce out. He supposed he disliked Joyce so much that he could almost wish she had killed her. He certainly wished he could blame her for the mess he had made of things on Sunday with Mr Takahashi, or Professor Takahashi as he was supposed to say, but not even his powers of self-justification would rise to that. Joyce was merely contributing generously to the sum of things not going very well.

*   *   *

SARA GREETED James in the gazebo overlooking the garden with concern that was mixed with gratitude for his thoughtfulness in arranging for his needs to be met by others. After more than a week of caring for Joyce and the strain of pretending to Andrew that doing so was not easy but Basically Absolutely Fine, she was not merely exhausted but more aware than was comfortable of her constitutional inability to nurse someone like Joyce with any degree of true grace. It was also constitutionally compulsory for this awareness to leave Sara feeling guilty and inadequate.

The Sulis seemed, on the face of it, to be doing a splendid job. James was stretched out on a recliner in the shade of the rose-covered gazebo. He was alone, the climb up here through the terraced garden behind the house presumably proving too much for other patients. He was wearing a white dressing gown with 'Sulis' embroidered in loopy writing on the front, and a thin blanket lightly covered his legs and feet. The *Guardian*, some books and a jug of some fresh-looking cold drink sat on a small table next to him. But despite it he looked almost as unhappy as he did unwell.

'Fine bloody friend you are,' James growled. 'What kept you?'

'I'm here now so stop moaning. You're not a good colour,' Sara said, sitting on the edge of the empty recliner alongside and peering into his face. James looked as if he were about to give a bright smile to show how mistaken she was, but did not. Instead he smiled with closed lips and said, 'Glad you came. I'll be fine just as soon as I'm out of here and had something decent to eat. I've given it a try and I don't like it and I'm not staying. You'll pack for me, won't you? There isn't much. I would have done it already but I've been a bit light-headed.'

'*Pack?*' Sara exclaimed. Surely if Medlar Cottage became James's personal recuperation ward, Joyce and Pretzel would have to go? She took less than a second to weigh up the merits of one against the other as house guests. But she was also wondering how James could be contemplating leaving when he was clearly so ill. But how could she find the strength to withstand those beseeching, unhealthy eyes?

James, seeing her difficulty but not understanding the reasons for it, at once adopted the mental stance of one who wants something so badly he refuses to ask for it. He raised both hands, showing his palms. 'Sorry. Forget what I said. Never mind.'

'It's a lovely place, this, James. Why would you want to leave? It's so peaceful. You'd never even know it was here, from the road. All those trees. And you can see for miles.' Sara picked up the book. 'What are you reading Coleridge for? You must be ill.'

'Reading it for? *For?* It's Art, sweetheart. It's not *for* things. When did you get to be so brutally prosaic?'

'I think that life with PC Plod must be draining the poetry out of you, Munchkin,' James said, smiling evilly. He took the book, opened it and leafed through it. 'Here's one just for you—it goes "*My pensive Sara!*" It's called the "Eolian Harp". Want to hear it? And yes, I'm ill. I suppose.'

'No, I don't. And I wish you wouldn't be rude about Andrew. And I'm not pensive, I'm shattered. Honestly,' Sara muttered, 'I wouldn't mind staying here myself. I don't think I *am* very well. And I've got Salzburg in a few days, and you wouldn't believe what else I'm having to deal with.'

James would have laughed if he hadn't thought it would hurt his stomach. Oh, Sara, Sara. Barely a minute into a visit to a sick friend and she's telling you *she's* shattered and unwell. You had to love her, sitting there twisting her dark, shining hair in her fingers, her big eyes looking if anything more beautiful for the touch of sulk and self-pity in them. Pure, unreconstructed diva that she could sometimes be, you had to love her because she was born to play the cello and did so with brilliance, sensitivity and passion as well as, of course, the international recognition that suited her natural glamour. She could be sensitive also in friendship, as well as fierce, selfless, loyal and bloody funny. But James had seen that unless her considerable intelligence or emotional luck intervened in time to prevent it, it could sometimes appear that she was also born to conduct her love affairs in a manner that was clumsy, distracted, impetuous and extreme. And up to a point she understood this about herself, so you had to love her, and in any case she somehow made you, anyway.

'You do seem a bit tense,' James said. 'Andrew trouble,

is it?' In James's private opinion Andrew and Sara were in for trouble, sooner or later.

'Yes, I suppose it is. Partly,' Sara sighed, loyalty mixed with dismay. 'I didn't tell you on Tuesday. I thought we should concentrate on getting you in here. But he's got an awkward case, a man they should have charged with murdering his wife. He's Japanese. A professor. He was here for a conference and he killed her, Andrew's sure of it.'

'Why is that difficult? I mean, any more difficult than usual?'

'There's not enough evidence. The bloke practically admitted it but they can't use it as evidence because he hadn't been cautioned before he said it. And now his lawyer has told him not to repeat it, and Andrew's in a permanent fury about it.' She did not add that his fury, because it was directed mainly at himself, was all the fiercer and more painful to watch. 'Then there's all the guilt about his children, and Valerie being vile. Then the question of that flat he bought and hardly ever uses. And I don't know where any of it leaves me. Do you know, I don't even actually know whether we live together or not?'

James sighed. 'Oh, he'll sort it out,' he said, without much enthusiasm. 'Perhaps you're too involved. Perhaps you should just try letting him get on with it. You've got other things to think about, after all. What about your Dvořák? I missed your Prom, sorry. How did it go?'

'And Andrew says this man, the husband, is the only real suspect and the forensic evidence isn't conclusive. I mean, if one of his hairs is found on her cardigan, it doesn't prove he killed her. Anyway, look, I don't want to talk about Andrew's problems. What about yours?'

'Look, there they go,' James said, raising a hand to

point. 'That's Jane and some Welshman, forget his name. Down there.' Sara looked down across the garden and saw two figures in robes identical to James's make their way round a pretty stone fountain towards what looked like a miniature parthenon, partly obscured by trees, at the end of a broad grass walk to the left of the house.

'Nice fountain.'

'There are fish in it. They're the only meat in the place.'

'Where are they off to now, those two?'

'Oh, down to the pool. That place that looks like a temple. It's all marble inside. Listed building. It's divine. They'll be there all afternoon, lying around.'

'Is that part of their treatment?'

'Supposed to be. Rest is important, apparently, as is nutrition. All those tricks with massage, hydrotherapy, yoga, the dog's bollocks, they're quite pleasant, but I think they're mainly just to pass the time.' He snorted. 'That's all it is. Waiting till you feel better. That's what they'll be doing round the pool now, just lying waiting till they feel better.'

'Why aren't you, then? Sounds nice. You are rather isolated up here.'

'Exactly. Isolation is better any day to the conversations they get you into. They want to tell you everything, and to hear everything, too. Medically, I mean. In forty-eight hours I've heard more words for bowel movements than any reasonable person could need in a lifetime.'

'And just how are they, by the way? In your own words?'

This time James managed a proper smile. 'Tired, but apparently I'm meant to be. Hungry, which I'm also meant to be, according to Dr Golightly.' His eyes brightened.

'Didn't you *love* Dr Golightly, Munchkin?' He sighed stagily. 'He almost makes all this stuff sound sensible, and it certainly works for him. He really is rather gorgeous. So I'm resting my system, apparently, and rediscovering a healthy mind and body balance, after the imbalances imposed on it by stress and my modern Western lifestyle habits. And as soon as my system is on its way to being rebalanced, then— get this—then I'm allowed to do art therapy.' A snarl had entered his voice. 'Only I'm not staying.'

'Yes, you are. And I have to say,' Sara said, 'that it doesn't sound too bad to me, for a week or two. Quite pleasant, sensible, even.' When James did not reply she turned her attention once more to the view. The foreground stone and greens of the garden fountain and the treetops above the swimming pool temple stretched away to the golds, greys and blacks of the city's spires and roofs, and the blue August hills beyond.

'Poussin,' she murmured. 'Reminds me of Poussin.'

'Hmm,' James concurred. 'Roasted with lemons. Skin all crispy. Chive and garlic butter . . .'

'I meant,' Sara said sternly, 'Poussin the artist. Nicolas Poussin. Blue backgrounds. Greens in the foreground. Trees, classical ruins. Arcadian vistas.'

'Big cavorting nymphs. Naked shepherds swigging from the keg. I should be so lucky. Fuck Poussin.'

'James, you've got to *try*. You've got to get well. It is a beautiful place, try and appreciate it.'

'Fuck Art. Fuck this place. I'm hungry and I want to go home.'

'You promised Tom. You *promised*.' Tom would expect a call from her. Was she going to have to say that James had been more unwilling and uncooperative, as well as more ill, than she had ever seen him before? But he was looking at her now with something of his usual expression, knowing he had gone too far.

'Sorry. Sorry,' he said, softly. 'I'll stay. I will.' Sara looked at him without trust. 'I will. I'll try, I'll even do the art therapy. Munchkin, I'll wear a smock and a black beret and paint you our own fucking Poussin, if it'll make you happy.'

Sara laughed and said as convincingly as she could, 'Art therapy might make a change for you. You might even like it.'

'I might. I'll have to find something to do if I'm not supposed to be playing the piano. *Although*,' he lowered his voice, 'they've got quite a decent piano here, a baby Blüthner. I sneaked a little go.'

'Aren't you supposed to give everything a rest? Tom said you hadn't packed any music.'

'I didn't. I only tinkled for a bit and anyway there's a nice lot of music here already. The last music therapist left some of her own stuff behind in the piano stool—tons of it actually—and they haven't got an address to send it on to, Yvonne says, so there's any amount of Schumann, Schubert, Brahms and all that.'

'Oh, yes. The one who left.'

'Yvonne didn't like her. Same as the art therapy, self-expression for the untaught. Yvonne says I'm lucky to escape. Banging and whanging away on recorders and percussion, finding their voices, imagine. She kept getting her name wrong. I remember now—her actual name was Alex Cooper and Yvonne kept calling her Alice and she didn't like it. According to Yvonne she was tight-arsed, couldn't take a joke. Anyway the music therapy's suspended. Alice Cooper only lasted three weeks.'

'Oh?'

'Yeah. Hated the living-in, Yvonne says. She went without giving notice. Dr Golightly was furious.'

'Living-in? You mean to say there's a vacancy here for a *live-in* musician and all they do is give a few lessons to complete beginners?'

'More or less, yeah. So? I hope you're not going to suggest *I* take them on. I'd rather die.'

She stood up. 'James,' she said, 'stay here. Don't move, I'll be back in a minute.'

'What are you— Sara?'

She was already five yards down the path when she turned. 'Nothing. I'll only be a minute. Just a little suggestion I have for him.'

James felt a little of his weary gloom dissipate, but not much. Unable to find enough curiosity to call after her to tell him what her little suggestion was, he lay back again, closed his eyes and listened to the birds, a fair number of which, he thought, he could cheerfully eat. With or without roasted lemons, crispy skin, chives and garlic butter.

CHAPTER 17

I'VE BROUGHT YOUR tea. Joyce? The thing is, Joyce, we do have to talk about a few things. I'm afraid I'm doing the Dvořák again.'

Joyce rose from the pillow looking askance and surprised in the offhand way that she had perfected since her arrival. 'Oh dear, are you? That's a great pity, in my view. It needs work.' She pronounced it WURK. Sara curbed a temptation to throw the tea over her head.

'I mean,' she said, with insincere patience, 'that I'll be away. There's a performance and live recording in Salzburg. In about ten days. So I'll be away, do you see? So it makes sense for you to get settled in at the Sulis before that happens . . .'

Sara was still standing in the doorway with the cup of tea, determined to get her message across this time. Joyce had proved to be a mistress of elective deafness on the subject of her moving from Medlar Cottage. She would nod in apparent understanding and then immediately try to draw them away from the subject with blatant non sequiturs about anything: the weather, Pretzel, her appetite. Sara had made her tea, wishing it were hemlock, and marched upstairs determined that she would be made to get the point.

'The house will be empty. And it's been lovely having you but it was only for a while, wasn't it? You'll want to be getting on with things, I expect. I mean, you were going to need somewhere more permanent some time, remember, and this is a wonderful chance.'

'But I could stay here and look after the place for you. Pretzel and me. A dog about the place, wouldn't that be a help, now?'

'You are too kind,' Sara said, 'but no, I'm not letting you spoil your plans for me.' Before Joyce could reply that the only person with plans was Sara, she went on firmly, 'You need to get yourself properly settled in and used to things. You'll love Dr Golightly.' As she handed Joyce her cup and saucer she looked doubtfully at her yellowish eyes, remembering Stephen Golightly's clear blue ones. 'You will. He's very kindly agreed to give you the nice little apartment that the last therap—resident musician had. And he understands that you need to take things very gently and get your own playing going again, and he wants you to think of it as your opportunity too, to get *really well* again.'

Even as she spoke a little dance started up inside Sara's head, celebrating the end of all the dishonest little euphemisms that now tripped out of her mouth, like 'really well' for 'sober' and 'properly settled in' for 'well and truly off my hands'. The greatest dishonesty of all, that she had spent half an hour in Dr Golightly's beautiful consulting room discussing with him how desperately Joyce needed help and that he had agreed out of pure kindness to take Joyce on or rather in, would remain her secret. The arrangement she had come to was that as well as board and lodging in the staff accommodation, Joyce would be paid a tiny amount of money, mainly for the sake of her pride, in return for leading her fellow patients in a little light music therapy and other, unspecified 'helping out'. Dr Golightly had graciously blurred the divide between staff and patient that he was making in her case by describing the Sulis as 'a mutually supportive, healing community which strives to respect each individual's contribution and meet his or her needs'. So Joyce would get treatment for her drink problem even though she was broke? Sara had asked, preferring plain words. Dr Golightly had reassured her. He could not allow anyone resident at the clinic and in need of its resources to go without, and certainly not for the want of money. He would consider that simply unethical. Waving aside Sara's offer to pay, he had proposed that he would devise and supervise Joyce's regime personally. Sara smiled, recalling how he had then explained to her that he was not a specialist in alcoholism but would apply the naturopathic principles of the clinic and that these might be tough but should prove effective. His face as he spoke, so serious and apologetic, had betrayed that he had no idea that at that moment she had been thinking how easily she could have kissed him for his unassuming compassion, if not for his blue eyes.

As Joyce sucked in her tea with a noise by this time as familiar to Sara as the wish to kill her which it now provoked, she thought happily that with Joyce gone she might also begin to look forward to Andrew being less deliberately preoccupied with the Takahashi case. She failed to notice that perhaps 'preoccupied' too was a euphemism for what might be a symptom of cooling passion.

Joyce fished out a handkerchief. Sitting on the bed and looking round the spare room she asked, 'So will I get a hand with my things, do you think? Will there be enough room for my things?' She lifted her eyes to Sara's. They were exactly like Pretzel's: wary, longing, and full of a fatalistic anticipation that at any moment the petting and fussing could stop and she would be hauled back to the kennel.

Sara sat down on the bed and placed a hand on her arm. 'Oh, of *course* you will. Of course we'll make sure you're comfortable and feeling at home.'

'Pretzel too?'

'Of course Pretzel too. He won't be allowed downstairs where the kitchens and staffroom are, or the dining room or the patients' bedrooms, of course . . .' Sara decided that it would be too cruel at this stage to add the drawing room, swimming pool, lawns, terrace, formal garden and treatment rooms to the list of canine no-go areas.

'They're all very nice at the Sulis,' she said. 'I've explained all about you, and Dr Golightly's right behind you. It's a wonderful chance, Joyce. They really want to help.'

Joyce slurped more tea with a disapproving noise. 'And who's helping whom, I should like to know? *I* was tutor to the Egyptian royal family. And a *professor* of music.'

'Well, yes! And they're absolutely thrilled to be getting you, they really are. They know you've been away from teaching for a while and that's fine. They want you to take it at your own pace.' There she went again, swinging from sympathy when Joyce came over all abject, to the grossest flattery when her tattered ego demanded recognition for what she once had been. Joyce had succeeded in making her alcoholism as unmentionable to Sara as it was to herself and now Sara, unable to refer to the drinking or its consequences directly, felt a glimmer, perhaps, of the same shame at the concealment.

'And I'll be seeing you lots,' she went on. 'Almost every day, as I'll be coming in to see James, anyway.' Dr Golightly had made a special point of that. Patients did best when they were well supported by family and friends, and he would like to suggest that he saw Sara each time she visited so that they remained closely in touch over Joyce's progress. Sara had thought this an utterly, tremendously sensible suggestion, and had simultaneously wondered what to wear when she next went.

A door banged downstairs. 'Andrew,' Sara said decisively, standing up. 'Better see what he's up to.' She was glad of the interruption but not sure, judging the ill temper of the door's bang, if she quite wanted it to be him. He had not taken it well last night when she had refused to leave Joyce alone for an evening, and had broken off their telephone call crossly before she had had time to explain that Joyce would not be around for much longer. And she was not feeling strong enough, she thought on the way downstairs, for the reproachful casting upwards of his eyes in the direction of Joyce's room, the ostentatious moving of Joyce's harmless things—her specs case or *Daily Telegraph* or handbag—from one place to another, or his pointed and laborious avoidance of any contact with Pretzel. He was in so many ways the complete opposite of Stephen Golightly.

In the kitchen Andrew glanced up from pouring himself a mug of tea from the stewed remains of Joyce's pot. 'Got the photographs back, the film that was in Mrs Takahashi's camera,' he said, and swallowed half of his tea. 'This is cold.'

'And?'

'Don't tell us a thing. A couple of snaps of Bath, but mostly they're of the place she was staying, the garden at the Golightly place. Runner beans, sunflowers, peas. She was quite taken with the countryside. Pictures of bloody cornfields, half a dozen of them. Field after field, close-ups, maybe even the same field. Perhaps they don't have organic smallholdings in Japan.' He drained his mug. 'Stewed as well. Doesn't matter.'

Sara watched him with her arms folded, trying to prevent her unfavourable comparison of him with Stephen Golightly from outlasting the pleasure she felt just to see him. She did love those brown eyes. And she was deciding all over again that she loved Andrew too, for trying not to let the expression in them betray his frustration, and even more for his being so hopeless at it. It was hard to love him sometimes but she did, even though he was so obsessed with this case he had not even asked how she was, or what was happening with Joyce.

'So, how are you?' he said. 'How's Baba Yaga? Found her a nice little house on stilts yet?'

'Joyce is leaving. I've found her a place to stay and a job,' Sara said, turning to the sink to empty the teapot. 'If you're at all interested.' A moment later the pot was nearly knocked from her hand by Andrew's arms, which had appeared round her and were hugging her so fiercely she squealed. He was clasping her so tightly she could barely laugh.

'Oh thank God for that,' he growled in her ear, kissing her as he spoke, his voice sending shivers through her. 'You star, you bloody wonderful star. God, Sara, we'll be on our own, our *own*. Oh, I can hardly wait . . .' She turned and prevented him from saying more with her mouth.

Just then Pretzel skeetered to his feet from underneath the table and tottered with wagging tail to the kitchen door. Unfortunately, since neither Sara nor Andrew was at that moment particularly receptive to the early warning, so it was that a minute later Andrew's tongue was in Sara's mouth, his penis in her left hand and the teapot in her right, when Joyce appeared in the doorway with her empty cup and asked, 'Er, would there be a wee drop left in that, dear?'

CHAPTER 18

DETECTIVE SERGEANT BRIDGER strolled down Green Street and paused at the empty window of The Sausage Shop. He would not have described himself as a big sausage fan, least of all of the ones sold here. Chicken with lemongrass, duck with oregano, no thank *you*. Did they do sausages in Japan? For all Bridger knew they did origami with raw fish ones.

He turned from the window and looked across the street at the Snake and Ladder. The town was buzzing with people, it being Friday night. Platoons of girls, three or four abreast, were marching along Green Street with their arms linked, conducting raucous and hilarious conversations. Quiet, darkly dressed young men wandered behind with less obvious purpose. Bridger looked at his watch. He could go in for a pint, but he decided against. The Snake and Ladder had no atmosphere and anyway, he did not want to turn up at Manvers Street with beer on his breath. He did, however, want to make very sure that DCI Poole saw him there or, failing that, that he got to hear that he had been. No point going the extra mile if nobody who mattered got to know about it.

He had already established that they were nine hours

ahead and that they worked Saturday mornings. So if he got down there now and put his face about a bit he could be on the phone by say, eleven. There was a good chance of speaking to the guy in the Police Department in Kobe, assuming they started at eight. There was a good chance that he would speak English as well as he emailed it. And a good chance, in the course of this and several more exchanges that he would engineer over the next few days, that he would be able to make a case to DCI Poole for going to Japan personally to pursue the investigation into Professor Takahashi. *Well, it'd take a couple of days but a one-to-one with the authorities on the ground there'd be the quickest way through this*, he'd suggest to Poole, sighing nonchalantly. *Bloody long flight and the climate's awful but it'd be worth it if it gets us our result I wouldn't mind going . . .* What's wrong with the Japanese consulate in Bristol, Bridger? Use them, man, that's what they're there for, he would say. *Ah, yes, the consular link's been useful but investigating one of their own citizens isn't their job at the end of the day etc. etc.*

Indeed the consulate had been useful. It was thanks to the consulate that Bridger had found out, with the suspect's cooperation, that Professor Takahashi had no previous convictions of any sort in his own country and that no complaint or charge had ever been made against him to the Japanese police. That had come as no surprise to Bridger. All the wife-beaters he had ever come across had been masters of intimidation and he assumed that this was a characteristic that crossed borders. What had been more of a surprise was the discovery that Takahashi, in his mid-fifties, had married his thirty-one-year-old wife in 1997. Bridger had taken heart at this because a little more digging would uncover, he was almost certain, not just an ugly divorce but a battered ex-wife. In that he had been wrong, of course. Bridger hugged himself. Just a simple thing like a copy of a marriage certificate had shown him that he had been wildly, blissfully wrong, because the first Mrs Takahashi was not divorced. She was dead.

Bridger could sniff a lead when it presented itself and there was something about this that cried out for further investigation. Why had Takahashi failed to mention that he had been married for only two years? Bridger would go cautiously, but he fully expected to find that the first wife was dead because her husband had killed her. Or maybe it was suicide, the final act of a desperate woman. He was a wife-beater. And if he was also a wife-killer, having got away with it once could he not, in another violent temper, have killed another wife?

He set off across the street but his footsteps slowed as he entered the alleyway at the side of the Snake and Ladder. One globe light shone above the side entrance to the pub, the door which Mrs Takahashi must have used to enter the building because the pub itself had been closed until ten-thirty that morning. Until then only the side entrance had been left unlocked for deliveries and for the kitchen staff who had been on duty since seven. Bridger had established all that himself, early on. It was the kind of useless detail you had to go into, he thought huffily, as he walked out of the other end of the alley and past the Photo-Kwik shop, to satisfy the likes of DCI Poole. It never produced anything. Nor did the scanning and re-scanning of security videos, although, he remembered with a smirk, they had not had too onerous a job there. The railway station's system had been down that day, in fact had been down for several days, along with all the station clocks, and for the third time in a month. The tape at Bristol Templemeads where Takahashi claimed to have boarded a train at 11.32 had been recorded over before they had even asked to see it. The image quality on the only other tapes, from Bath Abbey environs and the Guildhall, had been so poor that even if Takahashi had been present in the grey moving soup recorded between eight and ten o'clock that morning, not even his own mother could have said so. Complete waste of time and talent. It took Bridger's sort of applied intelligence to weasel out the kind of lead that he now had; the lead that was going to result not just in the suspect's conviction here, but in the solving of another and as yet undiscovered murder on the other side of the world. Now that was proper police work.

PART 2

CHAPTER 19

PETRONELLA CROPPER SAT beside her husband in silence on the way to the Sulis, while Hugh drove and exuded neutrality, two things he was good at. Their over-familiarity with the journey meant that the countryside they were passing through inspired no comment from either of them, although Petronella still and almost unconsciously scanned any field with ponies in it to see if there might be a grey. It was a silly habit after all this time, but she always looked out for a grey pony like Millie who had simply not been there one holiday when she had come home from school. Petronella was rarely exact about dates in her past but she thought it was when she was about eleven, and the habit had begun then as a doomed but genuine search, for Millie had been sold. She had found it unbearable to think that she might unknowingly drive past her in a field somewhere. Suppose Millie saw her and she *just drove past*? Even now, years after Millie must have died of old age, the thought could still sometimes make her cry, and the habit of scouring fields of ponies to see if there was a grey had stuck, even though Petronella's rational self knew that by now she was just looking for a pony *like* her beloved Millie. It was just a reflex thing, really.

She had never mentioned it to Hugh. She did not think she had even told him about Millie and, casting a look at him engrossed in his stolid piloting of the Range Rover through the Somerset lanes, she knew he would wonder what point she was making if she were suddenly to do so now. He seemed to accept without curiosity that she looked out of the passenger window when he drove her anywhere. Nor did he ever comment on how seldom she conversed in the car. She did not think she had ever explained that to him either (it was ghastly the way people go on about their childhoods) but as a child she had learned to associate cars with silence. There was a particular kind of silence that followed the cheery and insincere see-you-soons! because it never was soon. The yearning would begin the moment the car doors were slammed. The eventual end of the term that would just be starting lay too far in the future to hold any credibility for her whatsoever. There was so much to be got through first that she felt certain that the end would never come, yet the hopeless waiting for it began with the silence that would settle between herself and the hired driver within minutes of the start of the journey back to school. And although at the time she had believed that Mummy had had a terrible time with Daddy so that now she must not be selfish about boarding at school or jealous about letting Mummy have new friends, because of course Mummy deserved to have what she called Some Life Of My Own, she would also begin to hope as soon as her seat belt was fastened that next holidays (should they ever come) it would be just Mummy and her. Not that the holidays were exactly spoiled by a new boyfriend or husband. They went to lots of different places and it was lovely for Mummy, it was just the way they always assumed first claim on her mother's attention. She was sure that if they didn't do that then Mummy would have so much more time to give her. But Mummy had such exquisite manners she would always put them first. They were guests, after all.

It must be because she was pregnant again that she was wallowing in the past and that the recollection should be making her feel all blubby. Petronella couldn't abide self-pity and of course it couldn't have been all that bad. She wouldn't have had Millie at all if it hadn't been for that particular one's generosity and it was nobody's fault that he, and consequently Millie, had not lasted. How feeble of her to want to cry, but thank God the young were not here to see it. She had brought up Rupert and Miles not to be crybabies. That was so important, for their own sakes. She knew perfectly well that children who blub the minute they're left at prep school really do cop it from the others, so she agreed with Hugh there. She had been jolly lucky. Really, it had made her more independent. Meanwhile she was once again, this time aged forty-one and accidentally pregnant, sitting in a car watching out for grey ponies and being driven somewhere she didn't want to go.

Hugh took his hand from the steering wheel and patted her knee. 'Buck up, sausage,' he murmured. 'Only one more.'

'One more what?' Petronella asked, still thinking about her pregnancy.

'Visit, sausage. Visit to your mama. Just grit the gnashers, let her go on about toxins, listen to her symptoms and tell her she looks wonderful. After we've got it over with we'll be off to France and she can sit it out for the rest of August in the Sulis.'

'I don't know how you can be so callous. Poor Mummy.'

In the silence that followed Hugh felt like a brute, but dammit, it wasn't as if Petronella wouldn't, in another mood, say exactly the same thing herself. He did rather wish she would make her mind up about her mother. To know one's own mind on most matters was the mark of a sound chap. Petronella's ambivalence about her blessed mother was not the sort of thing one expected in a sound chap's wife. Some days it was all Poor Mummy and how she, with her little-and-often history with men, had never received real love from anyone except Petronella. On others it was Poor Petronella, rejected because her mother had never really wanted her and had been too taken up with the men to give her any proper love.

He said, 'But look, it's not as if she's not perfectly happy there, is it? Especially with the new admirer. She wouldn't want to come with us.'

'What was his name again? Warwick, that's it. It's sick.'

Petronella was fishing angrily in her Mulberry bag and brought out an envelope.

'Don't read it again, Pet. You know it just gets you all het up,' Hugh said mildly. Petronella ignored him and unfolded the letter.

'I should have known something funny was going on when she wrote at all. She's only written me about half a dozen proper letters in my life. This is the bit—' She began to read aboud but could have recited from memory.

Time just flies by & nobody can believe the change in me. I am writing simply masses & still doing Warwick's head did I tell you he has the most marvellous head. I don't think I told you he's ex-army of course he was terribly young and brave to be signed up in 1944 aged 16. He won't go into details to spare me but he was a prisoner of the Japs and damage was done & the army wont recognize that kind of thing its disgraceful. He says he gets by & he said he knew the Sulis would be a treat but he never expected to meet such a special lady! He's late 60s now, did I tell you.? Also Sister Yvonne agrees with me we all need spoiling so I shall take up Warwick's offer, he's good company & its nicer for me not to be on my own when I go home I'll carry on with his head & he is happy to be of service and you & Hugh will be away wont you and there's my grass and so much upkeep & so isnt it lucky Warwick hasn't firm plans.

Petronella waved the sheet of paper with annoyance.

'She's obviously going gaga. Look at her writing for a start, it's gone so shaky. It never used to be shaky.'

Hugh recognised that his role in this conversation was

to play things down. As he had already said many, many times in the three days since the letter arrived, he said again, 'She is in her eighties, now, Poppet. We have to expect things like shaky writing.'

'But I really do think she's going gaga. She can't remember a thing she's told me.' She was still waving the letter. 'I heard most of this last time we went anyway, before Warwick turned up to join us for tea. You remember, all about how she roped him into sitting for her stupid art therapy. "*Such a marvellous head*", how stupid that sounds. What worries me is this talk of afterwards. She doesn't say how long she's invited him for, he could almost be moving in. God, Mummy is the limit.'

This last comment clarified things, a little. Two minutes ago it had been a Poor Mummy day; now there was a definite gust of Poor Petronella in the emotional weather. Must be because she was in pod again. Hugh braced himself for another eight months of mood swings and resolved to keep a closer eye on the barometer. Earrings and lipstick before nine and a morning of competent soup-and-bread-making meant invariably a spell of Poor Mummy, whereas dressing gown at noon, scowling at the Aga and fried eggs for Sunday lunch were all clearly indicative of Poor Petronella.

'Well, it does mean we don't have to have her with us. He's doing us a favour, really.'

Petronella sighed with exasperation. 'Oh, I know. But she really is the limit. He must be at least ten years younger than she is. I can't think what he gets out of it.'

Hugh swallowed a snort at Petronella's apparent *naïveté*. He said, 'Perhaps he's in love with her. Plenty of men have been in love with her, after all, according to you. Perhaps it can happen, even at their age.'

There was a depressed silence until Petronella said, almost as if she had been taking the suggestion seriously, 'Not even Mummy could marry again at eighty-one.'

Hugh sighed and went on driving instead of asking out loud, *Oh couldn't she?*

After another three miles Petronella suddenly announced, 'Look, Hugh, we're mad going to France. We can't afford it. We should have cancelled when I found out about the baby, never mind the pig prices. We can hardly manage next term's fees. And soon there'll be *three* lots. And that's without,' her voice rose rather wildly, 'a new oboe for Rupert. And not counting Miles's orthodontics.'

'Poppet, we'll find a way. Everybody goes away in August and we need a holiday. I'll have a quiet word with ma-in-law today and get her to set up a trust for this one, too. That'll help.'

'She's not *made* of money, Hugh. I know she's done it for Rupert and Miles but she's not expecting to do it for another one.'

'Darling—' Hugh searched his lexicon of un-mercenary euphemisms for a way to say that actually his mother-in-law *was* made of money, but found it empty. He contented himself with thinking that at least Petronella was an only child and Bunny wasn't immortal, and by saying, 'You've got to look on the bright side. Don't want little sproglet in your tum-tum getting upset, do we? They can sense it, you know.'

Hugh had read something once in *Horse and Hound* about a mare's temperament affecting the hormones reaching the fetus in the uterus and was terribly pleased that the memory of it came to his aid now, and rather proud that he had managed to find the nursery terms, sproglet and tum-tum, that Petronella preferred when her own gynaecology was under discussion. So often he could not remember the point he wanted to make nor, even if he did, find the right way of putting it. In fact, it sometimes seemed to him that the more deeply he felt or believed in a thing, the less able he was to say a word about it.

CHAPTER 20

SISTER YVONNE STOOD fuming at the window of the empty drawing room and watched the progress of the black Saab up the rain-soaked drive. She had just reached a bad-tempered impasse with Hilary about what should be done about Bunny Fernandez and was still too cross to be curious about whose car it was and why it should be making its way towards the front entrance of the clinic and not heading for the small visitors' car park nearer the gate.

Five minutes ago Hilary had raised both hands pompously and said, 'Yvonne, it is not good for me to be having this conversation. I have been hurt by some of the things you have said, and I am going to leave the room now. You have the right to tell me that you are angry, but you do not have the right to insult me or my work. I shall come back when you are calmer. Goodbye.'

Bloody Hilary. The matter of Bunny Fernandez was quite clear. If Dr Golightly was not on the premises then she, Sister Yvonne Cartwright, the only other medically qualified person on the staff, was entitled to judge whether or not a patient required his attention. Not Hilary Golightly, who was not a nurse, who was nothing but a failed artist. Bunny Fernandez did not need the doctor and it was she, Yvonne, who was the one to judge, and having judged should have been listened to. But oh no, Hilary Golightly puffs herself up and suddenly she's the one arguing the toss and thinking she should be making the decisions.

Acrid bile rose in Sister Yvonne's throat. She reached into her uniform pocket for a couple of indigestion tablets because something, perhaps the bacon and egg butty she had bought at the garage halfway down Bathwick Hill on her way to work and eaten for lunch, had started striking matches in her intestines and was trying to set fire to itself. Not strictly along clinic guidelines, that sandwich (white bread, butter, smoked streaky, egg and mayo) but it wasn't as if the clinic employed her stomach, was it? And it wasn't as if she ate in secret, she just ate very quickly without bothering anyone in the basement staffroom while the others were busy preparing for the patients' lunch. And it was not strictly along clinic guidelines either to stoke up on Rennies throughout the day but this place got to you sometimes. She popped the tablets into her mouth, bit on them sourly, and as they crumbled in her copious saliva she went over the conversation with Hilary again. Although, Yvonne considered, it was not just a matter of what had been said, it was a question of what had been implied.

Mrs Fernandez' daughter and son-in-law had come for the day. That was the crux of the whole thing. They had sat with her during lunch—the daughter had even had a bowl of that chilled green soup, for some reason that must have been unrelated to either enjoyment or hunger—and almost straight afterwards Bunny had complained of feeling strange. She was a madam, that one. Yvonne had not bathed, massaged and pandered to her for all these years without spotting that. As she chewed and fumed, Yvonne's anger with Hilary writhed, rose up and grew tentacles which curled around and squeezed Bunny too, in a most satisfying way. The symptoms she had complained of had been delivered with her usual imperious certainty, but had been vague. With her head drawn back, she had described 'a sort of irritation' in her spine. She could sort of see things that she knew could not really be there: bright colours and sort of flashing lights. She was cold but sort of hot, thirsty and sort of wanting to go to the loo at the same time, restless and sort of wanting to sleep. Sort of asking for a smack round the face was Yvonne's professional opinion. Bunny was either getting a bit senile and confused or she was being a manipulative, attention-seeking old haddock and Yvonne knew which, and she could tell by the look she had exchanged with that Petronella that that was what she thought, too. Nevertheless Yvonne had taken her patient off to bed and Bunny had fallen into a half-sleep, or was faking it. She was definitely faking the occasional jerking of her limbs under the covers. The daughter and husband had followed, she looking guilty, he bemused, to sit with her.

It should have been the start of a quiet afternoon. The other patients had all taken themselves off to rest by the pool or in their rooms, leaving Yvonne and Hilary alone. But then in had jumped Hilary with her hand-wringing, clucking Yorkshire nonsense about how it was not like Bunny to miss her afternoon art therapy, especially now that her head of Warwick was coming along so strongly. So she must be really ill, and Dr Golightly (though of course Hilary said 'Stephen' with special emphasis) should be called in. Honestly—head of Warwick! Warwick was another one that Yvonne felt she could cheerfully drown in the hydrotherapy pool. The only head of Warwick that Yvonne could have cared anything for would be one on a platter with a kiwi fruit garnish, the fraudulent old goat. Not like Bunny to miss working on her head of Warwick, her arse. According to Yvonne, and she could tell Petronella Cropper agreed, it was *exactly* like Bunny to mount a little guilt-inducing drama for her daughter and son-in-law's benefit on the last visit they would make before going on holiday for three weeks.

The black car had now stopped and a lean, dark-haired woman dressed in jeans and an expensive-looking white shirt was getting out, making a wry face at the rain which was tipping down steadily. Yvonne thought she recognised her as Mr Ballantyne's friend, the one who'd visited yesterday. She was obviously bringing in some of his things (though what would James want with another table lamp, especially that one?) in anticipation of a long stay, so presumably her conversation with Dr Golightly the other day must have left her thinking that her friend was not going to be getting better any time soon. Well, she'd be disappointed if she wanted to see him today. Yvonne softened as she thought about poor Mr Ballantyne who really was quite poorly, so much worse than yesterday that he was having a day's juice fast and bedrest. That was the sort of patient she liked, a really ill one. There were hardly ever any properly ill people here, just over-indulged, hysterical hypochondriacs whose families didn't want them and who could blame them.

Now there was another woman, much older, and—oh

Jesus, Mary and Joseph—a dog. They were unloading so much stuff from the car it looked as though the three of them might be moving in. Yvonne sighed, supposed dimly that she should go to help and stayed where she was, just out of sight behind the tasselled turquoise curtain. Her thoughts returned to Hilary and with them returned a sense of grievance which began to swell and burst like yeast bubbles in fermenting dough, because this old woman outside, now that Yvonne could see her properly, looked very like another of Dr Golightly's lame ducks.

How many more were there to be? There was Leech, for a start. Yvonne, by inclination and training, was uncomfortable with loose arrangements, and she had tried months ago to explain to Dr Golightly that this casual set-up at the allotment, with that beggar Leech just turning up, squatting in the shed and practically being taken on, was dangerously loose. Anybody with any sense could see that he was a homeless down-and-out through choice. But Dr Golightly had been very firm. There was, he had said, nothing loose or dangerous about it, but a simple equilibrium. He was disappointed that Yvonne could not see it. Leech was not a beggar; he was damaged and in need. He had sought shelter in their shed. He had been made welcome and comfortable by Hilary, and now he repaid the favour with his labour in the garden. Ivan needed the help. Leech maintained his dignity. Hilary was happy because Ivan was under less pressure. Oh well, if *Hilary's* happy, she had said, and Dr Golightly had smiled in agreement. But Yvonne had gone on thinking that Hilary's handling of father and son over the matter of Leech had been disturbingly neat. And now it meant that they all had to put up with Leech sometimes rolling up in the van with

Ivan to deliver the fruit and veg, and probably giving the patients the creeps, any who might be up and about, anyway.

Yvonne, still watching the younger dark-haired woman struggle with baggage, dog and the old duck in the rain outside, swallowed. Her insides felt milky, soothed, and her feelings softened. It wasn't Dr Golightly's fault. He might even be right about Leech and, seen another way, Hilary was just another lame duck herself. The doctor was practically a saint and the trouble with saints was they sometimes needed saving from themselves. It was a further trouble to someone like Yvonne that they seldom knew this, and so she admitted that it rankled, Hilary's way of going to him at any old time of the morning or night with any trivial little thing she liked, using up his time. *She* never knocked and waited at his door, as everyone else had been instructed to, Yvonne had noticed. She was never asked to come back later, as others were, but was treated as if her bloody mucking about with clay and paint were of supreme importance.

Yvonne checked her anger just as it reached the dangerous stage of being transferred to Dr Golightly, territory on to which she would never stray. No, he was not perfect. Perhaps rather easily taken in but practically a saint, and a wonderful doctor. He was just being kind to Leech and to Hilary, too, and the only reason for that was because at the root of everything lay the matter of Ivan. Yvonne had heard enough about Ivan's past to understand why Dr Golightly took such pains to see that he remained well. She had seen the scars on Ivan's arms. And to give Hilary her due, she obviously cared about Ivan's health too, but honestly, as if art therapy mattered. Nobody in the place except perhaps that mad Bunny would give a celery stick for it.

Yvonne took several deep breaths to settle a new attack of dyspeptic belching. This place was bad for a person's health. It was ironic that she spent all day doing massages and whatnot to get people to relax, while the way that Hilary wound nice, gentle Ivan and his father round her little finger got her mad enough to explode. Yvonne clicked another two Rennies out of the foil packet and crunched them so loudly in her jaw that she hardly heard the door open and close behind her, and it was more the change in the room's atmosphere brought by an unwelcome presence that made her turn and acknowledge that Hilary had come back, as annoyingly sure of herself as before.

'I've just been up again. She's still asleep,' Hilary whispered, caringly.

'I don't want you disturbing my patients.'

'I've been down to the kitchen and told Ivan about our little talk earlier. And I'd like you to know that he's reassured me. He's very calm about it. He thinks if she's fallen asleep then sleep is what she needs. And so I said if he's happy I am, and we wouldn't call Stephen in to look at her.'

'Oh, so now she's *Ivan's* patient?'

Hilary folded her arms, then dropped them. 'Yvonne, I don't wish to be confrontational but we're supposed to work as a team. Anyway, of course she's *Stephen's* patient. You're a nurse.' She did not have to say 'only'; her tone inflicted the word's wound as surely as if she had. Yvonne realised that she hated not just everything Hilary said, but even her actual voice, that puddingy Yorkshire accent that made everything sound so smug and complacent. 'In my opinion, she is ill,' Hilary insisted, stepping forward and joining her at the window. 'But I always listen to Ivan.'

Yvonne continued to stare out, with her jaws locked. 'And in my clinical judgment, there is no reason to disturb Dr Golightly. At this stage, my patient's condition is perfectly manageable with nursing care. And whether you like it or not, my judgment goes.'

'Well, I feel sure that what Stephen would want— Oh! Who's that out there? That must be the new music lady. She's getting ever so wet.'

Yvonne turned and said, trying to hide her surprise with acidic courtesy, 'The new what?'

'The old one. With the cello case and the dog. She's the new music therapist. Stephen said she's moving in today, she's having the same room as what's-her-name had, Alex.' With a regretful smile which didn't fool Yvonne for a second she added, 'Aww. Hasn't Stephen told you?'

Stephen had not. He was practically a saint but at times a forgetful one. 'After all,' Hilary said graciously, 'I thought you and he made the clinical decisions. I'm very surprised he hasn't told you. He certainly told me.'

Yvonne could have punched her. 'We had other, more important things to discuss this morning. We don't deal with staffing trivia,' she said, tightly. 'And as I now have to attend to my patient, I'll leave you to your new colleague.'

'*My* new colleague? Ours, surely. We're a committed, multi-skilled therapeutic team, supposed to be, aren't we?'

'I'm clinical staff. You're support staff. And so's she, so you can deal with her. It's nothing to do with me, her being here.'

'Well, clearly. Since Stephen doesn't seem to have told you.'

'I suppose you persuaded him to have her. It's bad enough, having your creepy Leech around the place. Now we've got to have *her*.'

'I had nothing to do with it. I've never even set eyes on the woman. And Leech is not creepy. He's just quiet, and Ivan needs the help, and I don't want pressure building up on him. You try running a three-acre smallholding and a kitchen practically single-handed.'

'It's not single-handed! There are two chefs and three catering assistants!'

'They need managing. Ivan supervises the menus personally. And he makes the bread.'

'The chefs do the cooking and the assistants help to serve and clear up, and Dr Golightly advises . . .'

'That's not the point. Ivan's permanently exhausted, and all you have to do is stick people in hot and cold baths and run sprays over them and hand them their towels . . .'

'I'm a qualified nurse! I assist the osteopaths and acupuncturist as well as the doctor.' Yvonne began to count off on her fingers. 'I do the infra-red lamp, the hot packs, the inhalations *and* massages *and* general care. AND I'm nearly qualified to do stress counselling. And all you do is hand out paint brushes and clay and bang on about responding to colours!'

Most of the new woman's belongings were now on the tarmac of the car park. Hilary had read books on how to handle hostility and said mildly, 'Leech could help with that sort of thing. We need a porter-cum-handyman. He could be out there with an umbrella.' Hilary waved a hand in the direction of Sara, struggling to the door with boxes and making her way back to the car for the next load.

'Oh no, you don't. It's bad enough him working in the garden. You may think you've got Dr Golightly round your little finger but I'm going to speak to him again about Leech. He's off-putting.'

'You won't get anywhere. Stephen knows that Ivan needs the help. And I don't see it's any of your business anyway. Leech just pops in occasionally with the produce and goes away again. He's hardly ever out of that garden.'

'That's another thing! He shouldn't be allowed to sleep in that shed . . .'

Yvonne was interrupted by the clang of the front door bell. 'I'll go. I'm in charge.'

'Oh, no. I think I should. After all, I'm the owner's daughter-in-law.'

'I'm senior nursing staff.'

'I'm senior art therapist, and family. And this is a family-run establishment.'

'It's a professional establishment. Or *should* be.'

'With a family atmosphere.'

The bell clanged again, insistently, and the two women pasted on smiles and went together.

CHAPTER 21

J OYCE OPENED THE door quickly with her Yale key,
stepped silently inside and closed it. She would have to
see about Pretzel's claws. The small square stairwell
which rose up the height of the house from the main hall,
the 'staff stairs' as it was called, had a bit of an echo, and
while she could creep up without making a sound in the
trainers Sara had got for her, Pretzel liked to go up on the
bare boards next to the wall where it wasn't carpeted. His
feet as he climbed made a sound like a necklace breaking.
The door to Dr Golightly's flat on the top floor was just six
steps further up on the next half-landing and she did not
want him appearing and asking what the noise was. Less
still did she want any enquiries as to where she had been
and what she might have in her handbag. Just inside her
door she waited, her heart beating hard from the climb,
then turned and peered through the security spyhole that
gave her a view of the landing. Nothing. The only other visible door, down a half-flight on the landing below, led into
the upper corridor of the main house where the patients'
rooms were. It too was closed, as it had been when Joyce
had crept past, locked from the patients' side with another
Yale lock. She imagined that it was seldom used. Only Dr

Golightly might need it, she supposed, to reach a patient quickly from his flat during the night, although Joyce's impression of the clinic so far was that they did not expect emergencies. Dr Golightly's own door, just visible on the outer edge of the distorted circular view, remained closed. The strains of music that wafted down to her ears from behind it, presumably the sound that had drowned out Pretzel's claws on the stairs, floated on.

Safe now, she turned back. The room was at least potentially pleasant, painted uncontroversially in some yellow or other and carpeted in a polite green. It was not large but at least the tiny single bedroom and showerroom were separate. Joyce's suitcase and boxes stood in a row against one wall, her cello case and lamps beside them. The sofa was dark green and Sara had promised some cushions which would, she had said, make it a bit cosier. And the flowers she had brought from the garden, blowsy roses and aquilegias, were gradually overcoming the choking smells of air freshener and Mr Sheen with which the room had been hastily 'gone round' in preparation for her arrival. Actually, those smells would not last long against the perfumed onslaught of warm, live dog, the only consistent smell in Joyce's life and consequently the smell of home.

Leaning against the door and surveying her new room to try to make it familiar, she listened. Stephen Golightly had not struck her as a music lover, not at any rate a lover of Bach's unaccompanied cello suites. Joyce had Stephen Golightly down as more of a doer whose sort of doing—athletic, energetic, practical—seemed to preclude the sort of thinking that she considered not just a prerequisite to a proper appreciation of Bach, but an activity of an altogether higher order. It was not quite that she despised 'doing' per se, but she rather disliked the kind of doers who appeared to take pleasure in merely owning a physical body and to find entertainment in getting it to do things, not an attitude that had been encouraged in Monifieth. Sara and her ridiculous daily running, for example, and whose recording this was now being played. Joyce would know the sound of the Cristiani cello and that under-use of vibrato anywhere. The recognition was enough to move her further into the room where the music was fainter, but at that moment and unnervingly, rather as if she had made it happen, the Bach stopped. A few seconds later, some Beethoven started up. It was the Seven Variations in E flat Major from *Die Zauberflöte*, and it was Selkirk playing again. Joyce smiled. Ah, she wasn't bad at the wee easy stuff.

Suddenly the music grew louder. Dr Golightly's door was being opened. Joyce grabbed her handbag and looked round wildly. This little apartment had not been home long enough for her to have worked out her hiding places. But if Dr Golightly was making social calls he wouldn't go in the bedroom, surely? She shoved the bag into the bedroom and closed the door on it just as the volume of the music subsided again. She darted back to her outer door and opened it. Dr Golightly's door was closed and from behind it the Beethoven played on. But her eyes travelled down, caught by a movement, to the half-landing below. The door which led into the main house had just silently closed behind whoever had gone through it. What a silly thing to do, Joyce thought, to go out and leave your music playing like that. Dr Golightly hadn't struck her as a careless man, but it was hard to tell with some people.

She returned and lay on her sofa to wait until she could

be sure that her peace would not be disturbed. She realised that her heart was pounding again, with fear as well as excited, faintly criminal anticipation. The handbag's contents awaited. But even though she knew that Dr Golightly was not in his room she felt a little too flustered to make a start just yet, and of course the pleasure would be the greater the longer she withheld it from herself. Very few people understood this. Very few people understood that people like her exercised more control in an average day than they would muster in a lifetime dedicated to their sort of mundane self-indulgence. Yet she was flustered, possibly by the sheer proximity of Dr Golightly's living quarters, and Pretzel seemed to be feeling it too, since he had not made his usual seal-like leap on to the sofa to join her.

'C'mon, Pretzel.' She patted an empty patch beside her. 'C'mon up and give Mummy a wee cuddle.' Pretzel danced half-heartedly on his front paws but did not attempt to jump. He wandered away, head down and sniffing, and wound a straggly course which led him eventually to the tartan dogbed which Sara had bought for him, which was lying under a small, circular dining-table. Pretzel climbed in, circled it twice, lay down and sank his doleful head on to his front paws.

Joyce's mind was once again drawn away reluctantly from the package in her handbag, and she looked at him with concern. Sighing, she heaved herself to her feet and felt his nose, which was dry but cold. His ears felt cold, too. As she caressed them, he lifted his head, shivered sadly, gave a little whimper and let his head fall again on to his paws. She fetched a sweatshirt from the bedroom and placed it round him, but he still looked at her sadly. Kneel-

ing beside him, she looked back into his eyes and recognised what she saw reflected in them: humiliation, dis-
placement, the beginnings of bewilderment, the same
refugee's consciousness which she had grown adept at sub-
limating in herself, chiefly by forgiving herself her tres-
passes, blaming others and looking on the bright side.

'This is home now,' she crooned. 'For a while, anyway.
It'll be all right when we've got all unpacked, won't it,
son? Eh?' Pretzel, presumably lacking the conviction for a
proper tail wag, managed a weak wriggle of his bum.
Joyce muttered something, got up and stood with her
hands on her hips in front of the row of cardboard boxes.
Then she crouched down, rummaged for a few minutes
and brought out the Egyptian music box with a show of
elation that Pretzel witnessed non-committally.

'Here we are! A wee tune's what you need! Your
favourite wee tune, ready?' She wound the box up and set
it down to play. As the familiar, plinky melody started,
Pretzel rewarded her with a brief shiver and lift of his
ears, the canine equivalent of a brave little smile. Joyce
joined him again on the floor.

'Don't let me down now, son,' she whispered, stroking
him softly. Pretzel's body shivered again but he licked her
hand, and stirred his tail on the floor. Could he be hungry?
She had fed him earlier but perhaps he was unsettled by
the move, perhaps an extra meal would be reassuring. Sara
had placed the tins of dogfood and various supplies in a
cupboard in the neat little kitchen corner arranged with
worktop, sink, kettle and microwave. Joyce got up
again and tipped the remaining half of the contents of
the opened tin into a cereal bowl. As an extra treat she
crumbled over the top some of the bread and cheese she

hadn't eaten at lunchtime (it being so dry without butter) and cracked in an egg. As she put the bowl down Pretzel flumped over, sniffed it and began to eat. Joyce wanted to applaud. There couldn't be anything seriously wrong with a dog who still wanted to be fed, so it must just be a wee chill. She sank down on to the floor beside him and smiled as he went on eating, feeling herself blessed, granted for once the power to provide good things for the one she loved when countless times before and for others she had loved, it had been denied. And the music box's enfeebled tune, just one more time before extinction, twanked slowly round their ears as they sat together on the floor, while tears of relief filled Joyce's eyes and she began to cry.

CHAPTER 22

SARA YOWLED TOWARDS her top C and held it bravely, though it took longer to reach than she had expected and then seemed not to know what to do once it got there. And it was a tad harder to hold on to than real singers seemed to find it, she thought, as she heard herself slipping off it. But it was a forgiving audience (herself) and a kind acoustic (her large bathroom at Medlar Cottage). She was happy: utterly, wondrously alone and making a lot of noise. She sank back in the bathwater, took another deep breath and began *Vissi d'Arte* all over again.

In the mirror at the end of the bath she could just see the head of some mad, damp, naked diva (herself) above the surface of the bubbles, and she thought again what a shame it was that she looked so odd when she sang, adding unfairly to the tragedy of the sound she made. Her forehead puckered, the eyebrows straightened and rose like the two halves of Tower Bridge letting a tanker through, and it was close to obscene what happened to her lips. She sniggered and pulled herself up, sloshing water behind her on to the floor, reached over for the glass of champagne on the chair next to the bath and tipped it down her throat until it was empty. Then she reached further over, picked up the bottle from the floor and refilled her glass. Freedom. Freedom to sing atrociously. Freedom to drink champagne in the bath. Freedom to have the bath at the time of day when she would be cooking Joyce some nutritious but depressingly plain thing to eat for supper. Dammit, she thought, emptying her glass again, freedom to drink.

It was extraordinary how completely the removal of Joyce to the Sulis had restored Sara's susceptibility to the charms of her own house. She had spent nearly the whole of the afternoon in her music room working on the Dvořák, taking it apart and putting it all back together again, and by the end managing to play it really, even if she said so herself, much the way she thought it should go. Part of her enjoyment had lain in her renewed confidence in her judgment of the piece. The re-emergence of her disparaging teacher had unsettled her faith in her interpretation. But, as she had concluded as she was putting away the Peresson cello, she was playing it right, whatever Joyce's curling lips might be telling her. She was making it sound the way she wanted it, her way. And Joyce could go boil her head, lips and all.

Afterwards, with the mood of righteous rebellion still in her and yelling *My Way* above the roar of the vacuum cleaner, Sara had cleaned the house, less to pick up any remaining dog hairs than to expunge memories of her guest. For it was extraordinary how the apparently self-effacing Joyce had managed to exude a silent pessimism about everything, not just Sara's playing, in a manner so passive and yet so encroaching. It was not the result of anything she actually said or did, nor even the self-loathing in her eyes nor the diminished pride that soured her mouth, it was more a sort of miserable weather that attached to her and lingered, a dulling micro-climate of failure that hung stubbornly in the corners of Medlar Cottage after she had passed through, almost as if it were a noxious fog rather than a person that had been to stay.

Sara supposed, lying in her bath, that she now finally saw why Andrew had found it intolerable, but she would put everything right. She had not only fallen back in love with Medlar Cottage but with him too, and this evening was going to be wonderful. She had reclaimed the house for them both and filled it with flowers. It would be just the two of them, lots more champagne, amazing food of the kind that Joyce would not have touched, and then— well, not to put too fine a point on it, they would make love. Often, and variously. Or perhaps they would just make love and have the champagne and food later if there was time which, if they started the evening that way round, there almost certainly wouldn't be. A rush of excitement tumbled through her body and she sank, stretching, under the water. She somehow had to wait another three hours for him, feeling like this; tinglingly aware of every pore and dip and fold of her body was how she described it to herself, quite outrageously randy was what she knew it to be. She surfaced and lay soaking, planning, letting more minutes tick by, her excitement increasing. There was some delicious aromatherapy oil somewhere that she seldom used because it took so long to rub in to her skin and she was usually in a hurry to get dressed, but tonight, slowly and ceremoniously, she would anoint her body like an Old Testament concubine. She would paint her toenails again and wear no shoes, and her clothes would be soft and easy to shrug off, silk of course, and not too many.

*   *   *

BY ELEVEN o'clock Sara was still sitting cross-legged on the hearth rug with her empty glass. She had spilled champagne, the last of the bottle, down her dark red silk vest, the fifty or so candles burning in the drawing room were flickering their last, her skin felt unpleasantly slippery and her feet were cold. She had taken the overcooked Thai shrimps out of the oven over an hour ago and they were in the kitchen lying in their dish, curled in yellowing coconut and ginger sauce like dead baby mice awaiting a biology practical.

At five minutes past eleven Sara decided, practising her deep breathing, that she would get up very slowly, go to the telephone and ring Andrew very nicely and just ask, very reasonably, where the bloody hell he was and what the bloody hell he thought he was doing. But the telephone base, when she got to it, was flashing a new message. Knowing exactly what it would be Sara played it. Andrew was terribly sorry. Andrew would do anything to have it otherwise. Andrew couldn't make it because Valerie had just signed up for a Twelve-Step Women's Assertiveness Course on Sunday nights. He had to babysit. Valerie was also asserting her right to go for a curry with the girls afterwards so Andrew would have to stay until she chose to get back, which might be very late. Andrew thought that he would go to the flat tonight, remembering how Sara had objected to being disturbed the other day. Andrew hoped Sara would understand. Andrew was dead, Sara added silently as she clicked the machine off, and so was Valerie.

The message had been left hours earlier when she had

been either bawling Sinatra songs to the accompaniment of the Hoover, shouting Puccini in the bath or when her head was underwater, so it wasn't as if he were letting her down just at the very last minute, but nevertheless disappointment and rage were fighting it out in Sara's pounding head, and rage won. With a half-drunken shriek she stumbled into the kitchen, opened the back door, picked up the dish of Thai shrimps and hurled it outside where it crashed on to the path. Plates of fragrant rice, scallops, crab cakes, chilli dipping sauce and beansprouts went next. The champagne bottle went last, with the satisfying crump of exploding glass, followed by the startled yowl of a cat. Back in the drawing room she managed with difficulty not to kick over the burning candles and instead went round blowing them all out, noisily and furiously. Shaking, she stood in the dark, light-headed, panting, wondering what on earth she was going to do next. At what point had she conceded to Andrew—*had* she ever actually conceded?— the power to make her feel like this? How *dare* he make her feel like this? Actually, how dare Valerie do this? And the anger that they were making her feel had driven out not just any ability or desire to understand and forgive but also the capacity to think, sleep or eat. She looked round for something to destroy and realised with her last particle of reason that the only way to avoid trashing her own house was to get out of it. She tore upstairs, pulled off her clothes and changed into running gear.

*   *   *

IT WAS a pleasure, although not a soothing one, to drive when she had had too much to drink, in defiance of Andrew and his attitude to such things. It was a pleasure to know how much he would disapprove of what she was doing, so she resolved, as she drove with the concentrated diligence of a Sunday driver, that she would tell him, in detail, should she ever speak to him again. She parked in the car park of The George at Bathampton Lock. Other things she would tell Andrew, she thought, as she set off at an unwisely fast pace: how dark it was on the towpath, how deserted, how unprotected she was. How guilty he would feel if anything happened to her, because it was his and his ex-wife's fault that she was so angry and so also his responsibility that she was running off her rage in the dark, alone.

After five minutes Sara began to feel weary, as if she were tramping through water. She ran faster. After ten she was wearier, so she ran faster still. The sensation of running through water had gone; she was now struggling through deep tar which seemed to cling to her legs and would drag her down if she stopped.

The towpath was now darker for she had passed the last of the moored barges and houses of Bathampton long ago and on either side of the canal lay only fields, open to the moonless sky, harbouring silence. Sara felt almost afraid of her own laboured breathing, for although she was still too angry to feel frightened, it was impossible not to realise that somebody very frightened indeed would make a sound exactly like this. And somebody very frightened indeed would also be too short of breath to scream. She ran on.

At the end of half an hour Sara found herself more than three miles beyond Bathampton Lock and at the end of her strength. The champagne-charged rage which had surged through her, curiously like elation in its power to animate, had vanished, and she realised that she was actually quietly scared out of her wits. Then, just as she was thinking appeasingly that it was not Andrew's fault that she had failed to pick up his message and that she ought to turn round and go home, she saw the trembling, tiny, burning dot just feet away from her in the dark. It dawned on her. A fatalistic calm was sweeping fear out of her mind, although her body had begun to shake. She had already slowed her pace to a walk and now she stopped, watching the dot as it moved jerkily upwards, glowed brighter, and moved down. It would be no more than she deserved: alone on an empty towpath near midnight, wearing shorts and a T-shirt, undefended unless she could stick her car keys in his eyes. The kind of thing that when you read the Body Found On Towpath story in the paper you think, what did she expect? Yet it seemed a little cruel, she considered oddly without panic, that before she met her fate at the hands of some mad rapist who was just sitting here on a bench in case someone as stupid as she was should happen along, she should have to watch him enjoying a fag while he waited. She fingered the car keys in her pocket and wondered if, should she turn now and run, she would make it more than a hundred yards.

A frightened whimper broke from the direction of the glowing cigarette. A helpless voice in the dark called out, 'Oh oh, oooh—Ivan? Ivan? I hurt myself.' Despite the adult, male voice, it was the sound of a child in distress.

'Ooh, Ivan?' Fear or perhaps cold had reduced his speech to a squeaky whisper.

Sara called quietly, 'Hello? I'm . . . it's not Ivan. Are you . . . are you badly hurt?'

After a silence the voice answered, 'I hurt myself.'

Sara advanced. The man on the bench had thrown down the cigarette and it glowed on the path in front of him. He was shaking violently, yet was looking at Sara with neutral curiosity. For no especially rational reason, Sara's fear disappeared. It was just the shabby man. It was only the bearded, lost-looking bloke who was often on the towpath or in the field beyond, smoking roll-ups, watching the trains. True, this did not amount to a certainty that he was not also a mad rapist, but Sara's mind grasped at the recognition and took it as reassurance that he was harmless.

'Are you cold?'

He was wearing jeans and a jersey which looked warm enough, but perhaps he was feverish. His thin face certainly had a weakened look, as if softened rather than hardened by circumstances, and going by the state of his clothes he was probably sleeping rough. The weather this summer could have broken anyone's health. In reply the man simply held out one trembling hand to her and beckoned her with his eyes to take hold of it. Knowing she was mad, she did so. The fingers were freezing.

'Hurts,' he said.

'Have you got anywhere to go? Somewhere to sleep?' Sara looked up and down the towpath in despair. What was she supposed to do—walk with him, supposing he could walk three miles, back to her car and get him to a hospital?

'Have you got somewhere to sleep?' she repeated.

He was nodding.

'Is it far? To where you sleep?'

'Ivan . . . bad trip. Bad dream.' He glanced behind him and smiled through his shivers. 'I woke up,' he told her almost happily. He turned round again and then back to her.

Sara had the impression that he was now surer of his bearings. 'Bad dream. Over the track.' He waved an arm in the direction of the quiet darkness behind him, beyond the towpath where the railway line cut through between acres of farmland, wood and scrub.

'Perhaps you were sleepwalking,' she suggested. 'You woke up and got lost. Do you know where you are now?'

The man looked at her calmly, saying nothing.

'You're cold,' she went on, gently. 'I think you must have woken up and wandered off and lost your bearings, and you've been sitting here and got cold. Perhaps you should get back home now.'

The man listened and rose to his feet obediently. He held out his hand again.

In a flat voice he said, 'Kind.'

Sara took his quivering hand. 'Goodnight,' she said.

The man's fingers trembled in her closed palm.

'Hurt,' he said, before turning and disappearing into the darkness of the scrub beyond the towpath.

CHAPTER 23

STEPHEN GOLIGHTLY UNLOCKED the cabinet in his consulting room, removed the three folders marked *Mrs Barbara Fernandez (Bunny)*, *James Ballantyne* and *Miss Joyce Cruikshank* and took them over to the armchair where he intended to spend a quiet few moments reading and planning in peace, with a cup of ginseng and milk thistle tea. He slumped carelessly in the chair before correcting his posture, reminding himself that by sitting badly he was risking breathing problems from a collapsed chest, increased tension of the neck and lower back and depressed blood circulation leading to impeded venous return from the lower limbs. Asthma, slipped disc and varicose veins in other words, whose numberless, miserable victims he had picked up, dusted off and restored by naturopathic means for over ten years now. Again sitting up straight, he confirmed in his mind (for it was a thought of which he was fond) how avoidable and unnecessary most ailments were.

He wondered if he could track down in Bunny's notes something to show her daughter that would satisfactorily explain her present condition which, since its onset yesterday, was not improving. Then he would give careful consideration to Mr Ballantyne and how the news of his ulcer could best be conveyed so as to create sufficient anxiety for the patient to cooperate with long-term naturopathic treatment, but not so much that he would panic, jump ship and get himself opened up by some investigative butcher on the NHS. It would be a blow to the patient, of course, to learn that his problem was not simple IBS, but Stephen was confident that James would be amazed and grateful that naturopathy could still address this more serious condition. And the degenerative kidney condition outlined in Miss Cruikshank's notes since her medical examination and X-ray result this morning needed to be, as it were, fleshed out. It would take some explaining, and must be done gently so as not to alarm the patient. She too, if she cooperated, could expect a full recovery in time. Both of them would need the right handling and to his delight, his best hope of handling them right was to enlist the support of Sara Selkirk.

Stephen sank back luxuriously in his chair, again forgetting posture. Already he felt Sara was someone he could expect something from, perhaps even trust, largely because she had seemed after only one meeting to trust him. He recalled the look of entreaty that he had seen in those extraordinary eyes as she had petitioned him, five days ago, on the Cruikshank woman's behalf. Entreaty had been replaced by delight when he had agreed to give Joyce a trial as music therapist. He knew himself well enough to realise that it was really in pleasing Sara that his own gratification lay, and that while he was certainly not so crude a person as to be sexually aroused by mere gratitude from a woman, his pleasure in giving her what she asked for had not been entirely—what would the correct phrase be?—gender neutral. There had been quite simply something unthinkable in turning Sara down, and simultaneously something arousing in the notion that, as he was allowing himself to succumb to her persuasiveness, she might prove receptive to the power of his. And now that he had actually met Joyce Cruikshank it was surely undeniable that Sara owed him something.

With the complication of the weakness in the Cruikshank liver and kidneys which could, he was confident, keep Joyce under his medical supervision for some time, Sara might feel she owed him even more. He was already looking forward to her gratitude when, having first saved Joyce from the trauma of invasive conventional treatment, he would lead the old lady gently towards a slow but full recovery. Stephen, lying back in his chair, gazed at the ceiling without seeing it. He was indulging in a lewd and pictorial prediction of how Sara Selkirk might, should she be so encouraged, repay her debt of gratitude, and although correct posture was still far from his mind he, or part of him at least, was beginning to sit up very straight indeed.

The thought of Bunny Fernandez produced the necessary detumescence for Stephen to get on with his work. He leaned forward and picked up her folder. Barbara Grant, born 1918, in Hastings. What a long time ago that seemed, a time which one could imagine only in black and white, or perhaps in pastel colours. Stephen sipped some of his tea. It was inconceivable, somehow, that children born in such a time could break their parents' hearts as they do now except, perhaps, by dying. Scarlet fever, diphtheria, whooping cough: killers all. Perhaps it was the absence of routinely life-threatening conditions that accounted for people's slide into laziness where their health was concerned. Until, that was to say, some nasty consequence of their neglect began to bite (asthma, slipped disc, varicose veins) when suddenly they would be willing to subject themselves to any extremity of treatment in order to get well enough to go home, crack open a bottle of wine, swallow a large steak and start the whole process of decline into ill health once more. Stephen was realistic enough to acknowledge that it did him and the clinic no harm that it was so.

He sighed and drained his cup. He knew the irony of thinking it a pity that Sylvia could not be here to enjoy the clinic's success. It was her money that had set it up after she died, and in her lifetime she had enjoyed so little. She had been deeply pessimistic not just about naturopathy but about anything that doctors claimed to do. Perhaps she had been right, because it had not been until that extraordinary business with Lady Wallace, a terrific stroke of luck whichever way one looked at it, that word had got around and the clinic had really come into its own after five years on the brink of closing. Nothing like the miraculous cure of a voluble and well-connected patient to increase bookings, he had found. Sylvia would not have been amused at how that had come about, but then there had been few things that had made her laugh.

He remembered Ivan's arrival in 1964. Nobody had talked about post-natal depression in those days. Even he in his newly qualified ignorance had been keen to call it 'a touch of the baby blues', a phrase which miniaturised and prettified the big, ugly fact that for nearly two years following the birth of their son, Sylvia had been almost catatonic. He did not blame himself, but he had often wondered if Ivan's later mental history had its basis in those first two years of competent but unaffectionate handling by a succession of expensive nurses, paid for by Sylvia's parents. Or if his instability were innate, inherited from his depressive mother, in which case that would not be his fault either. But at least after Sylvia picked up again everything had been normal. He remembered a certain amount of parading in the park while Ivan, dressed in ruthless stripes, sat up in his Silver Cross pram and sucked on Scandinavian toys, the first to hit Britain. It seemed, and indeed in Sylvia's sad case truly was, a lifetime ago, and it did not help with the matters in hand. He sighed and turned back to his reading.

The notes began only at 1971 when Bunny, by then Barbara Cliborne, had presented to a private physician in London with (Stephen sighed again, this time with boredom) the usual: depression, weight gain, sleeplessness and thinning hair. The notes told him that she had one daughter of fourteen, smoked about twenty a day which he knew meant thirty, and that she drank 'wine, in moderation' which might well mean gin consumption in *im*moderation and in the afternoons, almost standard in a woman of her age, habits and social standing. Obviously the 'whole patient' philosophy had been doing the rounds in Harley Street by the seventies because the doctor had noted also that she had recently been divorced by her third husband and that this might be an underlying cause of his patient's indifferent health. Four subsequent appointments over the following year were kept, and the notes revealed nothing surprising about the progress of Bunny's mid-life symptoms under the ministrations of the standard, barbiturate-heavy treatment of the time. The last consultation revealed a thinner, happier patient, however, and the information that she would soon be leaving London to live in 'the Argentine' with her new husband. To help with onward referral, the doctor recorded that his patient's new married name would be Mrs Raymond Huntley-Crosse. No help whatsoever, in the event. He knew the rest: several years later Bunny, by that time Mrs Fernandez, resident in Bath with no Senor Fernandez in sight, had booked herself into the Sulis Clinic for three weeks that summer and every subsequent one, the only difference being that with each passing year she tended to be a little more fanatical and stay a little longer.

All that followed in the folder were the annual assessments of her reliably excellent health that he himself had made on each of her stays, because Bunny had consulted no other doctor. He closed the folder. In fact he was probably being over-cautious. Bunny Fernandez was one of those kippery, marinaded old women on whom nicotine and alcohol seemed to have acted as preservatives, while her indestructible constitution had gone its own sweet way no matter what she threw down her gullet. If at eighty-one, a good age by any reckoning, she was starting to show signs of wear and tear, could anyone be surprised? Dementia would be just what one could expect to strike Bunny Fernandez, so he should not allow himself to be unnerved by the woman's intermittent raving and loss of muscular control. Stephen reminded himself that the two people least surprised or concerned, except insofar as their own holiday plans were being scuppered, were the daughter and son-in-law. They were clearly taking the sensible view, and he had just satisfied himself that his patient's notes, as far as they concerned him, were in perfect order. There would be no comeback if Bunny Fernandez finally slipped away on his premises. Her symptoms were interspersed with periods of lucidity and calm; her decline would be gradual enough for them all to grow used to the idea that the old bird's synapses were ceasing to fire properly. Yvonne had better be warned that the nursing would become heavy. And although he would phrase it appropriately to the daughter when the time came for comforting words, his honest opinion was that it would be thanks to naturopathy that she would die so healthy.

Unlike his Sylvia. Petronella Cropper should be grateful that her mother would die after eighty-one years of undeserved good health and a brief spell of indignity. What was that compared with being so diminished and emptied of hope that you end your own life at forty-two? A knock at the door startled Stephen out of his speculation. Hastily he stacked the three folders together on the table and placed a paper weight on top. He rose and opened the door.

'Ivan! Come in, come in. Oh, come in!'

'You all right, Dad?' he asked as he sat down. 'I've only come to talk about nutrition plans for the new admissions. I've brought their menus for an update. I can come back if you like.'

Stephen waved this suggestion away and smiled broadly at his son without speaking for some moments. What Hilary had said was true. Since the news of her pregnancy Ivan had changed. No longer was he wearing, like some invisible T-shirt slogan, an air of having been so out of his head in the seventies and fucked up by the eighties that it was doing his head in to be functioning at all in the nineties. It seemed inconceivable that this was the same person who as a schoolboy had been fiddling with LSD, who had failed to get in to do medicine and who had, in between attention-seeking, psychotic breakdowns and a few not very bold suicide attempts, managed a poor pharmacology degree at the age of twenty-nine. He was the purposeful and outgoing Ivan who, Stephen had always known, lay underneath the pose of shambling reticence and who had not been sighted since about 1979. Now the younger, ganglier version of his tall, straight-backed, blue-eyed father smiled back shyly.

'So Hilary's told you, then?' Ivan asked.

'She has, indeed she has. I am delighted. You must be so happy.'

'I am, I really am,' Ivan said. More earnestly he added, 'You know, Dad, I'd never have believed the relief when I found out she really was. After all the worry, thinking perhaps I couldn't—'

'Oh, these things sometimes do just take their time,' Stephen said in an airy, doctory way. 'Nothing to worry about, usually. Now, the menus—'

'No, but Dad, honestly,' Ivan leaned forward confidingly, 'the relief, after what we went through. You know, after Hilary got checked out last year and we thought we'd be fine. And then it still wasn't happening and you remember what Christmas was like.'

Involuntarily Stephen glanced at Ivan's bare forearms. The marks would not have disappeared, of course, and never would. Like the memory of last Christmas they had merely receded, taking their places among the criss-crossing scars of twenty years of self-harm. Every crisis that Ivan had encountered or engineered since he was fifteen had provoked in him a compulsion to take a knife and make slow slashes into his own flesh, sometimes dozens of little slicings up his arms and legs. He did it as carefully and deliberately as a butcher scoring a piece of pork for crackling, except that this flesh was living, and his own. It bled, and it hurt. Stephen did not begin to understand it, nor could Ivan explain it beyond once admitting in a rare, lucid moment that he found some sense of release, a sort of peace, in watching his own blood run. After the first time, just after Sylvia's death, Stephen had thrown away every razor-blade in the house and grown a beard. The second time Ivan had used a kitchen knife. It was only after a particularly nasty session with scissors that Stephen had grasped that the availability of blades was not the issue. The cutting episodes were never in themselves life-threatening, unlike some of Ivan's escapades with drugs, and Stephen had had to learn to be grateful for that.

'Christmas Eve it was, when it got to me. All that new-born babe and "Away in a Manger" stuff. Remember, Dad?' Stephen looked up. Could Ivan really imagine that he would forget? The midnight mass at Freshford, the frosty walk back to Ivan and Hilary's house and the sight, barely ten minutes later, of his only son sobbing with pain in the bathroom doorway, blood running down both arms and poor, white-faced Hilary, holding the knife?

'Of course I remember. Ivan—'

'Maybe it was a blessing in disguise. Brought things to a head, because that was when I decided to have the sperm test, remember?'

'Well, afterwards. After you'd been patched up, wasn't it?'

'And the test was fine, wasn't it. Perfectly okay. No problem, the result said. Well, it's August now. So I just want to say I'm sorry. It's such a relief now she's pregnant and I realise how difficult I must have been. How much you've both put up with.'

Stephen shrugged and smiled. 'I don't want you to think about that. You've got to think ahead. If you want to thank me, try putting all this kind of thing behind you.' He nodded towards Ivan's scarred arms. 'Ivan, you'll soon be a father. Hilary needs you, so will the baby. Please—don't do it any more. Don't do it to them.'

'But it's funny it took all this time, January to August, when we were trying so hard. I mean, *really* hard.'

Something in Stephen froze. While he was flattered that Ivan should speak to him so openly he did not want to hear about his son and daughter-in-law's sex life and there was a confidentiality in Ivan's lowered voice warning him that any minute he was going to be told how often they 'did it'. And quite possibly when, where and how, unless he stopped him.

'Oh I don't think so,' he said, a little gruffly. 'Anything up to a year is good going. And of course Hilary—'

'Yes, Hilary. I was going to ask you something about Hilary.'

'Right now? We need to do our patient progress updates, too. And there's the Open Day on Friday—we need to talk about that. I've got a couple more for lunch.'

Ivan handed his father a sheet of paper from the pile he was carrying. 'Yes, but I just want you to take a quick look at this. Hilary's been taking the folic acid, of course, but now she's pregnant we decided that a raw diet would be best for her, certainly for the first eight weeks or so. It's the best time of year for it, the garden's full to bursting with stuff. I thought it'd help with rejuvenation and cell-building, boost her immune system.'

Stephen scanned the sheet, nodding. 'Very sound,' he said, handing it back. 'Excellent idea. Plenty of rest, too. It's limiting, of course. Might be a bit hard to stick to.'

Ivan beamed. 'That's why I'm going to do it too. Just to keep her company.'

Stephen nodded again, with surprised pleasure. 'Ivan, that's a great plan.' He hesitated. 'Look, I'm not even sure I should say this, I try not to interfere. But I'm so pleased,

I don't mean about the diet in itself, but because you're doing this for her. Supporting her. She deserves it, the way she's stuck by you.'

Ivan leaned forward and locked his father's eyes in his own blue gaze. 'Dad, I know. You've stuck by me, too. You and Hilary've been great.'

'Well, that's all right, Ivan. You know we just want—'

'You actually met Hilary over my hospital bed, remember. That episode in Dundee.'

'Of course I remember. That week we weren't even sure you would survive. When you were capable of speech you accused everybody of trying to kill you, Hilary, me, the nurses, we were all in some plot together. Even the person in the next bed.'

The two men exchanged a glance and a smile. Could it be that they were silently agreeing that Ivan's episodes might now be so far in the past that they could begin to pretend that there had been a funny side?

'I remember thinking afterwards it wasn't the way I wanted you to meet my future wife. Look, Dad, I've told Hilary this, too.' Ivan leaned further forward. 'I can't rewrite the past. But from now on, things are going to be very, very different. I promise.'

Later, when Ivan got up to go, Stephen followed him to the door, where they lingered long enough for a sudden charge of panic to shoot between them like an electric bolt, in which each felt a fleeting dread that the other was going to hug him. They concealed the moment with an exchange of twinkly blue looks and a handshake, but after Ivan had gone Stephen returned to his chair and began to wonder if he might dare to hope that Ivan might at last have stopped breaking his heart. It was the habit of twenty years for thoughts of Ivan to be shadowed by a sense of impotent pity, and the habit would be slow in taking its leave. He usually avoided any detailed recall of the blurred decade following Sylvia's death but it swam over him again now, the amorphous mess of grief that they had somehow lived through, and which now left its stain only on undisciplined moments of introspection such as these. It seemed to him that he and Ivan had each sucked the other down, each pouring pain on to pain and grief on to grief until they were both half-mad with it. The struggle to free themselves of each other had been fought through twenty years of Ivan's drugs and self-harm, false promises and dawns, twenty years of hysteria and dependence punctuated by silences and estrangement. It was a miracle that at last they had found the grace to forgive each other for their unconscious strivings to out-suffer each other. They had at last actually come together again as father and son, and even more closely than would ordinarily have been possible. The miracle-worker was Hilary.

Ivan had been a student in Dundee in 1986, going out of his mind for the fourth time since he was fifteen on a combination of drugs, alcohol and psychosis, although he had not been so far beyond reason six months earlier to fail to attach himself to Hilary, and it was she who had got him admitted to a hospital and contacted Stephen. Stephen, arriving when Ivan's raving was at its height, had been calmed on finding a capable, warm-hearted woman at Ivan's bedside, although in a passing way a little puzzled at what it was that Hilary herself was getting out of the liaison. Together, watching Ivan closely over the next two weeks as he had clambered back into his right mind, he and Hilary had grown close. She was a natural comforter. He saw how his son, just by looking at her, was made peaceful, and for that alone Stephen would have loved her. But he did wonder if either of them was aware that Hilary must remind Ivan of his mother.

There was certainly a glimpse of Sylvia in Ivan's new wife, more than a glimpse perhaps, in the dark hair that was always a little too thick and tousled for total respectability and in the large, full breasts that Stephen often had to stop himself from looking at, if not from thinking about. But Hilary's lips which, like Sylvia's, seemed designed for pleasure-seeking and also, although Stephen knew he should not think about that either, for pleasure-giving, were often pursed in vigilant self-discipline, as if her mouth disapproved of itself for being so sensual. After the wedding and as he got to know her better, Stephen began to understand that she placed a value on a quiet life for the three of them that was far greater than any ambition to be Ivan's *grande passion*, and she was sufficiently content with achieving that to be unconcerned by any possible resemblance to the departed one. With slightly brutal practicality, Hilary had pointed out that it was Sylvia who was dead and she who'd got Ivan now, so it was, in every sense, up to her to make him happy.

Stephen had reassured her that she was not alone. She could rely on him to do anything that would bring about Ivan's mental health and a lasting reconciliation, and from that moment had sprung the understanding that henceforth she and Stephen were benign co-conspirators in the arrangement of Ivan's wellbeing. Stephen smiled in spite of himself. What a team they made. Ivan was happy now. He got up, replaced the three folders in their correct places in the filing cabinet and locked it. Then, and with only the very slightest sense that he was risking something, he picked up the telephone and dialled Sara Selkirk's number.

CHAPTER 24

'WE JAPANESE,' STARTED Professor Takahashi's interpreter, not realising that the phrase had become Andrew's cue to stop listening. 'We Japanese . . .'

Andrew turned to Professor Takahashi. 'If you're about to tell me again that you Japanese have an overwhelming sense of duty and responsibility to the family that transcends any consideration of personal gratification or desire, or if . . .' Andrew sighed with weariness as the interpreter translated and Professor Takahashi nodded, '. . . you're about to insist again that it is quite normal for a Japanese wife to do as her husband tells her, or expect him to discipline her, let me assure you that all that is quite understood. You cannot, I'm afraid, avoid answering questions with the claim that being Japanese places you above suspicion.'

Andrew continued to stare at Professor Takahashi's face while the interpreter relayed all this, but it was difficult to know the effect it was having. Apart from a remarkable degree of tenacity in sticking to his original story, Professor Takahashi was displaying nothing other than a rather dignified, pained expression.

'What I want to hear from you is,' Andrew continued, 'exactly what happened on Saturday 31 July. Again. Because, Mr Takahashi, I think you did meet your wife in Bath early that morning, despite what you say. And I also believe that you pushed her, or persuaded her to enter the side door of the Snake and Ladder and that in the corridor you knocked her head against the wall and then strangled her.' He waited for the interpreter to rattle that lot back to him.

It was a stunt, of course, using the interpreter. Professor Takahashi's English was well up to the demands of delivering lectures and answering questions. He had had no difficulty either in understanding or expressing himself during their first bungled interview, although the possibility that he might have had was of course another arrow in the defence's nice fat quiver. Andrew was now being punctilious with every procedural nicety which meant that the interview room was rather crowded—with the suspect, the suspect's solicitor, the suspect's interpreter, the suspect's consular representative, DS Bridger, and himself—and consequently stuffy, and everything was taking at least twice as long as it should. It was also proving impossible to question the man with the kind of vigor that might produce off-guard, truthful and useful answers, because direct questions were being not so much translated as transmuted, via the complex choreography of nods and bows that signified careful listening, into what sounded like rather coy social chit-chat. And Professor Takahashi, behaving like some goodwill ambassador at a cultural exchange seminar, seemed more anxious to expound on interesting differences between the Japanese and the rest of the world than to clear any suspicion that he was guilty of his wife's mur-

der. Indeed he seemed embarrassed by Andrew's direct-
ness. Andrew was convinced that Professor Takahashi's
show of finer feelings was another stunt.

'My client has already answered that question,' Debbie
Trowbridge began, but Mr Takahashi interrupted with another volley at his interpreter.

'Professor Takahashi repeats that he spoke to his wife on
Friday evening by telephone and arranged to meet her at
the Royal Photographic Society at 12.30. He did not
arrange to meet her at the Snake and Ladder and has
never been there. He waited for his wife at the Royal
Photographic Society but she did not appear.'

Debbie Trowbridge said, with a look at Andrew that
was not unsympathetic, 'My client has cooperated fully
with your enquiries, and I have advised him not to answer
questions to which he has already given answers. Since you
appear to have no further lines of enquiry I have to ask on
what grounds you believe you should be allowed to carry
on questioning him. Unless he is going to be charged, he
must be released from all bail conditions.'

And as the interpreter spoke her words in Japanese
back to the client who had, Andrew was certain, understood it perfectly well in English, he had to concede that
what Debbie Trowbridge had said was perfectly and quite
sickeningly correct. He exchanged a look with Bridger
and felt any confidence that they would ever charge
Takahashi recede even further. Bridger's contribution so
far to the inquiry had been to run up a telephone bill getting pally with the Kobe Police Department, following a
hunch that Andrew considered spurious but which, in the
absence of anything better to go on, he had allowed him to
pursue. Bridger now surveyed Professor Takahashi with

what he clearly intended to be an expression of sardonic superiority.

'Professor Takahashi, tell us if you would about your first wife. Let's have the details. How *exactly* did she die?'

Long before the question had been put in Japanese, Professor Takahashi's composure collapsed in a gasp of appalled horror. He swayed in his chair as if the breath had been knocked out of him and with desperate eyes appealed to his lawyer.

'That's a totally unacceptable line of questioning! My client will not—'

'Must I answer? What is this matter to do with this? This is most difficult matter, one I do not wish to . . .' The rest of his sentence was lost in an outburst of weeping. As he fished for a handkerchief and struggled to control himself, Debbie Trowbridge repeated furiously that such a line of questioning was irrelevant. She was well within her rights to do so, Andrew thought, nodding reluctantly and concedingly, but nonetheless Takahashi's reaction had been very interesting indeed.

•   *   *   *

ANDREW LEFT the winding-up of the interview to Bridger and returned to the Major Incident Room. It was empty of people although stale with their flat, exhaled air. The team would be out on another round of interviewing which, Andrew thought hopelessly as he sank on to a chair, probably would not produce any new leads but, because it just might, had to be done and was indeed the only course open to them in the absence of anything more to go on. Andrew knew that at least one, probably more than one, witness was out there somewhere, and he knew too that unless he, she or they were tracked down there would be no chance of building a case. Numerous pleas to the public to come forward with information had yielded nothing except scores of possible sightings of the suspect which so far were turning out, on further enquiry, to be nebulous claims of 'noticing something a bit funny'. Yet all of them demanded a frustrating amount of time and effort which, Andrew now recalled with scorn, Bridger called 'officer input'. It had been an education to discover just how many Japanese (and Chinese, Korean, Malaysian, as well as Singaporean, Taiwanese, Peruvian, Turkish, French, Irish and Belgian) visitors had been in Bath drawing attention to themselves on that last Saturday in July. The enquiry team had also had, along with the sincere but mistaken majority of people responding with information, the usual small showing of prats whose weak-brained or malicious claims had wasted the usual amount of time, but they still had not found one essential, reliable witness who could give a pos- itive identification of Takahashi in Bath early that morning, at or near the scene of the offence, and whose willingness to be tested would allow them to proceed with an ID pa- rade. Not that that in itself would provide conclusive proof of anything, but it would at least enable them to punch some holes in Takahashi's claims about a missed lunchtime appointment.

Forensic had not helped. They had pulled, along with some of her own, a couple of deeply embedded hairs of her husband's from the dead woman's cardigan, which proved nothing except that at some point he had been in close contact with his wife. They had also found fibres from the bedspread at the B&B at Limpley Stoke, one of Hilary's hairs and a couple of white ones near the cuff, which had turned out to belong to Miffy. Miffy was the cat belonging to Mrs Heffer, the Golightlys' nearest neighbour, who confirmed that Mrs Takahashi had stopped to stroke the cat during one of her walks in the vegetable garden.

Andrew sighed and looked round the Incident Room, its walls covered with sheets of diligent, hopeless mapping, pictures, blackboard lists of names and numbers waiting for mechanistic, dogged checking and re-checking. The chalked Happy Birthday! message to one of the team in one corner of the blackboard was the only confirmation that the crew working here under DS Bridger's immediate supervision was not utterly demoralised, for the room seemed empty not just of people but of energy and optimism. Miffy's chances in hell seemed a better bet than Andrew's hopes of finding a worthwhile lead.

CHAPTER 25

BUNNY KNEW IT was Tuesday. She also knew 'it' was Petronella, for she knew no one else who spoke in that tinny tone. Bunny sighed but did not open her eyes. She had been able to see to it that Petronella acquired a decent accent, that being a matter simply of the right choice of school, but she had been unable to amend her daughter's needling voice, which had made Bunny itch to slap her almost from the minute she could speak. Before that, actually.

'It's Petronella,' went the voice again. 'Petronella's here, Mummy, so's Hugh. You're in the Sulis, and it's Tuesday. Mummy, are you awake?'

Bunny sighed again and opened her eyes. 'Of course I'm awake and I know very well it's Tuesday. What on earth's the point of telling me it's Tuesday?' The effort of pushing out the words started a fit of coughing. She allowed herself to be raised from her pillow until she was sitting up in bed. She rather guardedly took the cup of tea that Petronella was proffering and found to her private delight that the tremor in her hands had subsided. She drank in steady draughts until the cup was empty.

'Camomile and parsley,' she said, decisively.

'Dr Golightly thought it would help,' Hugh put in earnestly, from the other side of the bed.

'Help what?' Bunny asked. 'I'm perfectly all right. Except that I'm hungry.'

Petronella and Hugh smiled at each other across the bed. 'That's wonderful!' Petronella said. 'I'll go and find someone, shall I, and get something brought up.' She almost skipped to the door, watched by an unamused Bunny.

'Can't see what's wonderful about it,' she said crisply to Hugh after the door had closed. 'Perfectly natural. I haven't eaten since Sunday, so I'm bound to be hungry.'

Hugh smiled. 'Poor thing's relieved, that's all. You gave us a bit of a fright, you know. You have been rather out of it, shaking and whatnot, sleeping all hours and mumbling. Petronella thought you were er . . . seeing things. You did seem confused.'

Bunny looked pleased for the first time. 'My body and mind simply required rest. I keep telling you, the body heals itself when you let it tell you what it needs. And of course I wasn't confused. I'm not gaga yet. Where's Warwick?'

'He's—well, actually, I was hoping we could clear the air about Warwick. If you're up to having a little chat about him.'

'Chat about Warwick? Where is he? Warwick's my lifeline.'

'Well, that's rather it, actually. The thing is, Pet was rather worrying in case you'd got yourself into some commitment or other with the chap and we're not sure quite how things would lie then, you see. Vis-à-vis us, and the er . . . you know, your next grandchild. I don't know if you remember . . .'

'Of course I remember. There's to be another.' Bunny sighed heavily and shook her head. 'I was the same. *So* fertile men just had to *look* at me. I did get in some scrapes. At least Petronella is married, and one supposes to the father. That's something.'

Hugh cleared his throat and spoke with his eyes focused somewhere near the top of Bunny's headboard. 'You see, as far as things go with Warwick, we did wonder—I mean it's your decision of *course* but you haven't known him long and I'm sure he's good company and so on, but we wouldn't want you to be er . . . well, let down. If supposing, later on, I mean, we don't really know anything about him, after all.'

Hugh glanced at Bunny, saw her look of amused distrust and knew he was going to have to lay it on the line. 'I mean look, the new baby's going to wallop us hard, needless to say. In the old wallet. And we are so grateful for the help you gave for the boys and the decision's yours, of *course*. But really, I always feel one should treat them all the same if one possibly can, all fair do's, so to speak. Pet's worried sick quite frankly and she feels as I do that after all, family comes first and this one will be the last after all. Frankly, perhaps we should be a little wary of Warwick's motives, I mean I take it you do see that.'

'Warwick,' Bunny repeated slowly, 'is my lifeline.' She turned flinty eyes to Hugh and said, almost accusingly, 'You do know he had the most terrible time in the war. Terrible. Your generation doesn't understand. What is quite wonderful is the way he's always so cheerful. He can't do enough for me, you know.'

'Yes, I'm sure, but I mean has he—have you, er . . . shown your appreciation, in any *material* way? Has he suggested any kind of well . . . permanent arrangement?'

'Warwick is a gentleman,' Bunny said. 'I wonder that you can even ask.'

Just then Petronella returned, followed by Sister Yvonne who in turn was followed by Ivan, bearing a tray.

'*I* do any suggesting that is required,' Bunny went on. 'And I won't discuss it any more.'

'You *are* honoured, Mrs F. Feeling more yourself? The man himself has brought you some lunch,' Sister Yvonne said, giving the bedcovers some brisk smoothing down. 'All specially prepared.'

Ivan carefully placed the tray on the hospital table which swung over the bed. On it were three exquisitely arranged plates: one with a multicoloured salad, one piled with bread, crackers and lentil pâté, the last filled with scented summer fruits. A jug of viscous yellow juice stood next to them.

'Mango and orange,' Ivan said, smiling, as he poured some into a glass. 'Nice to see you better. Enjoy. Wait till you taste those strawberries. I'll let Warwick know you're feeling better. He's been missing you, he says.'

Bunny smiled complacently through a mouthful of bread and pâté. 'Tell Warwick to visit me this afternoon. I may feel up to some work on his head. And tell him'—she narrowed her eyes in Hugh's direction—'that I can't wait to see him and talk about our plans.'

CHAPTER 26

Poor old Dan had asked his dad to take him to Legoland on his birthday but Valerie had put a stop to that, designating the birthday treat to be in her gift.

'I'm taking them to Legoland on the Saturday. You're getting him on the actual day. Take them on a picnic or something,' she had told Andrew on Sunday, arriving back from her Assertiveness Course in a hostile cloud of vindaloo fumes, round about the same time that Sara was flinging a Thai dinner for two across her garden.

'But he asked me to take him,' Andrew said. 'He specially asked me and Sara to take him on Tuesday and it is his birthday, so if that's what he wants—'

'Oh, will you shut up about what *he* wants!'

Valerie's fuses, always short, were now the length of stubble. 'What about what *I* want for once? That's just the point! *You* get to do all the nice treats, don't you, while I get to do every other single bloody thing, every other bloody day of the week. All you do is breeze in and out at weekends with *her* and over-indulge them. Well, this time *I'm* doing the treat. It won't kill you to take them on a simple little picnic, will it? Or doesn't she do picnics?'

Andrew had opened his mouth to contest the justice of just about everything she had said, and closed it again. He desperately wanted to have the children with him for a night mid-week, but instead had to content himself with putting in short and cheerful visits to them on Tuesday and Thursday evenings. Valerie would not allow the children to go to him on school nights on the grounds that it would unsettle them. He saw them every weekend that he was not working and tried to ensure that they did something together, just as he had done with them most weekends before the divorce. It was sometimes no more than a country ramble and a funny tea back at his poky flat, but it was true that he now made more effort to think of places to take them and things to do. This was what Valerie described as over-indulging them.

Indeed, there was nothing wrong with a simple picnic. But when Valerie dropped the children off at ten o'clock on Tuesday morning at Medlar Cottage she had not actually told them that they were not, as they were expecting, going to Legoland with Daddy and Sara. That little piece of news had been left for Andrew to impart. 'Didn't Mummy say? She's taking you instead, on Saturday! Today, *we're* going for a walk and a picnic!' Not even the brightest tone of voice could sell a picnic over Legoland or convince Dan that he had not been betrayed by his father.

Sara happened to like picnics rather more than Andrew did, so it was she who had organised the food with what she privately thought was heroic selflessness and good humour. She had also picked up the broken china and glass from her garden, scrubbed the path clean of its food slick and hosed disgusting yellow spatterings off the surrounding shrubs. And she had not only not told Andrew of her encounter on the towpath, she had decided not to mention Sunday at all. So she was not altogether delighted when Andrew suggested the towpath for the picnic.

'Oh, why there? It's rather boring, isn't it? Why don't we take them up to Browns Folly?'

'Natalie hates climbing hills. The towpath's flat.'

'Well, what about going off to Bowood? There's an adventure playground.'

'Too far. Benji might be car sick.'

'But he could get car sick going to Legoland.'

'He's welcome to be sick in Valerie's car,' Andrew said, and sighed. 'All right, there's no point hiding it from you. I wouldn't mind just having another look at the Golightly place. Don't know why but it still bugs me. Why she should have been staying there, of all places. There's something we're not getting. I just want to take a look.'

Sara understood, not quite what the Golightly place might have to do with any of it, but how it was that part of Andrew's mind could not leave go, why he felt the need to pace the towpath again, thinking, wondering, looking, in the hope that he might finally see something. Although, she reassured herself sternly, it had been no such compulsion that had brought her there on Sunday night, for she was not involving herself in the case, difficult as it was to curb her natural nosiness. To do so only annoyed Andrew and diverted her attention from her work. Yet, had that not been part of it? That, even as she had felt herself lost in an irrational rage against Valerie, she had nevertheless brought herself, of all places, almost to the very spot that preoccupied her lover? And all she had found was a shivering vagrant. She really ought to leave the detective work to Andrew.

'Fine,' she said. 'The towpath will be fine. They'll like the locks and barges, won't they? Better than boring old countryside.'

She did not add that she was still curious about the shabby man and was hoping to see him again. And when she did she would nonchalantly point him out, and only then might she relate the story of Sunday night's little adventure. Andrew might, if she could pull his attention away from the Takahashi murder for a minute, be interested.

They had started at Bathampton Lock under a subdued sky which affected everyone's mood. Kicking along and saying little, every few yards stepping over the long fishing rods of the silent anglers who slumped at the canal side next to their horrifying tins of maggots, they had ended up, round about lunchtime and just as it looked as if it might rain, at the far side of the viaduct on the edge of Limpley Stoke. The anglers were now all behind them. Presumably the fish did not bite this close to the landing stages near the viaduct, where the traffic of tourist barges coming and going from their moorings kept the water churning in a dirty brown swirl. They were alone on the path, most other strollers and cyclists, Sara supposed, having taken themselves off to do something sensible such as have lunch in pub gardens.

Sara and Natalie stopped and turned to wait for the others to catch up. Andrew was still a long way down the path with Benji, and Dan, who seemed rather withdrawn for a birthday boy, trailed farther behind still. Sara put down the basket she was carrying and Natalie, freeing her hand from Sara's, danced off to the hedge to find unripe blackberries. She didn't much like blackberries, ripe or not, but she had to pick as many as possible in order to stop her brothers from getting them. Sara breathed in the sour green smell of crushed nettles and gazed past Natalie. Just on the far side of the hedge that Natalie was trying to reach, tramping down all the long grass in her path, and across a stretch of bramble scrub, lay the railway line. Down a steep slope on the far side of the tracks and across another narrow stretch of scrub was the start of the Golightlys' land. A sprinkler waved slowly, raining softly over some bright green plants, possibly lettuces. Compost heaps, polytunnels and various sheds were set at points among the rows of vegetables and brown bare squares, which stretched up to the back garden of the modern, rather ugly brick house. Another identical house stood some hundred yards off down a lane that connected the houses on the far side. A whirligig for drying clothes sprouted from the grass of the perfunctory back garden which sat between the house and the vegetables, where washing of nondescript colours lifted listlessly in the slight wind. The place was deserted.

'Don't bother 'cos I've picked all the best ones!' Natalie crowed in a sing-song, as the others reached them. 'There's only little ones left now!'

'Aw that's not fair,' Benji whined. 'Da-ad, that's not fair.'

'They're not ripe anyway, so they probably wouldn't taste very nice,' Sara said, as if that were the point.

'I've got *tons*,' Natalie said, defiantly.

'So? We'll get our own. They're not all yours you know. There's *loads* further up. C'mon, Benji.'

Dan pushed roughly past Andrew and trotted further on up the path, looking intently up and down the hedge for more blackberry bushes. Benji, thrilled to be summoned by his brother, followed. After a few moments, there was a happy shout and wave from Dan and a squeal from Benji, and then they almost disappeared into the hedge, delving for berries.

Andrew, just as Sara had done, had stopped and was now staring past the top of the hedge down to the smallholding on the other side of the railway.

'It's a big place, isn't it? They must grow lots more than they need at the Sulis,' she murmured.

'Hmm? Oh, yes. Yes, I think they said they're part of an organic box scheme. And I think they used to supply a couple of restaurants but the deliveries took so long they gave that up.' He carried on staring. As Sara watched him, a loose memory of something from Sunday night was beginning to flap in her mind, something in the shabby man's frightened voice as he had spoken blindly into the dark came back to her.

'Didn't you tell me the night after Mrs Takahashi was killed that the Golightly man was called Ivan? Ivan Golightly?'

'Ivan and Hilary Golightly. That's right. Why?'

'And your other suspects—yes, I know you say the husband did it, but you checked out other people who'd had a connection with her, didn't you? Like the Golightlys?'

Andrew hesitated and spoke slowly. 'Yes, of course. There's Ivan Golightly.' He began to count them off on his fingers. 'Ivan Golightly was working here all Saturday morning. He was seen by the woman who lives in the other house over there, Mrs Heffer.'

Sara gazed at the two houses. 'It's a long way. And

there's so much growing in between. Was she telling the truth?'

'You have such a suspicious mind. She's a damn good witness actually. She said the Golightlys are quiet neighbours, they mind their own business. She saw Ivan that Saturday and she even told us the almost exact time because she saw him coming down from the embankment just after the 9.23 went past. He waved.'

'She's on her own, is she?'

Andrew nodded. 'Widow, works in Waitrose. One son. She was in her own garden on the Friday afternoon and met Mrs Takahashi. They talked over the fence about cats. Mrs Heffer's son works for Dyson doing service calls, he stays with his mother quite often but he lives in Chippenham, and yes, we checked him out too. He was working.'

'What about the others?'

'Hilary Golightly? She gave Mrs Takahashi a lift into town on the Saturday morning, dropped her at a quarter to nine at the Abbey, nipped in to Abbey News for a paper. Then she drove on to the Sulis, where she arrived less than ten minutes later. All stories checked out and corroborated.'

'But there's another man. What was he doing? What about the shabby man, the man with the beard who hangs out round here? He's often round here. I've spoken to him. He mentioned Ivan.'

'*You* spoke to him? Why? Sara, what have you been up to? If I find you've been meddling in police business, I'll—'

'Yes? You'll what?'

Andrew grabbed her suddenly and kissed her. In a silly

voice he said, with his arms locked round her neck, 'I'll have you deported. To an uninhabited island.'

'If it's tropical and you're there,' she said back, 'I'll go quietly. And as long as it hasn't got a concert hall. No, but listen,' she pulled herself away, 'listen, the shabby man. I met him when I was out running, er . . . last week some time, I think it was. He said something about staying with Ivan. I spoke to him and I think he was saying he stayed over there somewhere, with Ivan. Who is he? I bet Bridger doesn't even know he exists. I bet he hasn't checked him out. *Have* you checked him out?'

In a voice that Sara recognised as one he used for the benefit of people not very clever, Andrew said, 'Police officers, Sara, are not entirely stupid. Even Bridger has his moments. Of course we've interviewed all the regulars along here. I am quite sure, if I go and check, that your shabby man's among them. And none of the barge-owners, anglers, dog-walkers or cyclists remember seeing anything that either corroborates or disproves what we think happened to Mrs Takahashi. Oh, and by the way, your shabby man has been known to us and to Julian House for years.'

'Oh.'

'He's been more or less homeless since the late eighties. He's never been in trouble. He's harmless.'

'What happened to him?'

'I'm not a social worker. Why would I know?'

Sara curled herself in under his arm. Whether it was the smell of his warm skin through the old cotton shirt or his growling pretence not to care about people like the shabby man that stabbed her suddenly with the knowledge that she loved him and, simultaneously, that she did not deserve him, she was not sure.

'You know all right. What?'

Andrew's arms tightened round her as they stood looking across towards the Golightly house.

'He's called Leech. He comes from Bristol. Had a car accident in his teens and suffered brain damage. He did live with his mother but she died young, in her early sixties. He had a place in a sheltered hostel until the funding was stopped and it closed. Hasn't settled since.'

'Poor Leech. Poor shabby man. Can't anyone help him?'

'There's nowhere for him to go permanently, not now. He's been sleeping rough round Limpley Stoke for a year at least. He goes to Julian House in the winter, when it's really cold. He gets by.'

'You make it sound as if it's all right.'

Andrew was still gazing at the smallholding across the railway. 'There are worse cases,' he said.

He had spent most of the evening before at Manvers Street police station, almost alone in the Incident Room, examining everything they had in the Takahashi investigation. Not that there hadn't been a development. The team had come up with two members of the public who were just about certain enough that they had seen a middle-aged Japanese male in Bath before nine o'clock on that Saturday morning. Certain enough to have a shot at an ID parade, which Bridger was now setting up. One of the witnesses, however, seemed to want to insist that his Japanese male had been wearing jeans. The other's had possibly been in shorts. Still, it was something, and meanwhile the question of the first wife remained interesting.

Bridger was digging, albeit with his usual snouty lack of finesse.

'A pregnant Japanese tourist is staying down there in that crummy little B&B. Six days after she arrives, she is murdered in the middle of Bath, early in the morning of one of the busiest days of the year. She was quickly overpowered, suggesting that her attacker was considerably bigger and stronger than she was. But,' Andrew exhaled dramatically, 'since the victim was under five foot and weighed less than a hundred pounds, that's most people. Man or woman. No sign of a sexual motive, and nothing taken.'

'Perhaps they were trying to rob her and were disturbed.'

'Doubt it. There was time to hide the body, and if robbery was the motive, you'd do that before you bundled the body in a cupboard. At the very least you'd take the camera, which was superb.'

'Film. You had the film that was in the camera developed, didn't you? What about others?'

'There were some new films back in her room, nothing more.'

'But—' Sara hesitated. Andrew seldom liked her flashes of insight. 'But she was a *photographer*. She'd been in Bath for six days. It's inconceivable that she didn't take pictures, isn't it? Where are the films?'

Andrew stared at her. 'She might have left film for developing somewhere. There might be films sitting somewhere, in Bath, uncollected.'

'She might even have left them at Photo-Kwik at the end of the alley, mightn't she? Or they might have been stolen from her bag, of course.'

Andrew looked dubious. 'We-ell . . . Look, thanks, I'll have all the developing places checked out. Might just work, might tell us more about where she was, when. Thanks. You have your uses, my darling.'

They stood in silence, listening to the plash of ducks on the canal behind them and the children's bantering commentary to one another among the bushes.

'And it might tell us nothing,' he added. 'That's the way this enquiry's going. And I wonder what the motive for stealing the film would be. Quite apart from the motive for killing, of course.'

Sara said, 'But you can't wait until you think you've got a motive, can you? You've got to start somewhere.'

Andrew shook his head and thought. 'Right. Suppose for a minute we forget motive. The suspects, apart from the husband who remains the prime one, are Joyce, Hilary and Ivan Golightly. You. Me. Everybody at the Snake and Ladder, that's the landlord, his wife, the waitresses, the kitchen porter, the chefs, all the punters. Any and every person Mrs Takahashi spoke to in Bath. And of course the entire conference in Bristol. Anyone. Just about anyone.'

'So where *do* you start?'

Andrew was not listening. 'That, of course, is how you tackle it if you make a very big assumption, which is that the murderer actually had a motive.'

'I thought you said we forget about motive.'

'I meant we don't concern ourselves for the moment with what the motive is. But we've still made the assumption there is one. Suppose there isn't?'

Sara frowned. 'You mean somebody just killing for no reason? Just somebody off their head? I thought you once told me that was the most unlikely thing of all.'

'It is. Category A murder—an unknown killer striking at random, for no apparent reason. They're unbelievably rare. And I have my doubts that that's what we've got here. To start with, there was an attempt to hide the body. No signs of uncontrolled frenzied violence, no sexual assault. That's why,' he looked with concern at her, 'I feel absolutely certain it was her husband.'

Sara nodded. 'You said it didn't seem right, her choosing to stay here. It's hardly the place you'd pick if you could afford better.'

'Which she could. The husband's an eminent academic, high status in Japan. Good salary.'

'So she was hiding. She ran away from him in Bristol and she was hiding out down there.' Sara nodded in the direction of the house. 'Perhaps he wanted her to go back to him and have the baby and she wanted out. He lost his temper, hit her and then strangled her.'

'Something like that. Although he hasn't once mentioned the pregnancy so it's possible he didn't even know she was pregnant. And one reason for that might be that the baby wasn't his.'

'What? You haven't told him? That his wife was pregnant? That's so cruel!'

Andrew looked surprised. 'It could be a material point in building a case, so of course we haven't told him, and we won't, as long as he's a suspect. If we don't charge him, of course he's entitled to see the PM report and he'll find out then.'

Sara's eyes had filled with tears. So the very existence of the small, dead, almost-baby was now a 'material point' for the purposes of convicting its putative father. It was not to be remembered for its own lost life's sake.

Andrew said, hugging her, 'My darling, don't ever join the police. You're far too emotional. But I'd swear that's how it happened. He admits, or at least did *once* admit, though that too is now inadmissible, dammit, that he hit her. Anyway, there's evidence he did. The bruises.'

'Evidence someone did,' Sara corrected quietly. 'Perhaps not him.'

Andrew smiled. 'You're learning. You're definitely learning.' He kissed her on the nose, but turned back to the view over the hedge. 'No. No, it was him. He hit her, that's certain. He slapped her because they had been having a row and she left him about a week before she died. And that, bugger it, that's all I've got. Not enough to charge him. Despite a dead first wife in the picture, too.'

'Sounds like it should be, somehow.'

'I *know* he killed her. I just know it. When you've seen a few of these cases—'

'That,' Sara said, poking him in the stomach, 'sounds exactly like the kind of thing you won't let me get away with. Forget instinct, don't bother me with intuition, where's the evidence—isn't that right?'

'That is quite right. Because I'm not talking about intuition, I'm talking about experience.'

'But it doesn't help, does it, if you haven't got enough to charge him? All you can do is keep up with appeals for information, is that it?'

'Yes,' Andrew sighed, 'and we ask around, we ask around some more and we check and we check again. It's what the *Bath Chronicle* calls "pursuing a number of lines of enquiry". They've been great, actually. We couldn't reach nearly so many people without their cooperation, even if we do have to allow them a few "Killer In Our Midst" headlines. Meanwhile I don't see there's much more I can do, except hope that the ID parade comes off. That would be a start.'

He placed his hands on her shoulders and looked at her. 'And you're off to Salzburg on Sunday.'

'I thought you'd forgotten.'

There was a yell from the hedgerow. 'I'm starving! When's lunch? Can we have it here?'

'Here would do, I suppose,' Andrew said to Sara, 'unless you want to get a bit further away from Cold Comfort Farm over there. Though you could always lead a raiding party and go scrump an organic turnip for us.' Sara laughed and he pulled her to him.

'Come here, you,' he said, kissing her loudly. 'I haven't kissed you all morning.'

'Not in the last two minutes,' Sara said. 'Do you think they mind, though, seeing us kiss? They might not like it.' The children all had their backs to them, but still.

Andrew let her go and spread one of the picnic blankets on the ground. 'Maybe not. But honestly, I sometimes think we should be able to expect a bit more of them. Dan's been poisonous all morning over bloody Legoland. The whole of the way along the path from Bathampton I was trying to explain to him why I'm not taking them, but of course I have to try to explain it without criticising his mother. He's still furious. With *me*. Bloody Valerie.'

'It must be hard. When he was looking forward to it so much.' They watched Dan, crouched by the hedge, picking blackberries.

'But he's still *going*, as I pointed out, just not today. He's got to learn to wait for things. He's old enough now,' Andrew murmured. Sara nodded, but felt she knew as well as Dan did that you might want a thing so badly you could never be old enough to be able to wait for it.

The children came out of the bushes, a little reluctantly, when Sara called them to come for something to eat. She was sitting on the blanket and filling baguettes from various plastic boxes around her when Benji raced up last, holding out both fists.

'I got better ones! I got special blackberries! Mine are special!' With a delighted smile he thrust out his hands and opened them. Sara stopped buttering bread.

'Andrew—'

Andrew quietly put down the bottle of beer he had just opened, crouched down, took both of Benji's wrists and tipped the deadly nightshade berries quickly on to his own hand. 'Darling, have you eaten any?' Benji shook his head.

'Are you quite, quite sure, Benji? Have you eaten any?'

Benji shook his head again, firmly. 'I was saving them for pudding.'

Andrew said, 'These aren't blackberries. They're a different sort of berry. I'm going to get rid of them.' His tone of voice had silenced all three children and they stood with serious faces, watching and listening. 'But first, all of you. Take a good look at them. See? Small and round, and very, very dark, nearly black.' Andrew passed his hand round under their solemn eyes and then flung the berries as far as he could across the path and back into the hedge, where they hit the leaves, pattering like hail.

'They are very, very poisonous.' Benji began to cry. Andrew, crouching once again, pulled him close. 'It's all right. I'm not cross, Benji. Don't cry. I want you to listen. I had to throw them away because they're poisonous, do you understand? If you ate them you'd be very ill and you might even die.'

'Sorry, Daddy. I didn't mean it. Don't tell Mummy . . . you won't tell Mummy, will you, Daddy, don't tell,' he sobbed.

'Darling, I'm not cross. I know you didn't mean it. I just want you all to recognise those berries another time and never, never touch them. All right? Come on, let's have lunch. Who wants Coke?'

'Can I open the crisps, Sara?'

'How many'd you have to eat to die, Dad?'

'C'n I have a cheese triangle?'

'Don't know, Dan, but probably not very many. That's why you mustn't ever touch them.'

Natalie made the first dive into the basket, followed by Dan. Food and drink restored the children's swaggering wellbeing and the adults' sense of ease. After a spit of rain which nobody took seriously, the sun actually came out. More birds, mallards, landed on the water. Andrew sat and threw little bits of bread to the ducks, who raced and squabbled with each other for each soggy lump, reminding him of his children, who lay or sat around. Still with mouths full of food, Dan and Natalie were making screeching noises through blades of grass between their thumbs. Benji sat humming parts of *The Snowman*, as he picked bits out of his baguette. The older children were given second baguettes and they wandered off with them in their hands to find better blades of grass.

'Don't go too near the bank,' Sara called after them. 'No falling in!'

But for the whisper of far-off traffic on the road half a mile away and the muffled drubbing noise of barges farther up by the viaduct, the only sound was the rustle of Benji working through his second packet of crisps. Sara moved the depleted food basket and plastic boxes off the blanket, lay down on her back and watched the clouds twisting in the sky, calculating when the next would cover the sun and bring the sudden, unwelcome cooling that would drain the blue from the water. Andrew was lying nearer the bank and she stretched down one bare foot, found his shoulder and made him jump. He grabbed the foot and tickled it until she squawked and pulled it away.

Dan appeared and squatted by the basket.

'Found any good grass?' Sara asked, with her eyes closed.

'Not doing that any more,' he said. 'We're watching ants now. Aw, Benji's got more crisps, c'n I have more?' He began foraging in the basket. 'D'you want any more to eat, Sara? There's more bread.' He looked up. 'Want another sandwich, Sara? I could do it.'

It was an impressive show of manners from a nine-year-old, Sara thought, still lying on her back and smiling up at him upside down. He had clearly calmed down and was trying to show there were no hard feelings. She did not want more to eat but it was important that she accept the offering.

'Yes, thanks, Dan, I will. There's a bit of pâté and lettuce to finish. Can you manage? Want me to do it?'

'No! I'm doing it. Shut your eyes and I'll surprise you.'

'Careful with the knife, then.'

Five minutes later, when there was almost as much mayonnaise between the pieces of bread as there was on the grass, Sara sat up in obedience to Dan's command, took her ragged sandwich and bit into it. After two or three chews she jumped to her feet and spat out the mouthful across the water. The ducks scattered, splashing.

'Oh! What's in this? Dan?'

Andrew got up. 'Dan, you little—! Was that a joke? Dan! Christ!'

Sara stared at the water where, among the floating, half-chewed white and green shreds of bread and lettuce, were the black tatters of berries. She had nearly swallowed a mouthful of deadly nightshade and was still holding in her hand the rest of a highly toxic sandwich. Just then Dan dashed forward and planted a kick on his father's shin.

'I hate you, I hate you! I hate you, Dad! I hate you!' Andrew now had hold of the flailing arms. Dan's face was unrecognisable with rage.

'Dan! Dan! What's this? What the—'

'I *hate* you! I hate you! You're horrible! You're a horrible Dad! Mum says you're horrible to all of us now because of Sara! You promised we'd go to Legoland and you're not meant to break promises! You're meant to keep a promise! Mum cries every day because you're so horrible and I hate you!'

'Dan, listen—'

'And I'm not called Dan any more! I'm DANIEL! It's not Dan, it's DANIEL! Mum told you and you can't even remember! So don't call me *Dan*!'

'Dan—Daniel, wait—'

But Daniel had already turned his tearful red face away from his father and was tearing off back down the towpath in the direction of Bathampton Lock.

*   *   *

NATALIE AND Benji took advantage of the stunned, silent condition of the grown-ups to crunch through almost a whole tin of travel sweets on the way home. Daniel too, having walked ahead furiously by himself to the car, stared out of the window without speaking. When Andrew delivered the children up at Valerie's doorstep, he waited until the three of them had trooped off into the house and out of earshot. Sara watched from the car as he raised a hand against Valerie's opening tirade for bringing them back at three o'clock when she had told him five. She was standing mouthing in the doorway, her arms folded like a bouncer, dressed aggressively in red trousers and a black sleeveless polo neck. Sara wound down the window and listened.

'No, *you* listen,' Andrew was shouting. 'I have something to say. Are you listening?' His voice was shaking with anger. Valerie uncrossed and crossed her arms and looked out distantly somewhere over his shoulder to indicate that she was, grudgingly.

'Ask Dan what he did today. See if he tells you. Just in case he doesn't, I will. He tried to poison Sara. Not very cleverly, but he tried, and the reason was because he was so angry with me. Not just about Legoland, though you fucked that up beautifully for us all, thank you very much.'

Valerie opened her mouth to speak but Andrew stopped her. 'No, no, don't tell me again it's natural he should be angry because we all know that. But whether he tells you what he did today or not, I want you to tell *him* something. Tell him why his father doesn't live with him any more. Tell him it wasn't just about Sara. Why not tell him you had an affair of your own, and you didn't even *want* me to stay. I really do hope you're listening, Valerie, because if you don't tell him I am going to contest the arrangement and get them with me at least half the time.

Do you understand? Oh, and that was another great job you did, not telling me he wants to be called Daniel. Only *he's* the one it hurt.'

Valerie responded just as he knew she would, with an absolutely predictable, bog-standard, averagely hostile slam of the door in his face. Andrew returned to the car. Sara had moved into the driver's seat. She drove off with a slight crunch from first into second gear. Andrew did not speak at first. He was half-wondering, now that he had said what he meant to Valerie for the first time in a while, why he should feel not in the least better for it.

'Thanks for driving. Sorry. This was meant to be a nice day.'

'I don't feel like going home yet, do you?' she asked, leaving aside the question of where home was, exactly. She had suddenly remembered that the kitchen in Medlar Cottage was bedecked with Happy Birthday banners and that Daniel's cake, saying 'Happy Birthday, Dan' was sitting on the table, awaiting the teatime return of five happy picnickers. She must spare Andrew the sight of it, if only for a time.

Andrew stared out the window at the rain. 'Eclipse day tomorrow,' he said, miserably. 'I thought of taking the kids to Cornwall for it but then I thought no, money's too tight. I wish I were, though.'

Sara did not reply, but turned the car down North Parade towards the centre of town.

'Where are we going?'

'Pump Room,' she said, with decision. 'We are going to drown our sorrows in tea and bury them under clotted cream. I am taking you to tea and I am going to get so fat

I'll have to wear a parachute instead of a dress in Salzburg and I don't care.'

Her stomach lurched suddenly at the thought of Salzburg and the Dvořák which had taken on, in her mind, the shape of a high wall. Her earlier confidence with it had gone. There was something now that she could almost hear in it that was demanding a gigantic leap of courage from her, a leap that she knew she should be able to make but did not always manage to. Something had raised the fence—but, please God, not Joyce's comments—and she felt afraid that she might be too small and weak, musically speaking, to clear the new height. She calmed herself with the thought that she had four days to work on it before Sunday. And if it was rather calculating of her to attend to Andrew's problems over tea for what remained of this afternoon because she was going to dump all concern for him for the rest of the week, well, that, she thought inarticulately, was just too bad.

For the next precious four days she was going to rid her life of clutter and do nothing but work. Except, of course, for meeting Stephen Golightly tomorrow, whose invitation to discuss 'one or two concerns', when he had telephoned yesterday, she had unaccountably found herself able to accept. After that, all distractions—a category into which she now ruthlessly lumped Andrew and his children along with Joyce and even James—in fact any other human being who might make the mistake of wanting something from her would not be tolerated. People were wrong to expect it; she was an artist, a musician, not the bloody fount of all compassion.

CHAPTER 27

THEY HAD SPENT a relaxing three-quarters of an hour over tea in the gracious Pump Room, listening to the pianist, eating cake and discussing methods of killing Valerie, when Sara, idly fingering the menu card, turned over the last page and read that today's pianist at afternoon tea was Alex Cooper. She looked behind her at the grudging girl as she plinked from *Summertime* to *Smoke Gets in Your Eyes*, and searched her memory. She was sure she had not met her before. Then it came to her. James, lying up at the top of the garden of the Sulis, had told her there was quite a good piano there, a baby Blüthner. And in the piano stool of the baby Blüthner he had found music belonging to the departed music therapist with the amusing name. The name which someone kept getting wrong—Alice Cooper instead of Alex Cooper. As the music trudged on, Sara looked more closely at the pianist. Alex Cooper's new job as Pump Room pianist did not seem particularly to agree with her. The tight little face with small, toffee-coloured eyes, the tense shoulders and decorous playing posture suggested someone who was not a natural performer, and the popular numbers being tapped out on the piano correctly, but devoid of grace, personality or swing, confirmed it. She wore no jewellery or make-up. Her clothes carried too little impact to offend; all that could be said of them was that they covered her body in the same way that her hair did nothing for her except cover her head. Alex Cooper's message to the world was not just that she was not a natural performer, it was that she would prefer not to be noticed at all.

But she would prefer, surely, to be told that several pounds' worth of her music was still in the piano stool at the Sulis when she must have given it up as lost. Alex Cooper was clearly not prosperous enough—who would be?—to lose it all, a collection probably acquired over years. Sara got up and approached the platform just as the few people in the Pump Room not holding teacups or cake forks began to applaud the last tinkling notes of the set. Alex turned her dead eyes towards Sara, expecting to deliver an indulgent reply to some standard question about the music.

'You used to work at the Sulis, didn't you?' Sara asked instead, which provoked in Alex a sudden, violent blush.

'The Sulis on Bathwick Hill? Didn't you use to work there?'

'The Sulis? *Oh*. Oh, well, yes. Yes, but not for very long.' She shook her head as if to indicate that this was all she knew on the subject, then turned and began to leaf through the music on the piano.

'It's just that when you left—'

'I left ages ago. I'm supposed to be playing,' Alex said with a nervous, managing smile, 'I'm sorry.' She launched with inappropriate aggression into *Edelweiss*. Sara, puzzled, thought for a moment about shouting above the racket but, concluding that the good turn she was trying to do Alex Cooper was one the girl did not deserve, shrugged and returned to her seat. Andrew raised an eyebrow and patiently poured her another cup of tea.

'What on earth were you saying to her? By the look on her face you were pointing out what a piss-poor pianist she is.'

Sara explained and then said, 'Don't know why she was so odd about it. She wouldn't even talk to me.'

'You told her who you were, I suppose?'

'Of course I didn't. Why should I?'

Andrew shook his head slowly, amused. 'You are hopeless. When will you ever learn to take advantage of your celebrity status?' He rose and made his way to the piano, where Alex was just gathering up her music.

A moment later he led a smiling but no less pink or embarrassed Alex to the table. 'I *thought* it was you! Then I thought, it *can't* be, then you asked me about the Sulis . . . gosh, it's great to meet you!' she gushed. 'I can see it's you now, of course! I heard you on the radio.'

She looked uncertainly back at Andrew, who nodded encouragingly. 'I can't believe you're asking *me* to join you for tea . . . but if you're *sure* . . . of course I'd love to, if you're really sure . . .'

Andrew had found another cup and chair. He put tea into one and Alex into the other and said, 'Sara said she wanted to meet you.' Alex beamed and glowed. 'Didn't you, Sara? So, Alex, how long have you been playing the Pump Room?'

Alex's face dulled for a moment before she took a deep breath and launched into a résumé of her life and musical education to date, its central feature being her college course (an indecipherable mix of music, therapeutic tools, expression and empowerment), culminating in a deeply felt commitment to exploring issues around creativity, serving the community, pushing back boundaries and breaking down barriers. Sara felt herself beginning to sink under the weight of this very old young woman.

'This is only a stopgap,' Alex said, nodding towards the piano on the platform. 'I want to do something worthwhile. I hate those stupid songs, they're so trite. And I get fed up playing for just tourists.'

'I'm off to Salzburg in a day or two,' Sara murmured. 'I should think I'll be playing to tourists there. But if you don't like it here, why did you leave the Sulis? You left all your music behind, you know. That's what I was trying to let you know.'

Alex coloured hotly again. '*Oh*. Oh well, I . . .'

'It's still in the piano stool. My friend found it. You could come up and collect it. Do you want me to tell them—'

'Sara,' Andrew cut in, 'I'm sure Alex can organise all that herself when she has time.'

Alex blinked gratefully at Andrew and relaxed a little. 'I haven't actually been back, not since I left,' she said confidingly.

Into the following silence Sara lobbed, conversationally, 'My friend heard from Sister Yvonne you left quite suddenly. Didn't you get on with Dr Golightly?'

'Oh, no, that wasn't it! He—he was fine, I suppose, only—look, I don't want you to think there's anything weird about me or anything.' She paused. Sara looked at her, trying not to look too interested. But what was it that made it impossible for this woman to discuss Stephen Golightly without expiring with embarrassment?

'I know I left my music behind. But I haven't been back for it because I didn't like what was going on there.' She gave a small sniff and drank her tea, hoping that that explanation would close the subject.

'Really? But Dr Golightly seems such a good doctor. Everyone says so. He's treating one of my dearest friends.' Sara was beaming with curiosity and goodwill, as if Alex Cooper were the most fascinating person ever to have honoured her by accepting an invitation to tea. And Alex fell for it, being too young and impressed to suggest that Sara mind her own business.

'No, no, I didn't mean that. He is a good doctor. It's just . . . other things. Things that weren't very professional. I . . . I didn't like the accommodation.'

Sara poured more tea into Alex's cup and lowered her voice. 'Tell me, go on. It's all right, I never betray secrets. But I really *must* know, I mean, if something unprofessional's going on. I don't want my friend suffering in any way. You do see, don't you?'

Alex mentally folded away the last shreds of her discretion under the flattering glow of Sara's attention. 'Oh, I don't mean unprofessional as far as the patients go. I mean other people, other things.'

'To do with the staff, do you mean? So what was wrong with your accommodation, exactly?'

'The staff were— Look, I can't go into it. But there was something going on. An affair. I didn't like that, I don't approve of things like that. Because I could overhear them when I was in my room. Him and the nurse—you know . . . Yvonne. I heard them—having an affair.'

'You mean Dr Golightly and Yvonne? You heard them making love in his flat? God, how *dreadfully* embarrassing!'

Sara stifled an urge to laugh. The thought of pretty, cheeky Yvonne and Stephen was rather sweet, if uncomfortably like a *Carry On* film. But why should the fact suddenly have increased his attractiveness?

Alex seemed a little peeved that her bombshell seemed to amuse rather than shock. Primly she said, 'I never actually saw them, but I—you know—heard noises. And she worships the ground he walks on, she's really obvious. But I wonder at *him*.'

'But perhaps he was lonely. Why shouldn't he? He's not married.'

'No, but *she* is, or she's got a partner, she was always going on about him, Chris this, Chris that. He drove a Securicor van or something. Anyway it's *disgusting* at her age and it's completely unprofessional. I couldn't very well go on listening to it, could I? So I left.'

'It was either soundproof your room or leave, then,' Sara almost giggled until a glance at Alex made it clear that levity was not welcome. 'Sorry, it wasn't funny for you, obviously.'

'I was *distraught*. I had to leave. I had nobody to turn to. Ivan saw I was upset and I told him. He's very sensitive. He's like his father the way he understands things, deep down.' Alex's voice had grown calmer.

Andrew asked, 'What did he say? I mean, what did he think about his father . . . you know?'

'He just said not to say anything to anybody because it could damage the clinic. He didn't seem all that surprised. I mean, he understood why I had to leave.'

Sara frowned. Why hadn't the silly little prude just made some noise of her own, played the radio very loud or just gone out? She looked at Andrew, whose eyes held the same concealed mirth at the farcical set-up, and then she knew. The reason why Alex Cooper had been unable to stand the sound of Dr Golightly making love with Yvonne was that she was in love with him herself.

'Poor you,' she told Alex, sincerely. 'Look, shall I get the music for you? I'm going there tomorrow.'

'Are you? I don't think you said,' Andrew murmured. 'I thought you were working.'

'Apart from that I will be. Dr Golightly asked to see me. He has one or two "concerns" to discuss, I *hope* not about Joyce. Shall I, Alex? I could bring it and leave it here for you if you like.'

'Oh you wouldn't, would you? Could you really? That would be wonderful.' Alex's eyes took on a luminous gleam like a spaniel's. 'I can't afford to replace it all but I can't go back. Would you *really*? And . . . do you think I could have an autograph as well?'

CHAPTER 28

THE ECLIPSE WAS a diversion. Sara took off her eclipse glasses and returned to the music room, sorry that the diversion had not been longer or more, well, diverting. The Dvořák still stood on the music stand and was still giving her trouble. Not technically, of course. Sara sat down and again told herself that if she worked on it a little more some elusive quality that she sought—something more supple and giving, nebulous, but more real than the notes of which the piece was made—would somehow manifest itself. Somehow she had to draw that quality out of the notes on the page and somehow she was not managing to do it. Nor had she managed it by the time she packed it in for the afternoon and set off for the Sulis.

*　　*　　*

SHE FOUND Hilary, Joyce and Yvonne staring without speaking at the heap on the floor. There wasn't much: an electronic keyboard, a glockenspiel, four or five recorders, two small guitars, five bongo drums and a triangle. The Welshman and Jane were sitting, unattractively tracksuited, in two of the chairs lined against one wall, waiting for the wonderful healing power of music to work its magic.

'No, but this is great! This lot could be fun!' Sara lied. She picked up a pair of drums and beat what she intended to be a rallying rhythm, which sounded stonily round the austere room. Nobody smiled. Joyce's mouth was clamped shut with distaste. The 'creative space' for music therapy at the Sulis—an almost empty high-ceilinged room which Yvonne had tried to cheer up with a few plants and pictures—had the air of a lost cause. The rebels appeared to have fled to the hills and left an assortment of musical instruments in the middle of the floor like surrendered weapons.

'No, I mean, people will love this. They will!' Sara insisted. 'It's a good start, isn't it, Joyce? You could make a start with the recorders, couldn't you?' She absolutely must get Joyce to stay, even if the descent from music professor to supervisor of toy instruments was a little humiliating. Joyce was not, she sensed from the disdainful lips, quite able to judge how few options she now had, nor willing to accept that any of even these few would involve some downward mobility. Bed, board and medical care at the Sulis in return for teaching music to morons was a damn sight less humiliating than the direction in which Joyce had been heading when Sara had found her.

Not that she had found the heart to spell this out, nor did Joyce appear to be troubled by any sense of obligation or gratitude to her for her intervention. Sara thought that while she did not exactly *require* thanks, it was irritating that Joyce seemed unaware that, but for her, she could by now be domiciled at the back of the bus station with the winos who sat around drinking an interesting range of industrial fluids in between peeing in their clothes and shouting at the walls. And even now, having saved her from that, she could not simply abandon Joyce to make the best of things here.

Joyce had seated herself at the electronic keyboard and was enjoying herself, experimenting with the *Skye Boat Song* on Hawaiian guitar with samba beat, her head down, concentrating. Watching her, Sara felt the weight of responsibility, for having picked Joyce off the street and shown her some hope, it would be infinitely more callous to let her sink now than to have walked by in the first place. Joyce would need her support to meet the challenge of teaching anything again, let alone music therapy. Then there was Joyce's own playing, which Sara had promised to help her with. And at the heart of it all was the little matter of keeping her off the bottle long enough for her to do any of it. And if it hadn't been for that damned pink suit catching her eye, she thought, trying not to grind her teeth, none of this would be her problem.

Joyce had switched to *Comin' Through The Rye* on pan-pipes with echo, and now looked up. She fixed Sara with a look which told her to push off and take her magnanimity with her. 'Would you mind if we got on? I've things to do and I want to get on and get back upstairs to Pretzel. I've a sick dog upstairs so I'd rather we didn't waste any more time. Now, is there no piano?' she said, turning to Hilary and Yvonne. 'Did I not see one in the dining room? I'll have that.'

'Ivan will be up later. Perhaps he can move it,' Hilary said, obligingly. To spite Yvonne, she was being Joyce's best friend. 'I'd love to help myself, but I daren't. Ivan won't let me lift a thing. I'm pregnant, you see.'

'Oh, *congratulations*,' said Sara. The two patients murmured their approval.

Hilary preened. 'Ivan won't hardly let me do *anything* actually, he's spoiling me rotten. Cups of tea, day and night, you name it.'

'My sister couldn't look at tea when she was carrying,' the Welshman said. 'Couldn't touch it, and she used to get through fifty teabags a week.'

'Oh, it's not ordinary tea, it's herbal. Ivan mixes it himself, it's got all the things you should have when you're pregnant. Tastes quite nice.'

'Er, may we discuss the piano?' Yvonne ventured, with insincere sweetness. She had overheard enough simpering accounts of Ivan's devotion to feel she need not acknowledge another. 'It belongs in the dining room. It's a baby grand.'

'But nobody plays it. Anyway,' Hilary said, turning to Sara but still, disconcertingly, talking to Yvonne, 'Miss Selkirk isn't here to listen to our arrangements, is she?' This was true. Sara had been seen into the house by Hilary and, walking ahead, had followed the sound of Joyce's voice through the open door. It was the sight of Joyce, watched by two patients, standing sourly with her hands on her hips over the instruments on the floor that had made Sara fear that she was about to become unbearably grand about the whole thing, and that had started her babbling about fun and recorders.

'It'll need tuning, I suppose,' Joyce was saying now. She looked sternly at them all.

'You're here to see Dr Golightly, aren't you?' Hilary said, this time actually to Sara. 'He was telling me. I expect he'll get you to sign a CD! I'll take you along.'

Sara smiled and turned to follow her. Just before she closed the door she heard the Welshman asking, 'Sign a CD? She famous, is she?' and Joyce replying. 'Och, no. She's just a wee lassie.'

*　　*　　*

STEPHEN GOLIGHTLY'S concerns seemed to be worrying him rather beautifully. He rose to meet Sara and showed her to a chair in his consulting room, and Sara noticed again that he and Andrew had the same sort of strong, long-legged, broad-shouldered body. The sort she could barely take her eyes off, she was now finding. Her two meetings with Stephen Golightly had been brief, and last time most of her energies had been concentrated on getting him to agree to try Joyce out as music therapist. It seemed like a careless oversight not to have noticed then how attractive he was, and it felt like an irrelevance now that he was at least twenty years older than she was.

As she sat down, he remained standing. She observed that where he and Andrew differed most was in the face. Andrew's deep brown eyes could chill or burn at twenty paces, but at times, like now, when he was in one of his patches of miserable inarticulacy over some difficult case or an emotional question concerning his children or both (or, Sara thought guiltily, the problem of where he and Sara wanted to live) his eyes became unreadable, seeming to absorb all available light and defy interpretation. Stephen Golightly's blue eyes were gentler. They invited if not instant trust (because she was not, either on principle or by inclination, as gullible as that) then at least the assurance that one could look for longer and further into them without too much danger, risking at most a pleasurable loss of peace of mind. So she did.

'I'm going to show you something,' he said. He turned to unlock his filing cabinet, allowing Sara to confirm to herself that his rear view was every bit as rewarding as the front. He returned to the armchair opposite hers with two files. 'I do have James's blessing to do this, of course.' He took his seat and opened one of the folders. 'It's rather more serious than we thought. He wants you to be completely in the picture, since Tom is away and can't be here.'

Sara instantly dropped her recreational appreciation of Stephen Golightly's bottom. Her mind seemed suddenly, true to all the clichés, to be simultaneously numb and racing ahead to hear the worst news she would ever hear in her life. She wondered if she was going to choke, or faint, and thought she could feel the colour leaving her face. Dr Golightly, without smiling, leaned towards her. 'I'm sorry I have to give you bad news,' he said. 'It's a shock. Try to breathe deeply, and you'll be all right in a few minutes. Lean back and breathe as deeply as you can.'

Sara obeyed, and in the silence he rose noiselessly, poured a glass of water from a carafe on his desk and returned. Sara took the glass and sipped. It seemed that Dr Golightly had, in the few seconds that her eyes had been closed, filled the room with quiet reassurance. After a moment he removed a piece of paper from the bottom of the pile in the folder. It had *Avon & District-Health Authority Screening Services* in turquoise at the top.

'It's not IBS after all. It's ulcers. I've had James's test results back and it's conclusively not IBS, which we were all hoping it was, since it's easily treatable, although distressing, of course. But I'm afraid there's quite severe ulceration of the duodenum.'

Sara's numbness began to give way to gratitude, perverse though she knew it to be, as if Dr Golightly himself had somehow personally intervened to prevent James's diagnosis from being cancer. She looked up at him and was absurdly comforted by the look in his eyes. Her own had filled with tears of relief.

'*Oh*. Oh, thank God. You're sure—it's an ulcer? Not—not, I mean, it's not worse, is it? It's just an ulcer? I mean, that's bad, I know, but you're sure that's what it is? Because he's going to be all right, isn't he? I mean—'

Dr Golightly said, 'Would you like me to explain?'

Sara closed her mouth and nodded. The eyes were telling her that everything was going to be just fine, so it was unthinkable that the mouth could be about to spout words which would contradict them.

'The duodenum is ulcerated, that's just where the stomach contents empty into the small intestine. James's stomach is producing too much acid which, added to his mucus production being somewhat compromised and probably abnormally high levels of *Helicobacter pylori*, added to psychological and emotional factors, is the cause of the problem.' Dr Golightly paused to make sure that Sara was following him. 'If conventionally treated, he would be stuffed with painkillers, antibiotics and antacids, plus pills to reduce acid secretion, plus pills to help coat the surface of the ulcers, and probably tranquillizers as well. And do you know what would happen then?'

'Um . . . he'd get better?'

'No! *No*. That's the point! Well, of course he'd get better in one sense. His symptoms would be alleviated. But the body would have been bombarded with chemical treatments to deal with the symptoms, while the underlying cause of the illness would not have been addressed. That would go unchecked. Do you see? But *that's* what we'll help him do here. Understand the reasons he got ill, and help him rebalance mentally and physically—spiritually, too, in a sense—so that he gets better *naturally*. And stays better.'

'So you mean he's agreed to this?'

'He has, yes. I've explained to him what we can do here, and what we can't. He doesn't smoke so that's a bonus, he's got to chuck the aspirin and the alcohol, also meat, salt and dairy foods. He understands all that. Then we have to work on mind and body awareness. Staying here and working on posture, breathing, nutrition, massage and relaxation is his best chance of avoiding deterioration, and surgery. And peritonitis, of course.'

'Peritonitis, of *course*? What do you mean?'

Dr Golightly's face grew grave. 'Sometimes, if an ulcer persists, it perforates. When that happens, the contents of the bowel can escape into the peritoneal cavity, causing peritonitis. Very serious. Sometimes fatal. Thankfully rare, though. With proper management, there's no reason not to expect that that can be avoided.'

He picked up one of the folders from the table and returned it to the filing cabinet. Sara rather mechanically drained the water in her glass and Stephen, noticing how shocked she still looked, returned to the chair carrying the carafe.

More gently he said, 'I am sorry to be landing you with this. James isn't feeling too well today, not surprisingly, and asked me to tell you myself how things stand.'

Sara nodded. 'Thank you. Now I must go. Can I see him?'

Dr Golightly filled her glass again. 'I really do think better not, just for today,' he said. 'He's very weary, and he's just making a gentle start on his treatments. He still has quite a lot to go through. Treatment can be quite demanding on a patient, that's why we advocate lots of rest. We wouldn't want to exhaust him, would we? And there's Joyce,' he added rather quickly, 'who I hoped to have a word with you about, too.'

Here it comes, Sara thought. In the interests of other users, please take your rubbish home. Do not leave your baggage unattended. Get her out of here. Bus station, here we come. But Stephen was opening the folder still on the table. 'She's had a full medical questionnaire and examination, of course,' he said, 'and she's put you down as next of kin.'

'But I'm not! We're not related at all,' Sara exclaimed.

Dr Golightly looked at her intently. 'Nevertheless, you are the person she wishes to have contacted in the event of any medical or other emergency. Wouldn't you wish to be contacted if anything serious should develop? Are you saying you're not willing to stand in that capacity, should there be any sort of crisis?'

A vision of an irate, thin-lipped ghost in a pink wool suit and a whining Pretzel scratching at the soil over an un-marked grave rose in Sara's mind. 'No, no, I'm not saying that,' she said, defeated. 'Of course I would want to be contacted. So, when do you want me to collect her things?'

'Collect her things? Oh, I do assure you, it's not as bad

as all that. Nothing we can't address, certainly. Of course I *am* only a doctor.' His lips were twitching.

He's practically laughing at me, Sara thought, and set her mind firmly against blushing. Or smiling back.

'No need to look so solemn,' Stephen went on, consulting the notes. 'Her nutritional status is poor. There's generally poor organ condition. Some spontaneous bruising, fortunately mild, but probably due to poor diet, mainly vitamin C deficiency.' He pulled an X-ray from an envelope in Joyce's folder and held it up for Sara to look at. 'Just got these back. Look here, do you see?' He tapped the larger and darker of two patches. 'The main problem is underlying kidney stress. If she continues to abuse alcohol, it'll be the liver next and she won't be long for this world.'

'Why,' Sara suddenly asked, 'are you telling me all this? About James, and now Joyce? I don't see what I can do.'

Dr Golightly replaced the X-ray in its envelope, raised his eyes and looked at her for a time without speaking. In his faintly surprised expression Sara saw not only that she had been judged, but that she had disappointed.

'Forgive me, of course you needn't involve yourself at all.'

'It's just that I'm very busy. I've got to go to Salzburg very soon, and I've got things I have to see to—at home, you see. Things.' She tailed off hopelessly. How could the current unresolved mess with Dvořák, the problem of Andrew (was that what he now was?) be explained to this stranger, except by some such inadequate phrase? She looked at him with defiance. Let Dvořák and Andrew be reduced to things to see to at home, then. It was still true.

Dr Golightly said gently, 'Joyce is possibly on the cusp, as it were. The body is a wonderful thing.' With you there,

Sara thought. 'Even after such neglect, the body will regenerate to a remarkable degree if it gets the right fuel. Everything here is home-made and organic, you know. If we can't source it easily we grow it ourselves, even some of our own cereals. Joyce could expect several more good years if she starts to look after herself now. Conversely, her body won't take much more if she doesn't.'

Sara bit her lip. 'But someone I know, who's seen a lot of this, says nobody can help an alcoholic who doesn't want help.' Andrew's point of view sounded like heresy in this humane, optimistic atmosphere and Sara knew she did not believe it, anyway.

'I haven't seen any evidence yet that she doesn't want it. And I was assuming that you would wish to help. The regime here is not always an easy one, and a supportive, loving friend can make all the difference.' He smiled. 'I'm only the doctor, I can only advise. The real healing is done by the patient, and patients who are supported by love do best of all. In that sense, you and I would be partners in helping Joyce and James heal themselves.'

Sara felt every bit as guilty as this was designed to make her feel. 'Of course I want to help them. I just don't see how I can. Much, I mean.'

'Oh, a little support goes a long way. Just be here, talk to them, encourage them? Help them feel they're getting better. Could you do that, Sara?'

He got up to replace the folders in the filing cabinet and Sara, watching him move across the room, supposed that Dvořák and Andrew notwithstanding, perhaps she could.

CHAPTER 29

AMES SAW SARA go, aching inwardly because he had
agreed to not having visitors today. Looking up from
his lump of clay he gazed out through the window of
the art studio across to the fountain and watched her stroll
with Dr Golightly around it. Both heads, inclined downwards in apparent contemplation of the formal planting
that surrounded it, were being raised from time to time,
perhaps to respond to whatever the other might be saying
but more likely simply to look at the other, a thing that
each of them seemed to find pleasurable, judging by the
amount of smiling that was going on. They were walking
much more slowly than was necessary and by the most indirect route to the car park. James watched their polite
orbit of each other, observing how mutual attraction
sometimes made people quite delectably uncomfortable.
Stephen Golightly and Sara were behaving like a man and
woman who had already undressed each other, at least
mentally, but were painfully conscious of having been too
recently introduced to have done so with any propriety.

If he could find the energy, he thought, he would tease
her about Stephen Golightly next time she visited. Then his
heart suddenly sagged as he remembered that she would be

off to Salzburg soon. It would not be for long, but at the thought of her being so far away a little more spirit leaked out of him. To the list of afflictions contributing to his general wretchedness he could now add a slight loss of balance, disturbing dreams and cramps in the extremities, all of which he had been given to understand were terrifically good things to have. These were signs that his body was responding to the naturopathic regime and ridding itself of toxins. It had also, he had pointed out weakly, rid itself of lunch today. He had been terribly sick, but not so terribly that he had failed to notice that the vegetable cobbler had looked much the same when it had reappeared as it had the first time. He wanted to grumble and moan and say evil, cynical things about naturopathy. He wanted Sara.

He turned back to his clay, pulled off a piece, whacked it around a bit and rolled it into a sausage. Prodding it around and sharpening one end, he saw that he had accidentally made a fairly passable vagina.

'Oh, how sweet!' croaked a voice nearby. Bunny, turning her attention from a mound of clay with one ear, was pointing at James's effort with a forefinger like a mudencrusted twig and peering at him with screwed-up eyes. James smashed his clay into a flat heap.

'Oh, you've spoiled it,' she cried. 'You've spoiled your little horse collar. Didn't you like it?'

'No.'

'Hilary says we need to accept our early efforts for what they are,' Warwick offered, from the other side of Bunny's table. 'Don't you, Hilary?' He was turning his head from side to side and rubbing his neck, seizing the moment when Bunny's attention had wandered to drop his pose. 'That's exactly what I did. My early efforts were total rubbish. That's what I told our Yorkshire lass, didn't I, Hilary? Total rubbish, never had any talent. Quite happy to let others get on with it. Quite happy to pose.' He smiled foolishly at Bunny. 'Bunny's forging ahead now with my head, aren't you? So glad to see you so much better, my dear. Quite your old self again.'

'Oh, quite,' Bunny conceded. 'I'm perfectly all right.' As long as she said she was, perhaps she would be. She was better, certainly, if not quite better. It was extraordinary, when one had learned how to listen, just what one's body could tell one. 'I *did* feel off, I can tell you. Poor Pet and Hugh are in high dudgeon of course. Do you know, the silly things cancelled their *gîte*? Why they did on my account I don't know, when I'm the last to ask . . .' She looked at Warwick. 'Actually I do know,' she said, in a louder voice. 'Between you and me and these four walls,' she seemed quite comfortable about including everyone else currently within the walls, 'it's all about M-O-N-E-Y. They can't wait for me to go because they think they're getting it all. Ha! And they think I don't realise.' Warwick coughed. Bunny pursed up her lips with satisfaction and looked back at James's clay. 'Are you going to make a horse with that? Hilary, look! I think James is making a horse.'

Hilary had been washing clay tools over at the sink. She made her way across the room.

'I'm not making a horse,' James said. 'Of course I'm not. But I don't really know what else to do. I don't know where to start.'

Hilary sat down on a stool opposite and gazed solidly at James. She preferred patients not to be artists of any sort themselves. They tended to have ideas, which could, as she liked to put it, cloud their responses. 'Remember what we said,' she began in her sensible voice, 'remember what we said about needing to forget what we already know. Don't think about what you know. It can cloud your responses. You don't need to know a thing.'

Behind her, Warwick was casting heavenward glances.

'We need to bypass, in a sense, what we know, and try to get on to a little side road of what we *feel*, physically and emotionally. Feeling is just another way of knowing, if you think about it. Only I don't want you to think about it. You're trying to get in touch. You're trying to tune in. That's where you found it hard, isn't it, Warwick?'

She turned just in time to see Warwick roll his eyes and draw a finger across his throat. 'Oh ignore him,' she said good-naturedly. 'Yes, *thank* you, Warwick.' She turned back, smiling. She found herself smiling more, now. People like Warwick, who once had made her job frustrating, now made her smile, because no frustration could touch her underneath her armour of happiness. She was safe from fools like Warwick. She folded her hands over her stomach. 'Now, James, just ignore Warwick. He's just trying to get a rise. I'll set Ivan on you, I will, you're an old cynic, aren't you?'

'Oi! Less of the "old", young lady!'

'Warwick! Don't move! Look at me. I'm trying to get your ear,' Bunny ordered.

'Now,' Hilary said gently to James, 'how the body *feels* is the issue. Once you have rediscovered how the body is feeling, the mind can help it recover.' She beamed. 'Try visualisation. Try to visualise your problem, in the part of your body that is unwell. Visualise in clay. Shape your health problem in clay, in any way you feel is right. Just let go.'

'You want me to sit here making clay ulcers all afternoon?'

Hilary would not be defeated. 'What I want is not the issue, James. It's what you want that counts. I'm going to leave you to try visualising, so if you're happy to get on, I think Jane needs some help.'

She rose and went to attend to the unhappy Jane who, alone in a corner of the studio, was silently wrapping coathangers together. Warwick broke the silence that followed by saying, 'Ulcers, hmmm. Had 'em myself. Four. Japanese rations. Painful. Lost a lot of weight.'

James was grateful for the sympathy but hoped Warwick was not going to elaborate.

'You can tell that was a long time ago,' Bunny said without irony. 'Have you lost any, by the way?' She scanned his torso with crooked black eyes. 'It doesn't look like it. And Dr Golightly's diets always work. You must be cheating.'

'You've seen what I eat, Bunny dear. Practically the same as you.'

'You don't eat your bread.'

'I do. I just don't eat it with meals. I keep it and eat it later.' Warwick coughed.

'I shall mention to Dr Golightly next time I see him that you're not losing weight,' Bunny said, loudly. 'He likes to know.'

'Oh, don't bother, please,' Warwick said. 'No need.'

Bunny had risen laboriously to her feet to refill the beaker of water that was keeping the clay damp. Something through the window drew her attention. 'Oh, look! There he is now, coming back from the car park! Let's catch him now. I'm sure if I wave—'

'Bunny, stop! Sit down! Please, sit *down*.' Warwick's voice was unusually fierce.

Bunny did so. 'But—'

He sighed. 'I'm having a bit of trouble, if you must know, getting into the swing of this diet.' Warwick's voice had dropped to a whisper, and his guilty eyes included James, perhaps in the hope that he would judge him more leniently than the iron-willed Bunny. 'Find the damned bread hard to take dry. Reminds me of the bad old days under the Japs, if you must know. So I've got myself a little supply. Just a little, you know, little picnic box, keep it in my room. Bit of butter makes all the difference.'

'You've been spreading the bread with butter? Ivan's lovely bread? *Butter?*' Bunny's scandalised voice made it sound as if Warwick had eviscerated his own mother and spread the bread with the proceeds. 'Hilary, did you hear that? Warwick's been spreading his bread with butter!'

'Good man, Warwick,' James said. 'Good man.'

Hilary turned. 'Oh *Warwick*,' she sighed. 'What are we to do with you?'

Warwick looked ashamed. 'Oh come on, you understand surely, a Yorkshire lass like you, brought up on best booter, eh? I mean, I'm happy to cooperate and all that. Quite see the importance. It's only a scrape, to help it down.'

'But really—*butter!*' Bunny said. She looked rather pale.

'Wouldn't like Dr G to know, rather not discuss it. Couldn't tell him a lie, such a nice fellow. So let it lie, eh, Bunny?'

Warwick coughed stiffly to indicate that no reply was necessary and resumed his pose. Bunny shrugged in James's direction and took up her modelling tool again. And as she lifted it in her trembling hand to cut into the clay, she looked at it a little longingly, rather as if it were a butter knife.

CHAPTER 30

LEECH HALF WOKE and stretched, feeling the sting of early morning cold on his bare feet as they pushed down out of the covers and dangled beyond the end of the folding bed. He was too long for beds and he did not really remember a time when he had not been, so the day's first sensation on his feet, which brought always the wearying thought that the hut was cold, was in order. He kept his face submerged in the jumper he used as a pillow but then came the second, the same chill stealing over his head. He turned and lay staring up, just in case today the jumper might warm rather than merely scratch the back of his skull a little and although it did not, he stayed there, his eyes searching the wooden ribs of the hut roof for anything unsettling, anything not as yesterday, as far as he could remember yesterday. His blocked nose was clearing now, with the softly rushing, itchy sensation that he had grown used to. He sniffed, and the mixed smells of dust and earth and salty feet gave him further reassurance that nothing had changed. So, secure in his mind that nothing had happened in the night that would call for any rearrangement of his expectations, quite sure that the hut was again freezing and that this day was so far consistent with others, Leech got out of bed.

Yet the day was different, or was going to be. Leech stepped on shaking legs out of the hut into the first light. Too early to say when the dawn clouds would shift, but today's happenings in the sky would go beyond mere weather. This day would be different. But when Leech tried to find words for the difference none came to him save those which he had heard others say: *momentous, epoch-making, historic, unique* and which, being other people's, remained just words. This day would also be, he remembered hearing, a once-in-a-lifetime experience, an idea which filled him with foreboding. Leech had had many of those. Once in a lifetime came horribly often, he found. For how long is a lifetime? Only as long as memory made it. It should be a long, unbroken tunnel between the very first thing he ever remembered—sunlight sparkling on the hairs on the sleeping dog's back that he saw from high up in someone's arms that day—and right now, today, the view of the hut roof when he opened his eyes on this August morning in 1999, aged thirty-one. But in Leech's tunnel there had been many rockfalls. His tunnel was a series of small dark chambers without doors, in every one of which a short lifetime had been lived.

Leech's lifetimes came by in turn and ended again once or twice a week, each lasting a few days at most. Once lived, the memory of them would remain close by for a time and then develop a tendency to stray, returning grudgingly, then not at all. His most loyal memory was his lifetime as a child. It remained somewhere not far off and lit by a weak, kindly beam, like the recollection of a story once read under the bedclothes about another boy a bit like him. Other lifetimes left no trace at all. He bore scars on his body from wounds he supposed he had suffered,

and sometimes deduced from the state of his fingernails
and hair, which continued to grow in what felt, impossibly, like his absence, that his life must somehow be passing.
He wore clothes which looked familiar, as if he had seen
them once on a long-dead relative who, he almost saved
himself from realising, was himself. Only his love for Ivan
joined up the days and gave him a part of his life that he
could feel was truly his.

Still barefoot, he strolled round to the water butt on
the side of the hut. It was almost full because it had rained
for most of July, although Leech was not up to that degree
of reflection on weather so long ago lived through. He
scooped up a handful of water and drank it, and with another handful loosened some of the grime on his face, and
used both hands to smear it into fresh streaks. Then he
weighed his scrotum inattentively in one cupped hand,
peed into the hedge, scratched his armpits and finger-
combed his hair, yawning. He returned to the hut, put on
his shoes, pulled on his jumper and came out again, dragging a blanket with him and pulling it round his shoulders.

Birds were starting to sing, and Leech could now see
the torn silver lace of night-spun cobwebs stretching
across between the rows of vegetables, down to the high
boundary hedge. Leech waited. Then, not knowing if what
he sensed were a movement from the ground or a sound
upon the air, he began to run, stripping and tearing the
threads of spider silk hanging between the vegetable rows.
He reached the bottom of the garden just as the scream of
the first train tore the curtain of the morning in two. He
stopped, gazed upwards and watched open-mouthed as
the silver and yellow train ripped past, unzipping the seam
between hedge top and sky.

It passed. Leech yawned again, rearranged his blanket round his shoulders and turned back down towards the shed. Skirting past the ranks of undisturbed beans, peas and lettuces, still trussed with the silver wire of the spiders, he tramped across the empty half acre of rye field until he reached the gap between the fruit cages where he could see the back of the house. There was nothing to see except the patch of poor grass, Hilary's whirligig for drying the flowered bed linen, a few herbs among the concrete slabs by the back door, and the outside tap. The curtains were closed. Good. Leech crouched down between the blackcurrants and the raspberries, picked a few and ate them. Then he sat down, wrapped his blanket round him, and waited. Ivan and Hilary were safe and sound, he could feel it. Safe and sound. Leech's eyes took in their curtained bedroom window above the dining room and scanned across to the smaller window whose curtains were not drawn. Nobody else, then. No B&B guests last night. Leech sighed with pleasure, fished in his clothing for his stuff, rolled a cigarette and lit it. He didn't like the B&B guests much. Ivan never said *come on down to the house after* when there were B&B guests around. There had been a nice one once whom he remembered for some particular reason, though the reason itself eluded him. She was nice. Very small she was, tiny. You could lift her like she was a doll or something. He did remember that.

*   *   *

HILARY LOOKED out the window as she filled the kettle and watched without surprise as Leech plodded across the grass and waited by the door. She opened it and nodded him in without smiling. It was too much to smile when she did not feel either fully awake or at all welcoming, and since Ivan was not yet down she did not have to find the energy to pretend. Ivan's raw diet seemed to be helping with the nausea though, or perhaps it was the ginger tea or the acupressure he regularly did on her arms. Quite possibly it was just the loving care he was now giving her that made her feel better. At the thought, she smiled fondly at Leech who, in answer, slid into his usual seat at the table in one corner. A smile meant there was a good chance of breakfast.

Hilary had already set out on a chopping board what looked to Leech like far too much fruit, when Ivan appeared in the doorway. He smiled at Leech, opened the fridge and pulled out from the back a torn plastic packet, holding it up between one finger and thumb.

'This wants using up,' he said. 'Leech can have this, can't he, Hil?' Hilary peered at the packet and nodded. She could not, either in conscience or in Health & Safety, put such elderly bacon before B&B guests, if they had had any. Ivan said brightly, 'I'll do it. Want some fried bread with that, Leech?'

Leech nodded happily. Breakfast, when it came a few minutes later, was the best he had ever had. The bacon was good. And the fried bread, although brown, had been fried by Ivan, which made it a once-in-a-lifetime breakfast.

'A once-in-a-lifetime breakfast,' he said throatily, watching Ivan and Hilary eat the last of their fruit. He had not noticed the silence, but noticed now that Ivan and Hilary exchanged a look. Hilary got up and began clearing plates.

'We've got something to tell you,' Ivan said, and hesitated. 'Something that's going to happen soon.'

But Leech was too clever for that. He nodded and spluttered, trying to talk too fast. 'I know. I know. A big thing's happening.' His voice was rusty from under-use. 'Today. The eclipse. That's happening today, yeah? Once in a lifetime. See? I know.' He sat back, beaming with pride.

Ivan and Hilary looked at each other again, worried. Ivan said gently, 'The eclipse was yesterday, man. Remember? You were with me. We watched it together. Hilary was at the clinic. All right, man?'

Leech stared at him. Slowly, he shook his head. He might remember and he might not. 'Yeah,' he said, so as not to disappoint Ivan.

'The thing is, the summer's going to be over soon, isn't it,' Hilary stated. 'The weather's going to change, isn't it? It'll be too cold for the hut, soon.'

She was now wiping round the sink with an antiseptic-soaked paper towel from a plastic box. Ivan watched while Leech, who may or may not have taken in what she was saying, looked down at his empty plate.

'I mean you've been very welcome,' she said, with the merest emphasis on 'been'. 'Ever so welcome, really, hasn't he, Ivan?'

Her eyes pleaded with Ivan to do the next bit for her. Ivan drew in a deep, reluctant breath. 'It's been good to have you, man,' he said. 'Really good. I mean, I really appreciated the help, it was great having you. The radicchio this year—wow!'

Leech's face brightened and he looked up, nodding. 'Yeah! And the . . . the strawberries! Yeah, they were good.'

'They were! They were really good. We don't want you to think that we don't really, really appreciate it. Do we, Hil?'

Leech nodded with satisfaction and returned to his plate, prodding up single crumbs of bread with one forefinger and putting them in his mouth.

'It's just that,' Hilary began again, knowing that Ivan had done his worst and she could look to him for no more, 'well, we did say. I mean, there's still lots of picking to do so maybe you could help out now and then but the really busy time's over, isn't it. And do you remember Ivan told you that we're going to have a baby?' She allowed herself a smile and a lift in her voice. She looked at Ivan and the now customary look of private joy was exchanged, a look which said in a glance, yes of course everybody's pleased for us but nobody else knows how happy we *really* are.

Leech frowned. There was a familiarity in the statement that made him suppose that it had cropped up before. Hilary lifted his plate away and wiped hard with her antiseptic paper at the place where it had been. Depositing the plate on the side of the sink she turned and looked hard at Ivan once more. He responded with an encouraging smile. She sighed. 'The thing is, we've been quite happy to have you here, you know, for meals and washing and the odd bath and so on.' Leech nodded as if to say it was nothing, he'd been pleased to oblige. 'Only with the baby, it'll be more difficult. Do you see?'

Leech did not, and was studying the table top. 'And as I say the summer's nearly over, so you couldn't go on staying in the hut anyway. It'll be too cold soon. It's been ever so cold anyway, this summer, you can't have been that comfortable. We wouldn't feel right, you staying in that hut much longer.'

Leech wiped his hand back and forth over his mouth, considering. He looked up at Ivan. 'Can kip in the house, then, can I?'

Ivan could tell by Hilary's face as she turned to the sink and turned on the hot tap that she was not going to say the next bit. 'Hilary's saying,' he said, looking at her back rather than at Leech's stone eyes, 'Hilary's saying that it's maybe time to think about where you're going to go next. After here. It's time to move on, do you see? Hilary's worried about you in the hut. Because we'll be a bit crowded with the baby, see what I mean?' When Leech did not reply he said as firmly as he could, 'You can't kip here. I mean, we'll see what we can do, getting you sorted and that, but you can't kip here really, no.'

'Oh, we'll definitely get you sorted with something,' Hilary cried quickly, turning back from the sink. 'I mean there's no question of throwing you out. I mean, we're not *like* that. But the baby . . . well, everything's going to be a bit upside down for a while, I expect.'

She drew breath to ask if he understood, and thought better of it. He would not, and if he said as much it would change nothing except how bad she felt, by making her feel even worse. But Leech had to go. It had crossed her mind earlier in the year that when she took in the B&B sign at the end of August, Leech could perhaps have the smaller room. She assumed, because he sometimes had a packet of cigs and the odd can of Coke, that he got a little money from somewhere, benefit probably, so she would be able to negotiate a bit from him to cover food and hot water. And even in the winter he could carry on being a real help to Ivan, so that he would never get over-tired and would be less prone to episodes. Three in the house would be quite bearable, she had anticipated, since Leech's company was no more demanding than having a soporific cat or a stuffed fox in the room with you. But baby put an entirely different cast on her plans. Her anxiety for the unborn child was being channelled into an obsession about keeping a spotlessly clean house, an aspiration incompatible with having as a lodger the likes of Leech, who did not have so much as a toothbrush let alone normal domestic standards. She was intent also on realising the picture she had created in her mind of herself, Ivan and the baby, as happy and self-contained as a secular nativity scene, the perfect nuclear family whose ruthless exclusivity she would protect from Leech or anyone else as if it were, indeed, holy.

It was not in Leech to make suggestions so he sat, awaiting orders. Hilary chose to take his impassivity for acceptance and said brightly, 'Good! So, suppose we said the end of August, then? That's enough time, isn't it? End of August,' she repeated.

'Coming?' Ivan was now at the back door, holding it open. 'There's plenty to lift.' Leech embraced the normality of being told what to do and stepped past him out on to the concrete path. 'I'll be along in a minute,' Ivan said.

Leech turned and made off across the grass to the gap in the hedge that led to the fruit cages and the garden beyond. His loping walk could have indicated that he was entirely relaxed about his impending homelessness, or that he had not taken it in.

Ivan wrapped his arms round Hilary and snuggled into her neck. His skin's scent reminded her of a lovely clean sheep. It was too early to feel any bump yet but Hilary, sheltering in the safety of her tall husband, imagined with quiet excitement what it would be like when Ivan would also feel, embracing her like this, the hard little pillow of fluid that their precious one was swimming in and later, the cheeky little kicks that he would take against his bony belly when she hugged him hard.

CHAPTER 31

FROM WHERE HE was lying under the white silk canopy in the Wisteria bedroom James could count any number of painted blossoms on the wall opposite, but he stopped at sixty-two and got up. He slipped off his bathrobe with an enthusiastic jerk of the arms that took him a little by surprise, turned sideways to the mirror and closed the connecting door into his bathroom firmly, as if to prevent the trailing flowers from following him in, set the shower on pulse and turned to the mirror to look at himself before it steamed up. On the mirrored wall a full-length, gloomier but slimmer James looked back at him. He had to conclude that his shape was somewhat improved. It must be the lack of caffeine that was encouraging his head to buzz slightly but this morning James felt, for the first time since his arrival, optimistic. The faint stirring in his limbs, sometimes quite a strong jerking that he could not always control, was the first sign of energy that he had felt since his moment of lust for Stephen Golightly.

He stepped into the shower. There would be plenty of opportunity to feast his eyes on the doctor again this afternoon, he recalled, lifting his face into the hot needles of water, because the clinic was having its Open Day. Sister Yvonne had been reassuring the patients all week that they would hardly notice a thing, dispelling the vision in James's head of fluttering bunting, a tea tent and wheelchair races, but he realised how bored he must be if, after just five days of enforced rest and no stimulation except visualising his illness in clay, the thought of a glimpse of people from the outside world seemed rather dazzling. For one afternoon in August when the clinic was generally quiet (most patients, it seemed, managing to fit in their physical collapses so as not to disrupt their summer holidays) Dr Golightly allowed a small number of visitors, invariably people 'interested' but so far resistant to the temptation of a stay, to make an accompanied tour of the premises. He and Sister Yvonne called it Awareness Raising, James called it Marketing and resolved, as he shaved, to find some amusement in it.

In his smaller room on the other side of the house Warwick too was shaving with even more care than usual, and deciding to wear his crimson and pale blue cravat in honour of the day. The blue was almost the same colour as his eyes, while his complexion, rather livid when he had first arrived, had now paled to a milkier tone which could even be flattered by the red. He leaned closer into the mirror and reassured himself that the red did not pick out the rims of his eyes too closely. Not that Bunny's eyesight would be equal to an observation of such nicety, Warwick knew, but she took a view about things like that. Naked but for the cravat, he hummed to his reflection in the mirror as he knotted it over his Adam's apple, enjoying the soft rasp of the silk, anticipating her reaction to its unusual pattern of exotic flowers. She would want to know exactly what the red flowers were—peonies, he thought—and she would ask where he had got it from. He now remembered with a slightly embarrassed cough that he had bought the cravat in Thailand at the end of a rather disgraceful holiday about five years ago, and now rehearsed the white lie that he had picked it up in a street market in Hong Kong or Singapore.

As he continued dressing he noted his still-fine legs, his hairy shoulders, and a barrel chest whose musculature was still basically firm under a layer of what he called cladding. Inevitably as the years wore on there were fewer items of personal attractiveness deserving of his daily mental tick, but Warwick could still take a pride, not least in the fine-looking appendage which dangled heavily beneath the slight overhang of his torso. As he fed it carefully into his underpants he hoped again that it would not be invited to see service in his conquest of Bunny Fernandez because sex with Bunny, while possible and perhaps even enjoyable, would definitely involve the use of his imagination. Although he hoped that she, too, was beyond all that sort of thing and like him, in pursuit of a partnership in which his flagging libido would be an irrelevance, he supposed he could, if she were to make it a requirement of their permanent liaison, be made use of in that way. He worried though, because it sometimes took him the best part of an hour to get a result, that it might call for more serious and sustained application than Bunny was capable of to coax a performance out of it, at least a performance that ended on a high note, as it were. But his fear that Bunny might take her affection and her share portfolio elsewhere if he were put to the test and found wilting, would be enough, he thought, smirking, to stiffen his resolve.

Now that he was almost genuinely fond of her and had grown bolder, sensing her obvious attachment to him, Warwick had begun to flatter himself that he sometimes understood her. He understood, for example, the compliment that she paid him in confiding her short-sightedness to him. And it was the only physical failing to which she was prepared to admit, because myopia was not for her a symptom of old age but a rather feminine, lovable little imperfection that brought out the protector in men. And about that, as about so many other things, she was right, of course. *Blind as a bat, darling! I can just about see to sign my name*, she had giggled in a secret whisper. Warwick hoped, more devoutly than it would be wise to let on, that she was right about that, too. All he would have to do would be to point out the dotted line and persuade her of the rest.

But at breakfast Warwick, entering the dining room at the same time as James, saw that there was more than poor eyesight affecting Bunny this morning. Bunny was sitting in her usual chair and judging by the food that had accumulated round her, appeared to have been there for some time. She was voraciously eating porridge, shovelling it in as if it were some sort of live slime that might evade capture unless she chased it round the bowl and worried it into the spoon with urgent jerks of her hand. And her appetite seemed to have brought with it a taste for peculiar combinations because, after glancing up from her porridge-guzzling with a cursory good morning, she busied herself with sucking hard on a slice of lemon which she lifted from the saucer of lemon slices on the table. The saucer was nearly empty and several strands of rind, nibbled clean of lemon juice and flesh, lay on Bunny's side plate.

'I simply must have something sharp to taste,' she muttered, sensing perhaps by the stunned silence of her admirers that an explanation was called for. 'Ivan's porridge is so good, of course, whatever you say, I think I could eat it all morning, but *this* morning I must also, I *must* have something sharp.' She leaned forward with a dry smack of the lips and seized the last lemon slice almost from under the nose of Jane, who sighed and stirred her lemonless herbal tea.

Bunny's improved appetite was not matched by any improvement in her appearance. Even under her chalky face powder, small livid spots were beginning to show and her hair had the dusty look of dead grass. When not actually eating she rubbed her hands together briskly as if she were cold. Her eyelids were weighted not just with her usual industrial quantities of tarry make-up but also with fluid, while her lips and eyebrows were puckering slightly, rising and falling as if engaged in a far-off conversation that only they knew about. She placed the last chewed lemon rind on her plate.

'My body is telling me something,' she announced with a twitch of the eyes, mainly to Jane. 'That's how it works, you see, once one is properly in tune. The body calls for what it needs—liquid, vitamins, sweet or sharp—and redresses its own imbalances! Our task—what I am doing now—is simply to listen and give it what it needs!'

James's body was at that moment telling him it needed bacon, eggs, toast and coffee, badly, and he did not reply. Warwick chewed bravely on a spoonful of dried nuts and seeds. Jane's was presumably telling her it needed to satisfy some cannibalistic craving, since the finger-ends of one hand had disappeared into her mouth and her jaw was hard at work on her nails. She rose from the table. Sighing again, and sliding the hand from her mouth she said dolefully, 'Dr Golightly's changed my balneotherapy prescription. I'm changing from seaweed to luma today,' and seeing James's face she added, 'to stimulate circulation. The seaweed was for body tension and high blood pressure.' She wafted towards the door and turned. 'I've got numb fingers. Though frankly after what I've been through, it's amazing I'm not numb all over.' Before anyone could respond she had left the room, leaving another sigh behind her.

'Divorce,' Warwick whispered to James. 'Recent. Taking it badly.'

'What a fuss,' Bunny said crossly. 'When you've been through it as often as I have . . .'

'But, dear lady . . .'

She waved away his concern. 'Warwick dear, we shall continue in the studio this afternoon, shan't we? The head!' It was half entreaty, half command. Speaking seemed to cost her some effort and loose porridge and saliva were now exiting from the corners of her mouth.

'But, dear lady, don't you feel that perhaps you're tiring yourself . . .?'

'Of course I'm not tired. I'm having massage and balneotherapy this morning. I'm having oatmeal, for my dry skin. We'll start as usual straight after I've had my rest, at three o'clock.' With a shaky smile she got up and cooed, with an ancient burble from somewhere deep in her chest, 'See you in a while, crocodile,' and then tottered from the room.

For several moments the only sounds were James's attack on his bowl of mixed cereals and Warwick's disappointed throat-clearing. James looked up.

'Nice cravat, Warwick,' he said, through a mouthful of husks.

*   *   *

IMMEDIATELY AFTER lunch, James's bowels expressed a violent objection to Ivan's ratatouille and wholemeal macaroni, and back up in the bathroom of the Wisteria Suite he groaned not only with pain but with the injustice of it, for the meal had been delicious and he had eaten lots. He himself would have used three times as much olive oil and thrown in parmesan but had reached the conclusion, after the first mouthful, that Ivan's was better for being without.

The dining room had been busier than usual, with half a dozen or so Open Day visitors, as well as Bunny's daughter and son-in-law who seemed to be permanent visitors. James had discovered, too late, that all of his fellow patients had opted to lunch in their rooms and so avoid scrutiny.

'D'you want to skip off back up to the Wisteria then, sweetheart?' Yvonne had asked confidingly, when she had found him hovering. 'We're run off our feet doing trays but we could manage one more if you like.' James had smiled bravely and stayed. But just as he had finished his plateful and was wondering about seconds, his innards had cruelly informed him that whatever he might think the ratatouille and macaroni were not going down well with *them*.

Rather exhausted and already late for his art therapy, he came downstairs again to find the hall milling with clinic staff and people holding neat little folders with the Sulis Clinic logo on the front. Dr Golightly was busy assigning them to members of staff for the guided tour part of the afternoon, one couple each to himself, Sister Yvonne, Ivan and Hilary, who were wearing evangelical smiles. James slipped past.

Halfway down the corridor which led to the art studio, the swell of voices from the hall grew faint. Just then, drifting out from the music room came the sound of quite good, *extremely* good, cello-playing. Boccherini, perhaps? He stopped and looked at his watch, because his first thought was that Sara must be here early (he was expecting her at four) but listening a moment longer he realised that neither the instrument nor the playing was hers. Not as sure, impassioned, intense; not, to be truthful, as good. Silently, he opened the door a fraction and slid into the room. At once the playing stopped. Joyce was sitting with her cello in a high-backed chair in front of the open french window. On a long table sat an array of instruments, enough to equip a small percussion band. Pretzel, covered loosely by a blanket, lay nearby with a bowl of water on a newspaper beside him. Joyce stared at James, startled. Her face was flushed and she was breathing rather hard.

'Sorry. Did I disturb?' he asked. 'Didn't mean to put you out.'

'I'm perfectly fine,' Joyce said, a touch defensively. 'I've just this minute got back in. I just popped out for a few messages. I had things to get. I'm just out of puff, getting back up that hill in a hurry.' James followed her eyes, which glanced behind her at the french window and then rather nervously at her large black handbag under the electronic keyboard. 'I thought you might be the visitors. I was supposed to be in here, playing when they come.' She drew herself up.

'I think they're probably on their way. It was very nice, anyway,' James said. 'Was that Boccherini? Lovely piece.' He did not know what else to say, it seeming to him inappropriate to congratulate a former professor on regaining a standard of competence. 'I'm very impressed,' he said, truthfully.

Joyce inclined her head graciously. 'It's what I'm here

to do. I'm to be here playing when the visitors come.' She had been tidied up quite effectively, James noticed, and a large shiny badge on her sweatshirt said *The Sulis Clinic—Naturopathy Works!*

'Really . . .' James hesitated, wondering if he was about to sound patronising, 'your playing was lovely. The visitors are going to come expecting concerts, not health treatments.'

'Music'd do most of them more good than the other stuff,' Joyce said with tired certainty, getting up and placing her cello against the wall. 'Music's good for you. Anyhow, when I'm playing I'm thinking about wee Pretzel here, not the visitors. I'm playing for him. He likes me playing to him when he's not well, don't you, son?'

Pretzel stirred at the sound of his name, and his tail gave one tired flip against the floor.

'I think he's got a wee chill. He's all trembly and thirsty. And his number twos, they're—'

'Oh, I think I just heard them,' James said, quickly, glancing over his shoulder. 'Your visitors are on their way. Must go. You get better now, Pretzel, you hear me?'

James made off down the passage and round the corner to the art studio on the other side of the building, where the atmosphere, the moment he escaped through the door and had closed it behind him, struck him as even more than usually calm. The bright sun streaming directly in set a silvery halo round the two silhouetted heads of the only other people in the room. Warmth and light flooded in through the line of three french windows opposite the door and for a moment it seemed that the specks of dust sparkling in the slanting beams of sunlight were all that moved. But Bunny, who was sitting with her back to

James, facing Warwick, who posed magnificently still in his usual chair in front of the french windows, was rather frantically shaving feathers of clay from her sculpture. No noise, except for the faint *pring-pring* of birds in the high trees outside, could be heard. If Joyce had resumed her little concert for her dog, the sound did not reach this far.

James drew breath to say good afternoon but thought better of it. Bunny was clearly in her fiercest mood, since Warwick had not dared even to lift a hand in greeting. And as he dithered, wondering whether to leave or settle quietly to his own laughable efforts with clay, he became aware that there *was* a sound, a slight, rhythmic, whistling snuffle, coming from Bunny's direction. She certainly was concentrating hard. James took a step to one side, and the change in viewpoint sent the sun's glare behind a section of wall between the windows. The room's black and silver stripes of shade and light and the haloed silhouettes of Bunny and Warwick solidified. Seeing her properly now, he saw also that Bunny was snuffling through trickles of dark blood which ran unchecked from her nostrils. She turned sunken eyes to his, desperate to speak but unable to, either because the dead tongue which flapped in her mouth was too paralysed or because the twitching, blinking, jerking of her face and neck prevented speech. She raised a hand in a gesture of entreaty or hopelessness, and James now understood that she had not been energetically sculpting at all, but trying to scrape blood-stained vomit from the half-worked clay in front of her. His eyes followed the shaking hand still clutching the scalpel which was now pointing, with terrible effort, towards Warwick, whose condition was much less distressing. He was merely dead, strangled with his pale blue and crimson cravat.

PART 3

CHAPTER 32

B Y THE TIME Sara arrived James had negotiated a pot of Earl Grey with sugar for himself and was lying on his bed under blankets, trying not to tremble. Just slightly aware of being able to insist, for a while at least, on having exactly what he wanted, he had refused to let anyone be with him except Sara. She sat debating whether or not to hold his hand, thinking profanely that despite the shakiness he looked rather better than when she had last seen him. The shock had somehow perked him up. She had already listened once to his animated sugar-fuelled account of what he had seen and had allowed him to lapse again into silence, thinking he might sleep. He was still staring at the ceiling, but his shakes had grown gradually less seismic and had now almost stopped.

She said, 'Andrew came with me, you know. The minute you rang, we both came. We got here before the police. Though they're here now, of course.'

James nodded and smiled palely. After a blurred ten minutes which started with his horrified dashing from the room, then shouts, which must have been his, and the stampede of hurrying feet, he had had the sensation of extraordinary calm, as if all that could happen had happened and the consequences would be for others to deal with. He had managed to use someone's mobile phone to ring Sara. A minute or two later the shaking had taken hold of him and he had had to be brought upstairs and fussed over by Sister Yvonne. Sara had arrived some time later.

'I'm glad you managed to ring us. Andrew's switched straight into work mode. He's downstairs now, handing things over.' She sighed. 'And getting in the way, probably. He won't be leading the enquiry, you see. Andrew knows too many of the people here personally. Somebody new called Askew's in charge. Want some more of your tea? It's just about still warm.'

James pulled himself up a little, took the cup and drank shakily. 'Oh, sugar,' he said, slowly. 'Shoo-gar.' He smiled with more certainty. 'Christ, Sara, it really was ghastly.' He drank some more.

'The police will want you to tell them everything you saw,' she said. 'Remember, it won't be Andrew, it might be—'

'Not Bridger?' James lay back and groaned. He and Bridger had met before, and not socially. 'How embarrassing.'

'Well, at least this time there's no need to invent your own alibi,' Sara said, and suddenly wondered if, Bridger being Bridger, that were true.

'What do you mean?'

'Well—' She looked hard at him. 'Well—from what you said. You found him, and with Bunny still there in the room. Warwick was just sitting there, wasn't he, and he was . . . well . . . dead.'

Not wishing to interrupt James's returning calm she had tried to speak the word softly as if it were something harmless, like 'tired' or 'off-colour', knowing it to be ridiculous. No mental ploy or careful tone of voice would prevail against the truth that a murder had been committed, just as other phrases such as 'resolving issues' or 'strains and pressures' (her current euphemisms, she realised now, for basic emotional dishonesty) should shield her from the unhappy possibility that she might not be up to the Dvořák, and that she and Andrew might be falling out of love with each other. She began to cry.

'Och, ye saft old witch,' James said. 'Don't take it so hard. Here, finish this.' He handed her his half-full cup.

Sara looked up. 'It's not that. Not just that. I don't know what it is. It's the Dvořák. I can't give it what it needs, I don't mean technically, it's not that. You know.' She emptied the teacup and blew her nose. 'Now, I want you to tell me again what happened,' she said. 'When you went in, you saw Bunny first, didn't you?'

James nodded. 'Didn't see either of them exactly at first, the room was so bright and the light was behind Warwick, and Bunny had her back to me. When I did see Bunny, she couldn't speak. She's probably had a stroke, that's what Sister Yvonne said.'

'Brought on by the effort of killing him.'

'Or the shock of finding him.'

There was a miserable silence, during which Sara considered that to all her other worries—starting with Joyce, including Dvořák and finishing with Andrew—she must now add this, another murder which would draw Andrew's attention. Would he now simply forget that she was struggling with the Dvořák, would he even notice, when she left for Salzburg, that she had gone? In the midst of the self-pity which always accompanied such reflections, Sara was suddenly struck by a truth so simple and overwhelming that she immediately felt stupid for not seeing it before: she could just as well order an incoming tide to go out as she could demand, plead or cajole Andrew into diverting his attention, at such times, towards herself. If she wanted to keep Andrew (more profoundly, if she wanted to stay in love with him) then she should give up and let the tide come in. What was the worst that could happen if she did? She suddenly said aloud, '*Wet feet*'. James looked at her. She laughed.

'You are weird,' James said. 'Whose feet?'

'I just worked something out. God, I've been stupid.'

'Cold feet,' James said. 'I've got cold feet. And my hands, they feel hot, then cold.' He squirmed under the blankets.

'That's shock for you,' Sara said, standing up. 'Where do you keep your socks?'

As James was settling back under his blankets with his feet wriggling in two pairs of socks, there was a knock at the door and Andrew came in.

'Bunny's had another stroke. She's completely unconscious now,' he said, settling himself on the white sofa. 'And I'm off the case, now Askew's here and they've got the SOCOs in. All the staff and visitors are waiting to give statements. They'll be sending someone up to talk to you in a little while, James.'

There seemed nothing to say. James murmured and closed his eyes, about to drift into sleep.

Sara met Andrew's eyes. 'Any idea yet if——?'

Andrew leaned forward with a shrug. 'Hard to believe she killed him. He's a sturdy bloke and she doesn't look strong. Although,' Andrew shook his head slowly, 'it's amazing what strength people can find.'

They thought about this for a while. James half-opened his eyes and said, 'Oh, she's tougher than she looks, I reckon. Warwick is a pussy cat, though.' He closed his eyes again. 'Was. Oh, God.'

'If she did kill him, if she had to find the strength some-how, do you mean it could have been in self-defence?' Sara asked. 'Do you think he might have been attacking her?'

Andrew shook his head again, indicating non-com-mittal rather than denial. 'It's a theoretical possibility, I suppose. The PM might tell us something, but I doubt it. There were no obvious signs of a struggle, no other obvi-ous injuries on either of them. You'd expect at the very least facial scratches, clothes pulled about and so on. No, it looks as if he died in his chair. Probably strangled from be-hind.'

'But he was facing the door. So that means he'd have seen whoever came in,' Sara said, sitting up. 'So that must mean he knew his assailant!'

'Oh brother,' Andrew said, casting his eyes to the ceil-ing, 'here we go.' He turned half-amused, half-irritated eyes on her. 'My darling, it means nothing of the sort. It *might* mean that. Or it might mean he was surprised by someone coming in behind from the french window. Or it might mean that he had nodded off to sleep, or had turned to look out the window, or he saw a stranger enter but saw no reason to move, or he wanted to move but wasn't quick enough, or was threatened in some way and told to sit still, or—'

Sara looked past him. 'I was only trying to help,' she said.

'And, of course, all that implies that Bunny wasn't in the room at the time, that she came in later and found him. If she was there at the time, the next question is what she had to do with it. We can't be certain that finding him dead brought the stroke on.'

'She could have witnessed it,' Sara said, stubbornly.

'Quite. Leave it to the police.'

'Oh, now, don't be mean to poor little Miss Marple,' James said. He turned to Sara. 'And you stick to your knitting, dear,' he mocked, 'and never mind him.'

'Actually, James, we shouldn't even have had this conversation. I wasn't thinking. I shouldn't have discussed any of this.' Andrew stood up with an impatient grunt and moved to the window. 'Look, when you give your statement, try to tell them exactly what happened, exactly what you saw. Forget anything I've said, I'm only speculating, anyway. At this stage it's wide open, and it's very important that your recall isn't affected by what we've been saying. Don't try to interpret things when you talk to the police, just try to remember accurately. It's very important. You do understand that, don't you?'

James pursed his lips and turned to Sara. 'Oooh, isn't he lovely? I could really go for him, you know, when he goes all *stern*.'

'Oh yes, ha ha. But James, I promise you, I am quite serious,' Andrew said, irritated with himself. 'This is a murder enquiry. You do appreciate the seriousness of that, don't you?'

James nodded, either exhausted or chastened. 'Don't worry. I can remember it all quite clearly. I rather wish I couldn't.' He wriggled his feet under the blankets and

•

closed his eyes again. 'I think I really might like to have a sleep now,' he said. 'Would you mind?'

Andrew nodded and walked to the door. Sara waved him goodbye. 'I want another minute,' she said, and after Andrew had left she came and sat on the end of James's bed.

'What is it? Tell Uncle,' James said. 'Not happy, are you?'

Sara hesitated to burden him with it, then did so, sighing. 'I can't get the Dvořák right. I know just what I want to do with it, and I can't get it. I can only do it *okay*. I'm not . . . *big* enough.'

As James considered, she went on, 'You did hear my Prom, didn't you? You said you didn't but you never forget. You *did* hear it.'

'All right. I did, yes. But as you were due to play it again and record it, I didn't think it was the moment to say anything. Or to lie, which you always spot.'

Sara groaned. 'It was that bad, then.'

'No. No, it wasn't bad at all, it truly wasn't. But it wasn't great either, not the way you could do it. Can't quite place why not.'

'I've tried and tried and tried to do the right things. I've *really* tried.'

'Maybe you should stop trying. Stop thinking so hard about doing the right thing and just love it a bit more. Maybe that was it—there wasn't much love in it.'

After a silence James said, 'Joyce seems to resent you rather, doesn't she? And I believe I detected a little frost between you and PC Plod?'

'Oh you are horrible to me,' Sara said. 'And don't call him that. All I try to do for them is the right thing, too.'

'And might that not be the problem? I think,' James said quietly, 'that you might try forgetting about the right thing, whatever that is. Do you want Andrew to do the right thing? No—you just want to be loved. So does he, I expect. And Joyce. And Dvořák. Forget the right thing and just love 'em. That's all they need.'

'You sound like *The Little Book of Vomit-Inducing Truisms*,' Sara said crossly. 'Love them? All of them? How am I supposed to do all that?'

'Fuck knows,' James murmured comfortably. 'Are you coming tomorrow?'

Sara got up and drew breath to say that she did not really have the time. 'I will if I can' was as much as she could manage. 'Look after yourself.'

James raised a theatrically limp hand. 'Bye-bye. Oh, would you mind asking Yvonne if she could find me a hot-water bottle? My feet are still cold.'

CHAPTER 33

THE NEXT DAY Andrew and Sara had reached the bottom of Bathwick Hill before Andrew said rather sarcastically, 'Saving all your conversation for James? You haven't spoken to me all day.'

'Of course I have. Anyway, you've only grunted back.'

'You've been in the music room for over seven hours. And now you seem unable to conduct a conversation.'

'I'm still thinking,' she said. The truth was that she was worrying, not just about the concert which was in itself too important for her to be anything less than brilliant, but also the live recording of it that would be made for release next year. Her inadequate Dvořák would be digitally enshrined for ever. 'And anyway, all you want to talk about is the Takahashi case or Dan. Daniel.' Realising how mean that must sound, she stroked his leg and said, 'Sorry. Don't mean to be so quiet. I completely understand. I'm just nervous, I think.'

'You'll be fine by tomorrow, the minute you're on that plane.'

'And you'll be fine too, as soon as you get Daniel to yourself for a few days. It's just what you both need.'

She hoped she was right. Since Daniel's murder attempt

Andrew's first bewilderment had mounted to something close to quiet panic that his familiar little boy had somehow been transforming before his eyes into a homicidal pre-teenager. Andrew felt responsible, and it filled him with horror to think that he may have driven Daniel to such an extremity without even noticing that he was inflicting such damage. With a feeling of sick urgency he had arranged to take his son on a cycling trip while Sara was away. He had had to argue hard, mainly with himself, to take leave in the middle of a murder case, but it was not as if they were overwhelmed with leads and the Warwick Jones case was a separate enquiry with its own momentum. The Takahashi case would not collapse if Andrew took a few days' leave, but his relationship with his son might if he did not. Daniel needed him, or so Andrew hoped. He needed his full attention, at any rate. They would be just a dad and his boy on their bikes, covering as many or as few miles as suited them, staying in B&Bs and bonding madly.

Andrew took Sara's hand and squeezed it. 'After we've seen James you can go back and do some more work. I'll cook.'

'Great,' Sara said. She was smiling to herself about how wondrously, unnaturally accommodating of the other's needs they were suddenly managing to be and questioning whether it could last. 'I'll probably do a bit. And I'll have tomorrow morning as well, don't forget. My flight's not till the afternoon.'

'I hope James appreciates it, us taking time to visit him again.'

'I think he does. Anyway, we don't mind, do we, as long as he's pleased to see us.'

James was not pleased to see them, however, being oblivious of their presence. Sister Yvonne came out of the treatment room to the left of the front door just as they came into the hall, and beckoned them in. In what Sara thought an unnecessarily hushed voice, she said, 'James is quite poorly still, after yesterday. Got a headache up the back of his head that won't shift. Couldn't sleep. Awake practically all night.'

'I'll go up and see him now,' Sara said.

'Well, actually, I wonder if you'd mind not. He's finally got to sleep, you see. In fact, I put my head round the door just a couple of minutes ago and he's out for the count. Really, it is what he needs. Dr Golightly looked at him at lunchtime and he says his whole system is crying out for rest in response to the shock of You Know What. And I've never known Dr Golightly to be wrong about these things.'

'But I'm going to Salzburg tomorrow. That means I won't see him before I go. I promised I'd see him before I went.'

Andrew said, 'We can't go and wake him up though, darling, can we? Look, I'll come and see him when you're away, and you'll be back on Thursday night anyway. I'll make sure he knows you were here. He'll understand.'

Sister Yvonne said, 'That does make sense.' Seeing that Sara's unhappy face had not brightened, she added, 'Look, tell you what. If you're not in a hurry now why don't you wait a while? You could sit out in the garden or in the drawing room and wait. And if he wakes up, well, he might feel up to seeing visitors.' Behind the magnanimous suggestion was the near certainty that James would be doing neither of these things within the next four hours.

'Or we can go and find Joyce. We came to see her, too. We can go up and see Joyce,' Sara said.

Sister Yvonne shook her head. 'Sorry, I happen to know she's just popped out. I saw her go down the drive after lunch. No music therapy today, you see, because so many of the patients are having bed rest.'

She looked intently at Andrew and her large brown eyes grew steely. 'I think the quicker the police find whoever it was and take themselves off again the better because it's upsetting us all very badly, you know. Dr Golightly's trying to run a clinic here. Now we've been told to be extra vigilant about security. How do you think that goes down in a place designed to reduce stress? Dr Golightly's frantic, deep down, though you couldn't tell if you didn't know him.'

Andrew nodded understandingly, and did not point out that in fact he had been impressed at how discreetly the police were conducting themselves. The remote possibility that the Sulis was being targeted by a madman was the main reason for the continuing presence of a uniformed officer down at the entrance lodge, who was taking a note of cars entering and leaving. The forensic work had been carried out immediately and completed within hours of the discovery of Warwick's body. The uneasy atmosphere had more to do with the event of the murder itself than with its investigation which—and nor did Andrew point this out—had barely got under way.

'Because you see, as well as James,' Yvonne went on, turning to Sara, 'there's Mrs Valentine not well. And Mrs Fernandez. Well, after yesterday, it's not surprising, is it? If you ask me it's all down to stress. You know, the shock of the whole business. And of course with them all in bed there are no art or music sessions so Joyce and Hilary have practically nothing to do while the kitchen staff and me—well, we're run off our feet taking trays up and down. Still, I prefer being busy and Dr Golightly relies on me.'

Taking the neat cue to push off and let her get on, Sara and Andrew found themselves back in the hall. Feeling unwanted, they shuffled off into the garden.

'Well, would you rather be her friend or her enemy?' Andrew asked. 'She's quite a little powerhouse, our Yvonne. D'you think she *is* having it away with the doctor?'

Sara considered. 'Oh, definitely. I think she gets what she wants, on the whole, and she obviously thinks he's a god, and she's very attractive. And I should think Dr Golightly goes for that dynamic type.'

'Especially if it comes knocking on his door. Lucky old sod.'

'Let's go and look at the pool,' Sara said. 'James says it's amazing.' As they crossed the garden her eyes took in the sloping lawn with the terraced shrubbery above and the gazebo at the very top, where James had been lying the first day. There was nobody there now.

Andrew pulled back the sliding door behind the row of columns at the pool entrance, and they stepped into the thick, steaming air. Not a breath disturbed the water. Sara saw as if through glass the Greek key pattern picked out on the pool floor in black and turquoise mosaic tiles. The leaves of tropical plants hung transfixed in glossy health. Empty loungers stood in rows across on the far side of the pool.

With a rustle of leaves and the sound of someone heaving themselves upright, a voice from behind some kind of potted palm said, 'Urghmm . . . urmm. Oh, gosh, sorry! Have I given you a fright? I'm *say* sorry!'

A woman with a smile too large for her face appeared round the plant. 'Hellay! I'm here to see my mother but she's gone off to sleep. Mrs Fernandez. She had a terrible fright yesterday. Did you hear? Hasn't woken all day! I was told to come and wait.'

'So were we,' Sara said. 'Our friend's asleep, too.'

'Oh. I mean . . . what I mean is, I'm waiting for that woman—you know—the old stick who does the music. I want her to play something for Mummy, I think it might bring her round.'

'Oh? Does she like music?'

'Well, you know, the classics. Actually, I think mainly she likes to be a little difficult. When I visit. You know, suddenly decides she needs a sleep or she's ill or something. But if *your* friend's asleep, well, perhaps they've given all the old dears a nap. Don't you think? Rather sweet! Like children.'

'Our friend's not an old dear.'

'Oh. It does bring people round though, sometimes, hearing music, doesn't it? Hugh thinks I'm silly but I'm sure it can. Well, anyway, I'm Petronella, by the way.'

Sara smiled, not with any warmth at the introduction, but with genuine sympathy. Anyone quite as stupid as this and so unguarded as to be willing to expose the fact to strangers really had to be pitied.

'Actually,' Petronella was saying now, in mock-confessional tones, 'you gave *me* a fright, if anything. I'd nodded off, when you came in. I do get awfully tired, it's because I'm pregnant, actually. Number three. It's *say* hot in here.'

'It is,' Andrew said. 'Actually, we were just taking a look at the pool. There are dozens of benches in the garden,' he now told Sara. 'Shall we go and sit outside?'

'Oh, good idea!' cried Petronella. 'I'm on my own to-day, and it is a bore waiting on one's own. Hugh—that's my other half—usually comes too. We were here practically all day yesterday. He's marvellous with Mummy. I'm too close, you see. One often is, isn't one, and really one needs to be detached. Hugh's terribly good at standing back.'

They reached a bench on the edge of the broad grass walk that led from the house down to the pool. Behind them, a wall of thick shrubbery shielded them from the sun. Petronella looked at her watch. 'If Hugh was here he'd get something done about that old bird who does the music. She was quite rude. I only wanted Mummy to hear her favourite tune, you'd think she'd be pleased to be asked, wouldn't you? Especially after yesterday. Hugh thinks it's *ridiculous*. We might complain.'

'What is her favourite tune?' Andrew asked, not giving a damn.

'I only asked if the woman could play it, and you'd think I'd insulted her. "The Dying Swan", is it? She just said no because she had to go out. Quite abruptly.'

' "The Swan",' Sara said.

'I mean I just asked. She said she wasn't here to give concerts. Quite rude.'

Petronella looked wanly into the trees on the other side of the walk. Sara said, to fill the silence, 'She likes "The Swan", does she, your mother?'

'Oh, *loves* it, yes. I do, too. She took me to *Swan Lake* once, when I was quite little. I can still remember that bit where the swan dies. Well, you do, don't you, at that age.'

Sara and Andrew exchanged a look of amusement. Neither was about to oust Petronella's cherished memory of hearing a piece of Saint-Saëns' *Carnival of the Animals* in the middle of Tchaikovsky's *Swan Lake*.

'Haven't you got it on a CD? Couldn't you play it to her on a CD?'

Before Petronella could get her head round that one Andrew said, 'Sara plays that piece. You'd play it for Petronella's mother, wouldn't you?' Sara gave him a dig with her elbow that nearly sent him off the bench. But he was squeezing her arm in order to draw her attention, and one look at him told her that his mind was working faster than hers. Sara sighed, trapped. Andrew, not being part of the enquiry, could not engineer a meeting with Bunny Fernandez. But Sara, if she were to answer the summons to play Saint-Saëns for the spoilt old trout, might be able to find out something about Bunny's experience yesterday. At the very least she could make an assessment of Bunny's condition and report back.

'Sara's a cellist,' Andrew told Petronella. 'In fact she's off to Salzburg tomorrow, to the festival.'

'Gosh! Salzburg! You are lucky!' Petronella exclaimed. 'How lovely, if you like that sort of thing.'

'Yes, isn't she! But I'm sure she'd play "The Swan" for your mother, wouldn't you, darling?' He was already on his feet. 'Come along. Joyce's cello will be in the music studio, won't it?'

'Gosh, really? Oh I say, you wouldn't, would you? I *know* it would help her pick up.'

'I don't think I should just use Joyce's instrument without asking . . .'

'Oh please! If you saw Mummy . . .'

'I'm sure Joyce wouldn't mind. It's not as if you don't know how to play it properly, is it, darling?' Andrew said smoothly. Sara's glare at him over Petronella's head told Andrew that her revenge was going to be unpredictable, as well as unspeakable and prolonged.

Sister Yvonne was coming out of Bunny's room on the top floor, quietly closing the door behind her, just as Petronella and Sara, carrying Joyce's cello, reached the top of the main stairs. Andrew had decided to wait in the hall, perhaps guessing that up here there would be police officers: two of them were sitting on hard chairs on the landing, a discreet distance from the door. Their embarrassment at having to hover there on the off-chance of interviewing, perhaps cautioning and arresting a sick old lady, was palpable. Yvonne mouthed a few words in their direction with a single movement of the head. They did not rise.

'Hellay! Is Mummy awake yet?' Petronella's voice boomed. If Mummy were capable of waking, that would surely do it, Sara thought.

Yvonne shook her head. She took a breath, looked uncertainly at Petronella's eager face and hesitated. 'I was just coming to find you. She's very peaceful,' she almost whispered. 'I've plumped her pillows up, and she's quite peaceful.' She did not suggest that they might disturb her by going in, but shook her head again in sympathy and said, 'Call me if you need me, won't you.'

'Mummy, it's me!' Petronella entered the room and walked swiftly over to the bed. She bent to kiss her mother, then straightened up and turned to where Sara hovered, a little distance off. The silly eyes were filling with tears.

'Oh, she *is* sleepy!' she said desperately, waving an arm towards the still figure under the covers. Sara steered Petronella, who seemed in danger of falling, to a chair at the bedside.

'Would you like to be alone with her? Shall I go?'

Petronella still had hold of her arm. 'No, stay! Oh please, if you don't mind.' Tears now ran down her cheeks. 'I'm no good at this kind of thing. Please stay and play her tune. Please. You never know'—she glanced at her mother—'you never know, it might bring her round . . . mightn't it? She just had a little turn. It might wake her up.'

Sara nodded quietly, fetched a chair to sit on and placed it a few feet from the end of the bed. She took the cello case to the side of the room and brought the instrument out. As she tuned it she glanced towards the bed, finding that she was shaking slightly, wondering why she was agreeing to this. Just before she drew her bow for the first notes of 'The Swan' she looked up and stared at Bunny, as if she had to impress upon herself the full—what? obscenity, pointless-ness, pathos, hilarity?—of what she was about to do.

Bunny was not having a little afternoon nap, being less in the Land of Nod than in a deep coma. The skin of her face was already tightening to reveal the bones beneath the flesh and her hands, like blue roots, lay still on the bed-spread. Her barely perceptible breathing was silent, yet before Sara reached the end of the piece, which she played as softly as she could and with more tenderness than she had believed she possessed, she sensed that it had stopped altogether. And, resting the bow gently across her knee as she looked with pity at the weeping Petronella, she felt also a slight sting of bitterness towards Andrew, for whose curiosity's sake she had just serenaded a cadaver.

CHAPTER 34

THAT NIGHT ANDREW slept badly, rising at around four and taking himself up to the hut at the top of the garden, the place where he could think best. Lying on the chaise longue, staring out across the valley but hardly seeing it, he ran over in his mind the few facts about the Warwick Jones case that were coming to light. There had been no widow to break the news to, in fact no family at all except for two nephews, both rather priggishly preoccupied with being good husbands and daddies in the Midlands, who had not seen their uncle since their own father had died. Several things about their uncle had been a mystery to them, chiefly the source of his largely unearned income and the phoney military accent. For it was their father, they confirmed, who had been the regular soldier and the prisoner of war for four years, not the older Warwick who they thought had been doing something in a factory near Birmingham during the war. Not that these small mysteries in themselves constituted a reason why he had been killed, for if every elderly gent who assumed a more honourable persona for the purpose of impressing old women were to be murdered for it, Bath would be all but empty of elderly gents.

Setting aside the why, Andrew turned fretfully to the
how of the case. It was certain that the short-sighted and
slightly confused Bunny had tottered into the studio at the
usual time, for two or three people had seen her on her
way there from her bedroom shortly before three o'clock.
It was possible, then, that she had noticed that Warwick
was in his usual place but not the state he was in, perhaps
the same trick of light beguiling her as it had James, and
had got herself into her chair before a proper look at him
had induced the first of the series of strokes. Warwick
himself had had lunch in his room, a slightly chaotic affair
that day because of the Open Day visitors, but his empty
tray had been among those cleared and washed before the
catering assistant Donna had gone off sink duty at two.
Ivan had taken his tray up, Hilary had gone up with his
dessert and Yvonne had brought his tray down. All members of staff had been helping with the service, except for
Dr Golightly, who had been hosting the table of guests,
and Joyce, who was considered too unreliable with trays.
Everyone else had been busy either in the kitchen, the dining room or up and down stairs, going to and from bedrooms. Any one of them could have been absent for as long
as it took quietly to throttle Warwick in his chair. And of
course, a complete stranger could have wandered on to
the premises at any time that day and done the same thing.
The main question in Andrew's mind was the uncomfortable one that he and Sara had been discussing last night
over supper (his very successful bouillabaisse, he recalled,
swallowing a garlicky belch). *There's got to be a connection,
hasn't there? Two stranglings in Bath, days apart? You can't think
they've been done by two different people*, she had said.
There was the obvious connection, of course, the B&B in

Limpley Stoke and the Sulis Clinic, but Andrew was not at all sure that this was not a red herring.

'A red herring?' she had said then, with something not unlike one on the end of her fork.

'All right, suppose we say there is a connection. Suppose we forget motive because we don't know what that is. Takahashi remains the main suspect for the first murder. He can't have committed the second because he was sitting all Friday afternoon with twenty-four other people, listening to the closing session of the seminar. Oh and by the way, your idea about the films hasn't helped. It was smart of you, though, to think that she would have taken more pictures, her being a photographer. But we've checked the places that do developing and Photo-Kwik doesn't keep records by name, only numbers. So unless films are paid for by cheque or card there's no record of names. Boots does it by name, though. There was a Takahashi.' Sara's face had brightened. 'But not ours. Another Takahashi, a student. We've seen him. No connection. Nice idea, though.'

When Sara had looked rather crestfallen Andrew had simply shaken his head. 'We just have to plough on. I still have my doubts that we're looking at motiveless murders, but that's the line that Askew's taking on the Jones enquiry. That's why he wants to bring in Leech for questioning, only I gather he's gone AWOL. He hasn't been seen since Thursday. The Golightlys say he may have been upset because they told him he couldn't stay on beyond the summer. We'll track him down in one of his haunts, he hasn't the wit to go missing. But please, don't go down to the towpath again, and certainly not at night.'

At seven o'clock in the morning Andrew closed the

hut, made his way down through the garden and returned to bed where he woke Sara up accidentally on purpose, by sliding one ice-cold foot against her leg. To stop him shivering, she turned, still half-asleep, wrapped her arms and legs around him and held him, without speaking, until he moved gently against her and into her, nudging his way slowly, without energy and almost sadly until he climaxed with a sigh and a tightening little shudder of his limbs. It was after nine when they woke again, still wrapped together, Sara with a crick in her shoulder, Andrew with a dead arm.

'Oh *Christ*,' she said, furious and tearful. 'Oh Christ, my shoulder! How the hell am I going to play like this? How can I play *Dvořák* like this! I must get a massage. I'll have to get a later flight. I'll need some physio. I'm supposed to be playing the hardest thing I've ever done in my life and you've mucked up my shoulder! You're an *idiot*—it's all your fault. Why did you *do* that!'

'Well, excuse me. But you did *rather* do it, too, I seem to remember,' Andrew snarled. 'And now I'll be late for seeing the kids. I don't suppose you noticed *that*, did you?' Was he ever going to be allowed to forget how important her bloody career was? What about his? What about his children?

'I was half-asleep!'

'Were you? I didn't notice the difference,' he said bitterly, slamming the door of the shower.

'That's an unforgivable thing to say!' she shouted. It was and he knew it, but Andrew said more unforgivable things as he pulled on his clothes without bothering to dry himself. The last of them was that he had had enough. Sara screamed that so had she and he could get himself and his bloody things out of her house. At that point Andrew dropped his voice to a civilised, hate-filled drawl and said that he would collect them when she was back from Salzburg at a time that did not inconvenience her, and Sara knew that he meant it. Fine, she replied in a voice just like his, so that he would know she meant it too.

After he had left Sara worked rather sheepishly in the music room, trying to ignore the feeling that his absence left behind. Here she was, the first day after the end of her relationship with Andrew, alone again in the house that had become exactly what it was after Matteo had died: a private, comfortable, beautiful mausoleum that she was screaming to be let out of. So, instead of sticking for as long as she should have done to the Dvořák, she decided that she did have time after all to go again to the Sulis to see James. The thought of Stephen Golightly had nothing whatever to do with it.

* * *

AT ROUGHLY the same moment Stephen Golightly was thinking about publicity and in particular how to avoid it. He had taken a nonchalant jog down to the main gate and satisfied himself that the police presence at the clinic entrance was as discreet as possible, reminding the officer to remain out of sight under the porch of the tiny lodge until any car should present itself. He then jogged as loosely as he could, in order to persuade the policeman of his unaltered calm, back up the drive. Stephen followed the curve as it rose around the knot garden on the south side to the almost empty car park. From there he climbed the terraced shrubbery and sat down on a recliner under the gazebo, breathing a fraction harder. As he checked his pulse, mentally giving his cardiovascular fitness a big tick, he surveyed the city stretching out beyond the garden, so apparently still yet seething, he was sure, with thousands of potentially grateful patients. He smiled involuntarily, already hearing accolades, hardly noticing that the imagined conversations were in fact rehearsals for real compliments that he would engineer later.

August could be rather a depressing month, with few patients and those there were being mainly converts and regulars whose adulation no longer carried much thrill for him. He was a good doctor. He knew that by the brisk turnover he did down in town at his NHS practice, providing relief for the unvarying complaints of infancy, maturity and old age. But these patients came and went as if both his prescriptions (which they took) and his advice (which they ignored) in some way disappointed; as if he were ministering to them inadequately and sending them away with rather less than they felt was their due. He sometimes wondered if they held him somehow to blame for their being ill in the first place, as if they thought that it was in his power to exempt, say, a two-year-old from glue ear, a teenager from acne, a septuagenarian from arthritis. When he saw, by contrast, the quite preposterous gratitude in the eyes of his Sulis patients, he was able then to see himself as they did. Then he also *felt* that he was good, as well as knowing that he was.

This August had looked no different from half a dozen others, to begin with. It had been no surprise to take Bunny Fernandez's booking, nor to see Dafydd Broadbent again, and there was always a patient or two of Warwick's type about the place. But James and Joyce, both ideal patients from the treatability point of view, as well as Jane Valentine in the kind of emotional post-divorce collapse that was usually responsive to lots of sympathetic attention, had been unlooked-for bonuses. So this August should have been gratifying both to his own self-esteem and to the effect on autumn bookings that could be expected when the walking adverts themselves, a new quotient of fit ex-patients, went home and expressed their conversion to naturopathy to their amazed relatives and friends.

So it was not the murder that was the worst of it in Stephen's view, bad as it was. The proper response, which he had been careful to give, to the death of Warwick was to agree that it was appalling, but his private calculation was that while the murder was regrettable, it was also forgettable. Warwick had not been a regular patient and had put 'None' after next-of-kin on his form. The nephews had been unearthed by the police in Solihull or somewhere, he believed, not a region that supplied a flow of Sulis patients in any case, so any word-of-mouth damage to the clinic would be minimal.

But now there was Bunny Fernandez, too. Until Warwick (and he hardly counted in that way) Stephen had never before had a death at the Sulis. It wasn't what people came for. He had decided, immediately after Bunny had been found in a state of mouthing semi-consciousness, to go for containment. The circumstance of her having been seen by the Open Day guests, a good half-dozen prospective patients, was unfortunate, but he could do no more about it. It was just possible that enough had been said subsequently to allay any fear that Bunny was in any way illustrative of what happened to you if you went to the Sulis, but he did not hold out much hope of a flood of bookings arising from the Open Day. Again unfortunate, but not disastrous.

And he had squared things pretty well with the family. Seeing at once that Bunny was unlikely to recover he had persuaded the son-in-law that she really should not be moved to hospital to undergo 'invasive, high-tech resuscitation procedures which would at best delay the inevitable for a few more painful days'. And the daughter had not needed persuading for she had lapsed into a kind of airy optimism, taking shelter behind his advice, or rather her own self-deluding interpretation of it, that if Bunny should stay at the clinic then her 'little turn' could surely only be something trivial. So luckily the worst possible eventuality—a patient being rushed more dead than alive into the Royal United from that posh Sulis place—had been avoided, and consequently no damaging gossip was currently buzzing around the entire city of Bath and its surrounding counties.

Nonetheless, once he had been able to get through to the daughter that her mother really had died it had offended him disproportionately, even as he was writing 'cerebrovascular accident' on the death certificate, that the old lady should have slipped away when in his careful hands. She had been loyal and rewarding to treat. That he had proved unworthy of her faith and ultimately undeserving of her gratitude swept through him as a kind of guilty sadness. He pulled the small bottle marked 'Gaia—energising compound of organic carrot and orange juices with extract of betel' from the front pocket of his tracksuit top and drank deeply from it. Clear liquid reassurance swam down his body. You are a good doctor, he breathed to himself.

And yet, he considered, casting watchful eyes across the empty garden and drinking swiftly from the bottle again, not even Bunny's strokes and subsequent death, which had been, as he had memorised for his own comfort, a peaceful end after more than eighty active years, were the worst part of this August. The worst of this most depressing of Augusts was the intractable nature of the other patients' complaints.

He tried to brighten the picture for himself by thinking about Joyce Cruikshank who, despite having the most sceptical attitude of anyone in the establishment, had been improving steadily. She had gained weight and condition, and even if she was not a specimen of glossy good health, she looked much less brittle. Her attitude may have softened, too, though it hardly mattered. She still took her meals in her room, preferring the company of her dog to that of the other staff and patients, but her admittedly undemanding work seemed to find favour with those who went to her sessions. He was no musician himself, but the jangles and twangs and hoots that reached him from the music room sounded jolly enough.

But Dafydd Broadbent had come to the end of his stay and gone back to Llandeillo with twitching hands, a clear sign, they had decided between them, of the body's ability to heal itself. Stephen, taking care not to call them convulsions, had said that the twitches must be the effects of deep muscle tissue realignment following trauma—Dafydd had had a nasty whiplash and wrist sprain last March following a prang on the A38—but, facing facts quietly to himself in the privacy of his garden, Stephen acknowledged that he had been relieved to see him go, for Dafydd had exhausted all the therapeutic possibilities in his pharmacopoeia and shown no real improvement. And Dafydd's increasingly vivid nightmares, which had woken him screaming on several nights in a row, were potentially unsettling for other patients. Thank God for thick walls.

And he hadn't liked the look of Jane Valentine this morning. The lassitude that she had displayed on arrival had deepened into profound exhaustion, though her appetite was still good, if sporadic. The alternating freezing, burning and numb sensations in the extremities might yet respond to massage and hot and cold spinal baths. He had known circulations lazier than hers though not, he conceded, in anyone as young as she was. Her intolerance of being covered even by the lightest of blankets was a tad hysterical and, in Yvonne's view, mainly for his benefit. She could be right about that. Mrs Valentine would not be the first female patient keen to make sure that he saw how pretty her breasts looked under a silk nightdress, and she might be just at that stage following divorce when a forbidden, avenging affair on her own terms might appeal to her. Not that she would be up to much, physically, for the moment. Stephen smiled. There was no reason why he should not enjoy being regarded as quarry, but there was forbidden and forbidden and he drew the line at affairs with patients.

But not necessarily at patients' friends, he pondered, watching unseen from his vantage point the progress of Sara Selkirk's car up the drive, yet a mere affair, avenging, half-forbidden or otherwise was not what one could contemplate with a woman like that. Sara Selkirk was the sort of woman with whom there could be no paddling about in the shallows but only the deepest, headlong plunge into dark water. He could tell that 'casual' would simply not be in her vocabulary, which made her the most intoxicating and also the most dangerous of prospects. There was the policeman, of course, Andrew Poole. Stephen contemplated how much of an obstacle he might turn out to be. Her being attracted to him physically was easy enough to understand and the fellow was certainly no fool, but it was impossible to judge how strong the bond between them was. He found that this only added to the enjoyable sense of danger surrounding Sara. Perhaps his hope that they were not truly close arose more from his own need than from anything he had detected between them. Yet there was nothing remotely coquettish about her, so Stephen could not believe that he mistook altogether, when Sara looked at him, the merest shadow in her eyes that conveyed that she might not necessarily be completely committed elsewhere.

He watched her move into the building, thinking how good a red dress looks on a dark-haired woman, and feeling also neatly unavailable to answer her worried questions. He would not have to explain that James was much as before and see the disappointment in her eyes. James was, if anything, slightly worse, he reminded himself, slipping fretfully back into his original line of thought. Patients with major rebalancing to accomplish before the body's own healing power prevailed often did get worse before they got better. It was a salutary reminder, Stephen thought, of the devastating effects that shock and stress can have on a body, because it was since Warwick's and Bunny's deaths that James had relapsed. Sometimes, he justified, the body needed a dose of the most effective natural relaxant known to man, and it was a pity that someone had not tipped a large brandy down James's throat on

Friday. After another careful look round he unscrewed the top off the juice bottle and drained the last of the vodka. It wasn't as if it was a habit with him, after all, but it would not play well with either his loyal staff or adoring patients if they learned that from time to time he allowed himself to break his own rules. He was human, and it was not his fault, he thought peevishly, if people sometimes forgot that.

CHAPTER 35

'YOUR CLIENT WHAT?' Detective Sergeant Bridger asked Debbie Trowbridge.

'I have advised my client that this identity parade contravenes the law and that even if he were to be positively identified, that would be inadmissible. Consequently my client is unhappy. And so am I,' Debbie Trowbridge said in her official voice, with a barely discernible tremble of anger in it. That was the way this kind of guy got you, by making you so angry you showed it. His body language, which she translated accurately as *I've got a cock and you haven't*, made her so furious that she was in danger of losing the cool professional edge that she had trained herself to add to her voice, which she considered too light for a solicitor. She cleared her throat and raised her eyebrows. By concentrating on the farce for which this idiot was responsible, she could direct her anger where it belonged.

'The conduct of this identity parade contravenes— Sergeant, are you listening to me?'

Bridger, about to fish in his pockets for cigarettes and matches, was raising a hand in greeting to someone behind her, who had presumably just entered the corridor by the doors at the end. Bridger stood up straighter.

'Sergeant, I don't seem to be getting through. I want to see DCI Poole. He's leading this enquiry, isn't he?'

'I am. And good morning, Miss Trowbridge. Are we all set, Bridger? I hope your client's ready?'

Thank God for a sane person to talk to. Debbie Trowbridge shook her head. 'Sorry. I've been trying to get through to your sergeant here.' DCI Poole was about to be as appalled as she had been, and it was she who was about to appall him.

'My client, as you know, has been bailed pending further police enquiries into the murder of his wife. He has met all bail conditions in good faith and cooperated fully, at a time of considerable distress and difficulty for him. He should have returned to Japan last Friday. My client—'

Andrew interrupted indulgently. 'Yes, yes, yes, understood. I'm not the magistrate, Debbie. What's your point?'

'My point,' Debbie said, shaking her blonded hair and allowing herself to crow, 'is that this identity parade has been rigged in a way which will put my client in an unfair position. All those taking part in an identity parade, if I may just remind you of your obligations under PACE—'

'What's the matter with the parade? Bridger? You've had a whole week to set this one up. What's wrong with it?' Andrew asked sharply, turning to Bridger.

'You haven't seen the line-up yourself, then?'

'Of course I haven't. I can't organise an ID parade when I'm the officer leading the enquiry, you know that.'

'It was the best I could do. I tried to tell you it'd be impossible,' Bridger appealed to them, simultaneously defensive and pathetic. 'You try getting hold of twelve middle-aged Japanese men who'll cooperate. Most of them didn't understand what we were asking, even with the interpreter. The ones that did didn't want to come in to a police station on a Monday morning, why should they? They're on holiday. I had to improvise.' He looked accusingly at Debbie Trowbridge. 'If you ask me, she's making too much of it.'

Debbie looked hard at DCI Poole. 'Six out of the ten men waiting to be in the line-up are English. Your sergeant could only find three other Japanese apart from the suspect. So the other six are wearing eyeliner. Two of them have black wigs on.'

She spoke slowly so as to spin out the effect, but was not enjoying the sight, much as she had hoped to, of Andrew Poole's effort to control his rage while the fact of Bridger's idiocy sank in. She returned down the corridor, trying not to make the clack of her heels sound unpleasantly triumphant. Poor Andrew Poole. She admired his control, really. It was not until she was just through the swing doors that she heard his voice shouting something, she could not be sure *exactly* what, but she fancied it was something about not the fucking D'Oyly Carte.

*   *   *

ANDREW STEPPED through the doors out of the police station and took a deep breath of air. He had left Inspector Lovesey, the officer in charge of the ID parade, reeling with amazement at Bridger's crassness. Andrew, knowing him better, was not. Lovesey had been apologetic. He had rather let Bridger get on with it, he conceded to Andrew, who had pointed out that that was always, with Bridger, a mistake. And, he had gone on, the aborted ID parade had been his last and only hope of getting enough evidence to charge the suspect. The only other evidence was

circumstantial, insufficient to charge, and Debbie Trowbridge had not had to point out that if after more than two
weeks the enquiry had come up with nothing new then
the police could not justifiably claim to have 'reasonable
grounds to suspect'. And without those grounds her client
could not be charged and must be released. Professor
Takahashi was going back to Japan. And so was Mrs Takahashi. They had released her body for burial and her sister
would be arriving the next day to take her home.

Beyond the wall of the station the ordinary-looking mix
of people in Bath in summertime trooped past on heavy
feet, a disproportionate number weighed down with
backpacks and luggage. The pedestrian crossing peeped
intermittently, the traffic slowed, people walked, pushed
pushchairs, pedalled bikes. Some, like the man edging out
the door of Comet with a microwave the size of a large
kennel, would be local. Others carried leaflets and cam-
eras, their worn faces betraying the drudgery of European
city-hopping. Probably not one of them had wasted, nor
would now waste, a single second of their lives worrying
about the murder of a thirty-one-year-old Japanese wife,
or the husband who killed her.

Still standing on the steps of the station, Andrew
yawned. It was tempting, for a moment, to think of spending the rest of the afternoon either drunk, asleep, or both,
but he had promised Sara that he would look in on James
before he set off with Dan. Despite their having parted
yesterday in mutual rage (such a goddam fuss over a stiff
shoulder) he would do so. Sighing heavily in a useless attempt to breathe the anger and disappointment out of his
body, he set off for the Sulis.

Andrew took the entrance to the clinic almost at a run

and made swiftly across the empty hall for the stairs. It had been Sara's idea that he should get in and up to James's room as quickly as possible and so avoid any imperious advice not to disturb the patient, but the hall remained silent. Sister Yvonne and her colleagues must be standing guard over some other ailing inmate, Andrew supposed, and framed the idea in his mind to tell James this as amusingly as he could. But the moment he entered the room he could see that James, who was awake and would have preferred not to be, would be neither receptive to the joke nor capable of laughing. Andrew stifled a gasp. In the space of three days James seemed to have lost half the air in his body. He lay on top of his bed like a half-deflated, greyish container for a human being rather than a person who properly filled his own frame. His breathing was short. In his eyes Andrew saw relief rather than pleasure to see him, and fear. James raised both hands, which were trembling violently. Beneath the covers his legs and torso kicked and jerked.

'It feels like things are crawling all over me. It's disgusting. All over. I shut my eyes and I see things, it's horrible. I haven't slept.'

'But—' Andrew gathered his wits just in time to remember that it would not be a good idea to let James see how alarmed he was. 'What does the doctor say? Dr Golightly's seen you, surely?'

James nodded. 'Didn't say much. Try to rest. Body needs time. Keep fluids up.' He closed his eyes. 'But I feel sick all the time. I can't control my hands. Can you get Tom? Please get Tom.'

Andrew considered for a moment, and spoke calmly.

'The first thing I think I should do is get you to a hospital. Don't you think that's where you should be?'

'I told them that, I said I've never ever felt this bad. Dr G said highly inadvisable. Yvonne says nursing's appalling at the RUH, I'm better off here. Dr G doesn't want—'

'To hell with what Dr G wants.' Andrew felt his earlier anger rise up again and this time he directed it, rightly or wrongly he did not care, towards Stephen Golightly. He was too furious to waste time arguing. 'I think a little direct action is called for. Come on. Get that blanket round you. Now—that's it. Put your arms round my neck and hang on.'

James breathed thanks, before allowing himself to be wrapped in the blanket and lifted from the bed. On a better day he might have managed some facetious remark about Andrew's butch arms but he said nothing more, simply hoping he was not too heavy and that he would be able to lie still. On the hazardous way down he hung on and kept his eyes closed, nervous in principle but almost doubting if the experience of landing on the hall floor, having been dropped down five flights of stairs, would in practice make him feel any worse than he did already.

From the window of the treatment room Sister Yvonne saw the large, fluttering white bundle being carted down to the car park, opened her mouth to squawk and closed it again. For there was nobody she could squawk to. Dr Golightly was upstairs seeing Mrs Valentine, Joyce was in her room with her damn dog who, she claimed, was still sick, and the only other people on the premises also had problems of their own. She turned from the window and looked closely at Hilary on the couch.

'Feeling a bit better, now?' she asked, with genuine

concern. She had surprised herself by finding that she could actually feel tenderly towards the woman.

Hilary, lying white-faced, began to cry again and tried to sit up.

'Oh, dear, dear, dear,' Yvonne said, settling her back down. 'Don't try to move yet. Just you lie there, dear, till Ivan gets back. You're going to be fine. No pain, is there? No? Now remember, that's a very good sign.' She smiled a smile of professional optimism. 'Spotting's terribly common in the first few weeks, remember. It's usually nothing to worry about at all. I know it's upsetting, of course you're worried, but staying calm's the best thing you can do for Baby. Isn't it?'

The door opened and Ivan entered, carrying a cup and saucer. The sight of his face, as white as Hilary's and scarcely less frightened, brought a lump to Yvonne's throat. He must want that baby as desperately as Hilary did. She squeezed her crossed fingers in her uniform pocket, begging some imagined, consultant-like deity, the great Obstetrician in the Sky, that Hilary's unexpected slight show of blood should not be the start of a miscarriage. Please make it all right for them, poor things.

'Has it stopped?' Ivan asked anxiously. 'There's no more, is there?'

Hilary shook her head. 'It's only the bit I saw when I went to the loo.'

'And it's bright red, not thick and dark,' Yvonne said comfortably. 'That's another good sign. And when you're feeling better, we'll ring your midwife. I expect she'll want to check you over.'

Hilary managed a weak smile to Ivan as he handed her

the cup of tea. He sat gingerly on the side of the couch and stroked her hair.

'Poor Hil. Poor, poor Hilly. You mustn't be frightened. You've had a dreadful shock, but it's going to be all right. I *know* it will.' Ivan's eyes were glowing with love and confidence. Hilary sipped her tea and mustered her strength. If Ivan could overcome his own fear in order to reassure her, then she must do the same for him. She smiled.

'It will, pet. I'm sure it will. Baby's going to be fine, aren't you?' she said, addressing her belly in a cooing tone. Ivan placed a hand on her stomach tenderly and she covered it with her own and let it rest there, feeling her love pulsing like a pleasant sort of ache into him, through his hand and down into the wet cave under her skin where the baby lay.

Sister Yvonne had been a nurse too long to feel any medical shyness but she averted her eyes from them and turned again to the window. She was past all the wanting babies business, now. Babies hadn't been an option for her and Chris but hey (as Chris would say), they had so much else going for them. They had each other, a nice house, good jobs and good friends. Eleven years now. Nobody got absolutely everything they wanted in this life, she thought, sighing and turning back from the window. And right this minute she had better concentrate on what to do next. Ivan and Hilary had better stay together here, which meant that she and Joyce would have to oversee the catering girls and the preparation of supper, though she was willing to bet that Joyce would either refuse to leave her dog, or not be in her room. Where did that woman go? She could, Yvonne supposed, manage by herself if necessary. There weren't all that many to feed now, after all. She had already thought better of going up to Dr Golightly, who was still with Mrs Valentine, to tell him of James's departure. The doctor had enough to worry about already, because quite apart from the possible miscarriage of his grandchild, Mrs Valentine was really not at all well. In fact, Sister Yvonne did not like the look of her at all.

CHAPTER 36

Yuko Matano placed the lilies on the floor by the door to the Ladies and stood quietly with her head bowed. Andrew waited behind her, appalled at her dignity, appalled too that the poignancy of the gesture had to compete with the squalor of its setting. There could be no comfort in Mrs Takahashi's meeting her end here. Her eyes had not rested on anything beautiful in the seconds before her killer took her forever beyond beauty. She had died in a dirty corridor outside a lav, and there was nothing in that fact that could elevate it to the status of a place of pilgrimage. Only the love of a sister inspired to leave lilies did that. Andrew's eyes filled with tears.

Mrs Matano turned and signalled that she was ready to leave. They were walking back towards Manvers Street, the formalities over, when Andrew glanced down at her and saw that tears were running silently down her face. Not caring if he was meant to or not, he took her elbow and steered her into the coffee place in the Podium. When they were sitting down with cups of espresso Mrs Matano smiled and apologised. Andrew saw how tired she was. His shame at not being able to report that her sister's killer had been charged left him almost unable to say anything at all.

'Please, don't apologise. I should apologise. We . . . I wish . . . what . . . what will you do now?'

'Oh, first get back home. Consulate is helping me. We have funeral to arrange. Our parents . . .' She broke off to wipe her eyes. 'I did not tell them about the baby, now I am glad they do not know. Mitsuko wanted to tell them herself. After she had told Kenichi.'

'You mean, he didn't know?'

Yuko looked at him sadly. 'No. I tell her this is wrong, I tell her she should. When she call me those times, I say she should tell him and he would understand. Understand everything.'

'Understand what?'

She sighed. 'I can tell you now. There is no secret now, no point. When she marry Kenichi they agree at first no children, Kenichi did not want more children. So my sister is afraid to say, and she is so, so sick with the baby. She cannot stand it.'

'I don't understand. What couldn't she stand? Didn't she want to be with him? Is that why she left?'

'No, no, she love him. But Kenichi is much older and old-fashioned. He believe that a Japanese wife takes care of a husband, she serves him food, sit with him always when they eat, this is the old-fashioned way. And Mitsuko, she cannot do this when she is sick. She tell me on phone. She cannot bear to watch him eat. She feels even sicker.'

Andrew's mind flew back to his first meeting with Professor Takahashi over breakfast and felt in complete sympathy. 'You don't mean she left him because she couldn't bear to watch him eat?'

'No, no—not so simple. She is so upset he does not understand and still she does not tell him why. She is screaming and he slapped her on face, *pah!* once like that, to stop her. She wanted time to be by herself and plan what to do. She was worried, also a little jealous.'

'Jealous? How come?'

Yuko hesitated. 'My sister very much younger. She hoped her marriage will put all sadness and unhappiness away from Kenichi. But inside he is still unhappy, getting better only very slow. My sister is jealous that she does not make him so happy as his first wife. And he does not want a family, he is still . . . what word to use . . . in pain. For what happened. For his first wife.'

'What do you mean? What did happen?'

Yuko began to cry again. 'For him it is too much, it is too much for one man in one life. His two children, his wife, they died. In Kobe earthquake.'

CHAPTER 37

Next day when the wailing first started, it came almost as a relief.

*   *   *

Yvonne had never known an atmosphere like it in Dr Golightly's consulting room and for the first hour of the day she had been trying to conduct herself in a whispering, indirect manner towards him, which she hoped signalled that she understood he would prefer it if she were not present. But she had to be, of course. Just because things were not going well was no reason to skip the daily updates on each patient; if anything it was more important than ever. But she had found it very difficult to express the view that Mrs Valentine seemed worse today without it sounding as if she had lost faith in Dr Golightly, whose reproachful eyes seemed to be saying that he knew that, actually, she had.

'Highly likely to be viral, I would have said. Wouldn't you say, Doctor?'

Stephen Golightly's eyes flickered for a second, but he shook his head slowly, less in disagreement than impatience.

'Hmm? Oh, yes, possible that her immune system's compromised by stress, divorce and so on,' he said tightly. 'I suppose she might be prone to viral infection. But this . . . this . . .'

'You see, I was wondering, if it's viral, then perhaps she really should be moved . . . you know, put in isolation somewhere. And if it's viral, it'd explain why James—Mightn't it?'

Dr Golightly replied at once, wishing to rid himself of the need to engage with Yvonne's slower mind, because of course he had already considered the viral question and dismissed it, attractive though it might have been as an explanation. Although now that James had probably been admitted to hospital he hoped that he was not going to have to go public with any reassurance which, however it were phrased, would immediately sound as if there were something to worry about. He could see the *Bath Chronicle* now: PRIVATE CLINIC DISMISSES SUPERBUG FEARS.

'No, it's not viral. We have no airconditioning, which is how these things proliferate. The heating system is off. And anyway, if it were viral, we should have a great many more than two patients unwell. Furthermore, their symptoms were only superficially similar—raised temperature, for example. That's too general a symptom to aid diagnosis. I should have thought you'd know that.'

'Yes, of course I do see what you mean,' Yvonne said, rather hotly. She had never seen Dr Golightly tense and angry; he always made you feel safe. But the greatest surprise was just how unfair he was being. She determined to jolly him out of it and with a sympathetic wrinkle of her nose she said, 'Do you know, I think we worry too much. I mean, people come here unwell, don't they? It's just because usually everybody gets better that it seems so terrible when a couple don't, at least not straight away. You're a victim of your own success really, aren't you?'

It was almost tempting for a moment to succumb to such a cosy point of view, but Stephen Golightly shook his head again. 'It's not viral. I think Mrs Valentine is showing early symptoms of Parkinson's.'

Yvonne's mouth dropped open. 'Oh heavens. She's only thirty-seven.'

Dr Golightly nodded. 'Onset's been very sudden. It can take years, though of course we don't know for sure that she simply hasn't noticed a gradual weakening in her hands.'

The room seemed physically to darken with the unrelenting bad news. Dr Golightly broke the silence by saying, 'Some people really don't seem to have much luck, do they?' It almost sounded from the bitterness in his voice that he was not referring to his unfortunate patients. And it was just as Yvonne was composing in her mind a rallying remark about how effective drug treatments for Parkinson's were nowadays, that the wailing reached their ears.

*   *   *

STEPHEN, CLOSELY followed by Yvonne, was first to arrive in the hall, where Joyce, newly emerged from the staff staircase, was staggering about, her face contorted and a high-pitched, windy pibroch of noise wheezing from her thin lips. She was cradling in her arms a stinking bundle of brown hide, wrapped in a green sweatshirt. The keening screeches of a deranged, elderly Scotswoman were too much for Yvonne. She brought them to an abrupt stop with a competent crack of her palm across Joyce's face and followed up the assault, in her most professionally sooth-ing voice, with the suggestion that she come along and sit down.

'Pretzel,' moaned Joyce, holding out the bundle. One blackish ear slapped out over her hand. 'My wee Pretzel. My wee dog's gone. He's dead, eech augh waaugh . . .'

Stephen's serenely arranged face collapsed and red-dened. Two of the cleaners had now arrived in the hall. 'For God's sake! This is a stress-free environment!' he shouted. He swung round, haranguing the air. 'Christ, is there not enough going on here already! I will not put up with this nonsense in my clinic, least of all over a fucking dog! Get her out of here,' he shouted to Yvonne. 'And that filthy corpse. Out! Get her back upstairs!'

Yvonne had turned from the sobbing Joyce and stared, astonished. Three of the catering assistants arrived at the top of the kitchen stairs, poured into the hall and stood, staring. Stephen was not so lost in anger that he was not able to count to five: that made five members of staff, ex-cluding Yvonne and Joyce, watching him lose control; five people with families, friends, neighbours, who now had a lovely, shocking, gossipy story to go home with about how Dr Golightly and the Sulis Clinic were falling apart.

'But, Dr Golightly, she's upset. She needs to be treated for shock. Don't you think we should—' At that moment Yvonne caught sight of Ivan. Drawn by the noise he stood in his apron, immobilised by surprise, in the doorway of the stairs to the kitchen. Yvonne still had hold of Joyce's heaving shoulders. She wondered how long he had been there watching her cope alone, too stunned to offer help.

'Look, Ivan, I think you'd better try and help your fa-

ther calm down. Take him along to the drawing room. Stay
with him. I'll deal with this one.'

Ivan hesitated just long enough to tempt Yvonne to
shout to him to stop blinking like an idiot and behave like
a man. But just as she was restraining herself from upsetting him too, which would leave her the only person in
control and seriously outnumbered by the hysterics, he
heaved himself off the doorframe and took Stephen's arm.
He was trying to mimic the expression of benign calm that
truly belonged on his father's face.

'Come on, Dad. You mustn't get so upset. Joyce didn't
mean any harm, she's just upset. And so are you.' He
smiled kindly. 'You've been overdoing things.'

Stephen looked slightly shamefaced and nodded.

'Come on,' Ivan went on, confidently, 'we'll go and sit
down for a moment. No need to get so upset. Joyce hasn't
disturbed any patients, has she, because there aren't any
here.'

CHAPTER 38

THE BEST CITIES are surrounded by hills, Sara thought, bored by the unoriginality of her observation but not by the view of Salzburg and the Salzach River that she was looking down upon from the Hohensalzburg Castle. A large board had informed her that the castle was eleventh century and that she was standing 120 metres above the city.

'The best cities are surrounded by hills,' declared the second viola from somewhere behind her. Sara edged away, to avoid having to respond. She was not being grand in avoiding a mere second viola, it was just that this second viola, Bernadette Xavier, happened to be a tedious Liverpudlian who, when she was not displaying grotesque maternal importance by bringing 'my two' into every conversation, was fond of announcing yawn-inducing clichés which she clearly thought were insights, about music, travel and life in general. Bernadette had attached herself to the group consisting of Charlie (the leader of the orchestra), Jeff and Geoff (first violin and principal viola), and Mel (Geoff's girlfriend, second viola and desk partner of Bernadette, to whom she was almost allergic) and Sara.

So far during their lunch and free time between rehearsals and that evening's concert they had been enlightened thus by Bernadette: Austrian beer is very good, it's not the salad that's fattening it's the mayonnaise, the Salzburg festival attracts an awful lot of tourists, and her two would have loved the cable-car ride up to the castle on top of the rock. By the time Sara was being told that the best cities were surrounded by hills she was ready to hurl Bernadette off it. She strolled away and joined Charlie, who was sitting on a bench at a viewing platform enjoying a fag. He smiled, seeing Bernadette now some way behind.

'Sorry about her.'

'Oh, never mind,' Sara said, sitting down. 'We couldn't have told her not to come with us, could we?' They listened as Bernadette accosted the others who were catching up. 'She's got no idea, has she?' Sara said quietly.

'None. She thinks she's fascinating. Still, doesn't really spoil it, does it? Great up here. Have you got your luggage yet, by the way?'

Sara nodded. It had gone astray on Sunday somewhere between Heathrow and Salzburg so she had simply *had* to go out on Monday and buy quite a few new clothes and shoes. Such a nuisance. And a coincidence that she had bought things which Andrew would probably not like (have liked, rather, since his opinion of how she looked no longer concerned her). 'It arrived last night. No problem, except I might not get all the new stuff in to go home.'

Charlie laughed and inhaled on his cigarette. 'Won't offer you one. Don't smoke, do you?'

'No. But I drink a lot. And gamble recklessly, and lose,' Sara said, thinking of Dvořák and Andrew, in that order.

Charlie laughed again. 'That reminds me. What happened to your wino? You know, that old dear you rescued when she fell over pissed at the Albert Hall. What happened?'

Sara gave a sudden laugh which she had not intended to sound as bitter as it did. 'Come on, let's wander on before Bernadette catches us up. Leave her to the others for a bit. You do realise, don't you, who the wino was? Is, I mean.'

Charlie shook his head. He had gone straight off home at the end of the concert because his partner, Cathy, on maternity leave from her place in the orchestra, was coping with the baby alone and it was his turn to be the one up in the small hours.

'Joyce Cruikshank. You know—Royal Scottish Academy?'

'Get away. Get *away*. Wait till I tell Cathy. There was quite a story, wasn't there?'

'I don't really know. I managed to get something out of her about losing someone, someone close to her. She wouldn't tell me any more.'

They strolled on. Charlie said, 'Cathy was there at the time, you know. She only did second study cello so she didn't get Crookie but she knew the bloke. She'd always wondered what happened afterwards. Poor old Crook didn't have many options.'

'After what? What bloke? You don't mean she had a *man*?'

'Well, no, not quite. He was one of her students, very good-looking, very, very talented. The story was she was a bit obsessed with him. You mean to say you never heard, then? The thing with the bloke and the biscuit?'

'I didn't keep in touch after I left,' Sara said, shaking her head. 'I only heard she'd retired a bit early. I do remember her biscuits, though. She made very good biscuits.'

'Yes, well, she retired as in resignation required.'

'I don't think I really liked her much, not even then. I learned a lot but I was always uncomfortable. What happened?'

'Apparently she had a student, this bloke who she taught at home, one of her stars. He had a nut allergy. You know, the really serious kind where you go into severe shock. And Crookie always had tea and home-made biscuits, all that stuff, after the lesson.'

Sara groaned. 'I do remember that.'

'Right. Well the bloke never ate anything without asking first if it had nuts in. He wouldn't risk it, would he, especially home-made things. But he ate one of her biscuits this particular day and went into shock.'

'She *poisoned* him?'

'Either she must have known he had the allergy and forgotten about it, or she forgot she'd put nuts in the biscuits.'

'Or did it deliberately,' Sara suggested, wondering even as she said it if perhaps she had spent too much time with a detective. 'Perhaps out of jealousy, because he had a young beautiful girlfriend, maybe. Or pique, or blind rage, because she declared herself and he rejected her. What a tragedy.'

'I remember now, it was all to do with ground almonds. It was shortbread. He was about twenty, I think, damn good player. He died.'

'Oh, God. Poor guy. Poor *Joyce*.'

'The police got involved. It wasn't very clear, you see, because his parents claimed he knew how to avoid that kind of accident and must have been told it was safe. They blamed Cruikshank. There was talk of a possible manslaughter charge, but the coroner—'

'Procurator-fiscal,' Sara corrected him. 'In Scotland.'

'Yeah, anyway, they decided at the inquest—'

'Fatal accident enquiry, in Scotland.'

'Do you want to hear this or not? They couldn't prove negligence or malice, so they decided on accidental death. Crookie retired early, moved away from Glasgow, disappeared. Couldn't handle it, Cathy thought.'

'Poor, poor thing,' Sara said. A picture of sad-eyed Joyce standing in the spare bedroom at Medlar Cottage, stooped in her disgraceful old underwear with the rag of filthy pink suit on the floor at her feet, swam into her mind. 'Poor thing.'

As they continued down the steps and terraces that wound gently down the castle rock Sara found herself hoping very much that Joyce had not been in love with her beautiful, clever boy. Her pain at causing such an accident would be enough in itself, enough to demolish her self-worth and trigger the drinking. Sara did not see how it could be borne at all if she had killed not just a student in her care, but also the thing she loved.

More than halfway down was a booth selling ice creams and drinks, surrounded by half a dozen wooden picnic tables and wasps doing reconnaissance flights. They bought ice cream and bottles of water and waited until the others caught them up and folded themselves into the uncomfortable benches.

'There's a church worth seeing, according to the book,' someone said after they had been sitting for a time over their drinks, trapping wasps and getting too hot. 'Down in the square.'

'I'm burning,' Sara said. 'Anywhere cool and dark sounds good to me.' There was a groan or two and nobody moved. 'Isn't anyone else coming?'

'Oh, I am,' Bernadette said brightly. 'I never miss a church, when I'm abroad.' Sara could not think of any way of stopping her from coming, short of nailing her cheek to the table, which flashed for one joyous instant through her mind. But the others surely would not deliver her up to Bernadette's sole company? She stared at them until they all, even Charlie, looked guiltily away. As well they might, the traitors.

Sara's extravagantly pious crossing of herself on entering the church did not put Bernadette off. She followed closely.

'It's quite old, isn't it? Oh, there's a pulpit!'

And no amount of slow intaking of breath and raising of the eyes, hinting at a private burden patiently borne, not even the lighting of a candle, was going to signal to this woman that Sara might have some personal matter to discuss with Our Lord and would like to be left alone. Not that she had, but really, with a name like Bernadette, should she not have been at least a little responsive to the idea of prayerful solitude in the lady chapel?

'Oh, isn't that *funny*?' cried Bernadette. 'St Anton, it says. That means St Anthony. The church is dedicated to St *Anthony*.' She was pointing up at a vast, filthy oil painting which hung almost in the dark in one of the side aisles. It was the seventh or eighth image of him that Sara had noticed, apart from the sign outside which gave the name.

'What's funny about that?'

'Well——St Anthony. When we're playing the St Anthony

Variations tonight. And the cello concerto by *Anton Dvořák*. Don't you think that's a really weird coincidence?'

'No, not really.'

'Oh, where's your imagination?' Bernadette said, pushing her arm gently. They were not quite alone in the church, so as Bernadette continued pointing out features in her loud voice, as if she were regaling a friend in Marks and Spencers with something she had just spotted on the separates rail, Sara felt both embarrassed and bored.

'I wonder if we should be a bit quieter,' she whispered. 'We might be spoiling the atmosphere for other people if we're too loud. Don't you think?'

Bernadette smiled pityingly. In fairness, the other visitors in the church were also tourists forced in out of the sun. 'The Temptation of St Anthony,' she whispered, pointing at the canvas, 'see?'

Sara looked, wondering what was supposed to be tempting about grappling bare-handed with a toothed serpent the length of a fireman's hose, which was what the beleaguered saint was doing. For fear of prompting an explanation, she kept quiet and moved on.

'The devil sent him visions,' Bernadette supplied. 'He lived on bread and water in the desert, and he fasted in the wilderness to get rid of them.'

Sara ignored her and gazed at the next picture, in which St Anthony was simply standing with a cross or a crutch in one hand and with the other raised, blessing things. Bernadette shuffled along beside her and pointed again. 'There he is again. He's always got a pig with him. My two always find that funny.'

It was the first almost imperceptibly interesting thing that Sara had ever heard her say. She looked hard at the picture and indeed saw, peeping round St Anthony's robe, a pig.

'Why does he, I wonder,' she said, not really asking.

'Oh, patron saint,' Bernadette said airily, 'he's the patron saint of swineherds. Every litter used to have a piglet named after him, I think. Third-century hermit, Anthony was, lived in Egypt.'

'You do know a lot,' Sara said.

'Oh, we certainly know our saints in my family,' Bernadette said. 'Because of our name. We changed it, you know. You see,' she dropped her voice at last to a tolerably low volume, 'I wasn't born a Xavier, none of us were Xaviers at all. Our surname was Thick. You wouldn't believe it, would you, imagine being saddled with a name like that!'

Sara nodded sympathetically, not trusting herself to say anything.

'It was fine until my parents moved to Liverpool and we came along, my sister and brothers and me. We were all teased, well, hardly surprising. Not a lot of fun, a Liverpool playground, when your name is Thick.' She sighed heavily. 'So we decided, all of us, to change our name. My mum wanted us to take a saint's name, she's quite religious, and we all agreed. Trouble was, we couldn't agree which one.'

'So how did you decide? Did you just toss a coin or something?'

'Good Lord, no. We're Liverpool Catholics, remember. We went through the whole of Butler's *Lives of the Saints* and fought it out over every single one. We couldn't agree on one we all liked. By the time we got to Xavier my dad put his foot down and that was that.'

They both laughed. Sara looked again at the dark picture. 'So who are those people, then? What are those flowers they're holding out?' she asked, pointing to three tiny
figures reaching up to the saint and offering in their out-
stretched hands what might have been huge yellow
dahlias.

'Oh, can't remember,' Bernadette said. 'Don't remember anything about flowers. Although maybe that was the
other St Anthony.'

Sara looked blank.

'You know, St Anthony of Padua,' Bernadette said
breezily. 'Twelfth century. Devoted himself to the poor, I
think.'

They gazed in silence for a few more moments and began to make their way slowly back down the nave to the
West door.

'It does matter, you know, what you're called,'
Bernadette said seriously. 'Do you realise, before I
changed my name, people really did treat me as if I *was*
thick?'

'Disgraceful,' Sara murmured, strolling ahead of her
out of the church and back into the sunshine.

CHAPTER 39

SARA TOOK A taxi from the Osterreichischer Hof. Her concerto was not until the second half of the concert so she had allowed herself the pleasure of lying in her bath right up till the moment when she knew the orchestra would be lifting their bows, blowing out their horns and fretting about their reeds, about to start the gracious St Anthony Chorale. She arrived backstage just as the first half was finishing and the orchestra was clattering in off the platform for the interval.

'There you are!' Bernadette was at her side. 'It came to me later! I thought, she'll really want to know that so I just had to find you and tell you.'

'Tell me *what*?' Sara wanted, needed and did not usually have to insist upon complete isolation and quiet before a performance. Her dressing room door was another twenty yards away. She did not stop walking, but Bernadette followed.

'Bernadette, if you don't mind—'

'I knew you'd want to know, you were so interested, so I got them to look it up when I rang home. I always speak to my two at six o'clock. Anyway, St Anthony was supposed to have power over fire. People used to get this

illness where their hands felt like they were burning and
they went mad. In the Middle Ages they thought it was the
devil or witchcraft and they prayed to St Anthony for intercession. Those people in the picture were praying for
relief. St Anthony's Fire it was called.'

'Lovely. Now——'

'But it wasn't witchcraft! It was caused by bad harvests.
Something in the grain, a blight or something, ergot poisoning, but then they didn't know that——'

Sara had reached the door of her dressing room and
opened it.

'Whole fields were affected. Imagine——field after
field . . .'

'Thank you, Bernadette,' she said without smiling,
stepping through and closing it almost in her face.

She breathed thankfully in the quiet of the room, relaxed her shoulders, cracked her knuckles and looked at
her watch. They had long intervals at these concerts, allowing plenty of time for the European great and good to
sip champagne and be seen sipping champagne in their expensive evening clothes. Still a clear half hour. Sara sighed
and tried to relax. All she had to do was step into her dress
and shoes, tune up, warm up and breathe deeply. And stop
worrying about being big enough for the Dvořák. Just
love it more, whatever that meant. And Andrew less.

It was after she had changed and tuned up and was
blowing on her fingers to keep them warm that
Bernadette's drivel suddenly came into her mind. Burning
hands. *Field after field*. Was it a line from a poem or something, like 'amid the shining corn'? Cornfields? There *was*
something about cornfields, field after field . . . Damn
Bernadette. She needed this space in order to prepare her-

self if she was going to give any kind of performance. *Mrs Takahashi's photographs*. Andrew had said it—bloody cornfields, field after field. Mrs Takahashi's pictures of the smallholding. She blew on her hands again. She thought of James and his strong pianist's hands. 'They feel hot, then cold,' he had said. She heard Stephen Golightly's words, 'Everything here is home-made and organic, you know. If we can't source it easily, we grow it ourselves, even some of our own cereals.'

'*Something in the grain, a blight or something, ergot poisoning*'. And she was on in ten minutes. If she had more sense than heart, she told herself, she would stay right here in her dressing room until it was time to go on. She would keep calm, play her Dvořák and deal with this admittedly very long shot (what Andrew would call jumping to conclusions) afterwards. Sense told her that another two hours could make no difference. Heart, however, seemed to be telling her calmly that there was no telephone in her dressing room and that her mobile would probably be useless in this city surrounded by mountains, so she must bring her address book and all the money she had. Out in the corridor she followed the sound of voices to the crowded backstage hall where most members of the orchestra were sitting out the interval. She made her way to the side of the room where the smokers congregated next to a line of open windows.

'Charlie, Charlie, help me find a phone, quick. I've got to speak to someone. It's urgent.'

Thank God for burly, tall, competent people. Charlie took one look at her face, stubbed out his cigarette and grabbed her by the hand. 'Must be, if you can brave smokers' corner. Come on.'

Charlie worked his competent magic on a steward who

seemed to understand his experimental German and led
them behind the counter of an unused cloakroom. A pay-
phone that took coins only was mounted on the wall. Sara
stacked up all the money she had and flicked her address
book open under 'S'. She would not be able to reach
Andrew on his cycling trip anyway, even if she could have
brought herself to speak to him. Charlie watched for a
second before returning to the crowd in the hall. As Sara
dialled the number of the Sulis she could hear him holler-
ing for quiet and telling his colleagues to start fishing in
their pockets because La Selkirk needed their loose
change and not to argue. An amused murmur rose behind
her as the phone was answered. By the answering machine. Sara hesitated. How the hell was she to put it? Why
was nobody answering? Before Yvonne's official voice had
fully finished thanking her for her call, she hung up. She dialled again. This time it was answered by a croaky voice.

'Hello?'

Sara shoved in all the money she had. 'Joyce? Joyce, is
that you? Are you all right? It's me, Sara.'

'Oh. Oh, Sara.' Joyce seemed to need a pause in which
to recollect who Sara might be. 'Pretzel's dead.'

'Joyce? Oh Joyce, I am sorry. I'm really sorry but I've
only got a few seconds.'

There was a muffled grunt from the other end. Had
Joyce been drinking? There was no time to ask her to go
and bring someone more competent to the phone. 'Joyce,
listen. Tell Dr Golightly—'

'Och, Dr Golightly?' Even long distance, Joyce's con-
temptuous spit was audible. 'You should have heard him
going on, and my poor wee dog dead. Fat lot of use.

'Course I knew he was no good, he can't even read an X-ray.'

'Joyce, that isn't the point right now—'

'Reading X-rays is basic. There he goes, pointing away at the kidneys, can't even tell I've only got the one. I had one out in 1937. That was the year of the Abdication you know. Och, ruddy doctors, honest to God—'

'*Joyce!* Listen, Joyce, tell . . . Yvonne then, tell *anyone*— I think I know what's wrong with James. I think he might ttch have got er ot poi nin g, it's a thing you g t tt sksk grai s that makess you chcch—Jo ce, ar yo on a mo ile?'

'Eh? Oh, uh-uh. Right enough. Uh-uh, I know what it is, I remember now. That's what the thing was in Egypt, the epidemic. A while ago, mind. Did you know I was tutor to the Egyptian royal family?'

'Joyce, I have to go. can't tt sksk chch now but it might well be and you've got to find and stop chch tt ssk ssk the br cad and make sure James gets—'

She was interrupted by soft, pitiful wailing. 'Oh, Pretzel! He's dead! My wee Pretzel!' Joyce said something else but Sara was pushing in more coins and she couldn't hear what.

'Hello? What? Did you hear me? Are you chtt sts still there? Hello?' A pile of coins was building up on the counter beside her as Charlie came and went. She pushed in more. 'Joyce, I can't ssh chtt chtt you. What's that noise in the background? Wha ssh chttt chttt are you?'

'I can't hear you krr krr chtt I tt you James isn't here.'

'Isn't there? What? Chtt krrkrr you've got to tell them it's ss ch er got ch er ch. Hello?'

'Nobody's here. James IS IN THE RUH,' Joyce shouted.

'*What?*' She was running out of time again. As she

jammed more coins in she screamed, 'What? Tell *them,* then! Joyce?You need to tell the hospital.Then the Sulis— make sure they know. Can you hear me?'The line clicked and the dialling tone buzzed in her ear. Charlie stood nearby, concerned.

The members of the orchestra were slowly moving about, picking up their instruments, combing hair, waiting. Two minutes. Frantically, Sara summoned the steward again and together with Charlie she managed to get the number for international directory enquiries. She dialled it, got through at once on a perfect line and after only a few seconds' wait heard a mechanical voice giving her the number of the Royal United Hospital, Bath.

The agitated concert hall manager was now at her elbow. 'The audience is seated, Fräulein Selkirk.The orchestra is ready to go on.'

'Just a minute. I'll only be a minute.'

'Fräulein Selkirk, the recording team is ready. And the audience must not be kept waiting—'

She was through, but the line was echoey. The Austrian manager had been joined by the orchestral manager.

'Eh, Miss Selkirk, is there a problem? Would you get ready to go on stage, please?'

'RoyalUnitedHospitalhowmayIhelpyou?' said someone who sounded like a toy, her voice miniaturised by the bad line.

How may they help her? Christ, where would they like her to start? She took a deep breath, raised a finger to indicate one minute to the furious and now sweating concert manager and said, 'I'm ringing about a friend of mine. I'm ringing from abroad. Can I speak to him? James Ballantyne.'

'What ward?'

'I don't know. The name is James Ballantyne.'

She paused to shove in coins.

'When was he admitted?'

'I'm sorry, I don't know that.'

'Miss Selkirk, I really have to ask you—'

'*One* moment.'

'*SSH!* I won't be long, promise. Sorry.'

After eight rings and more coins a female voice said,

'GeneralEnquiriesvisitorshelplinehowmayIhelpyou?'

'I want to speak to a patient but I don't know the ward. James Ballantyne.'

'Fräulein Selkirk, Sir Simon is asking if all is well and wishes you please to get ready to go on stage at once.'

Sara answered by cramming more coins in the box.

'Hello? I'm calling from abroad, can you possibly hurry?'

'Onemomentplease. When was the patient admitted?'

'I don't *know*, I already told someone that—'

'Do you know what the patient was complaining of?'

'Fräulein, with Sir Simon's approval I am now sending the orchestra on stage. You must come now.'

'No, well, I mean, not for sure—that's why . . . Look, the name is James Ballantyne.'

'I don't need *your* name onemomentplease.'

'That's the patient's name! James Ballantyne!'

'Onemomentplease trying to connect you.'

More rings, then 'Ralph Allen Ward Nursing Assistant Harris speaking.'

The last members of the orchestra were now disappearing through the doorway leading to the stage and the last of Sara's coins was disappearing into the box.

Her voice and hands were now shaking. Trying not to

scream, she asked to speak to James Ballantyne. There was a pause, during which Sara heard the distant applause as the leader took his chair. Tuning started. Simon would be waiting to follow her on, his benign face thunderous.

'Are you family?'

'No, I'm a friend. I'm ringing from abroad, so if you could—' Christ, she must be mad, she couldn't stand here a moment longer. She had to go and play the Dvořák concerto. Oh God she couldn't . . .

'And the name of the patient again?'

'James Ballantyne. I'm a close friend.'

'Pardon me? Oh er, yes. Oh yes, right. Just a minute, I'll just get Sister to speak to you.'

While Sister was being got, Sara realised that she needed to pee again, and wouldn't be able to.

'Hello, Sister Banda speaking.'

'Hello, look, could I please speak to someone about James Ballantyne—'

'Oh yes, I'm sorry, you're a friend, is that right? You haven't heard, obviously.'

'Heard what?'

'I'm very sorry to have to tell you by phone, but I have to give you some bad news. I'm afraid your friend passed away yesterday. There were complications following surgery. And as there don't appear to be any—'

'Oh no. No, no no no—'

'I am sorry, but the end was—'

Sara had dropped the phone so the sister's careful words, that death when it came had been peaceful, pinked tinnily out of the swinging receiver, unheard.

CHAPTER 40

IT HAD BEEN a choice between throwing up on the stage or managing to wait until she got off the platform and back into her dressing room, so Sara retched luxuriantly into her dressing-room loo with a sort of numb self-congratulation that she had held on until the end of her fourth return to the stage. The outrageous bouquet that she had just accepted lay slumped against the wall where she had flung it, fearing she might be sick into it. The audience was still applauding, as if determined that she should go back for a fifth time, but gave up at around the same time as she finished groaning and was lifting her head to the mirror.

She did not know how she had managed to play the Dvořák at all but it appeared, as if it mattered, that she had played it rather brilliantly. She had been thinking only of James, though thinking was not quite what it had been, nor had it been totally its supposed opposite, feeling. It had been thinking and feeling fused into suffering of such intensity that it amounted to a kind of *knowing*. She splashed cold water on her face and tried to stop shaking. So, she thought, looking at her wrecked face, she had played the Dvořák brilliantly because she had played it in pain, knowing both love and loss, or rather getting to know them again. The good years since Matteo's death seemed less like the achievement of happiness than the mere wandering of her attention. How could she have forgotten what it was like? How was it possible that she loved James enough to feel like this, but not enough to have saved him? Love was powerless except to create pain. She pushed Andrew out of her mind. Would James have considered that tonight she had loved the Dvořák enough? Yes, probably, but she never would again.

She showered and changed into jeans and retched once more, and called through the dressing-room door to yet another enquiry from Charlie.

'Truly, Charlie, I'm all right. You go on with the others, I won't join you for dinner. No, I'm going straight back to the hotel, I've got a car.' Somehow, to join the others and send the news of the death of James Ballantyne round the orchestra would make it real. For as long as only she knew about it, she felt she could contain it, that she could make it somehow not quite the case. She stood no chance of bearing it at all unless she could fool herself that James was becoming dead a little bit at a time, in tiny pieces, until she was able to cope with the fact in its entirety.

She ought to tell Simon. He had been more puzzled than angry at her behaviour before the performance, though clearly quite delighted *by* the performance, but she had fled the minute she had got off stage and for that alone Sara knew that she owed him a proper explanation. But she could not trust herself to give it now. The kindness in his eyes would finish her, and she had to keep a hold on herself in order to negotiate a way of getting home tonight rather than waiting for her flight in the morning. She would write to him, she decided, she would write him a letter after she got home, which was the thing she had to concentrate on doing now.

At the Osterreichischer Hof she set the desk staff into a flurry by demanding information about flights that night, went up to pack and came down again fifteen minutes later. No flights that night from Salzburg.

'From somewhere else, then!' she almost shouted. 'What about Munich?'

There was no scheduled flight that night from Munich to Heathrow, but there was a charter to Stansted, leaving at 1.30 am. She could make it, just, as there was a train to Munich at 10.45. Would Madam like to book the flight? There was availability.

'Two,' Sara said, patiently. 'Two seats. I must have a seat for the instrument.' The concierge nodded without raising his eyebrows. Cellists, he'd seen them come and go: Cohen, Wallfisch, Isserlis. Very nice, some of them. Very fussy, all of them, about their instruments. This one was positively easygoing, next to some.

People who are travelling to attend to a death are the most efficient travellers, being if not quite intolerant, then indifferent to everyone else; to be in public with a privately breaking heart induces a particular stand-offish dignity. They must be constantly moving, as if by concentrating all energy on the process of getting there they can shrink the distances between destinations. Sara sat upright in the train, comforted by the speed of it. She drank water and ate peanuts, until she was sick again. As she brushed her teeth in the lurching train cubicle she deliberately did not look at her face, anticipating that it would show her her own wretchedness. In the plane she managed to doze for a short time, so that when the flight landed at Stansted she felt able to drive and hired a car.

As she drove out of the airport and into the dark countryside she found herself relaxing and smiling until she realised that she had been travelling under an odd, vague delusion that her unhappiness, too, would end when she arrived. She had been unconsciously taking comfort from the knowledge that she was drawing closer to the place where James would be as if she believed, in some ludicrous way, that he would be waiting for her, interested to hear all about her appalling journey. For the first time she wanted to cry. Instead, she turned her mind to practical considerations. James would (she recoiled from the thought of James's body) still be somewhere at the hospital, she supposed. She had not found out exactly when he had died, but now that she thought about it she realised that Tom must already know and could even be in Bath.

She reached the edge of the city at four o'clock in the morning. Now it was suddenly intolerable that she had arrived, for she was too early to do anything. As well as exhausted and on the edge of hysterical tears, she now also felt stupid. What difference could it have made to James if she had spent one more night in a comfortable hotel in Salzburg and arrived home on her booked flight—she added the hours up—only ten hours from now? Now there would be at least a five-hour wait in her empty house before she should even try to get in touch with Tom. The streets were deserted. She had rushed home as if James would be waiting and now there was nobody here, nobody who knew what she had done and nobody who cared. There was no Andrew and never would be, not after what they had said to each other. He did not even know about

James. Nobody did. There should be some sign that would show people what had happened, and how somebody felt about it.

Behind Bathwick Hill the pink and silver promise of light was stealing into objects and buildings. The day had almost begun, the first whole day and the first of thousands that Sara would see in the knowledge that another person dear to her was dead and would not see it too. She seized at a reason for her frantic journey home. She would watch the sunrise from James's look-out at the top of the Sulis garden, the place where she had last heard him laugh. She would think about him for a while and leave her flowers there. She would place them just where he had lain, the beautiful, wilting flowers she had been given for the performance that only James, because she loved him, had made it possible for her to give. How unbearable it was proving to be, loving. No private ceremony with flowers altered that, yet she would leave them in the way that people marked the place of a fatal event, a gesture she had never until this moment understood the point of.

CHAPTER 41

To SARA'S SURPRISE the gates to the Sulis were open, so she drove straight up and parked. The house was in complete darkness, not even an outside light shone. In the half-dark she set off, making for the terraces that led up to James's gazebo. She supposed, not really having thought about it until now, that if she were challenged by anyone she would simply tell them to fuck off and leave her alone, feeling somehow quite able to insist that wandering round someone's garden at four o'clock in the morning carrying a bunch of flowers was a perfectly reasonable thing to do.

The stillness of the garden was broken by a disturbance, or more the sense of a disturbance, from the direction of the swimming-pool temple. Until now it had not occurred to Sara to be frightened, but she did now dimly think, though curiously without much concern, that the person who had murdered Warwick Jones less than a week ago was still at large and might have killed for no reason. Turning towards the temple she saw a faint gleam of light, and as she watched there came a faint sound like a *hush*! Then the light broke into dancing specks and darts which lit up the pillars and sparkled out across the dim stone steps almost to the grass in front of the entrance. Somebody had just dived into the pool. Or was drowning.

Still clutching her flowers, Sara made her way swiftly across the grass and pulled open the sliding door. She was at once stilled by the atmosphere inside that was created by hundreds of candles, single tealights, set out on the floor and on little tables around the water's edge. Feeling that her entrance violated some almost divine, ceremonial atmosphere, she pulled the door closed behind her lest any breeze should blow them out. Hundreds of flames flickered and twisted in obedience to the gust that she had brought with her, righted themselves and burned true. It was so beautiful, so warm and quiet that Sara, as her eyes gazed at the golden light which gleamed off the water, wondered if she had been mistaken about the noise. No one was here. Just then, the dark water shivered. She followed with her eyes the darker line below its surface which, as it moved, sent a gentle wake which lapped up to the pool side. Someone was under water, swimming the entire length of the pool. The water broke when the shape reached the far end. The naked figure which emerged with its back to Sara, not quite far enough away to escape the candlelight which cast its glow along the body's edge, flattering or perhaps just showing it as it was: male and strong. Stephen Golightly stepped over to a chair and picked up his towel. Turning and peering, he laughed with surprise and called, in a voice that boomed sonorously across the water, 'Oh, you shouldn't have.'

'Whu-uh? Sorry? Uh?'

'For me?' He gestured at the bunch of flowers which hung half wrecked and forgotten in Sara's hand. As she stared, Stephen Golightly continued to stand smiling at her as if entirely unaware that he was naked. Then he took his towel and began to dry his face. While his head was covered, Sara took a long, involuntarily fascinated look at his groin, whose main attraction was wobbling rather endearingly as his arms energetically pummelled his hair dry. Stephen pulled the towel away from his head and began to walk a little unsteadily towards her end of the pool. As he walked he knotted the towel, as an afterthought, round his middle.

He had stopped smiling by the time he reached one of the tables from which he picked up a bottle. Sara had not noticed it, or the glass, behind the candles. Stephen was now looking at her seriously.

'Come on, I don't bite,' he said, gently. His speech was not slurred, exactly, but his tongue sounded thicker than it should be. 'You've heard, obviously. I'm so sorry. I'm sorry about everything.'

Sara stood rooted, tears now beginning to pour down her face, still clutching the damn flowers. Stephen took them from her and laid them down, then led her by the hand to a pile of lounger mattresses and towels spread out on the floor. She took the glass he offered and drained it. When she had finished the vodka she covered her face in her hands, feeling rather pointless, so she asked for another. She had not eaten for hours and had only dozed on the plane, so the fabulous stuff was hitting her just where it needed to. Stephen gave her more and when she had drunk it, he refilled the glass and drank that himself.

After a silence he said, rather unnecessarily, 'I've had quite a lot of this already.'

Sara nodded. She could see now that his smiles had

been rather forced. With his face now in repose he looked almost as bad as she did.

'It's all over,' he said, waving an arm loosely. 'All these lights, they're for the aromatherapy burners. We buy in bulk. This is the whole damn lot. Go out in a blaze, I thought.'

'It's very pretty.'

'There's no one left now. I've cancelled new admissions. The clinic's gone. I'm leaving—'

'Have they found out any more about Warwick?'

Stephen shook his head. 'They're looking for Leech. They seem quite sure it was him. They're interviewing people, people he knew, people from here.' After a silence he said, 'But they've let that other man go, the husband of that Japanese woman. It was in the *Chronicle*. He didn't do it, he's gone back to Japan.'

'Oh *no*. Really? But he *did* do it. They just can't prove it. Andrew was— Oh, God, it doesn't matter.'

'To be honest, I've had my mind on other things.'

'Of course.'

'Sara, I'm so sorry. I'm so sorry about James. I promise we did all we could.'

'Don't tell me about it, I can't bear to hear it. Not yet. It's too late. What are you doing swimming at four o'clock in the morning, anyway?'

'I love this place. It's my last night. One last night, and I thought I'd spend it here. Clinic's finished. One last night before I leave.' Stephen smiled unhappily.

'You sound very final about it.'

'Well, I'm realistic.' He poured himself another drink and sipped it. 'The clinic's finished. Everything happened rather quickly down at the RUH. The police came and took medical files for the coroner, before I could, well, tidy them up. Yes, they'll look into everything very thoroughly, I have no doubt.'

He looked earnestly at Sara. 'I'm human, too. I make mistakes. Doctors do make mistakes. But I want you to know I've genuinely tried to help my patients. I didn't want anyone to die. I hope people will at least give me credit for that, afterwards.'

'After what? The inquest, you mean?'

'No. I mean after I'm struck off. I'm leaving, of course. I have to leave. I'll be struck off, but I have always genuinely tried to help my patients.'

Sara half sat up, indignant. 'But why? Are you saying you were negligent? Do you mean it didn't need to happen? They said complications following surgery, that's all. What—'

'No, no. No, there's been no negligence.' Stephen sighed heavily, sat up and filled the glass from the near-empty vodka bottle.

'That's not why I'll be struck off,' he said, sipping and handing the glass over. She drank, waiting for him to explain while he stared across the pool.

'Why will they, then?' she challenged him, not understanding.

He looked at her, thinking about her usefulness. 'I'd like to tell you. Of all the people who could have walked in here tonight, I'm glad it's you, do you know that? It might be good to tell you. I'd like to think you understood, even if you didn't forgive. I haven't hurt anybody.'

'*Why* will you be struck off?'

After a silence in which they both drank some more vodka, Stephen said, in a voice now definitely slurred, 'I set up the Sulis a few years after my wife died. I used all of the money she left. It was a lot, but barely enough. We struggled. The first two years I don't know how we stayed open. I had a patient called—I shouldn't tell you her name, but she was local, she had a title.' He turned to her earnestly. 'What happened was an honest mistake. This lady—she'd been to see me in town down at the surgery and I'd sent her for some tests. When the results came back they were with lots of others and it was a busy morning. I saw her to discuss her results which were not at all good. A bowel problem. Intestines.'

'Intestine? Oh God, not Lady Wallace?'

Stephen nodded. 'She raised the idea of spending time at the Sulis. It was her own idea. I have never, ever tried to sell my clinic to my NHS patients. It would be completely unethical. I manage to keep the two things separate because I don't make any money from the Sulis, it's non profit-making. I only intended to take a salary from the Sulis after I'd retired from the NHS.'

'Don't talk to me,' Sara said, pouring herself another drink, 'as if I were a bloody medical ethics tribunal.'

'Sorry. Anyway, I didn't bring up the idea of the Sulis to Lady Wallace because I honestly didn't think it would help, but she was desperate, and I agreed the relaxation and diet might help her palliatively, so to speak, so in she came, the next day.'

'And?'

'Well, she began to get better immediately. Quite spectacularly better. I was astonished. So I went back to her notes, and I found that I'd made a mistake. I'd discussed someone else's results with her. They'd somehow got into

her notes, clipped to her own results, which were fine. You
see? She wasn't really all that ill to begin with.'

'What about the poor sod they did belong to? They *were*
ill. What happened to them?'

'Oh, I put that right. I said they'd been delayed, had her
in to give her the news within a couple of days. She did
quite well for several months. Dead now,' he said.

'Oh, well, that's all right, then,' Sara said sourly.

'But Lady Wallace, she was very well connected, she
knew everybody. I know it was wrong, but since she was
getting better anyway I decided not to tell her about the
mistake. I just couldn't risk the blunder getting out. It
might have finished the clinic off. I wasn't seeking to gain
anything for myself. You do see that, don't you? I wasn't
trying to get anything out of it.'

'Except,' Sara said, slurring, 'her undying gratitude. I
suppose she went home and told everybody about the
wonders of naturopathy. And did the clinic no harm at all.'

'That was the general effect, yes, but I promise you I
didn't plan it that way. I just wanted the mistake covered
up and as she was better there seemed no harm in keeping
it from her that she wasn't ever really ill. I've always
played down the notion of miracle cures. But she didn't.
She told everybody. And the clinic took off. I wasn't comfortable about it, at first.'

Sara sighed. There was something self-important in the
seriousness he attached to his misdemeanour. 'I don't see
why you're talking about leaving. I think you should stick
around and explain this yourself. Nobody suffered, not really, not even the patient who died, if you gave her the
right news straight away. Here, have a drink.'

Stephen took the glass and drank. After a short silence Sara said, 'I must go. It's getting light now. I'm so tired.'

'No, wait. I'm going to tell you the rest. That wasn't the end of it. The reputation I got after that—it was hard to let it go. So I did it again. Only with a few patients of my own, of course, not with referrals. I couldn't risk another GP's interference. I would just sometimes paint a rather worse picture of the condition and its prognosis, you see. If it involved hospital tests from outside the practice I would just rewrite them, do a similar letter with different results. I even did pretty good logos you know, you can on a PC. Or I'd show the patient someone else's X-rays—I've got dozens now. And a spell at the Sulis would produce an amazing benefit, then, you see? It kept the clinic's reputation up and my patients were so grateful when they got so much better. I felt good, too. I really was helping them.'

'You were deceiving them!'

'But I made them feel *better*!'

There was another silence. Sara said suddenly, 'Joyce. Joyce's X-ray—that was a fake, wasn't it?'

'How did you know that?'

Stephen's stricken face and the farcical story seemed suddenly, through the vodka, bitterly funny. She snorted, 'Because, Doctor, she's only bloody well got *one* kidney. And you showed her, and me, an X-ray with two.' She sniggered at the tawdry, idiotic deception.

'You have to admit, though, she was getting better.'

'You sound almost proud of yourself.'

'I'm not, not after what's happened. But I was trying to keep the place going, for Ivan, too. He needs the stability. You do understand, don't you?'

'You haven't told anyone else this?'

Stephen shook his head. 'Nobody knows, but they will. They'll soon find out.'

There was another pause. 'What about Alex Cooper?'

'Who? Oh, *Alex Cooper*. I thought you were talking about a patient. Oh, Alex was a strange girl. I've no idea what made Alex tick.'

'Really? She had a crush on you, didn't she? Is that why she left?'

Stephen cleared his throat. 'She got very silly one night, and after that she said she couldn't stay. I certainly didn't encourage her, by the way. I was her employer. And it was extremely annoying, her leaving so suddenly.' He smiled wanly at Sara. 'Not my type anyway. Too thin, too young. Boring girl.'

Sara allowed herself to feel indirectly flattered by this. 'When she left, I suppose she couldn't say why, could she? If that was the real reason, you rejecting her, she couldn't say so.'

'I suppose not. She just left. Why are you interested anyway?'

Sara shrugged. It didn't much matter to her now. James was dead and she was dead drunk. They drank in silence. The candles' reflection burned on the pool's shining water, and the plants hung graceful in the golden light. What matter if paradise be false, if it be paradise?

Stephen said, 'The water's lovely. Why don't you go in?'

Sara could not really think why not after seven or eight vodkas, but managed to say that she had no swimsuit before she realised how very Alex Coopery it sounded. He was a doctor, for God's sake, he'd seen bodies before and anyway, had he not just told her that he had other, more serious things on his mind? He was looking at her now with a look of slight, amused disappointment.

'You go on up to the shallow end,' he said, 'and get yourself into the water, and I'll stay here and promise not to look. All right?'

Of course he was not interested in her, not sexually. She'd observed as much when he was drying his hair. And no wonder, she thought, since she was showing herself to be more of a provincial prude than a free-spirited water goddess, but she got up and walked down the length of the pool to the steps at the far end. Stephen was lying on the mattress staring up at the roof where the candles reflected their watery light. She stripped off to her knickers and then calculated that she would feel much less ridiculous with them off than on, so got rid of them too.

The water folded over her like cold silk and she murmured, dipping her face and head as she swam while the water pulled out her hair and dragged it like black fronds down her back. She knew she must be drunk, but how could this amazing feeling, as if her body were being stroked by cool water for the first time ever, have anything to do with the muddy flattening of sensation that usually came with alcohol? It was not simply that the feeling of the water seemed new, her whole body felt new as well, like a rather nice present she had just been given, a body capable of any number of delicious sensations that she had hitherto only heard about. She glanced up. Stephen was still lying on his back, possibly even asleep. She turned on to her back and floated, raising one arm, then the other, letting them flop heavily back into the water like oars, watching the drops of water flick off her hands and splash back to the surface. With a kick she turned again and slipped under, slithering along close to the bottom of the pool, listening to the silence.

She swam back to the shallow end and without making the least noise she rose from the pool and paused there, luxuriating now in the feel of warm air on her body just as she had loved the sensation of her skin meeting the water.

'Like Aphrodite rising from the waves, Miss Selkirk. Quick now or I'll see your bum. There are robes somewhere,' Stephen said. He was laughing at her. Sara turned round very slowly. He was sitting up now, watching.

'Thanks,' she said, languidly pulling her hair up into a wet roll on the top of her head. She looked round and saw the pile of bathrobes, took one, and just as Stephen had done with the towel, set off down the pool side carrying it, pausing every few steps to put it on, one arm, then the next, and last, carelessly, tying the belt which held it together. She flopped down beside him and they sat in silence but for the subsiding laps of the water against the pool side. Stephen poured out a drink and handed it to her. She drank half and handed it back. He put the glass on the floor and pulled her down on to the mattress.

'You're tired,' he said, looking down at her. 'Very, very tired.'

Sara nodded and closed her eyes. She was tired, but it was worse than that; she was the same. Everything was the same. The beautiful water had not changed anything. The magic, transforming pool was a delusion. She had emerged from it as battered and heartbroken as she had entered it.

'It's so awful. Everything's awful.' She began to cry again, vodka tears for all of it: James, exhaustion, Andrew, Dvořák, Stephen laughing at her.

'Don't talk about it. You're too tired to talk about anything,' he said, making it sound almost like medical advice. Almost, until the hand resting on her forehead began to smooth her hair off her face, travelled down her throat and slipped under the edge of her robe and reached a shoulder. Sara's eyes were still closed when his mouth came down over hers and his tongue began pushing gently. She drew away and looked at him. His hand moved down, loosened the robe and found her breast.

'Lie still. Lie still. And you'll feel better.' The voice was now in her ear and she was aware of his skin, scented like hers with pool water, but warm, human, male, and very close to hers, and his fingers slipping down.

'Better than what?' she murmured stupidly, knowing for certain now that she was drunk, and glad to be. She pulled away the towel from Stephen's body. He was kneeling between her legs. Sara pulled her robe away. She closed her eyes again, wondering though not caring whether it was his fingers or his tongue on her nipples, just as long as he was going to do this for ever. Not, not for ever. With a sudden surge of need she rose and reached for him. He hesitated for a second above her, then he pushed into her. He pushed again, and again. Then he paused above her and looked at her, gauging his effect. Watching her, he slid back and forth, infinitely slow, never taking his eyes from her face. And slowly, so slowly, with infinite slowness, looking back into his eyes as he sank into and melted out of her, Sara began to realise what he wanted. He didn't want her, not beyond the want of engorged muscle and nerve endings (not that that, she was the first to concede, should be underestimated). He wanted her gratitude. He wanted it so badly he had almost stopped making love and was hovering in neutral, ticking over, withholding her pleasure until he got it, like the class bully holding sweeties out of reach. She smiled beatifically up at him and whispered, 'You're wonderful.' Three thrusts and two grunts later he shuddered and collapsed on her shoulder.

After an interval long enough, she hoped, to convey adequate respect for his orgasm, she shifted gently and sighed. He rolled off her and lay on his back, holding her hand. The hand-holding was ominous. She hoped to God he wasn't going to thank her.

'I wish I still smoked,' he said. 'I still miss the one afterwards.'

Sara laughed with relief. She was almost too weary and uninterested to express surprise that he ever had. 'What, a healthy specimen like you?'

He looked pleased. 'I'm not bad, am I? I work at it. Eight vitamins a day, no alcohol—tonight's an exception—exercise, organic vegetarian diet—'

Sara yawned to shut him up. She was exhausted as well as miserable, now that the tension between them had been extinguished, and she wondered how soon she could get away. She was appalled but not altogether surprised by the realisation that now that they had made love (actually, the phrase 'had sex' was more accurate, and the words 'one-sided, mechanistic fuck' could have been appropriately applied) she had lost not only desire but any interest in him whatsoever. She had learned more about him during the few seconds that he had lingered above her, waiting for her praise, than he could ever tell her or wish her to know. She wanted to get away from him before her indifference showed, before it grew into contempt. Already she could see that really, he was rather pathetic.

He had stood up and was forcing his arms into a robe. He tied the belt and knelt beside her. 'I've lost everything. I have nothing left to offer anyone. All I wanted was to help people and get a bit of recognition. Ivan's got Hilary and soon she'll have the baby and they won't need me any more. Ivan will get a fortune when he sells this place. My usefulness is past.'

For the first time he sounded almost pitiable. Sara struggled to open her half-closed eyes. Before she could say anything he whispered, 'It's amazing, you being here, appearing like that. I was feeling so desperate, I had, well, I had been thinking if I got drunk enough I might have the courage to drown myself. Then you came.'

He squeezed her hand. 'I have to go. Could you, would you please do one more thing? Go to Ivan tomorrow and tell him why I've gone. I've never told him, but the building's not mine, it's in trust, in his name. Tell Hilary—' Stephen's eyes were bright with tears, 'please tell her that I'm—that I send all my love to her and to the baby. Will you do that?'

Sara could barely raise her head. 'I will.'

He kissed her lightly on the lips. 'Goodbye.'

CHAPTER 42

WHEN SARA AWOKE, the sun was up and glaring off the surface of the pool. She got up dazzled, still dazed with sleep and groggy with the headache and thirst that reminded her, as if her sticky thighs did not, of how drunk she had been. She remembered, very unwillingly, everything that had happened, including her promise to tell Ivan and Hilary that Stephen had gone. Her clothes, she also remembered, were down at the far end of the pool. She dived in and swam the length, washing off all she could of last night's lunacy. She dried herself and got dressed, found some bottled water and took that with her. The flowers for James had gone.

She arrived at the Golightlys' house before eight o'clock. Ivan answered her knock in the clothes she imagined he had slept in, looking hostile and dirty. He stood in the doorway and looked past her, frowning, his eyes taking in her car and the otherwise empty lane. Sara's weak social smile turned to one of appeasement.

'I'm really sorry to disturb you, especially so early, but—'

Ivan's look challenged her to make the disturbance worthwhile. Sara felt suddenly angry.

'Look, I know this can hardly be convenient and I promise you I'd rather not be here but I promised your father I'd let you know—'

'Yeah—what,' he interrupted, folding his arms, looking past her again. There was no curiosity, simply the wish to be told what and have her go.

'Look, I'm *terribly* sorry it's obviously deeply inconvenient, but actually this is pretty inconvenient for me too. I promised your father I'd let you know he's had to . . . he's gone away for a while. He . . . I think he wants you to decide what to do about the clinic, whether to sell it, or whatever. He said to tell you the building's yours, it's in your name.'

'Yes, I know,' Ivan said, with a mirthless little smile.

'Oh. He said you didn't.'

'I do, though. My father tends to underestimate what I know. Old habit.'

'Well, anyway, he asked me to tell you he's had to go away.'

'Of course. Well, that's that, then. Thank you for telling me.'

Sara now saw weariness rather than indifference. He shook his head and looked at her properly for the first time. She wondered if he had been crying.

'I've been awake all night, worrying about things,' he said. 'You know, the patients, and poor Warwick. I keep thinking there must be something I should have done. We've put our whole lives into that place. It's been such a shock, and now it's getting to Hilary, too. The baby—' To her horror, his eyes filled with tears, which he wiped away with a sleeve. He pressed the fingers of one trembling hand into his eyes and stood on the doorstep, gulping.

'You need to sit down,' Sara said.

'No. No, I'm all right.' He swayed, with his face hidden in his hands, and gulped some more. But Sara simply had not the energy for compassion. While she did not blame him, it would have felt like effort misapplied to spend too much time helping Ivan feel better for the death of *her* friend.

'Is Hilary around?' she asked, considering that the tea and sympathy routine was really his wife's department. 'Part of the message was for her, too. Your father says that he—'

'She's upstairs. She's had another threatened miscarriage. She has to rest, or she may lose it.' Ivan's voice was swallowed by his sobs. Sara had heard about how long they had waited for this baby. She made another effort to feel compassion and even managed to say some of the right things, but as she took her leave she could not help herself thinking, well, now you might have to find out what it's like to lose somebody you love.

CHAPTER 43

SARA LEFT HER case, cello and bag in the hall of Medlar Cottage, went upstairs, closed her curtains and fell into bed. When she woke six hours later she got up at once, stumbled down in her dressing gown and dialled James's number. Tom's number, as she must now learn to think of it. The answering machine was on but she hung up without leaving a message. There are messages too fragile for machines. Tom might well be staying at his mother's, or could even be at the hospital. Should she go to the hospital? But Tom might not be there. She thought of James lying somewhere in its impersonal vastness and shivered. She could not go, not yet, not alone.

She went back upstairs, showered and dressed, without noticing what clothes she put on. Back in the kitchen she moved slowly, sedate in her misery, and steadfastly made an omelette using up some sad tomatoes, basil and the good half of a red pepper that was going mouldy. It was odd, she thought, how she could continue to function, how the brain still insisted on her noticing daily trivia such as things in the fridge that needed using up. She ate her omelette with more enthusiasm than she thought possible, feeling guilty to be hungry.

It was nearly five in the afternoon when she wandered up the garden to the pond and swung herself into the hammock. Through the diamonds of the netting she could see the bamboo curtain on the far side of the pond and recalled the sound of James's voice two summers ago, calling her as she had lain in the hammock then, the rustle of the leaves and his hot face appearing round it, pleased to have tracked her down and reached the top of the garden on a sweltering day. She lay until long after the sun had sunk behind the garden, lighting up the far side of the valley, and eventually she fell asleep again.

She woke this time shivering with cold. The green of the leaves and grass was receding behind the charcoal gleam of twilight. The pale flowers of the roses and meadow sweet held the last of the brightness. Birds called late in the trees; insects were silent. Sara wandered back down to the house, which seemed suddenly too large. Tom's answering machine was still switched on and again she could think of no message to leave. She wandered from room to room neither tired, rested, hungry nor satisfied, her mind numb yet in a storm of incoherent protest.

Why should James be the one to die? In the music room she took out her cello and tuned up. The Dvořák which she wished to forget had been played on her Peresson cello, the big Romantic instrument that Andrew liked so much. Her need to be soothed called for the Cristiani's creamy, gentler sound. She would play something that James liked, perhaps. She began Fauré's Élégie in C Minor, and the soft tug of the notes loosened tears which ran down her face as she played. An almost physical ache was beating in her at the thought that she would never hear James play, or play with him again.

She began to play the theme of the St Anthony Variations. Despite the measured, gracious calm of the music she found herself beginning to grow angry. It enraged her, suddenly, to think that James had been persuaded, by her as much as by Tom, into staying at the Sulis. Had he gone to a proper hospital, his ulcers would have responded to the insult of conventional treatment and he would be alive now, mangled by surgeons and stuffed with drugs, but alive. She put down her bow and blew on her hands. They were still cold from her long sleep in the cooling air of the garden and too stiff to deal with the first variation.

She got up and put away the cello. In the kitchen she ran the hot tap, turning her fingers in the water as they began to tingle, and recalling James's hands and his poor cold feet. Hot and cold, burning and freezing at the same time. It was now almost twenty-four hours since she learned of his death, and she was only now allowing her mind to turn to the manner of it. She had been too shocked to ask the hospital, but she considered now that it would be almost as if she had stopped caring about him if she did not find out in detail exactly what had happened and what he had gone through. Had he suffered? She had to know. It was a silly idea, she knew, but finding out might be the last thing she was able to do for him. Had the poor darling suffered? Her mind returned to the agonising picture of the struggling St Anthony with the serpent, his livid face gleaming in the shaft of innocuous sunlight hitting the canvas, and next to it the other, reassuring image of St Anthony the benign father, with his crutch, the sweet little piglet and the tiny people entreating his intercession for relief for their poor burning hands. What else happened to people poisoned by ergot and what exactly was it? Bernadette had not known. In her maddening voice during the interval (another lifetime ago) she had only yapped in her self-congratulatory way that she had found out that the people in the picture were suffering from St Anthony's Fire, from grain blighted by ergot. And that was all Sara knew: nothing much except two names for what had killed James.

The *Compact Oxford Dictionary* told her little else though it told her in a different way:

A diseased transformation of the seed of rye and other grasses, being really the sclerotium or hardened mycelium of a fungus (*Claviceps purpurea*) . . .

'*Mycelium*' sounded familiar. Was it its similarity to 'mycology symposium'? Professor Takahashi's exact area of academic research had seemed not just inpenetrably arcane but an irrelevance to the fact of his wife's murder. Andrew would be interested in the connection and she might find a way of letting him know of it, without speaking to him herself. Some time. Right this minute she had no interest in his unsolved murder. She needed to understand what had happened to James and she only knew of one mycologist who, even if he had killed his wife, might be able to help her.

CHAPTER 44

'HELLO, I'M CALLING from England, I'd like to speak to Professor Takahashi.'

Sara had spent most of the previous hour on the telephone, trying to track down someone at Bristol with responsibility for extra-mural programmes and summer schools. She had spoken to someone who clearly expected to be congratulated for being in the office late at night because she was *snowed under*, and as a reward for doing so Sara had been given a name and an extension number, which was not answered. She went back to the first person, got another name of someone who was definitely in the building as he taught Adult Learners Intermediate Methodology on Thursday evenings, whose number was answered by a security officer who had never heard of him. She tried a few minutes later, got the person who had been missing who said that actually he was not the person Sara wanted but the person Sara did want was on holiday. Sara went back again to the first person, who turned out to have the summer school records on her database if that was all she wanted, so wasn't that lucky. Sara explained how she had loved the mycology symposium but she had lost the list of delegates' contact addresses and she was just about to start work in an area suggested to her by Professor Takahashi. Wasn't Professor Takahashi from Kobe University? Didn't he have an email address there? He turned out to have not just an email address but a fax and telephone number, too.

As she waited for somebody to answer the telephone she allowed herself to feel rather clever. Just as she was thinking that if only her reasons for being clever weren't so appalling she might laugh, she was put through and a voice said, very fast, '*Takahashi.*'

'Professor Takahashi, I hope you don't mind, I know it's early for you.'

'It is eight, yes. I am extremely busy, I begin early, at seven-thirty. You are?'

'I'm ringing you from England. I was a student on your course at Bristol.'

'Ho, yes, hello. Your name is?'

'Oh, I'm er . . . M-m er Mary Morrison. I expect you remember me? I certainly remember *you.*' Fingers crossed. 'I felt there was a great deal of overlap between our er . . . two areas.'

'Yes, yes. Your area yes, of course, that is?'

'And it was a *wonderful* symposium. I'm ringing because I'm looking at my notes and . . . er . . . wondering if you could clarify a point or two. If you can spare five minutes. I'm interested chiefly in ergot?'

There was a short silence. 'Well of course, my entire contribution to the symposium was in field of the larger Ascomycetes.'

'Of course! But I'm hoping to concentrate mainly on ergot, and the question of human poisoning?'

'Oh, you mean my historical overview of European and

British outbreaks? But this is basic! Manchester outbreak, if you recall, of 1927, was characterised by ergot's effect on a working-class population . . .'

'Yes, I remember that.'

'. . . and the strange phenomenon of a considerably lesser effect of the same amount on better-off, lower middle-class population who were nevertheless eating bread from the same source?'

'Errmmm . . .'

'Do you remember—the toxic effects were lessened or totally absent in the second group. This is now thought to have been the effect of spreading butter on the bread which the better-off group was in the habit of doing. The relevant inhibiting factor in the butter is vitamin D and other compounds, of which the most important are, of course— But you surely have the transcript of my lecture?'

'I don't! Oddly enough, I don't seem to have it! I wouldn't need to bother you otherwise.'

'You wish me to fax it to you?'

Sara gave him the number and thanked him over-profusely, which was somehow what she gathered was expected. 'Yes, well, that would be *wonderful*, if you would fax it straight away, I'm working on it right now.'

'Yes, I have copies. I shall fax right now and if there is problem you can call, okay?'

'I am so grateful. *Thank* you. Now I do have just another quick question, if I may. I hope you don't mind my asking but did your late wife, who I believe was your assistant and picture researcher, did she . . . did she take as great an interest in this area as you yourself? What was the extent of her involvement?'

There was a long silence.

'Professor Takahashi, I do hope you don't mind my asking. It's just that I'm writing up the symposium for my department and I wanted to include a brief appreciation of your wife's work. A tribute, in view of the dreadful thing that happened. I've got most of what I need from the course literature, but I just wondered if I could put in some biographical details, that she was a dedicated researcher who shared your passion for the subject. Are you still there, Professor?'

'My wife was a wonderful woman.' Professor Takahashi's voice was husky. 'She was . . . she made my work *her* work. I undertake much work since . . . since 1995, I am working extremely hard when she comes to be my assistant and she involves herself completely. Just before her death she—' The professor's voice faded. 'She was most passionate about the subject but she never . . . please, your name was? I would like a copy of your tribute, please. I do not think I remember your name. You are?'

'Oh, I'm here and there, you know, guest lecturing mainly, writing, reviewing. So, you've got my fax number? I would so much like a copy of your lecture. Thank you so much.'

CHAPTER 45

*D*ARLING, CAN YOU *hear, can you hear me, pet?* Hilary was having a lovely dream, not such a strange thing to have when you're in bed—she knew for a certainty she was in bed because if she moved she could feel soft material slipping under her feet—that bit wasn't in the dream. So she was in bed but not at home. It did not feel like her bed at home . . . *You can hear me, can't you, pet, it's me.* Hilary smiled and shook out her long black hair, lovely hair she had, right down her back, exotic-looking for York-shire, she was. Everyone said so. Except Dad, who said you look like god knows what. You could be an exotic dancer you, her mates Denise and Carole said, you could, you've got the figure. Hilary tossed her dark hair again and wriggled to the music, forgetting of course she was in bed where dancing is difficult. Actually, her body felt far too heavy to dance and she wouldn't swear there was really any music. That must be in the dream, too.

She wished they would make themselves known. She wished they would declare themselves, the dream and the real bits, and stop mixing her up. Was her hair quite as long and as black now? *Hil, you're in hospital, remember? They put you to sleep.* Of course. That's why she was dreaming, then. She'd been asleep. And of course, that's why her body was so heavy she could hardly move. Someone had surely filled her lap with stones, and whatever happened to Carole and Denise? It was sad the way you lost touch as you got older. Hilary moaned, remembering that her black, swinging hair was not like that any more and her body, it wasn't what it had been at seventeen. Still. She smiled again—strange how normal it felt to smile with your eyes shut—never mind. She remembered now, and realised half-sadly that she had left the dream behind. How daft of her to make a mistake like that. Of course she didn't have stones in her lap. She wasn't dreaming now. That delicious, heavy, burdensome weight in the middle of her body was her baby. She smiled again, happy to have left the dream. Real was better. She was having a baby. *Hil, you can hear me, can't you?*

And that was Ivan speaking to her. Hello you. That was herself speaking now, she was almost certain. Possibly she only thought she had said it, she wasn't opening her eyes to find out. *You keep still and rest. They've given you something to make you nice and sleepy after the operation and it's very late.* Everybody's asleep. I know, even me, she thought she said, laughing.

I'm going to tell you a story. The voice was not just faint, it seemed to be coming from all directions and from nowhere, its meaning sounding in her head like soft breaking waves. Yet it must be Ivan's voice. *About a woman.* Some story about a woman. *Now, this woman, we'll call her Hilary, all right, pet?* She smiled. It was Ivan's voice so the story would come right. *Well, this Hilary and her husband wanted a baby so badly, and a baby just wouldn't come, and they were so worried the woman's husband had a little sperm test and that turned out to be fine so they stopped worrying and soon after the baby was on its way. Isn't that a nice story?* She smiled, then frowned a little. *Please stay, voice, stay with me.*

Ivan got up and checked through the clear glass in the door that there was nobody in the corridor. It was fortunate that Hilary had been put in a side room on her own, more than he had hoped for. The sister in charge had confided in him that she didn't hold with mixed ante- and post-natal wards. 'It's pure cruelty, miscarried ladies in the next bay along from ladies with newborns. Anyway I've got a side room free because my last placenta praevia's just gone. I'll pop your wife in there.' Hilary and he would not be disturbed. 'It's open visiting here, you stay as long as you like. You need to grieve together. Talk. She'll need to let it all pour out,' the sister said. Ivan resisted the temptation to observe that that, surely, was what Hilary had already done.

He sat down next to Hilary again and sighed. It had been difficult for him, and nobody recognised that. Nobody in his whole life knew how difficult it was, not until Hilary. That's why it had been so very difficult.

Hello, pet, still nice and sleepy? Back to the story. Now, Hilary's husband—the husband's called Ivan, by the way—he has this test and everything's okay. Or at least his father says it's okay. Oh, his father's a doctor, did I mention that? A nice doctor that everyone loves but that really is another story, I mustn't lose my thread, must I. So, into a little bottle the sample goes and the doctor gets it sent off for him because he knew what problems they'd been having and being a doctor he can 'fast-track' it for them. They were a nice open caring sharing lot, this family. So, the result comes back and it's fine.

Ivan bent over close to Hilary's face. Her eyelids were closed and still, but behind the thickening flesh of her cheeks he thought he detected a tremor of muscle. *Now where were we? Oh yes. Well, we skip to Easter. That's when little Alex comes to be the new music lady at the clinic. And there's a nice room for her just below the doctor's flat at the big smart clinic. But all is not well, because guess what. Very soon after Alex hears noises coming from next door. Can you guess what they were, Hilary? Can you?* Hilary was whimpering. Ivan hissed in her ear. *They were fucking noises.* Hilary's moans grew loud and her head tossed from side to side. Ivan bent forward and grabbed her hair so tightly that her head stopped moving. *Understand? Yes! Yes! Yes! Fucking noises. And Alex is a nice girl, far too nice to spy or pry, but she isn't stupid. She doesn't see anyone but she can work out who it is—Yvonne, of course. Yvonne loves Dr Golightly, you can see that.*

Ivan rose and poured himself water from the jug on Hilary's locker, sat down again and drank. *So,* he began, his voice breaking, *so.* He took several deep breaths and swallowed more water. *Alex thinks, very naughty of them, because the doctor's the boss and Yvonne's not really single, she lives with Chris. Poor Alex can't put up with these embarrassing, awful noises coming through the walls, not when it's her boss and the senior nurse. Alex is so upset she gets another job but feels bad about leaving like that, she thinks someone should know what's going on. So she has a word with Ivan. You remember who Ivan is, don't you. The husband. Ivan, the nice, kind, gentle one that she can talk to.*

Ivan watched Hilary's eyes twitch behind the tightly screwed up eyelids. Tears welled into his own eyes and he pressed his hands hard into them and rubbed. The next bit would cheer him up.

So Ivan says there there I understand and don't you worry. But he worries. You know why, don't you? Because it couldn't be

Yvonne, that's why. And he wonders who else it could be, and then he thinks back to the sperm test, because he knows things about the way his father deals with tests. His father's a bit naughty with tests, though he doesn't know Ivan knows this, but Ivan knows a lot of things, starting with where his father keeps the key of his filing cabinets. And Ivan does a bit of research because he is not stupid, people forget he did pharmacology even though that's not as good as medicine so it doesn't count. And he finds out a sad thing. Men like him who use naughty drugs, sometimes they can't have babies. So he goes off and has another test done all by himself and guess what? His sperm's next to useless, very low count, not quite impossible to make a baby but unlikely, especially as his wife is so OLD—oh, did I mention that?

Tears ran from the corners of Hilary's eyes into her hair. She appeared to be trying to swallow. Ivan hoped she was trying to scream. When the test had come back as borderline, she and Stephen had discussed what to do. How to prevent Ivan from losing hope. He must never be allowed to lose hope that there would be a baby.

Not absolutely sure you're concentrating, pet, but never mind, I'll be telling you this story lots from now on. Anyway, Ivan works it out. Hilary and his dad decided not to tell Ivan the result of the first test because they think he might get so upset he'll have another breakdown and start hurting himself all over again. So they don't tell Ivan that his juice is as much use as a Cup-a-Soup for making babies. Can't manage anything, can he?

Ivan's head sank on to the side of the bed. He did not see, as he cried noisily into a scrap of green hospital paper towel, the lifting of Hilary's fingers lying across her stomach. She moaned, hearing his weeping somewhere very distant. *So Hilary will carry on giving Ivan lots of screws and pretend they're making babies and then when husband's not looking Doctor Dad will shoot his four-star, tried and tested spunk up her until she's pregnant. Dad and son look so alike, you see, nobody will ever know the difference! And they have always wanted to screw each other, you see, Hilary and the dad. Ivan has seen that and thinks they might even have done it before. So what fun they will have and all in a good cause.*

Hilary's eyes were wide open. She gasped, trying to find her voice, while her lips worked like two small landed fish. Ivan stood up and whacked her hard across the face with the flat of his hand. She gurgled and moaned. *Now shut up, pet, and listen to me, or I'll have to do that again. If you make me cross like that again I won't tell you the rest of the story. Well, then, everything goes along nicely for a while, but—oh I should have mentioned—the clinic's had it and Dad has scarpered—until guess what. One day, splosh! Out tumbles disgusting red slippery bag of giblets and that's the end of baby. Not Ivan's, though, that's the point. I did make that clear, I hope.*

Hilary's screaming brought a nurse who listened to Ivan's white-faced explanation that his wife appeared to have had a nightmare and had woken up saying all kinds of upsetting things. After she had brought the doctor, soothed and sedated her patient, the nurse tiptoed away. Poor things. It was late now, but there would be no point trying to suggest that this one leave to get some rest, even though his wife would be dead to the world for the next few hours. He was obviously devoted to her.

Her footfalls faded to silence. *And do you know what?* Ivan whispered, holding Hilary's hand. *Now that the story's over, the husband doesn't feel anything. He thought he'd feel so many things but he doesn't feel anything at all, he doesn't even feel real.*

CHAPTER 46

DR TAKAHASHI'S FAX came scudding through Sara's machine at a quarter past eleven. She pulled each page off as it came in, assembled the fourteen slippery, curling sheets and sank into the sofa to read. The first dozen pages were filled with the relevant botany, history and folklore. Within ten seconds of starting to read the final two pages, on the pathology of ergot, she was almost retching.

She read that the pretty-sounding *Claviceps purpurea* fungus commonly known as ergot could produce in humans not only burning hands but, in addition, any or all of the following symptoms: debility, anxiety, insomnia, emaciation, excessive appetite, great thirst, cravings for acids, cramps, dry and flaky skin, dilated pupils, sunken eyes, falling out of the hair, cracked stiff tongue, red facial spots, vomiting of blood, 'eructations of bad odour' and 'small painful boils with green contents'. These symptoms were to be got through, apparently, before the victim could hope for the fatal onset of haemorrhages of 'oozing, fetid, watery black blood', gangrene, hallucinations and dementia. And if any doubt remained, diagnosis could be facilitated by examining the patient's stools which might be olive-green, thin, putrid and bloody, as well as involuntary.

James. Was it possible that James could have been reduced to this? She could not countenance it. Please let her be wrong. She might, she prayed, be completely wrong about the whole thing. Please let it be that James died of some swift but kinder disease that had just washed through him and overcome him painlessly in sleep. Perhaps she *was* wrong. Since her frantic hypothesising in the dressing room last night and her desperate telephone calls she had gone almost past caring. Sara suddenly sat up straight, her heart pounding, remembering. What if Joyce had not actually got the meaning of what she had tried to tell her from Salzburg? What if, in an alcoholic haze, she had not heard properly or not understood? Sara had no idea, now that she stopped to think about it, whether or not Joyce had acted on the message at all, either at the Sulis or at the RUH. Stephen had not, after all, said anything about ergot. He had not actually used the word and nor had she. He had said only that no patients were left. She tried to slow her mind, searching for coherence, and wondered if Andrew was the only person she knew who would make better sense of this than she could. The deaths of Mrs Takahashi and Warwick Jones were slipping in and out of her calculations, too, yet she could see neither how nor even if they had anything to do with it. If indeed 'it' was really accidental ergot poisoning. And while she might be wrong (she clutched at the possibility for her own sake almost as much as for James's) she might also be right. Joyce, quite apart from any other staff who could still be there, might still be eating ergot by the handful, completely unaware.

She reached the gates of the Sulis at half-past eleven.

Once again, the grounds were in darkness and the roofline of the unlit house stood out dark against the indigo sky. Looking up she tried to see the house as she knew it to be, graciously proportioned and golden stoned. But it was the daylight version that now seemed the illusion, while the cloak of Gothic gloom that the house wore under the dark sky seemed real. It was reassuring, then, that as Sara was locking the car she could see that there were lights on in the basement. Joyce was perhaps cooking something for herself. She broke into a run.

The smell of burning oil and the sound of voices rose up the stairwell to the hall. Sara tore down the stairs and arrived breathless at the bottom. All talking stopped. Sara stood, staring, seeing from the half-dozen or so faces staring back how insane she must look. One or two looked positively frightened. 'What—what are you doing here?' Sara gasped, getting in first with the question that could more justifiably be directed at her.

Ivan swirled the heavy frying pan once expertly in the air and replaced it over the flame. He turned back to the stove, where the rasp of sizzling began and grew louder. A tray of fat, raw sausages sat by the side of the cooker. Baskets of fresh-looking rolls and bowls of bright salad stood nearby.

'Having a party,' Yvonne said from the sofa. 'Sausages and pancakes. Hot dogs French style. I'd have thought that was obvious. Have a drink.' She picked up a bottle. 'Ivan's made all these lovely pancakes, haven't you, Ivan?'

'Galettes,' Ivan said, smiling and turning round. 'Pancakes are made with wheat flour. This is a mixture of buckwheat and other things. Better for savoury fillings.' He nodded to Sara. 'A sudden impulse. Hilary's in hospital and I couldn't face being on my own so I rang Yvonne and she got everyone round.'

'Via the pub, mind you!' Yvonne said. Sara smiled weakly as everyone laughed.

Ivan said, 'Do stay. I'm using up all our stocks: tomatoes, cheese, garlic, salad, rye and caraway rolls, there's plenty.'

'Ivan thought we should have a little impromptu farewell party. I brought meat! And all cooked in lovely, lovely oil,' Yvonne said, breaking into a shrieking laugh. 'We don't care, do we!'

Sara looked round. She now recognised some of the laughing faces as the kitchen and cleaning staff. One or two young men, obviously partners, sat or stood with glasses in their hands. Bowls of crisps and salted nuts were being passed round. Yvonne placed a hand on the shoulder of the younger, short-haired woman beside her on the sofa. 'Meet Chris, my other half,' she said jovially, 'and come on, have a drink. There's gallons. What the hell? Do it properly, we thought, as it's probably our last night. Here.'

Sara, too confused to speak, watched as the flushed and shiny Yvonne took a glass and Chris, smiling broadly, filled it with red wine. She handed Sara the glass with a wobbly smile. 'Cheers!'

'Where's Joyce?' Sara asked.

'Gone. I went up to get her to join us but she's not there.'

Sara's despair was almost too deep for words. 'Oh, no,' she sighed, picturing her insensible in a stairwell somewhere. 'Did she . . . talk to you about anything? Say anything at all?'

'What about? No. I haven't seen her today. Oh, don't you go worrying,' Yvonne said, comfortably. 'Why shouldn't she go out?'

'She might— She'll— She's not meant to drink.'

Yvonne looked at her with a nose wrinkle and a confidential smile. 'You are a worrier, aren't you? Come on, we've all had a terrible time. Time to put it behind us now, isn't that right? That's what Ivan says and he and Hilary have had an awful time too so if *he* can stand there, making pancakes . . .'

'Galettes,' Ivan said, nodding, and slipped the hot soft disc from the pan on to a plate already high with others. He dribbled more oil from a bottle on to the pan, turned it over the flame and swirled a ladleful of batter into it. A glorious smell and loud sizzle filled the air. Orange flames flicked and danced up from the stove as the oil caught at the edges.

'Whoa!' Chris whooped. Yvonne clapped her hands, on balance a mistake, as she was still holding her glass.

'Stop, *stop*! You mustn't—it's dangerous, you mustn't!' Sara stepped forward to the stove, as far as the heat allowed her to go.

Ivan grinned. 'Don't worry. I've made hundreds of these. The flame improves the flavour.'

'No, no, I don't mean that. It's the flour. It's poisoned. You mustn't eat it, it's dangerous.'

Ivan laughed. Sara pulled his sleeve and he turned again, shaking his head. 'Come off it. You are joking, aren't you? It's a hundred per cent organic.'

'I'm not joking. I think it's contaminated. You've got to listen.' Ivan turned off the flame under the pan. The happy sizzling died away to a stunned silence, which Sara knew she must fill with an explanation. Everyone was looking at her with amusement or distrust.

'Is there rye flour in that? From the smallholding?' she asked, pointing towards the bowl of batter.

Ivan nodded. 'A little.'

Yvonne picked up the basket of bread rolls. 'And these are rye and caraway, aren't they?'

Sara took a deep breath. 'I think it may be infested with ergot. It's a fungus. It's rare nowadays, you don't get it on anything that's been sprayed, but on organic rye— I think it may have affected yours. That's why James got so ill. It was the bread. Some of his symptoms—I've checked all this—some of them were the same as ergot victims in the Middle Ages.'

The silence had somehow grown even more stunned. Yvonne had sat up and turned and was now kneeling, looking at Sara over the back of the sofa. 'Come off it. You mean, the tremors, the hands and feet? The appetite? Oh, the poor souls. Bunny, Mrs Valentine too. Ivan, that can't be right, can it? Poisoned rye?'

Ivan's face was the colour of his batter. He had put down his spatula. 'My God, I . . . I don't know . . . I've never heard of—Wait, wait though,' he said, his face lifting slightly. 'Everybody ate the bread. Not everyone was ill, were they? Yvonne, you weren't ill.'

'Trust you to ask,' Yvonne said. She sighed with resignation. 'I'm sorry, Ivan, I never had the heart to tell you, but it bunged me up, that bread. I never touched it after the first time. I'm fine with the salads, but as far as the bread goes I used to bring my own or buy a sarnie and eat it in the staffroom. I'm a Kingsmill and Flora girl, inside and out, aren't I, Chris?'

Ivan looked over her head to some distant point, presumably the moral high ground, with a hurt expression on his face. 'Joyce,' he said. 'She wasn't ill either. If anything she got better, put on some weight.'

They waited. There was another heavy sigh from Yvonne. 'Sorry to grass on her, but she didn't eat it either. She told me she held with proper hot meals, meat and two veg. Scotch people don't believe in salads and brown bread.'

'So what did she eat then? She definitely put weight on.'

'The garage halfway down the hill. I told her about it. She popped out every day and sneaked back a steak and kidney pie in her handbag. They even heat them up for you. She got quite a taste for them.'

'And she fed the bread to Pretzel, I suppose,' Sara said. 'That's why she took trays up to her room, so she could feed it to him and nobody would know she wasn't cooperating with her treatment. Poor little dog.'

Ivan looked even worse. He had been staring at Yvonne, then at Sara and back to Yvonne. Yvonne pointed out, 'You're all right. Didn't you eat it, Ivan?'

He shook his head. 'Hilary and I switched to a raw diet when she got pregnant. Juices and leaves, mainly. To maximise vitamin and mineral absorption in the early weeks.' He wiped at his eyes with his tea towel. 'Inner cleansing. We were encouraging Hilary's digestive system into optimum functioning for the sake of the baby. I did it too, to encourage her. I might have known it wouldn't work.' He sobbed noisily into the towel, then looked up.

'What about everyone else?' he said, challengingly, with a wave toward the little knot of people in the room. 'They're all fine. Aren't you?'

Quietly Yvonne said, 'Ivan, they're all part-timers. They don't eat in. Everyone brings a biscuit or something for their breaks.' There were murmurs and nods.

Ivan turned to Sara. 'Look, how can you be sure about this?' he asked, aggressive in the way of a wounded, weakened animal. 'Don't you have any idea how careful we are about nutrition? We are *healers*. Nutrition's at the core of all we do, and now you're practically accusing us of . . . of *poisoning* people. It's a terrible thing to say.'

Sara felt cornered. Of course she was not sure. Nor was she finding it easy to think of appropriate things to say to this idiot Ivan, who seemed to have turned the act of eating into a self-immolating religion of quite Tantric complexity. 'I'm suggesting it's a possibility,' she replied, as quietly as she could, for she felt like shouting. 'Surely it's better to know, one way or the other? Of course I hope I'm wrong.'

'Well, I'm quite sure you *are* wrong,' Ivan said, looking round the room for support.

'Well, we've got to find out,' Sara said, 'haven't we?'

'Yes, absolutely,' Ivan said, with surprising energy and determination. 'The rest of the grain's back at the store on the smallholding. We ought to go and look at it, and destroy it at once if you're right. It must be burned.'

He looked round the room again. 'Yvonne, there's alfalfa, peppers and tomatoes, and there's some bought organic pasta you might as well use up. Will you stay here and give everyone something to eat? I'll take Sara to the smallholding, just as soon as I've binned all this lot.'

The batter, along with the pancakes and the rolls, was dispatched to the kitchen bin and the dishes and bowls submerged in hot soapy water. Ivan pulled off his apron and picked up his car keys.

'On second thoughts,' he said to Sara, 'I've probably had too much wine. Would you drive me? Then you can leave me there and go on home, can't you? I'll walk in along the towpath in the morning, not that there's much to come in for, except to start the clear-out.'

CHAPTER 47

I N THE CAR Ivan said, looking straight ahead through the windscreen, 'If you are right—I hope you're not, but if you are—I'm sorry. Desperately sorry.'

Sara drove, saying nothing, feeling mean, small and in the right. Forgiveness for what had happened to James might one day be possible, even appropriate, but for now her original dubiousness about the Sulis and its precious philosophies had swollen into an anger that she dared not express. Ivan's feeling sorry was no less than he ought to feel, yet his saying so was enough to make her want to scream with rage at the inadequacy of it. 'Sorry', even 'desperately sorry', was not going to bring James back nor begin to make her feel less bereft.

'I've been thinking,' she said. 'If we do find that the crop's affected, we mustn't burn it. People have died and been injured, and that means there could be legal action by them or relatives. The clinic could be sued, and the rye is evidence.' She thought about Tom, about how hopeless an idea it was that money could compensate for anything. But money could start a trust fund in James's name, an award for pianists, perhaps. She knew, remembering Matteo's death, that the business of setting up such a thing would at first displace some of Tom's grief and would even, eventually, come to comfort him.

'If you really are sorry, you won't stand in the way of people claiming some sort of compensation, will you? If the clinic's sold, the proceeds could be used to pay damages. You wouldn't try to prevent that, would you?'

'Of course not,' Ivan said. 'You're quite right. And there's something else. If we can get ergot here, it must be a risk on other organic farms. Anywhere growing organic grain. People should know about the risks, shouldn't they? We tend to think organic must be safer than conventional. If *any* good can come out of this,' he said, fiercely, 'it's making people aware of the danger. It will at least bring it out into the open.'

A mile or two further on Ivan spoke again. 'How do you know so much about this? I thought you were just a musician.'

'I made some enquiries, that's all. There's a fax on the back seat.'

Ivan stretched behind and got it. They were not yet clear of the city, and by the orange street lights he scanned the pages. 'There's a picture of it here as well, I see.'

'Yes. Even on a fax it's not that difficult to spot. Little black hook-shaped things, growing out from between the husks. I suppose if you knew what it was you couldn't miss it. We'll soon know if your rye has it or not.'

After a further silence Ivan said cautiously, 'I'd never even heard of it till today. But look——you don't suppose—— I mean, if it's not that difficult to spot, suppose someone knew it was there and said nothing?'

Sara snorted. 'Oh for God's sake. Who, for instance?'

'Well, Hugh Cropper, possibly? If what you say about

damages is right. Look, he's a farmer, and according to Bunny he was always short. Suppose he knew and said nothing? One dead mother-in-law, I suppose the daughter benefits there, plus a lump sum in compensation?'

'Don't be stupid,' Sara snarled, finding her anger rising still further. In the hurt silence that followed she stopped to consider the accusation and satisfied herself, as coolly as she was able to, that it was absurd. 'Bunny's been dead over a week and he's said nothing. In fact, he agreed that she should be cremated, if you remember.'

'What's her being cremated got to do with it?'

Sara sighed. Surely innocence of this order in a man of thirty-five was contrived. 'Hugh wouldn't have agreed to a cremation if he'd been planning to bring an action, would he? Because he'd know that if it came to court they might want to disinter her, to get evidence of ergot in the body. If you can trace it in a body, that is. But without that sort of evidence he might not be able to prove his case.'

'Yes, I see. Gosh, you do know a lot,' Ivan said. 'I'm sorry. You're right, of course. I've no idea how these things are worked out. But look, if it wasn't Hugh, what about Joyce? Yvonne? Or even my father?'

'Oh come on! You think Joyce poisoned her own dog, the only living creature she cared about? And what did Yvonne have to gain? And why on *earth* would your father knowingly have fed contaminated food to his patients? Forgive my bluntness, but I really do think it's time to stop looking round for a scapegoat and start facing up to a huge, tragic accident for which you are at least partly responsible. It's quite bad enough, without you behaving like a little boy casting around for some sensational explanation and someone else to blame.'

Ivan said meekly, 'I'm sorry, I'm really sorry. I do honestly want to get to the bottom of it all. I do want to do my part. You can count on that.' He turned to her with a guilty and apologetic smile which partially worked its blue-eyed, small-defenceless-creature magic.

She smiled ruefully back. 'Let's keep our heads, then. No wild theories. We'll stick to the facts. First we've got to look at the rye, haven't we?'

They were now driving into darkness that stretched out on all sides below the buzzing, sodium-lit main road, a country of dark fields separated only by paths and lanes between farms and hamlets. The land lay open and still under the moon, yet secret, its mysteries deep and centuries old. These fields would have once produced rye. And when the fields were ploughed and the good seed scattered on the ground, it was not God's almighty hand nor the devil's, nor any human alchemy or skill that determined whether the crop would be sweet and plentiful, or sour with the black, toxic ergot. It was the rain, the cold and the ready spores meeting in a dire configuration with the seasons, a precise admixture of water, temperature and time that would draw up from the ground a crop so casually lethal that households and whole villages would be wiped out. Yet as it grew it would look the same, waving palely under the sun, a blight year masquerading as a good one, and the crop would be harvested with gratitude. And the same fields had been planted again this year by people who had never heard of ergot. It was as if the earth had now been turned over so many times that all the old stories of the land's arbitrary evil were buried too deep for telling.

When Sara parked and switched off the engine she was

startled for a moment by how completely the darkness surrounded her. Her eyes adjusted as she clambered out and joined Ivan at the edge of the smallholding. He pointed to a long low concrete building on the far side.

'See it? You'll manage, won't you? Let me go ahead and switch the lights on.'

'Don't you have a torch in the house? It's so dark.'

'It might freak out Mrs Heffer to see a torchbeam down the field at this time of night,' Ivan whispered. 'And it would be a kindness to keep quiet, so we don't wake her up. She's been very shaken up, with one thing and another.'

He walked ahead. Just as they reached the door he said, 'Damn! Just remembered, the key's in the house. You wait here, I'll only be a minute.' He turned and tramped back down between the rows of vegetables, leaving Sara outside the hut. She watched lights go on in the house, as she moved from foot to foot and hummed a tune that came into her head. The lights went out. After a minute she was surprised to hear, and then to see, two figures returning. Walking directly in front of Ivan was Leech, the shabby man. Before Sara could say anything Ivan unlocked the door, pushed Leech in ahead of him and pressed switches on the wall just inside. The entire shed was flooded inside and out with a burst of light which revealed the building in its almost overpowering ugliness. Sara was standing on a shallow concrete ramp which sloped up to the door of the breeze-block building. From the central doorway, where a flat, cheap, interior door with an aluminium handle now stood ajar, and through the flat metal-framed windows, the bleaching light from a double row of fluorescent tubes mounted on the ceiling shone out. Ivan's head appeared. 'C'mon, hurry up. Aren't you coming in?'

Sara stepped forward into the brightness, bewildered by the idea that such a visually polluting dump could be used for anything as healthful as an organic food store. She looked around. Wooden staging ran the length of the back wall, on which stood labelled cloth and paper bags of varying sizes. She read onion, celery, runner, dwarf. Gardening tools were hung on a side wall, along with netting, canes, wound up hoses, sprinklers and watering cans. Several trugs and wooden boxes containing what looked like onion sets and seed potatoes stood about. On the far side of the room the outline of small round objects could be seen laid out under sheets of brown paper. Tomatoes, perhaps, or onions. Two small, thick sacks stood under the staging.

Leech was sitting on a mound of cloth on a camp bed in one corner. Pushing both hands through his hair, he stretched, nodded at Sara and Ivan and looked round without the slightest curiosity. Then he leaned over to take off his shoes, lay down and pulled the assortment of blankets and old quilts over himself. He was shivering.

'I told him he's to come down here. I just woke him up and now he thinks he's going back to bed. No grasp of time, not much grasp of anything. He's been staying down at the house, in my attic, eh, haven't you? Keeping you safe, haven't we, eh?' Ivan said, with what sounded like amusement in his voice.

'But the police want to talk to him. About Warwick. Do you mean you've been hiding him?'

Ivan appeared not to have heard her, but Leech did. He got up and stood by his bed, looking at her.

'No grasp of time,' Ivan repeated. 'I think that's why he likes the trains. They're nice and regular. Isn't that why you like the trains? You like the trains, don't you?'

'Is he deaf as well?' Sara asked, because Ivan had raised his voice, insultingly she thought, to speak to him. And strangely, mention of the trains brought to mind something that Andrew had said. *He was coming down from the embankment just after the 9.23 went past.* But he had not been talking about Leech. Leech was now grinning grimly at her as he scratched extravagantly at his long torso, pulling his clothes around and revealing the white, frail skin over his ribs. He was still shivering, and the sight of his, to her, unbearably vulnerable, cold and uncared-for body created a slight tugging feeling in Sara's throat.

'Here Leech, put this on.' Ivan had pulled a blue checked shirt from a peg on the wall. 'You can wear my shirt, you like that, don't you?' Leech smiled and caught the shirt clumsily as he flung it across. He pulled it on, but still shivered.

'Leech, get the rye, would you? The sacks of rye, over there,' Ivan said, not unkindly, gesturing with his head. Sara watched, puzzled that Ivan should be making what amounted to a ceremony out of the dismal business of inspecting the rye. He was standing very straight now, his back to the wall where the garden tools hung, his hands clasped behind his back. His face had assumed an almost military formality and the chin, usually soft, was thrust forward. Sara watched as Leech shuffled to the staging at the far side of the room, bent down and brought the two sacks from under it to the table in the centre. He pushed aside the courgettes laid out on newspaper, the mugs and teabag box, the folded newspaper and biscuit packets and placed the sacks in the space he had cleared.

'Leech, go back and sit on your bed,' Ivan said. Leech's submissive turning and doing so was craven, and Sara realised that he was familiar with the tone of voice Ivan was using. She said as much.

'But he likes clear directions,' Ivan replied, slightly irritated at this digression. 'He likes to know what's expected of him. He's quite happy. Now, shall we get on?' He nodded towards the sacks but remained where he was, standing by the wall, as if afraid of what they might contain. 'Sara, open them, would you?'

As she stepped forward and did so, a sharp, damp, rotting yet not quite rotten smell rose from the sacks. She brought out a handful and stared at the grains in her palm, turning them under her thumb. When she looked up and saw Ivan's face she could see that beneath the formality he was frightened.

'Let's see, then,' Ivan said. 'Come on, I might as well know the worst.'

Sara advanced, her hand held out. Ivan grabbed her by the wrist, scattering the grains in her palm over the floor. With his other hand he had reached to the wall behind him, and was now holding a small scythe. Sara gasped. Leech was sitting wide-eyed on his bed, his mouth opening and shutting. He rose with a frightened moan and made ditheringly for the open door, wringing his hands. Ivan moved swiftly and stepped across his way, dragging Sara with him, his grip on her wrist tightening. 'Get back,' he commanded. 'Leech, get back over there.'

Leech did so, sinking with a creak on to the bed from where he continued to stare at Ivan and through the open door behind him into the dark. Sara tried with her other hand to free the fingers digging into her wrist, until the scythe swung over her arm. 'Let go or I'll slice you up,' Ivan told her. She had no doubt that he would.

'What's going on?' she gasped. 'What's all this about?'

'Leech. Stand up.' Leech did so. 'Leech, go and get the other scythe. Behind me on the wall, hanging up. Go and get it.' Leech seemed relieved to be given instructions, and obeyed. Sara heard a clatter and rasp as the scythe came off the wall and the shuffle as he returned to the camp bed where he stood, scythe in hand.

'What's going on?' she whispered. 'What about the rye?'

Ivan said, ignoring her, 'Remember the Jap lady, Leech? See? He doesn't. Remember the little Jap lady you lifted over the hedge so she could get to the towpath?'

Leech was nodding mechanically, without recognition.

'He doesn't remember. But she took photographs of the rye to show her husband. Very serious, you see. She wanted his opinion. She was prepared to meet him to tell him, even though she'd left him. Because an ergot out-break is a natural disaster and we must be quite, quite sure before we go burning crops and raising the alarm, mustn't we?'

'She knew? She told you?'

'Of course she did. She didn't have to go into detail. I know enough pharmacology to know what ergot does, once she pointed out it was all over the rye.'

'But what do you mean? You're making a mistake. You must be ill.'

'Leech could tell you, if he had any sense, which he doesn't, of course. He doesn't mind me saying, do you,

Leech? Leech? Leech, come on, you'll do anything for me, won't you? See your sleeping bag there, Leech? I want you to cut it up. Now. Go on. Cut it up with the scythe, like I tell you. Just do it, Leech.'

Leech wavered, whimpering, looking from Ivan to Sara. She said, as gently as she could, 'Don't, Leech. You don't have to. It's all right, don't get upset.'

Leech lifted the scythe and began slicing. The blade split the fabric like skin and white clouds of stuffing escaped. Ivan sniggered.

Sara turned her eyes away and tried again to free her arm from Ivan's grip. She said, 'I don't understand what you're trying to prove. Mrs Takahashi didn't find ergot on the rye at all, did she?'

'Of course she did! You're nearly as stupid as Leech. And she's desperate to tell her husband. All I had to do was tell her he rang on Friday night after she was asleep to tell her to meet him at 9.00 instead of 12.30. And then I bike it in along the towpath, find her outside the RPS and tell her there's been another phone message and she's to meet him outside Photo-Kwik instead, so they can develop the pictures she's taken to show him. And of course I can show her a little shortcut. We used to supply herbs to that place, you know, before it was the Snake and Ladder. Side entrance in the alley always open, first thing.'

'Let me go, please. Please.' Sara looked round desperately. Under the stark light the bags of rye sat on the table and Leech whimpered from his bed like an unhappy dog.

'Isn't nature wonderful? A lovely organic way of wiping out my father's fucking clinic and his fucking reputation. Sad really, she didn't deserve it. But my father deserves to lose his fucking patients and his fucking clinic. You know he lies to his patients? He fakes tests and lies to them. And you know he's impregnated my fucking wife? *My* wife!' Ivan's voice had risen and now carried the screech of a guilty, thwarted child's defensive zeal to be understood. Tears of rage were running down the baby face.

Sara's legs were trembling wildly. Her voice, when she tried to speak, was lost in gulps of panic because the diminishing portion of her mind that was still rational was telling her, almost detachedly, that she was being told these things because Ivan was confident that she would not have an opportunity to repeat them.

'That's nonsense. Absolute nonsense. As if your own father would—'

'He did! The pair of them have been at it for months, to get her knocked up! It's just the kind of thing they'd do, they're shits! Alex Cooper heard them at it—oh of course she didn't realise, she thought it was Yvonne! But I knew who it had to be! I *knew*!'

Sara's voice was remarkably slow and calm. 'You bloody fool. Oh no, it wasn't Yvonne. Maybe it wasn't *anybody*. Maybe Alex Cooper made the whole thing up, can't you see? Your father turned her down. Maybe that's why she left, because she came on to him and he turned her down. She was just spreading her bit of poison before she went. Maybe it made her feel better. She fooled you.'

'That's a fucking lie! A fucking lie! My father—my *father*—' Ivan's mouth twisted on the word, 'he never kicked anybody out of bed in his life! He had it coming! It would have got them all in the end, except for stupid fucking Warwick and his butter. I was mad when Hilary told me about his butter. I had to go and look it up. It's the vitamin D in butter, it stops the ergot working, did you find that out, you smart-arsed bitch? So I took direct action with Warwick, on a nice busy day when the place was full of strangers.'

'Ivan, I don't believe you. You're making up some awful story and I don't know why, please let go of me . . .'

'Interesting about the vitamin D, don't you think? I'd forgotten it's in butter. That's why my father wasn't ill, he takes vitamin tablets. So he was just sitting on his well-toned arse in his fucking clinic watching them die. That was so funny. And he couldn't do a thing about it. That clinic's not really his anyway, it was my money as much as his, my *mother's* money. Then you come along talking about ergot and compensation, you bitch. Nobody else had a clue.'

'But Leech does, now,' Sara said, softly. Her eyes were burning into Leech, willing him to make a run for it. But he did not move his gaze from the open door.

Ivan snorted scornfully and turned the scythe slowly in the air. 'Leech comes in very useful. Warwick is killed and Leech disappears, and later, when he's found dead, every-one will think it was Leech. Because when we arrived here, or so I will say, Leech leapt on us with the scythe. He injured me first.'

Slowly he drew the scythe down along the outside of his thigh. The denim fell open; blood seeped out of the sliced flesh. He shifted his weight on to his other leg, pant-ing. Then he cut again. And again. He swallowed hard and gave a deep, groaning sigh which Sara thought, sickened, was one of relief. Although tears were running down his cheeks, his wincing face wore a smile of gratification.

'Oh, bloody painful. Bad business. But eventually, of course, I manage to overpower Leech and get the scythe from him, which I use to defend myself, unfortunately killing him. But not before he's hacked you to bits, tragically. A frenzied attack, the third person he's killed, do you see? Bad business.'

'But, Ivan, I don't know what you mean,' Sara managed to say. 'Ivan, listen.' She could hardly bear to look at him. His face was twisted with the effort of speaking through his pain. Blood poured from the three wounds on his leg. 'Listen to me. You know none of this is true, don't you? Ivan . . .'

Something she had heard about using a person's name to reduce tension swam into her brain. 'Ivan, just stop a minute. I've got this all wrong, so have you. The rye—the rye over there on the table. I looked at it. There's nothing wrong with it. It's perfectly okay. It's clean.'

Ivan snorted and adjusted his grip, glanced at the rye and back at Sara's face.

'Honestly, it's not contaminated, that's what I was trying to show you. There's nothing wrong with it. Honestly, I swear, it's perfectly all right.'

She was wide-eyed, bewildered, terrified. 'Ivan, I've made some sort of awful mistake, jumping to stupid conclusions. It's because I'm so upset about James, I suppose. I wanted some kind of reason for it. Only please, let me go.'

Ivan stared at her distrustfully. He did not let go.

'I've just grabbed at an explanation and it's wrong. The rye's fine. Go and look.'

Still he did not let go. Sara tried again. 'You've done the same thing, jumped to the wrong conclusions, made up all that stuff and got us all scared for nothing. Come on, let me go. Leech wants you to as well. There's no need for this. Let me go. I promise you, look at the rye and you'll see for yourself. It's fine. Whatever made people ill it certainly wasn't the rye. The rye's fine. You can just sell the clinic and put all this behind you.'

Leech's whimpering had stopped and he was gazing past Ivan into the darkness beyond the open door. It was impossible to tell whether he stared with longing, hopelessness, or complete insensibility.

'Leech, come here,' Ivan shouted. 'Come here, you stupid bastard. Cut her. Cut her, Leech. With the scythe. Go on!'

Leech raised the scythe and grunted as he lurched forward. His eyes were wild with incomprehension. He swung the scythe once, whined in desperation and let it fall back to his side. He looked at Sara blankly.

'Just fucking do it, Leech! Cut her!'

Leech nodded. 'Kind,' he said. Then he swung the scythe up again into the air behind him and brought it down hard on Ivan's shoulder.

Sara's scream came like an explosion as Ivan's blood hit her face. She pulled herself away, screaming to Leech to run, as she made for the door and dived into the darkness. But instead of the open, empty ground, the night air and safety, she ran straight into the hard, upright wall of someone's chest.

CHAPTER 48

THREE O'CLOCK IN the morning can be a good time to drink a large brandy, or it can be bloody awful. Sara, sipping hers, had not decided. Andrew sat opposite her across the kitchen table in Medlar Cottage, whose shaded lamps and familiar, faint smells of wood and bread were gradually reducing their sense of crisis and soothing them with a warm, approving atmosphere.

Sara put down her glass. 'I'm too full of tea,' she said. There had been gallons of it, as well as blankets over her shoulders, and questions, in the previous two hours of talking to the police. Ivan was in hospital under arrest, saying nothing, apparently overwhelmed by grief at his wife's miscarriage and the confusing events in the shed. Leech also was in hospital, also under arrest. Sara had given her story at least twice and insisted on coming home. Andrew had insisted on coming with her. She looked across at him warily.

'So how did you know? How did you know to come to the smallholding?'

Andrew looked slightly blank. 'Dan. Daniel, I mean. We got back to the flat tonight, knackered. We had a good time on the bikes, or rather he did. I was miserable about you. But until tonight he hadn't mentioned the picnic once. So when I put him to bed I just asked him why he'd tried to feed you the poisoned sandwich. I said I thought he was fond of you.'

'What did he say?'

'He was nearly asleep. He told me not to be stupid, of course he was fond of you, it was me he hated. Then he threw his arms round me and said he didn't any more so I gave him a big hug and tucked him in.'

Sara said, 'I don't get it.'

'Neither did I at first. Then I thought about it. He didn't hate you but he tried to kill you because it would hurt his father. It made me think of Warwick, being killed on the Open Day when it'll hurt Stephen Golightly most. Not because Warwick's done anything to anyone. I just thought it might be worth following up, that's all.'

'Good God! You realise what you've done, don't you? You've acted on intuition! How *awful* for you. I'm *so* sorry.'

'Shut up, you. So I rang the Sulis to speak to Ivan's father and that's when I found out about Hilary, and Ivan going off to the smallholding. With you. I didn't much like the sound of that so I took Daniel to Mrs Thing in the flat upstairs and said something urgent had come up. She thought I was insane.'

'Well, I'd say it was above the call of duty.'

'Duty? *Duty?* That had nothing to do with it. I've thought of nothing except you and those things I said. I'm sorry. I don't know what made me do it. I love you. And I can't bear it that I wasn't with you when you heard about James. When I left him in the hospital on Sunday I had no idea it was that serious.'

'I don't think anyone did. I'm sorry, too, for everything, all of it. I love you, too.'

'We've both been stupid, haven't we?'

Sara nodded wearily. 'And we won't do things like that to each other again, will we? We've agreed that. We shouldn't keep saying it.'

He smiled at her. 'But how much I love you, that'll bear repeating. I do love you.'

Sara said, 'I love you, too.' Before she could say any more Andrew said, 'And no more sorry, either. You should drink your brandy if you can. It'll help you sleep.'

'The thing that'll keep me awake is what you said about all that stuff Ivan said in the shed probably being inadmissible as evidence. It's so wrong.'

Andrew sighed. 'It does seem that way. But we won't get a conviction on the basis of what little I overheard—not when it's the story of an off-duty police officer looking for a conviction, confirmed only by his girlfriend. Leech's evidence won't be any good, obviously, even if he managed to give it. And there's no conclusive forensic proof that Ivan murdered Mrs Takahashi or Warwick.'

'But what about the Snake and Ladder! He said he knew about the side door being open, and he would have known about the radio in the kitchen, that nobody would hear anything. Surely—'

'It's not evidence.'

'Well, what about the alibi, then? When Mrs Heffer saw him on the embankment. Why would he be up there? It's Leech who went up to watch the trains. You ask her, see if she was sure. It could have been Leech in the blue shirt, couldn't it? He's tall and thin, they both wore hats.'

'Yes, it sounds like we could throw some doubt on his

alibi. We'll check. But that's not evidence either. Even the rye itself—you were very convincing, by the way, you almost had me believing it *was* clean—even though it's riddled with ergot, it doesn't prove any criminal intent. We can't prove Ivan knew that it was contaminated, less still that he set out to use it to kill people or damage them. We can't even prove he knew what ergot was or anything about what it does. Unless he confesses, and there's no reason to suppose he will, he'll get away with it.'

'What about the photographs? Ivan knew Mrs Takahashi had taken pictures of the ergot and that no used films were found in her bag. Don't you think he could have taken them and had them developed?'

'We'll search the house, of course. It's possible he took them and forgot about the one in the camera, or didn't have time to get it out. We've checked the pictures again, by the way, the ones that were in the camera. They were close-ups of the rye, not just pretty views of the field. You can see the ergot if you know what you're looking for.' He sighed. 'I doubt if we'll find any others in the house, though. Even if he did have them developed it would have been mad to keep them. My guess is he destroyed them, or more likely just destroyed the films. But we'll look. It's the only thing we've got to go on.'

Sara sank her head on to her hands and yawned. Staying awake seemed only to be prolonging a succession of painful, hopeless injustices. For that reason alone she welcomed sleep. On their way upstairs, walking past the open study door, Sara spotted the white gleam of a piece of curled paper on the floor. 'There's another fax,' she said, picking it up. In the light of the landing she read Professor Takahashi's neat typing:

Miss dear Morrison Mary

I reflect that perhaps your interests lie not exclusively in human poisoning region. Here is supplementary informations, with my courteous sentiments.

As you will know, active component of *Claviceps purpurea* (ergot) comprises several compounds of lysergic acid, having some pharmacological applications in animal and human treatments.

As follows, histamine, tyramine and acetylcholine all are present in small amounts and have no medicinal importance. Specific active constituents are ergotamine and ergometrine (much details I will leave out, concerning on six pairs of stereoisomeric alkaloids in three chemical groups). Liquid extract of ergot is prepared by maceration and percolation. In human, dihydroergotamine is use in treatment of migraine, pruritus and shingles. In veterinary application it has been used to treat interdigital cyst, foot swelling in dog. In larger animal ergometrine is indicated in treatment of post-parturient uterine inertia, involution of the post-parturient uterus and post-partum haemorrhage. It is contra-indicated in the pregnant animal and also human of course, its circulatory and ecbolic action and effect on unstriped muscle produce swift expulsion of uterine contents! Ergometrine only is soluble most readily in water. With hope these supplementary informations assist you. Good luck!

Takahashi Kenichi

'We've got him,' Andrew said.

'Who? What?'

'Ivan. Lysergic acid. The pharmacology.'

Sara read the fax again and murmured, 'I don't know what you mean.'

'Lysergic acid. That's the main constituent of LSD, my darling. There can't be a seventies pharmacology student who doesn't know that, least of all Ivan Golightly. He probably made the stuff.'

'And lysergic acid is in ergot, too?'

'Yes, that's what Takahashi says. So even if Ivan didn't already know about ergot, as he is claiming, once Mrs Takahashi told him about it he'd be on familiar ground with lysergic acid. He'd know how dangerous it was and what he could do with it. He must have decided at once. The same day Hilary told him she was pregnant.'

'You still can't prove it, though, can you?'

'It wasn't just the ergot he baked into the bread, listen: "ergometrine only is soluble most readily in water", "contra-indicated in the pregnant animal", "swift expulsion of uterine contents".'

'What? The *baby*? You don't mean he—their baby? The herbal tea?'

'He's convinced the baby's not his.'

'But only because of what Alex Cooper said about Stephen having an affair with Yvonne. She *might* have been making all that up.' She did not add that she believed Stephen Golightly to have been telling the truth about Alex.

'And she might not. But Ivan believed her, and he also knew Yvonne was gay so it couldn't be her. And Hilary and her father-in-law are close, so he convinces himself they're having an affair and trying to get her pregnant. Remember he said something about faking tests.'

'I can probably tell you more about that. Ivan must have known about them, too.'

'So when Hilary tells him she's pregnant he doesn't believe it's his.'

'But it *could* have been. He said his count was borderline, that's all. Not impossibly low.'

'But he's had paranoid episodes before, hasn't he? So he gives Hilary ergometrine in herbal tea and gets rid of the baby. He knew what he was doing. He knew.'

He looked at his watch. 'We can only hold him for forty-eight hours without charge. If we can run some tests on Hilary . . . if there's a way of tracing ergometrine in the body, proving that's why she miscarried . . . look, I know it's nearly half-past three—'

'Go, go,' Sara said. She was shaking. 'I'm going to bed. I'll sleep for hours anyway, I don't mind, truly. You go.'

It was true that she did not mind, but she did not sleep for a great many hours. At eight o'clock her telephone rang. Thinking it would be Andrew, she picked up the telephone by her bed.

'Hello?' she croaked, and sank back into the pillow smiling, waiting, grateful for Andrew, knowing she loved him. There was no voice on earth that she would rather hear.

'Fine bloody friend you are,' growled James.

CHAPTER 49

'FOR A START, Ralph Allen's a *female* ward. This is Beau Nash,' James said, when Sara had stopped hugging him. He was sitting up in bed and looking remarkably well.

'How was I to know that?' Sara said. 'I asked for you by name because I didn't know what ward you were in. The line was hopeless and this woman looked on some list and found Jane Valentine's name and just put me through.'

'Poor Jane,' James said. 'Poor Jane. Bitter as hell, desperately unhappy. That can't have helped. Gangrene set in, I heard. She died the day of the operation. Both feet. They thought they might have to do her hands, too. I should think the thought was enough to kill her.'

Sara's stricken face seemed, if anything, to encourage him. 'But Joyce came up trumps. Have you seen her?'

'I'll pop in when I've left you,' Sara said. 'I can still hardly believe it.'

James had told Sara the story that he had got from Gerry, a nice gossipy charge nurse who knew everything. Joyce, unable to make herself understood on the telephone, had turned up at the main entrance of the hospital late on Wednesday night and eventually got someone to listen to her ergot story. She had been drinking, but had made herself clear enough. Then, as a result of hunger (she had not eaten that day), the three-mile walk to the hospital, grief, mental exhaustion and the booze, she had collapsed and been admitted. She was now in another ward, wolfing down three meals a day and talking to Social Services. But not yet, according to Gerry, to Alcoholics Anonymous.

James said, 'I've been learning quite a bit about ergot in here. They've had to bone up, apparently. I'm rather a change from routine for them. I'm *quite* important.'

'Oh, God, when I think of what it was like, and you weren't dead at all. If you *knew* how it felt—' Sara burst into tears, crying and half laughing, for the fifth time. She felt recklessly relieved.

'And Gerry's seriously cute. Got a body to die for . . .'

'You *are* better.'

'Sure am. I haven't even got ulcers, by the way, it was only IBS. And ergot poisoning. But I had the convulsive form, you see, easier to treat. Muscle relaxant drugs. It helped that I threw up, apparently. Main reason I'm better of course is that I'm not taking my daily ergot by the mouthful any more. The other form that Jane had, that's the gangrenous one. According to that tome in there that the consultant brought in to show me,' James waved towards the recess in his locker.

Sara took the book out and read, '*Compendium of Mycological Poisoning in Humans.*'

'There's a great bit somewhere about some woman's leg dropping off on the way to have it amputated. Give it here.'

'Poor Mrs Takahashi. Just trying to have a few days to

herself to stop feeling sick and she finds the ergot and tries to help. And poor Professor Takahashi.'

'Do you want to hear this or not? Or should I just linger alone on my bed of pain *again*?'

'You sod. I thought you were dead, or of course I'd have been in touch.'

She seized his hand. Every few minutes she was realising again that James was not dead so it seemed pleasantly prosaic, given that James had just been delivered back to her out of the jaws of death, that Gerry should now appear and say that if James didn't mind giving him a cheek he would do his next injection and perhaps Sara had stayed long enough for a first visit.

Just as she was leaving James called, 'How did the Dvořák go, by the way?'

Sara said, 'The Dvořák went just fine, thank you very much.'

CHAPTER 50

SARA FELT SHE knew herself mind, body and spirit, after a couple of decades thinking about it. She was well up on her body rhythms, attuned both to her own and, after seven weeks of living with him, also to Andrew's, but while he continued to sleep like a boy (a very indulged one) and wake up with a mind emptied of ordinary care, she was waking earlier and earlier. She knew she had undergone some change. So of late she had taken to lying until morning came, listening to the incessant summer rain and praying, although she was too practical to address any particular deity, that the change she felt was not the one she dreaded and for which she would risk so much. What had not changed, unless to increase, was her feeling that she was so stupid.

She was still ever watchful. She needed these hours spent beside Andrew but alone; silently, in the dark, she was collecting her faculties in preparation for the next big thing, gathering enough strength for both of them. It was a habit formed even before their first break-up, but there was something else now that was making her protective, cautious of mind and more careful in her movements.

The last day of September was wet and cold and Sara

rose silently, exchanged her nightie for a skirt and shirt and went downstairs, there being no reason now, except the hope that she might be mistaken, to delay. Gazing across the kitchen sink to the garden and the vibrant parsley patch, she pondered, calculating for the thousandth time. Sunday morning: Andrew. Sunday and Monday: Pills in lost luggage. Tuesday: Take three. Wednesday night: Violently sick. Thursday morning: Stephen. Thursday night: Forget to take pill in midst of other goings-on. Friday: Discover have left last remaining pack in bedside drawer of hotel in Salzburg. Saturday: Bury head in sand. So stupid. Wilfully (deliberately?) stupid. She felt also newly responsible in a way that was as yet untouched by anxiety; stronger in some way and paradoxically more vulnerable. Oh yes, and as sick as a dog. She turned on the cold tap and held her wrists under the water, a natural, healthful remedy for nausea she had read about and which today, as on the preceding six days, did not work.

She sank into a chair at the kitchen table, opened the box and pulled out its contents and the instructions. There was a lot to read. Andrew would not stir for a while yet.

ABOUT THE AUTHOR

MORAG JOSS grew up on the west coast of Scotland. She began writing in 1996, when her first short story won an award in a national competition. She then wrote three Sara Selkirk novels, set in Bath, and with her fourth novel, *Half Broken Things*, she won the 2003 CWA Silver Dagger Award. Her work has been translated into several languages.

Morag Joss lives in the country outside the city of Bath, and in London.

Don't miss any of Morag Joss's tantalizing
mysteries featuring cellist Sara Selkirk

FUNERAL MUSIC

FEARFUL SYMMETRY

FRUITFUL BODIES

And read on for an exciting preview of

HALF BROKEN THINGS

BY

MORAG JOSS

Winner of the Crime Writers' Association
Silver Dagger Award

Available in hardcover
October 2005

Morag Joss

Half
Broken
Things

a novel of suspense

HALF BROKEN THINGS

On Sale October 2005

Walden Manor
August

T HIS IS NOT what it might look like. We're quiet people. As a general rule extraordinary things do not
happen to us, and we are not the type to go looking
for them. But so much has happened since January, and I
started it. Things began to happen, things that I must have
brought about somehow without quite foreseeing where
they would lead. So I feel I must explain, late in the day
though it is. I'm going to set out as clearly as I can, in the
order in which they occurred, the things that have happened here. And I shall find it difficult because I was
brought up not to draw attention to myself and I've never
been considered a forthcoming person, never being one to
splurge out on anything, least of all great long explana-
tions. Indeed Mother always described me as secretive.
But that was because, with her, I came to expect to have
my reasons for things not so much misunderstood as overlooked or mislaid, and so early on I stopped giving them.

Father was usually quiet, too. When I think back to the
sounds of the house in Oakfield Avenue where I grew up, I
do not remember voices. I think we sighed or cleared our

throats more often than we spoke words. I remember mainly the tick of Father's longcase clock in the dining room that we never ate in, and then after the clock had gone, a particular silence throughout the house that I thought of as a shade of grey. And much later when I was an adult, still there looking after Mother, the most regular sound was the microwave. It pinged a dozen times a day. In fact, until recently, whenever I heard a certain tone of ping, in a shop or somewhere like that, I would immediately smell boiling milk. But when I was a child there was just the clock, with silences in between.

Mother had few words herself. She often went about the house as if she were harbouring unsaid things at great personal cost, with a locked look on her mouth. That being so I suppose Father and I felt unable to open our own very much. What happens to all the things you might say or want to say, but don't? Well, they don't lie about in your head indefinitely, waiting to be let out. For a time they may stay there quite patiently, but then they shuffle off and fade until you can't locate them any more, and you realise they're not coming back. By then you're past caring.

So I grew to think of myself as someone not in particular need of words. I did not acquire the habit of calling them up, not many at a time at least, not even to myself in my own head. Things in my head had been very quiet for a long time, before all this.

But I have been wrong about this aspect of myself, as about others. I find that there are words there after all. Now that I need them, my words have come crowding back, perhaps because I have a limited time in which to get them all down (today is the 20th, so only eleven more days). I am pleased that my hands remember the old touch-typing moves without seeming to involve me at all.

The letters are hitting the paper in this old typewriter almost as if they were being shot out of my finger ends. Which is just as well, because I'm busy enough dealing with all the clamouring words that are flinging themselves around in my head, fighting over which gets fired out first. I'm in a hurry to let them loose. I want to explain, because it is suddenly extremely urgent and important that, in the end, we are not misunderstood.

And I shall try to put down not just what, but *why* things have happened and why none of it could have turned out any differently. But until now I really haven't thought about the why. Time's the thing. I haven't had time, not time of the right kind, to ask myself why things have gone the way they have. I've been too busy being happy; even now I'm happy although the time left is of the other kind. But I'm quite content to spend it trying to puzzle it all out and write it down. It's a pleasant way to pass time, sitting over the typewriter at the study window and looking out now and then to wave at them (that's Michael, Steph and Charlie) down there in the garden. They're not doing much. Steph is singing to Charlie and rocking him on her lap: 'Row, row, row the boat'—that's one of Charlie's favourites and the more she rocks the more he likes it. They're waving back now. I've told them I've got to write a report for the agency and actually, in a way that's almost true, so they're making pretend-sad faces up at me because I can't spend the afternoon with them. And now Steph's got hold of Charlie's wrist and she's making him wave too. Behind them, I can see three different kinds of Michaelmas daisy in the border, three nice shades of purple. But the roses are on their second flowering now and look as if the air's gone out of them, as if they've stayed too long at the party.

Anyway, I'm going off the point. I was saying that I'm going to explain everything. And while I cannot imagine any explanation for anything that does not also contain an element of justification, I am not trying to offer excuses for what we have done. But nor am I apologising, quite, except for the mess and inconvenience which are bound to be considerable.

So how did it start? With the letter from the agency? Or with the advertisement I placed? Perhaps much, much earlier, years and years ago, with Jenny. Jenny is the niece I invented for myself. Yes, perhaps that reveals a tendency. She started as just a little, harmless, face-saving white lie which of course led to others, and in no time at all the fact that she did not exist was neither here nor there. My niece became quite real to me, or as real as somebody living in Australia ever could be, in my mind. I haven't travelled abroad.

No, now that I reflect, it started with this place, with the house itself. Because the house made me feel things from the very first which perhaps I should find strange, it being my fifty-eighth. Memories are a little blurred after fifty-seven in eighteen years, but I do know I never felt things before. This is the fifty-eighth house, although I've sat some houses more than once because people used to ask for me again. I specialise, or I did, in long stays. 'We have the perfect lady, flexible and no ties, usually available' was how I was recommended. I spell this out just so that it is clear that I have been well thought of. Inexperience has nothing to do with it. Nor was it anything to do with malice or jealousy.

The house when I came was full of old things, fuller than it is now for reasons I will come to. Many of them were anyway not in mint condition, and I liked them like that. I liked the way they sat about the house in little settlements, as if they had sought one another out and were sticking together, little colonies of things on small island table tops. There were the boxes: workboxes with velvet linings and silver spools and scissors and dear little button-hooks, boxes with tiny glass bottles with stoppers missing, writing boxes still cedar scented and ink-stained on the inside, yellowed and ancient carved ivory boxes, painted and enamel ones, I suppose for snuff, those ones, but I wasn't concerned about their original purpose. Then there were the small silver things in the drawing room, the heavy paper knife with a swan's head, the magnifying glass, a round box with a dent, the filigree basket with the twisted handle, a vase for a single rose. The blue and white porcelain in the dining room, some of it chipped, and the fans in the case in the library, of beaded lace, faded painted parchment and tired looking feathers. Even some of the books: nearly everything else was modern, but on three shelves there were sets of very old books with cracked spines and faded titles. They all had that look of being dusted in cinnamon and gave off a leafy smell that reminded me of church. Inside, many of the pages were loose, and so thin that the print on the other side grinned right through the words when I tried to read, as if they were not unreadable enough already.

But all these things seemed content in their imperfections, they were not shouting out to be mended the way new things do. New things so often break before there has been time for them to fade and crumble. Here, it was as if the things had simply been around long enough to be dropped or bent or knocked, and every one of these minute, accidental events had been patiently absorbed, as if the things knew themselves to be acceptable and thought beautiful just as they were. If objects could give contented sighs, that's what these would have done. I wanted to be like that. I wondered if I, also fading and crumbling as everything does in the end, could be like that. Yes, I remember I did wonder that right from the start, in those first few days of January.

The third day, like the first two, slipped away and got lost somewhere in the folds of the afternoon. As before, Jean had made the dusting of the objects in the house last for most of the morning. She had vacuumed the floors again and cleaned her bathroom, unnecessarily. After her lunch of milky instant coffee and biscuits she tidied round the kitchen. When she could fool herself no longer that there was anything left to do she mounted the carved wooden stairs and walked the upper floors, again feeling mildly inquisitive, as if the house and the rest of the day might be conspiring to withhold something from her. And again, pointlessly, she tried the three doors she knew to be locked. Then she wandered with less purpose, pausing here and there, her vague eyes watching how light displaced time in the many other rooms of the house. Light entered by the mullioned windows, it stretched over floors and panelled walls and lay down across empty beds. It lay as cold and silent as a held breath over furniture and objects and over Jean lingering in each doorway; it claimed space usually taken by hours and minutes which, outside, continued to pass. Through windows to the west Jean saw how the wind was moving the bare trees that bordered the fields; through the south windows she watched grass shivering in the paddock, watched as clouds pasted on to the sky bulged and heaved a little. Inside, the afternoon aged; its folds sank and deepened, closed over the last of the daylight and sucked it in. When it was quite dark Jean walked again from room to room, touching things gently and drawing curtains. So the third day passed, with Jean watching as it seemed not to do so, unaware that she was waiting.

She was keeping the letter from the agency with her in the pocket of her thick new cardigan, the Christmas present she had bought and wrapped for herself so that she would have something to open 'from my niece Jenny in Australia' in front of the other residents on Christmas morning. For this year, finding herself again between house sitting jobs over the holiday, she had been obliged to spend Christmas at the Ardenleigh Guest House. It was Jean's fifth Christmas there in eighteen years, and Jenny had sprung into being the very first time when, one day at breakfast, a depressed old lady had invited Jean to agree with her that Christmas was quite dreadful when you were getting on and nobody wanted you. It had sounded like an accusation; Jean had then been in her late forties and suspected that she looked older. She ignored the clumsy assumption about her age and concentrated on the 'unwanted' allegation. She heard herself saying loudly, *Oh, but I didn't have to come here! In fact my . . . my niece begged me to come to her! But I told her oh no, I shan't come this year, thank you, dear. Thank you, Jenny dear, I said, but no, I'll make other arrangements.* And then of course the old lady had asked her why. *Oh, well. Well, she's having a baby soon, her third. So I thought, it wouldn't be fair to add to the workload this year.* Then she added, in a voice loaded with dread, *You see, she's Not Having An Easy Pregnancy.*

Several of the residents were permanent, and the next time Jean had to spend Christmas there, one of them asked, surely too eagerly, how the niece was getting on. She could not bear to disappoint—it was as if for the intervening two years the residents had been on the edge of their seats waiting for news—so she found herself telling them about the baby (*quite a toddler now, into everything!*) adding that this year they were away, spending Christmas with Jenny's husband's family. And it was the same the next time, at which point Jean lost her nerve and sent them all off to live in Australia. But she discovered that the Ardenleigh residents had formed a high opinion of Jenny, and it did not seem right to Jean to sully her niece's reputation by allowing her, just because she had emigrated, to forget her old aunt in England. It did not seem the kind of thing Jenny would do. So for Ardenleigh Christmases she always produced Jenny's thoughtful present, relieved not to have to produce also another reason, beyond the unbearably long flight (at her age), for not spending Christmas 'down under'.

But this year it seemed that Jenny had slipped up, because the cardigan was not a success. Jean had chosen it thinking its colour 'amethyst' and realised, now that it had been hers for over a week, that it was just a muddy purple. But it did not occur to her not to wear it even though it now disappointed; she wrapped herself snugly into her mistake just as she kept the letter close as a reminder to be at all times braced against the temptation to forget it. It lay in her cardigan pocket. In the mornings, bending to dust the feet of a table or to unplug the vacuum cleaner, Jean would sometimes feel it crackle next to her, as if a small, sharp part of herself had broken off and was hanging loose against her side. It puzzled her, almost, to find that she was not actually in pain. Sometimes she would take the envelope from her pocket and look at it, but she did not read the letter again.

Yet, somewhere in the course of these afternoons, Jean would arrive at an amnesty with the presence of the letter. As daylight took its leave, it seemed to wrap up and bear away also the threat that seeped from her cardigan pocket. She could feel that the letter itself was still there, but she would begin to regard it with a sort of detached astonishment, which grew into simple disbelief, that marks on a piece of paper should hold any power over her. Walking from room to room, switching on lamps, it seemed amazing to her that only this morning she had thought the letter had any meaning at all. Here, in this soft lamplight, how could it? And as the day darkened further, the picture of herself accepting some pointless words in an envelope hidden inside her cardigan grew more and more improbable. By night time, when she had settled at the drawing-room fire and the peace of the house was at its deepest, the very notion of eight months hence was simply incredible. Here, if she wanted it, the future could be as dim and distant as she preferred the past to be.

On the fourth day Shelley from the agency telephoned.

"Hello?"

"Is that Walden Manor?"

"Hello?"

"Who is this? Jean? Jean, is that you? It's Shelley, from Town and Country Sitters. Did you get our letter?"

"Oh. Oh yes. Yes, I got the letter."

Jean disliked Shelley. She had met her in person only once, when a householder had insisted that his keys should not be sent through the post to the sitter and Jean had had to travel to the office in Stockport to collect them. She knew she ought to try to feel sorry for her. Shelley was burdened both by asthma and by a disproportionately large chest, which together gave the impression that her breasts were actually two hard-working outside lungs, round and wide, inelastic and over-inflated. Jean now pictured them rising and falling and pulled her purple cardigan round her own neat shoulders, swaying in a wave of panic that suddenly washed through her. She waited with the receiver held some distance away, trying to calm herself, while Shelley caught her breath at the other end. She guessed that Shelley would be at her desk, winding the telephone flex around the ringed index finger of her free hand, her unbuttoned jacket of the navy businesswoman sort skimming the sides of her blouse-clad bosom with the whish and crackle of acetate meeting acetate. Possibly this was adding to the gusts of noise that Jean could hear now, as if some battle that she could not see were being fought somewhere in the distance.

"Right, well, Jean," Shelley managed at last, "so you've had our confirmation. Basically I just wanted to check if you've got any queries. You're OK as regards the contents of the letter, are you? Unfortunately we won't be in a position to offer you any further employment after the expiry of this current contract. I mean, we had said, hadn't we. I did say."

Jean said nothing, realising that her silence would be considered a difficult one.

Shelley told her, "We don't like terminating people but it's company policy. Town and Country's not in a position to keep people on past retirement age, we're not allowed. It's the insurance." Breathing of a struggling, bovine kind followed this long speech. "I mean you've done sterling work. But you've already had four years past sixty. Right. So."

Still Jean said nothing, so Shelley changed tack. "So, you're doing OK, are you, Jean, as regards the location of the property, OK popping out and getting your bits and pieces? Because they did say it'd be better for a car owner as you've got over a mile to the village and it might be lonely. They said really it'd suit a slightly younger person with a car and maybe a part time job in the area, though I did tell them you were very professional and OK with a mile. You are OK, Jean, are you?"

"There's been a breakage," Jean announced. "Today,

while I was dusting. A teapot on the sideboard. Blue and white, Chinese, with silver mountings. Not very large."

There was another wait while Shelley prepared the tone of her reply and Jean heard the breathing grow unmistakably irritated. "Well you've just proved my point. We have to fork out the excess on that now. You'll need to find it on the inventory and notify us and we'll have to tell the owners. You have got the inventory, haven't you? It was in with the rest of the paperwork, with our letter and the owners' list, you know, all their do's and don'ts?"

"Yes, I've got the paperwork. And the list, all the do's and don'ts. Plenty of *them*."

"Yes, well, that's their prerogative. People can go a bit over the top especially when they can't meet the sitter themselves. The Standish-Caves had to fly out the day before you arrived, that was all explained, wasn't it?"

The list of instructions and grudging permissions for the house sitter that had come from the owners, via the agency, filled several typed pages. They were wide-ranging: no open fires, no candles, do not use the dining room or drawing room, use TV in small sitting room, use only kitchen crockery, do not use the cappuccino machine or the ice cream maker, always wear gloves to dust the books, beeswax polish only no silicone sprays, you are welcome to finish any *opened* jars, unplug the television at night. Jean hugged her cardigan closer.

"You'd think I'd never house-sat before. You'd think I don't know the first thing."

"Well you can't blame them, can you, especially not now something's broken. It is their house."

"I could have a go at mending it. I've still got the bits."

"Don't touch it! They'll want it properly mended, if it's even worth doing. These clients are very particular, that's why they're using us. That's why you're there. Oh, *Jean*."

There was more laborious breathing from Stockport until Jean finally cleared her throat and said, "Sorry."

Shelley said, rather quickly, "Well I'm sure you are but I mean this is the point, isn't it? This is just the point. You are sixty-four. Suppose it happens again? Suppose you had a fall or something, well our clients are paying for peace of mind, which they'd not be getting, would they, not in that particular scenario. No way they'd be getting peace of mind if Town and Country let their sitters go on too long."

"It's only small. They probably won't even miss it, there are hundreds of things here."

"Jean, you're in a *people* business. The client's needs come first. That's key. Isn't it? You're in the client's home."

Jean sniffed. "You don't have to tell me that. I have been doing this eighteen years."

"Yes, and maybe that's why it's time to call it a day, isn't it? After all, we've all got to retire sometime, haven't we? I should think you could do with a rest! Where is it you're retiring to, again?"

There was another wait while Jean said nothing because she did not know, and Shelley shored up her elective forgetfulness against the disturbing little truth that for eighteen years the agency had corresponded with Jean, on the very rare occasions when there was a gap between house-sitting assignments, care of a Mrs Pearl Costello (proprietrix) at the Ardenleigh Private Guest House in East Sussex somewhere. St Leonard's, was it? That this year Jean had asked as usual for an assignment that would span Christmas, and they had nothing for her until this one at Walden Manor, beginning on January 3rd. Shelley sighed with an audible crackle as her jacket shifted on her shoulders. All right, so Jean had no family. But today was Shelley's first Monday back from 'doing' Christmas for fourteen people of four generations in a three-bedroomed house, and she told herself stoutly that family life could be over-rated. Jean probably had a ball at the Ardenleigh.

"Going to retire to the seaside, are you, Jean?"

"I'm looking at a number of options. I haven't decided."

"Good for you. Right, well, I'll let you get on. Send us on a notification of the breakage. Oh, and can you remember in future when you answer a client's phone, you should say, 'Walden Manor, the Standish-Cave residence, may I help you?' It's a nice touch. You don't just say hello, all right? Company policy. And careful with that duster, at least till you're enjoying a long and happy retirement!"

Jean put down the telephone in the certain knowledge that Shelley in Stockport was doing the same with a shake of the head, a crackle of her clothing and a despairing little remark to the office in general about it being high time too, getting Jean Wade off the books.

That evening Jean lit a fire in the drawing room. When it was well alight, she drew the agency's letter from her pocket and laid it carefully over the flames. Its pages curled, blackened and blazed up as the logs underneath settled with a hiss and a weak snap of exploding resin that sounded to Jean, smiling in her deep armchair, more like an approving sigh followed by faint and affectionate tutting. Only as the flames died, and to her surprise, did she become aware of a dissatisfaction with the emptiness of the room. Jean did not acknowledge loneliness. She had long recognised that two states, solitariness and a kind of sadness, were constants in her life, merely two ordinary facts of her existence. The two things might have been related, but as far as she could she left that possibility unexamined. Because even if they were, what could she do about it? Like many people who cannot abide self-pity, Jean sometimes felt very sorry indeed for a deeply buried part of herself whose very existence irked her. And of course she was alone now, sitting in the glow of the fire and of warm-shaded lamps, in the low, beamed drawing room with its dark rose carpet and the heavy drapes pulled against the dark outside. She occupied a solid wing armchair, one of several chairs in the room which, along with two sofas, were covered in materials that were all different but belonged to the same respectable family of chalky old shades of green, pink and grey. She had never been more comfortable in her life, and she was, of course, alone. And so what dissatisfied her suddenly, she thought, could not be simple loneliness, not some unmet desire for a companion, but more a feeling of regret that she was the only person in the world who had seen the short but satisfying burning of the letter. For it had been a ceremony of a kind, watching the maroon, swirling print of the letterhead 'Town & Country Sitters *for total peace of mind*' go up in flames. And ceremonies should be witnessed even if they are not quite understood, Jean thought, because she could not say exactly what the significance of hers had been, whether it marked an end or a beginning, a remembrance, an allegiance, a pledge. But it had been in a way purifying, and there should have been somebody else here to watch it with her. Somebody who might afterwards stay a while, and to whom she might talk in her underused voice, all about the letter, and Mother, and houses and growing old, and who, occupying the other chair by the fire, would nod and understand. And who, later perhaps, almost carelessly admiring her cleverness and good taste, would assure her that one smashed teapot among so many half broken things did not matter, that all would be well, even that her ill-chosen cardigan was, in fact, a beautiful shade of amethyst.